MW01244538

ROYAL REBELS

FORBIDDEN TO THE CROWN

Caitlin Crews

Amanda Cinelli

Jennifer Lewis

MILLS & BOON

ROYAL REBELS: FORBIDDEN TO THE CROWN © 2021 by Harlequin Books S.A.

THE BILLIONAIRE'S SECRET PRINCESS
© 2017 by Caitlin Crews
Australian Copyright 2017
New Zealand Copyright 2017

First Published 2017
Third Australian Paperback Edition 2021
ISBN 978 1 867 23757 0

ONE NIGHT WITH THE FORBIDDEN PRINCESS
© 2018 by Amanda Cinelli
Australian Copyright 2018
New Zealand Copyright 2018

First Published 2018
Second Australian Paperback Edition 2021
ISBN 978 1 867 23757 0

AT HIS MAJESTY'S CONVENIENCE
© 2011 by Jennifer Lewis
Australian Copyright 2011
New Zealand Copyright 2011

First Published 2011
Second Australian Paperback Edition 2021
ISBN 978 1 867 23757 0

Published by
Mills & Boon
An imprint of Harlequin Enterprises (Australia) Pty Limited (ABN 47 001 180 918), a subsidiary of HarperCollins Publishers Australia Pty Limited (ABN 36 009 913 517)
Level 13, 201 Elizabeth Street
SYDNEY NSW 2000
AUSTRALIA

FSC
MIX
Paper from
responsible sources
FSC® C001695
www.fsc.org

® and ™ (apart from those relating to FSC®) are trademarks of Harlequin Enterprises (Australia) Pty Limited or its corporate affiliates. Trademarks indicated with ® are registered in Australia, New Zealand and in other countries. Contact admin_legal@Harlequin.ca for details.

Printed and bound in Australia by McPherson's Printing Group

CONTENTS

The Billionaire's Secret Princess

Caitlin Crews

USA TODAY bestselling and RITA® Award–nominated author **Caitlin Crews** loves writing romance. She teaches her favorite romance novels in creative writing classes at places like UCLA Extension's prestigious Writers' Program, where she finally gets to utilize the MA and PhD in English literature she received from the University of York in England. She currently lives in California, with her very own hero and too many pets. Visit her at caitlincrews.com.

To all the secret princesses cruelly stuck working in horrible offices: as long as you know the truth, that's what matters.

CHAPTER ONE

ACHILLES CASILIERIS REQUIRED PERFECTION.

In himself, certainly. He prided himself on it, knowing all too well how easy it was to fall far, far short. And in his employees, absolutely—or they would quickly find themselves on the other side of their noncompete agreements with indelible black marks against their names.

He did not play around. He had built everything he had from nothing, step by painstaking step, and he hadn't succeeded the way he had—building the recession-proof Casilieris Company and making his first million by the age of twenty-five, then expanding both his business and his personal fortune into the billions—by accepting anything less than 100 percent perfection in all things. Always.

Achilles was tough, tyrannical when necessary, and refused to accept what one short-lived personal assistant had foolishly called "human limitations" to his face.

He was a man who knew the monster in himself. He'd seen its face in his own mirror. He did not allow for "human limitations."

Natalie Monette was his current executive assistant and had held the position for a record five years because she had never once asserted that she was human as some kind of excuse. In

point of fact, Achilles thought of her as a remarkably efficient
robot—the highest praise he could think to bestow on anyone,
as it removed the possibility of human error from the equation.

Achilles had no patience for human error.

Which was why his assistant's behavior on this flight today
was so alarming.

The day had started out normally enough. When Achilles
had risen at his usual early hour, it had been to find Natalie already hard at work in the study of his Belgravia town house.
She'd set up a few calls to his associates in France, outlined his
schedule for the day and his upcoming meetings in New York.
They'd swung by his corporate offices in the City, where Achilles had handled a fire he thought she should have put out before
he'd learned of it, but then she'd accompanied him in his car to
the private airfield he preferred without appearing the least bit
bothered that he'd dressed her down for her failure. And why
should she be bothered? She knew he expected perfection and
had failed to deliver it. Besides, Natalie was never bothered.
She'd acquitted herself with her usual cool competence and
attitude-free demeanor, the way she always did or she never
would have lasted five minutes with him. Much less five years.

And then she'd gone into the bathroom at the airfield, stayed
in there long enough that he'd had to go find her himself, and
come out changed.

Achilles couldn't put his finger on *how* she'd changed, only
that she had.

She still looked the part of the closest assistant to a man
as feared and lauded as Achilles had been for years now. She
looked like his public face the way she always did. He appreciated that and always had. It wasn't enough that she was capable of handling the complications of his personal and company
business without breaking a sweat, that she never seemed to
sleep, that she could protect him from the intrusive paparazzi
and hold off his equally demanding board members in the same
breath—it was necessary that she also look like the sort of

woman who belonged in his exalted orbit for the rare occasions when he needed to escort someone to this or that function and couldn't trouble himself to expend the modicum of charm necessary to squire one of his mistresses. Today she wore one of her usual outfits, a pencil skirt and soft blouse and a feminine sort of sweater that wrapped around her torso and was no different from any other outfit she'd worn a million times before.

Natalie dressed to disappear in plain sight. But for some reason, she caught his eye this odd afternoon. He couldn't quite figure it out. It was as if he had never seen her before. It was as if she'd gone into the bathroom in the airport lounge and come out a completely different person.

Achilles sat back in his remarkably comfortable leather chair on the jet and watched her as she took her seat opposite him. Did he imagine that she hesitated? Was he making up the strange look he'd seen in her eyes before she sat down? Almost as if she was looking for clues instead of taking her seat as she always did?

"What took you so long in that bathroom?" he asked, not bothering to keep his tone particularly polite. "I should not have to chase down my own assistant, surely."

Natalie blinked. He didn't know why the green of her eyes behind the glasses he knew she didn't need for sight seemed... too bright, somehow. Or brighter, anyway, than they'd been before. In fact, now that he thought about it, everything about her was brighter. And he couldn't understand how anyone could walk into a regular lavatory and come out...gleaming.

"I apologize," she said quietly. Simply. And there was something about her voice then. It was almost...musical.

It occurred to Achilles that he had certainly never thought of Natalie's voice as anything approaching *musical* before. It had always been a voice, pure and simple. And she had certainly never *gleamed.*

And that, he thought with impatience, was one of the reasons that he had prized Natalie so much for all these years. Because he had never, ever noticed her as anything but his executive assistant, who was reasonably attractive because it was good business to give his Neanderthal cronies something worth gazing at while they were trying to ignore Achilles's dominance. But there was a difference between noting that a woman was attractive and *being attracted to* that woman. Achilles would not have hired Natalie if he'd been attracted to her. He never had been. Not ever.

But to his utter astonishment that was what seemed to be happening. Right here. Right now. His body was sending him unambiguous signals. He wasn't simply *attracted* to his assistant. What he felt roll in him as she crossed her legs at the ankle and smiled at him was far more than *attraction*.

It was need.

Blinding and impossible and incredibly, astonishingly inconvenient.

Achilles Casilieris did not do inconvenience, and he was violently opposed to *need*. It had been beaten into him as an unwanted child that it was the height of foolishness to want something he couldn't have. That meant he'd dedicated his adult life to never allowing himself to need anything at all when he could buy whatever took his fancy, and he hadn't.

And yet there was no denying that dark thread that wound in him, pulling tight and succeeding in surprising him—something else that happened very, very rarely.

Achilles knew the shadows that lived in him. He had no intention of revisiting them. Ever.

Whatever his assistant was doing, she needed to stop. Now.

"That is all you wish to say?" He sounded edgy. Dangerous. He didn't like that, either.

But Natalie hardly seemed to notice. "If you would like me to expand on my apology, Mr. Casilieris, you need only tell me how."

He thought there was a subtle rebuke in that, no matter how

softly she'd said it, and that, too, was new. And unacceptable no matter how prettily she'd voiced it.

Her copper-colored hair gleamed. Her skin glowed as she moved her hands in her lap, which struck him as odd, because Natalie never sat there with her hands folded in her lap like some kind of diffident Catholic schoolgirl. She was always in motion, because she was always working. But tonight, Natalie appeared to be sitting there like some kind of regal Madonna, hands folded in her lap, long, silky legs crossed at the ankles, and an inappropriately serene smile on her face.

If it wasn't impossible, he would have thought that she really was someone else entirely. Because she looked exactly the same save for all that gold that seemed to wrap itself around her and him, too, making him unduly fascinated with the pulse he could see beating at her throat—except he'd never, ever noticed her that way before.

Achilles did not have time for this, whatever it was. There was entirely too much going on with his businesses at the moment, like the hotel deal he'd been trying to put together for the better part of the last year that was by no means assured. He hadn't become one of the most feared and fearsome billionaires in the world because he took time off from running his businesses to pretend to care about the personal lives of his employees.

But Natalie wasn't just any employee. She was the one he'd actually come to rely on. The only person he relied on in the world, to be specific.

"Is there anything you need to tell me?" he asked.

He watched her, perhaps too carefully. It was impossible not to notice the way she flushed slightly at that. That was strange, too. He couldn't remember a single instance Natalie had ever flushed in response to anything he'd done. And the truth was he'd done a lot. He didn't hide his flashes of irritation or spend too much time worrying about anyone else's feelings. Why should he? The Casilieris Company was about profit—and it was about Achilles. Who else's feelings should matter? One of the things he'd long prized about his assistant was that she never, ever reacted to anything that he did or said or shouted. She just did her job.

But today Natalie had spots of red, high on her elegant cheekbones, and she'd been sitting across from him for whole minutes now without doing a single thing that could be construed as her job.

Elegant? demanded an incredulous voice inside him. *Cheekbones?*

Since when had Achilles ever noticed anything of the kind? He didn't pay that much attention to the mistresses he took to his bed—which he deigned to do in the first place only after they passed through all the levels of his application process and signed strict confidentiality agreements. And the women who made it through were in no doubt as to why they were there. It was to please him, not render him disoriented enough to be focusing on their bloody *cheekbones.*

"Like what, for example?" She asked the question and then she smiled at him, that curve of her mouth that was suddenly wired to the hardest part of him, and echoed inside him like heat. Heat he didn't want. "I'll be happy to tell you anything you wish to hear, Mr. Casilieris. That is, after all, my job."

"Is that your job?" He smiled, and he doubted it echoed much of anywhere. Or was anything but edgy and a little but harsh. "I had started to doubt that you remembered you had one."

"Because I kept you waiting? That was unusual, it's true."

"You've never done so before. You've never dared." He tilted his head slightly as he gazed at her, not understanding why everything was different when nothing was. He could see that she was exactly the same as she always was, down to that single freckle centered on her left cheekbone that he wasn't even aware he'd noticed before now. "Again, has some tragedy befallen you? Were you hit over the head?" He did nothing to hide the warning or the menace in his voice. "You do not appear to be yourself."

But if he thought he'd managed to discomfit her, he saw in the next moment that was not to be. The flush faded from her porcelain cheeks, and all she did was smile at him again. With that maddeningly enigmatic curve of her lips.

Lips, he noticed with entirely too much of his body, that were remarkably lush.

This was insupportable.

"I am desolated to disappoint you," she murmured as the plane began to move, bumping gently along the tarmac. "But there was no tragedy." Something glinted in her green gaze, though her smile never dimmed. "Though I must confess in the spirit of full disclosure that I was thinking of quitting."

Achilles only watched her idly, as if she hadn't just said that. Because she couldn't possibly have just said that.

"I beg your pardon," he said after a moment passed and there was still that spike of something dark and furious in his chest. "I must have misheard you. You do not mean that you plan to quit this job. That you wish to leave *me*."

It was not lost on him that he'd phrased that in a way that should have horrified him. Maybe it would at some point. But today what slapped at him was that his assistant spoke of quitting without a single hint of anything like uncertainty on her face.

And he found he couldn't tolerate that.

"I'm considering it," she said. Still smiling. Unaware of her own danger or the dark thing rolling in him, reminding him of how easy it was to wake that monster that slept in him. How disastrously easy.

But Achilles laughed then, understanding finally catching up with him. "If this is an attempt to wrangle more money out of me, Miss Monette, I cannot say that I admire the strategy. You're perfectly well compensated as is. Overcompensated, one might say."

"Might one? Perhaps." She looked unmoved. "Then again, perhaps your rivals have noticed exactly how much you rely on me. Perhaps I've decided that I want more than being at the beck and call of a billionaire. Much less standing in as your favorite bit of target practice."

"It cannot possibly have bothered you that I lost my temper earlier."

Her smile was bland. "If you say it cannot, then I'm sure you must be right."

"I lose my temper all the time. It's never bothered you before. It's part of your job to not be bothered, in point of fact."

"I'm certain that's it." Her enigmatic smile seemed to deepen. "I must be the one who isn't any good at her job."

He had the most insane notion then. It was something about the cool challenge in her gaze, as if they were equals. As if she had every right to call him on whatever she pleased. He had no idea why he wanted to reach across the little space between their chairs and put his hands on her. Test her skin to see if it was as soft as it looked. Taste that lush mouth—

What the hell was happening to him?

Achilles shook his head, as much to clear it as anything else. "If this is your version of a negotiation, you should rethink your approach. You know perfectly well that there's entirely too much going on right now."

"Some might think that this is the perfect time, then, to talk about things like compensation and temper tantrums," Natalie replied, her voice as even and unbothered as ever. There was no reason that should make him grit his teeth. "After all, when one is expected to work twenty-two hours a day and is shouted at for her trouble, one's thoughts automatically turn to what one lacks. It's human nature."

"You lack nothing. You have no time to spend the money I pay you because you're too busy traveling the world—which I also pay for."

"If only I had more than two hours a day to enjoy these piles of money."

"People would kill for the opportunity to spend even five minutes in my presence," he reminded her. "Or have you forgotten who I am?"

"Come now." She shook her head at him, and he had the astonishing sense that she was trying to chastise him. *Him.* "It would not kill you to be more polite, would it?"

Polite.

His own assistant had just lectured him on his manners.

To say that he was reeling hardly began to scratch the surface of Achilles's reaction.

But then she smiled, and that reaction got more complicated. "I got on the plane anyway. I decided not to quit today." Achilles could not possibly have missed her emphasis on that final word. "You're welcome."

And something began to build inside him at that. Something huge, dark, almost overwhelming. He was very much afraid it was rage.

But that, he refused. No matter what. Achilles left his demons behind him a long time ago, and he wasn't going back. He refused.

"If you would like to leave, Miss Monette, I will not stop you," he assured her coldly. "I cannot begin to imagine what has led you to imagine I would try. I do not beg. I could fill your position with a snap of my fingers. I might yet, simply because this conversation is intolerable."

The assistant he'd thought he knew would have swallowed hard at that, then looked away. She would have smoothed her hands over her skirt and apologized as she did it. She had riled him only a few times over the years, and she'd talked her way out of it in exactly that way. He gazed at her expectantly.

But today, Natalie only sat there with distractingly perfect posture and gazed back at him with a certain serene confidence that made him want to…mess her up. Get his hands in that unremarkable ponytail and feel the texture of all that gleaming copper. Or beneath her snowy-white blouse. Or better yet, up beneath that skirt of hers.

He was so furious he wasn't nearly as appalled at himself as he should have been.

"I think we both know perfectly well that while you could snap your fingers and summon crowds of candidates for my position, you'd have a very hard time filling it to your satisfaction," she said with a certainty that…gnawed at him. "Perhaps we could dispense with the threats. You need me."

He would sooner have her leap forward and plunge a knife into his chest.

"I need no one," he rasped out. "And nothing."

His suddenly mysterious assistant only inclined her head, which he realized was no response at all. As if she was merely patronizing him—a notion that made every muscle in his body clench tight.

"You should worry less about your replacement and more about your job," Achilles gritted out. "I have no idea what makes you think you can speak to me with such disrespect."

"It is not disrespectful to speak frankly, surely," she said. Her expression didn't change, but her green gaze was grave— very much, he thought with dawning incredulity, as if she'd expected better of him.

Achilles could only stare back at her in arrogant astonishment. Was he now to suffer the indignity of being judged by his own assistant? And why was it she seemed wholly uncowed by his amazement?

"Unless you plan to utilize a parachute, it would appear you are stuck right here in your distasteful position for the next few hours," Achilles growled at her when he thought he could speak without shouting. Shouting was too easy. And obscured his actual feelings. "I'd suggest you use the time to rethink your current attitude."

He didn't care for the brilliant smile she aimed at him then, as if she was attempting to encourage him with it. *Him.* He particularly didn't like the way it seemed too bright, as if it was lighting him up from the inside out.

"What a kind offer, Mr. Casilieris," she said in that self-possessed voice of hers that was driving him mad. "I will keep it in mind."

The plane took off then, somersaulting into the London sky. Achilles let gravity press him back against the seat and considered the evidence before him. He had worked with this woman for five years, and she had never spoken to him like that before. Ever. He hardly knew what to make of it.

But then, there was a great deal he didn't know what to do with, suddenly. The way his heart pounded against his ribs as if he was in a real temper, when he was not the sort of man who lost control. Of his temper or anything else. He expected nothing less than perfection from himself, first and foremost. And temper made him think of those long-ago days of his youth, and his stepfather's hovel of a house, victim to every stray whim and temper and fist until he'd given himself over to all that rage and fury inside him and become little better than an animal himself—

Why was he allowing himself to think of such things? His youth was off-limits, even in his own head. What the hell was *happening*?

Achilles didn't like that Natalie affected him. But what made him suspicious was that she'd never affected him before. He'd approved when she started to wear those glasses and put her hair up, to make herself less of a target for the less scrupulous men he dealt with who thought they could get to him through expressing their interest in her. But he hadn't needed her to downplay her looks because *he* was entranced by her. He hadn't been.

So what had changed today?

What had emboldened her and, worse, allowed her to get under his skin?

He kept circling back to that bathroom in the airport and

the fact she'd walked out of it a different person from the one who'd walked in.

Of course, she wasn't a *different person*. Did he imagine the real Natalie had suffered a body snatching? Did he imagine there was some elaborate hoax afoot?

The idea was absurd. But he couldn't seem to get past it. The plane hit its cruising altitude, and he moved from his chair to the leather couch that took pride of place in the center of the cabin that was set up like one of his high-end hotel rooms. He sat back with his laptop and pretended to be looking through his email when he was watching Natalie instead. Looking for clues.

She wasn't moving around the plane with her usual focus and energy. He thought she seemed tentative. Uncertain—and this despite the fact she seemed to walk taller than before. As if she'd changed her very posture in that bathroom. But who did something like that?

A different person would have different posture.

It was crazy. He knew that. And Achilles knew further that he always went a little too intense when he was closing a deal, so it shouldn't have surprised him that he was willing to consider the insane option today. Part of being the sort of unexpected, out-of-the-box thinker he'd always been was allowing his mad little flights of fancy. He never knew where they might lead.

He indulged himself as Natalie sat and started to look through her own bag as if she'd never seen it before. He pulled up the picture of her he kept in his files for security purposes and did an image search on it, because why not.

Achilles was prepared to discover a few photos of random celebrities she resembled, maybe. And then he'd have to face the fact that his favorite assistant might have gone off the deep end. She was right that replacing her would be hard—but it wouldn't be impossible. He hadn't overestimated his appeal—and that of his wildly successful company—to pretty much anyone and everyone. He was swamped with applicants daily, and he didn't even have an open position.

But then none of that mattered because his image search hit gold.

There were pages and pages of pictures. All of his assistant—except it wasn't her. He knew it from the exquisitely bespoke gowns she wore. He knew it from the jewels that flowed around her neck and covered her hands, drawing attention to things like the perfect manicure she had today—when the Natalie he knew almost never had time to care for her nails like that. And every picture he clicked on identified the woman in them not as Natalie Monette, assistant to Achilles Casilieris, but Her Royal Highness, Princess Valentina of Murin.

Achilles didn't have much use for royals, or really anyone with inherited wealth, when he'd had to go to so much trouble to amass his own. He'd never been to the tiny Mediterranean kingdom of Murin, mostly because he didn't have a yacht to dock there during a sparkling summer of endless lounging and, further, didn't need to take advantage of the country's famously friendly approach to taxes. But he recognized King Geoffrey of Murin on sight, and he certainly recognized the Murinese royal family's coat of arms.

It had been splashed all over the private jet he'd seen on the same tarmac as his back in London.

There was madness, Achilles thought then, and then there was a con job that no one would ever suspect—because who could imagine that the person standing in front of them, looking like someone they already knew, was actually someone else?

If he wasn't mistaken—and he knew he wasn't, because there were too many things about his assistant today that didn't make sense, and Achilles was no great believer in coincidence—Princess Valentina of Murin was trying to run a con.

On him.

Which meant a great many things. First, that his actual assistant was very likely pretending to be the princess somewhere, leaving him and her job in the hands of someone she had to know would fail to live up to Achilles's high standards. That suggested that second, she really wasn't all that happy in her position, as this princess had dared to throw in his face in a way he doubted Natalie ever would have. But it also suggested that third, Natalie had effectively given her notice.

Achilles didn't like any of that. At all. But the fourth thing that occurred to him was that clearly, neither this princess nor his missing assistant expected their little switch to be noticed. Natalie, who should have known better, must honestly have believed that he wouldn't notice an imposter in her place. Or she hadn't cared much if he did.

That was enraging, on some level. Insulting.

But Achilles smiled as Valentina settled herself across the coffee table from him, with a certain inbred grace that whispered of palaces and comportment classes and a lifetime of genteel manners.

Because she thought she was tricking him.

Which meant he could trick her instead. A prospect his body responded to with great enthusiasm as he studied her, this woman who looked like an underling whom a man in his position could never have touched out of ethical considerations—but wasn't.

She wasn't his employee. He didn't pay her salary, and she wasn't bound to obey him in anything if she didn't feel like it.

But she had no idea that he knew that.

Achilles almost felt sorry for her. Almost.

"Let's get started," he murmured, as if they'd exchanged no harsh words. He watched confusion move over her face in a blink, then disappear, because she was a royal princess and she was used to concealing her reactions. He planned to have fun with that. The possibilities were endless, and seemed to roll through him like heat. "We have so much work to do, Miss Monette. I hardly know where to begin."

CHAPTER TWO

BY THE TIME they landed in New York, Princess Valentina of Murin was second-guessing her spontaneous, impulsive decision to switch places with the perfect stranger she'd found wearing her face in the airport lounge.

Achilles Casilieris could make anyone second-guess anything, she suspected.

"You do not appear to be paying attention," he said silkily from beside her, as if he knew exactly what she was thinking. And who she was. And every dream she'd ever had since she was a girl—that was how disconcerting this man was, even lounging there beside her in the back of a luxury car doing nothing more alarming than *sitting*.

"I am hanging on your every word," she assured him as calmly as she could, and then she repeated his last three sentences back to him.

But she had no idea what he was talking about. Repeating conversations she wasn't really listening to was a skill she'd learned in the palace a long, long time ago. It came in handy at many a royal gathering. And in many longwinded lectures from her father and his staff.

You have thrown yourself into deep, deep water, she told herself now, as if that wasn't entirely too apparent already. As if it hadn't already occurred to her that she'd better learn how to swim, and fast.

Achilles Casilieris was a problem.

Valentina knew powerful men. Men who ruled countries. Men who came from centuries upon centuries of power and consequence and wielded it with the offhanded superiority of those who had never imagined *not* ruling all they surveyed.

But Achilles was in an entirely different league.

He took over the whole of the backseat of the car that had waited for them on the tarmac in the bright and sunny afternoon, looking roomy and spacious from the outside. He'd insisted she sit next to him on the plush backseat that should have been more than able to fit two people with room to spare. And yet Valentina felt crowded, as if he was pressing up against her when he wasn't. Achilles wasn't touching her, but still, she was entirely too *aware* of him.

He took up all the air. He'd done it on his plane, too.

She had the hectic notion, connected to that knot beneath her breastbone that was preventing her from taking anything like a deep breath, that it wasn't the enclosed space that was the issue. That he would have this same effect anywhere. All that brooding ruthlessness he didn't bother to contain—or maybe he couldn't contain even if he'd wanted to—seemed to hum around him like a kind of force field that both repelled and compelled at once.

If she was honest, the little glimpse she'd had of him in the airport had been the same—she'd just ignored it.

Valentina had been too busy racing into the lounge so she could have a few precious seconds alone. No staff. No guards. No cameras. Just her perched on the top of a closed toilet seat, shut away from the world, breathing. Letting her face do what it liked. Thinking of absolutely nothing. Not her duty. Not her father's expectations.

Certainly not her bloodless engagement to Prince Rodolfo of Tissely, a man she'd tuned out within moments of their first meeting. Or their impending wedding in two months' time, which she could feel bearing down on her like a thick hand around her throat every time she let herself think about it. It wasn't that she didn't *want* to do her duty and marry the Crown Prince of Tissely. She'd been promised in marriage to her father's allies since the day she was born. It was that she'd never given a great deal of thought to what it was she wanted, because *want* had never been an option available to her.

And it had suddenly occurred to her at her latest wedding dress fitting there in London that she was running out of time.

Soon she would be married to a man in what was really more of a corporate merger of two great European brands, the houses of Tissely and Murin. She'd be expected to produce the necessary heirs to continue the line. She would take her place in the great sweep of her family's storied history, unite two ancient kingdoms, and in so doing fulfill her purpose in life. The end.

The end, she'd thought in that bathroom stall, high-end and luxurious but still, a bathroom stall. *My life fulfilled at twenty-seven.*

Valentina was a woman who'd been given everything, including a healthy understanding of how lucky she was. She didn't often indulge herself with thoughts of what was and wasn't fair when there was no doubt she was among the most fortunate people alive.

But the thing was, it still didn't seem fair. No matter how hard she tried not to think about it that way.

She would do what she had to do, of course. She always had and always would, but for that single moment, locked away in a bathroom stall where no one could see her and no one would ever know, she basked in the sheer, dizzying unfairness of it all.

Then she'd pulled herself together, stepped out and had been prepared to march onto her plane and head back to the life that had been plotted out for her since the day she arrived on the planet.

Only to find her twin standing at the sinks.

Her identical twin—though that was, of course, impossible.

"What is this?" the other woman had asked when they'd faced each other, looking something close to scared. Or unnerved, anyway. "How...?"

Valentina had been fascinated. She'd been unable to keep herself from studying this woman who appeared to be wearing her body as well as her face. She was dressed in a sleek pencil skirt and low heels, which showed legs that Valentina recognized all too well, having last seen them in her own mirror. "I'm Valentina."

"Natalie."

She'd repeated that name in her head like it was a magic spell. She didn't know why she felt as if it was.

But then, running into her double in a London bathroom seemed something close enough to magic to count. Right then when she'd been indulging her self-pity about the unchangeable course of her own life, the universe had presented her with a glimpse of what else could be. If she was someone else.

An identical someone else.

They had the same face. The same legs, as she'd already noted. The same coppery hair that her double wore up in a serviceable ponytail and the same nose Valentina could trace directly to her maternal grandmother. What were the chances, she'd wondered then, that they *weren't* related?

And didn't that raise all kinds of interesting questions?

"You're that princess," Natalie had said, a bit haltingly.

But if Valentina was a princess, and if they were related as they surely had to be...

"I suspect you might be, too," she'd said gently.

"We can't possibly be related. I'm a glorified secretary who never really had a home. You're a royal princess. Presumably your lineage dates back to the Roman Conquest."

"Give or take a few centuries." Valentina tried to imagine having a job like that. Or any job. A secretary, glorified or otherwise, who reported to work for someone else and actually *did things* with her time that weren't directly related to being a symbol. She couldn't really wrap her head around it, or being effectively without a home, either, having been a part of Murin since her birth. As much Murin as its beaches and hills, its monuments and its palace. She might as well have been a park. "Depending which branch of the family you mean, of course."

"I was under the impression that people with lineages that could lead to thrones and crown jewels tended to keep better track of their members," Natalie had said, her tone just dry enough to make Valentina decide that given the right circumstances—meaning anywhere that wasn't a toilet—she'd rather like her doppelganger.

And she knew what the other woman had been asking.

"Conspiracy theorists claim my mother was killed and her death hushed up. Senior palace officials have assured me my whole life that no, she merely left to preserve her mental health, and is rumored to be in residence in a hospital devoted to such things somewhere. All I know is that I haven't seen her since shortly after I was born. According to my father, she preferred anonymity to the joys of motherhood."

And she waited for Natalie to give her an explanation in turn. To laugh, perhaps, and then tell her that she'd been raised by two perfectly normal parents in a happily normal somewhere else, filled with golden retrievers and school buses and pumpkin-spiced coffee drinks and whatever else normal people took for granted that Valentina only read about.

But instead, this woman wearing Valentina's face had looked stricken. "I've never met my father," she'd whispered. "My mother's always told me she has no idea who he was. And she bounces from one affair to the next pretty quickly, so I came to terms with the fact it was possible she really, truly didn't know."

And Valentina had laughed, because what else could she do? She'd spent her whole life wishing she'd had more of a family than her chilly father. Oh, she loved him, she did, but he was so excruciatingly proper. So worried about appearances. His version of a hug was a well-meaning critique on her latest public appearance. Love to her father was maintaining and bolstering the family's reputation across the ages. She'd always wanted a sister to share in the bolstering. A brother. A mother. *Someone.*

But she hadn't had anyone. And now she had a stranger who looked just like her.

"My father is many things," she'd told Natalie. It was too soon to say *our father.* And who knew? Maybe they were cousins. Or maybe this was a fluke. No matter that little jolt of recognition inside her, as if she'd been meant to know this woman. As if this was a reunion. "Including His Royal Majesty, King Geoffrey of Murin. What he is not now, nor has ever been, I imagine, is forgettable."

Natalie had shaken her head. "You underestimate my mother's commitment to amnesia. She's made it a life choice instead of a malady. On some level I admire it."

"My mother was the noblewoman Frederica de Burgh, from a very old Murinese family." Valentina watched Natalie closely as she spoke, looking for any hint of...anything, really, in her gaze. "Promised to my father at birth, raised by nuns and kept deliberately sheltered, and then widely held to be unequal to the task of becoming queen. Mentally. But that's the story they would tell, isn't it, to explain why she disappeared? What's your mother's name?"

Natalie sighed and swung her shoulder bag onto the counter. Valentina had the impression that she'd really, truly wanted not to answer. But she had. "She calls herself Erica."

And there it was. Valentina supposed it could be a coincidence that *Erica* was a shortened form of *Frederica.* But how many coincidences were likely when they resulted in two women who'd never met—who never should have met—who happened to be mirror images?

If there was something in her that turned over at the notion that her mother had, in fact, had a maternal impulse after all— just not for Valentina—well, this wasn't the time to think about that. It might never be the time to think about that. She'd spent twenty-seven years trying her best not to think about that.

She changed the subject before she lost her composure completely and started asking questions she knew she shouldn't.

"I saw Achilles Casilieris, out there in the lounge," she'd said instead. The notorious billionaire had been there on her way in, brooding in a corner of the lounge and scowling at the paper he'd been reading. "He looks even more fearsome in person. You can almost *see* all that brash command and dizzying wealth ooze from his pores, can't you?"

"He's my boss," Natalie had said, sounding amused—if rather darkly. "If he was really oozing anything, anywhere, it would be my job to provide first aid until actual medical personnel could come handle it. At which point he would bite my head off for wasting his precious time by not curing him instantly."

Valentina had been flooded with a rash of follow-up questions. Was the biting off of heads normal? Was it fun to work for a man who sounded half-feral? Most important, did Natalie like her life or merely suffer through it?

But then her mobile started buzzing in her clutch. She'd forgotten about ferocious billionaires and thought about things she knew too much about, like the daredevil prince she was bound to marry soon, instead, because their fathers had agreed regardless of whether either one of them liked it. She'd checked the mobile's display to be sure, but wasn't surprised to find she'd guessed correctly. Lucky her, she'd had another meeting with her husband-to-be in Murin that very afternoon. She'd expected it to go the way all their meetings so far had gone. Prince Rodolfo, beloved the world over for his good looks and devil-may-care attitude, would talk. She would listen without really listening. She'd long since concluded that foretold a very happy royal marriage.

"My fiancé," she'd explained, meeting Natalie's gaze again. "Or his chief of staff, to be more precise."

"Congratulations," Natalie murmured.

"Thank you, I'm very lucky." Valentina's mouth curved, though her tone was far more dry than Natalie's had been. "Everyone says so. Prince Rodolfo is objectively attractive. Not all princes can make that claim, but the tabloids have exulted over his abs since he was a teenager. Just as they have salivated over his impressive dating history, which has involved a selection of models and actresses from at least four continents and did not cease in any noticeable way upon our engagement last fall."

"Your Prince Charming sounds…charming," Natalie had said.

Valentina raised one shoulder, then dropped it. "His theory is that he remains free until our marriage, and then will be free once again following the necessary birth of his heir. More discreetly, I can only hope. Meanwhile, I am beside myself with joy that I must take my place at his side in two short months. Of course."

Natalie had laughed, and the sound had made Valentina's stomach flip. Because it sounded like her. It sounded exactly like her.

"It's going to be a terrific couple of months all around, then," her mirror image was saying. "Mr. Casilieris is in rare form. He's putting together a particularly dramatic deal and it's not going his way and he…isn't used to that. So that's me working twenty-two-hour days instead of my usual twenty for the foreseeable future, which is even more fun when he's cranky and snarling."

"It can't possibly be worse than having to smile politely while your future husband lectures you about the absurd expectation of fidelity in what is essentially an arranged marriage for hours on end. The absurdity is that *he* might be expected to curb his impulses for a year or so, in case you wondered. The expectations for *me* apparently involve quietly and chastely finding fulfillment in philanthropic works, like his sainted absentee mother, who everyone knows manufactured a supposed health crisis so she could live out her days in peaceful seclusion. It's easy to be philanthropically fulfilled while living in isolation in Bavaria."

Natalie had smiled. "Try biting your tongue while your famously short-tempered boss rages at you for no reason, for the hundredth time in an hour, because he pays you to stand there and take it without wilting or crying or selling whingeing stories about him to the press."

Valentina had returned that smile. "Or the hours and hours of grim palace-vetted prewedding press interviews in the company of a pack of advisers who will censor everything I say and inevitably make me sound like a bit of animated treacle, as out of touch with reality as the average overly sweet dessert."

"Speaking of treats, I also have to deal with the board of directors Mr. Casilieris treats like irritating schoolchildren, his packs of furious ex-lovers each with her own vendetta, all his terrified employees who need to be coached through meetings with him and treated for PTSD after, and every last member of his staff in every one of his households, who like me to be the one to ask him the questions they know will set him off on one of his scorch-the-earth rages." Natalie had moved closer then, and lowered her voice. "I was thinking of quitting, to be honest. Today."

"I can't quit, I'm afraid," Valentina had said. Regretfully.

But she'd wished she could. She'd wished she could just... walk away and not have to live up to anyone's expectations. And not have to marry a man whom she barely knew. And not have to resign herself to a version of the same life so many of her ancestors had lived. Maybe that was where the idea had come from. Blood was blood, after all. And this woman clearly shared her blood. What if...?

"I have a better idea," she'd said, and then she'd tossed it out there before she could think better of it. "Let's switch places. For a month, say. Six weeks at the most. Just for a little break."

"That's crazy," Natalie said at once, and she was right. Of course she was right.

"Insane," Valentina had agreed. "But you might find royal protocol exciting! And I've always wanted to do the things everyone else in the world does. Like go to a real job."

"People can't *switch places*." Natalie had frowned. "And certainly not with a princess."

"You could think about whether or not you really want to quit," Valentina pointed out, trying to sweeten the deal. "It would be a lovely holiday for you. Where will Achilles Casilieris be in six weeks' time?"

"He's never gone from London for too long," Natalie had said, as if she was considering it.

Valentina had smiled. "Then in six weeks we'll meet in London. We'll text in the meantime with all the necessary details about our lives, and on the appointed day we'll just meet up and switch back and no one will ever be the wiser. Doesn't that sound like *fun*?"

"It would never work," Natalie had replied. Which wasn't exactly a *no*. "No one will ever believe I'm you."

Valentina waved a hand, encompassing the pair of them. "How would anyone know the difference? I can barely tell myself."

"People will take one look at me and know I'm not you. *You* look like a *princess*."

"You, too, can look like a princess," Valentina assured her. Then smiled. "This princess, anyway. You already do."

"You're elegant. Poised. You've had years of training, presumably. How to be a diplomat. How to be polite in every possible situation. Which fork to use at dinner, for God's sake."

"Achilles Casilieris is one of the wealthiest men alive," Valentina had pointed out. "He dines with as many kings as I do. I suspect that as his personal assistant, Natalie, you have, too. And have likely learned how to navigate the cutlery."

"No one will believe it," Natalie had insisted. But she'd sounded a bit as if she was wavering.

Valentina tugged off the ring on her left hand and placed it down on the counter between them. It made an audible *clink* against the marble surface, as well it should, given it was one of the crown jewels of the kingdom of Tissely.

"Try it on. I dare you. It's an heirloom from Prince Rodolfo's extensive treasury of such items, dating back to the dawn of time, more or less." She smiled. "If it doesn't fit we'll never speak of switching places again."

But the ring had fit her double as if it had been made especially for her.

And after that, switching clothes was easy. Valentina found herself in front of the bathroom mirror, dressed like a billionaire's assistant, when Natalie walked out of the stall behind her in her own shift dress and the heels her favorite shoe designer had made just for her. It was like looking in a mirror, but one that walked and looked unsteady on her feet and was wearing her hair differently.

Valentina couldn't tell if she was disconcerted or excited. Both, maybe.

She'd eyed Natalie. "Will your glasses give me a headache, do you suppose?"

But Natalie had pulled them from her face and handed them over. "They're clear glass. I was getting a little too much attention from some of the men Mr. Casilieris works with, and it annoyed him. I didn't want to lose my job, so I started wearing my hair up and these glasses. It worked like a charm."

"I refuse to believe men are so idiotic."

Natalie had grinned as Valentina took the glasses and slid them onto her nose. "The men we're talking about weren't exactly paying me attention because they found me enthralling. It was a diversionary tactic during negotiations, and yes, you'd be surprised how many men fail to see a woman who looks smart."

She'd freed her hair from its utilitarian ponytail and shook it out, then handed the stretchy elastic to Valentina. It took Valentina a moment to re-create the ponytail on her own head, and then it was done.

And it really was like magic.

"This is crazy," Natalie had whispered.

"We have to switch places now," Valentina said softly, hearing the rough patch in her own voice. "I've always wanted to be...someone else. Someone normal. Just for a little while."

And she'd gotten exactly what she'd wanted, hadn't she?

"I am distressed, Miss Monette, that I cannot manage to secure your attention for more than a moment or two," Achilles said then, slamming Valentina back into this car he dominated so easily when all he was doing was sitting there.

Sitting there, filling up the world without even trying.

He was *devastating*. There was no other possible word that could describe him. His black hair was close-cropped to his head, which only served to highlight his strong, intensely masculine features. She'd had hours on the plane to study him as she'd repeatedly failed to do the things he'd expected of her, and she still couldn't really get her head around why it was that he was so...affecting. He shouldn't have been. Dark hair. Dark eyes that tended toward gold when his temper washed over him, which he'd so far made no attempt to hide. A strong nose that reminded her of ancient statues she'd seen in famous museums. That lean, hard body of his that wasn't made of marble or bronze but seemed to suggest both as he used it so effortlessly. A predator packed into a dark suit that seemed molded to him, whispering suggestions of a lethal warrior when all he was doing was taking phone calls with a five-hundred-thousand-dollar watch on one wrist that he didn't flash about, because he was Achilles Casilieris. He didn't need flash.

Achilles was something else.

It was the power that seemed to emanate from him, even when he was doing nothing but sitting quietly. It was the fierce hit of his intelligence, that brooding, unmistakable cleverness that seemed to wrap around him like a cloud. It was something in the way he looked at her, as if he saw too much and too deeply and no matter that Valentina's unreadable game face was the envy of Europe. Besides all that, there was something untamed about him. Fierce.

Something about him left her breathless. Entirely too close to reeling.

"Do you require a gold star every time you make a statement?" she asked, careful not to look at him. It was too hard to look away. She'd discovered that on the plane ride from London—and he was a lot closer now. So close she was sure she could feel the heat of his body from where she sat. "I'll be certain to make a note to celebrate you more often. Sir."

Valentina didn't know what she was doing. In Natalie's job, certainly, but also with this man in general. She'd learned one thing about powerful people—particularly men—and it was that they did not enjoy being challenged. Under any circumstances. What made her think Achilles would go against type and magically handle this well?

But she couldn't seem to stop herself.

And the fact that she had never been one to challenge much of anything before hardly signified. Or maybe that was why she felt so unfettered, she thought. Because this wasn't her life. This wasn't her remote father and his endless expectations for the behavior of his only child. This was a strange little bit of role-playing that allowed her to be someone other than Princess Valentina for a moment. A few weeks, that was all. Why not challenge Achilles while she was at it? *Especially* if no one else ever did?

She could feel his gaze on the side of her face, that brooding dark gold, and she braced herself. Then made sure her expression was nothing but serene as she turned to face him.

It didn't matter. There was no minimizing this man. She could feel the hit of him—like a fist—deep in her belly. And then lower.

"Are you certain you were not hit in the head?" Achilles asked, his dark voice faintly rough with the hint of his native Greek. "Perhaps in the bathroom at the airport? I fear that such places can often suffer from slippery floors. Deadly traps for the unwary."

"It was only a bathroom," she replied airily. "It wasn't slippery or otherwise notable in any way."

"Are you sure?" And something in his voice and his hard gaze prickled into her then. Making her chest feel tighter.

Valentina did not want to talk about the bathroom, much less anything that had happened there. And there was something in his gaze that worried her—but that was insane. He couldn't have any idea that she'd run into her own twin. How could he? Valentina had been unaware that there was the faintest possibility she might have a twin until today.

Which made her think about her father and his many, many lectures about his only child in a new, unfortunate light. But Valentina thrust that aside. That was something to worry about when she was a princess again. That was a problem she could take up when she was back in Murin Castle.

Here, now, she was a secretary. An executive assistant, no more and no less.

"I beg your pardon, Mr. Casilieris." She let her smile deepen and ignored the little hum of…something deep inside her when his gaze seemed to catch fire. "Are you trying to tell me that you need a bathroom? Should I ask the driver to stop the car right here in the middle of the George Washington Bridge?"

She expected him to get angry again. Surely that was what had been going on before, back in London before the plane had taken off. She'd seen temper all over that fierce, hard face of his and gleaming hot in his gaze. More than that, she'd felt it inside her. As if the things he felt echoed within her, winding her into knots. She felt something a whole lot like a chill inch its way down her spine at that notion.

But Achilles only smiled. And that was far more dangerous than merely devastating.

"Miss Monette," he said and shook his head, as if she amused him, when she could see that the thing that moved over that ruthless face of his was far too intense to be simple *amusement*. "I had no idea that beneath your officious exterior you've been hiding a comedienne all this time. For five years you've worked at my side and never let so much as a hint of this whimsical side of your personality out into the open. Whatever could have changed?"

He knows. The little voice inside her was certain—and terrified.

But it was impossible. Valentina knew it was impossible, so she made herself smile and relax against the leather seat as if she'd never in her life been so at her ease. Very much as if she was not within scant inches of a very large, very powerful, very intense male who was eyeing her the way gigantic lions and tigers and jaguars eyed their food. When they were playing with it.

She'd watched enough documentaries and made enough state visits to African countries to know firsthand.

"Perhaps I've always been this amusing," she suggested, managing to tamp down her hysteria about oversize felines, none of which was particularly helpful at the moment. "Perhaps you've only recently allowed yourself to truly listen to me."

"I greatly enjoy listening to you," Achilles replied. There was a laziness in the way he sat there, sprawled out in the backseat of his car, that dark gold gaze on hers. A certain laziness, yes—but Valentina didn't believe it for a second. "I particularly enjoy listening to you when you are doing your job perfectly. Because you know how much I admire perfection. I insist on it, in fact. Which is why I cannot understand why you failed to provide it today."

"I don't know what you mean."

But she knew what he meant. She'd been on the plane and she'd been the one to fail repeatedly to do what was clearly her job. She'd hung up on one conference call and failed entirely to connect another. She'd expected him to explode—if she was honest, there was a part of her that wanted him to explode, in the way that anyone might want to poke and poke and poke at some kind of blister to see if it would pop. But he hadn't popped. He hadn't lost his temper at all, despite the fact that it had been very clear to Valentina very quickly that she was a complete and utter disaster at doing whatever it was that Natalie did.

When Achilles had stared at her in amazement, however, she hadn't made any excuses. She'd only gazed right back, serenely, as if she'd meant to do whatever utterly incorrect thing it was. As if it was all some kind of strategy.

She could admit that she hadn't really thought the job part through. She been so busy fantasizing herself into some kind of normal life that it had never occurred to her that, normal or not, a life was still *a whole life*. She had no idea how to live any way but the way she'd been living for almost thirty years. How remarkably condescending, she'd thought up there on Achilles Casilieris's jet, that she'd imagined she could simply step into a job—especially one as demanding as this appeared to be—and do it merely because she'd decided it was her chance at something "normal."

Valentina had found the entire experience humbling, if she was honest, and it had been only a few hours since she'd switched places with Natalie in London. Who knew what else awaited her?

But Achilles was still sprawled there beside her, that unnerving look of his making her skin feel too small for her bones.

"Natalie, Natalie," he murmured, and Valentina told herself it was a good thing he'd used that name. It wasn't her name, and she needed the reminder. This wasn't about her. It wasn't her job to advocate for Natalie when the other woman might not wish for her to do anything like that. She was on a fast track to losing Natalie her job, and then what? Valentina didn't have to worry about her employment prospects, but she had no idea what the market was like for billionaire's assistants.

But maybe there was a part of her that already knew that there was no way Natalie Monette was a stranger to her. Certainly not on the genetic level. And that had implications she wasn't prepared to examine just yet, but she did know that the woman who was in all likelihood her long-lost identical twin did not have to work for Achilles Casilieris unless she wanted to.

How arrogant of you, a voice inside her said quietly. *Her Royal Highness, making unilateral decisions for others' lives without their input.*

The voice sounded a little too much like her father's.

"That is my name," Valentina said to Achilles, in case there had been any doubt. Perhaps with a little too much force.

But she had the strangest notion that he was...*tasting* the name as he said it. As if he'd never said it before. Did he call Natalie by her first name? Valentina rather thought not, given that he'd called her *Miss Monette* when she'd met him—but that was neither here nor there, she told herself. And no matter that she was a woman who happened to know the power of titles. She had many of her own. And her life was marked by those who used the different versions of her titles, not to mention the few who actually called her by her first name.

"I cannot tolerate this behavior," he said, but it wasn't in that same infuriated tone he'd used earlier. If anything, he sounded almost...indulgent. But surely that was impossible. "It borders on open rebellion, and I cannot have that. This is not a democracy, I'm afraid. This is a dictatorship. If I want your opinion, I'll tell you what it is."

There was no reason her heart should have been kicking at her like that, her pulse so loud in her ears she was sure he must be able to hear it himself.

"What an interesting way to foster employee loyalty," she murmured. "Really more of a scorch-the-earth approach. Do you find it gets you the results you want?"

"I do not need to breed employee loyalty," Achilles told her, sounding even lazier than before, those dark eyes of his on hers. "People are loyal to me or they are fired. You seem to have forgotten reality today, Natalie. Allow me to remind you that I pay you so much money that I own your loyalty, just as I own everything else."

"Perhaps," and her voice was a little too rough then. A little too shaky, when what could this possibly have to do with her? She was a visitor. Natalie's loyalty was no concern of hers. "I have no wish to be owned. Does anyone? I think you'll find that they do not."

Achilles shrugged. "Whether you wish it or do not, that is how it is."

"That is why I was considering quitting," she heard herself say. And she was no longer looking at him. That was still far too dangerous, too disconcerting. She found herself staring down at her hands, folded in her lap. She could feel that she was frowning, when she learned a long, long time ago never to show her feelings in public. "It's all very well and good for you, of course. I imagine it's quite pleasant to have minions. But for me, there's more to life than blind loyalty. There's more to life than work." She blinked back a strange heat. "I may not have experienced it myself, but I know there must be."

"And what do you think is out there?" He shifted in the seat beside her, but Valentina still refused to look back at him, no matter how she seemed almost physically compelled to do just that. "What do you think you're missing? Is it worth what you are throwing away here today, with this aggressive attitude and the childish pretense that you don't know your own job?"

"It's only those who are bored of the world, or jaded, who are so certain no one else could possibly wish to see it."

"No one is keeping you from roaming about the planet at will," he told her in a low voice. Too low. So low it danced along her skin and seemed to insinuate itself beneath her flesh. "But you seem to wish to burn down the world you know in order to see the one you don't. That is not what I would call wise. Would you?"

Valentina didn't understand why his words seemed to beat beneath her own skin. But she couldn't seem to catch her breath.

And her eyes seemed entirely too full, almost scratchy, with an emotion she couldn't begin to name.

She was aware of too many things. Of the car as it slid through the Manhattan streets. Of Achilles himself, too big and too masculine in the seat beside her, and much too close besides. And most of all, that oddly weighted thing within her, rolling around and around until she couldn't tell the difference between sensation and reaction.

And him right there in the middle of it, confusing her all the more.

CHAPTER THREE

ACHILLES DIDN'T SAY another word, and that was worse. It left Valentina to sit there with her own thoughts in a whirl and nothing to temper them. It left no barrier between that compelling, intent look in his curiously dark eyes and her.

Valentina had no experience with men. Her father had insisted that she grow up as sheltered as possible from public life, so that she could enjoy what little privacy was afforded to a European princess before she turned eighteen. She'd attended carefully selected boarding schools run strictly and deliberately, but that hadn't prevented her classmates from involving themselves in all kinds of dramatic situations. Even then, Valentina had kept herself apart.

Your mother's defection was a stain on the throne, her father always told her. *It is upon us to render it clean and whole again.*

Valentina had been far too terrified of staining Murin any further to risk a scandal. She'd concentrated on her studies and her friends and left the teenage rebellions to others. And once out of school, she'd been thrust unceremoniously into the spotlight. She'd been an ambassador for her kingdom wherever she went, and more than that, she'd always known that she was promised to the Crown Prince of Tissely. Any scandals she embroiled herself in would haunt two kingdoms.

She'd never seen the point.

And along the way she'd started to take a certain pride in the fact that she was saving herself for her predetermined marriage. It was the one thing that was hers to give on her wedding night that had nothing to do with her father or her kingdom.

Is it pride that's kept you chaste—or is it control? a little voice inside her asked then, and the way it kicked in her, Valentina suspected she wouldn't care for the answer. She ignored it.

But the point was, she had no idea how to handle men. Not on any kind of intimate level. These past few hours, in fact, were the longest she'd ever spent alone in the company of a man. It simply didn't happen when she was herself. There were always attendants and aides swarming around Princess Valentina. Always.

She told herself that was why she was having such trouble catching her breath. It was the novelty—that was all. It certainly wasn't *him*.

Still, it was almost a relief when the car pulled up in front of a quietly elegant building on the Upper West Side of Manhattan, perched there with a commanding view of Central Park, and came to a stop.

The late-afternoon breeze washed over her when she stepped from the car, smelling improbably of flowers in the urban sprawl of New York City. But Valentina decided to take it as a blessing.

Achilles remained silent as he escorted her into the building. He only raised his chin in the barest of responses to the greeting that came his way from the doormen in the shiny, obviously upscale lobby, and then he led her into a private elevator located toward the back and behind another set of security guards. It was a gleaming, shining thing that he operated with a key. And it was blessedly without any mirrors.

Valentina wasn't entirely sure whom she'd see if she looked at her own reflection just then.

There were too many things she didn't understand churning inside her, and she hadn't the slightest idea what she was doing here. What on earth she hoped to gain from this odd little lark across the planet, literally in another woman's shoes.

A break, she reminded herself sternly. A vacation. A little holiday away from all the duties and responsibilities of Princess Valentina, which was more important now than ever. She would give herself over to her single-greatest responsibility in a matter of weeks. She would marry Prince Rodolfo and make both of their fathers and all of their subjects very, very happy.

And a brief escape had sounded like bliss for that split second back there in London—and it still did, when she thought about what waited for her. The terribly appropriate royal marriage. The endlessly public yet circumspect life of a modern queen. The glare of all that attention that she and any children she bore could expect no matter where they went or what they did, yet she could never comment upon lest she seem ungrateful or entitled.

Hers was to wave and smile—that was all. She was marrying a man she hardly knew who would expect the marital version of the same. This was a little breather before the reality of all that. This was a tiny bit of space between her circumscribed life at her father's side and more of the same at her husband's.

She couldn't allow the brooding, unreadable man beside her to ruin it, no matter how unnerving his dark gold gaze was. No matter what fires it kicked up inside her that she hardly dared name.

The elevator doors slid open, delivering them straight into the sumptuous front hall of an exquisitely decorated penthouse. Valentina followed Achilles as he strode deep inside, not bothering to spare her a glance as he moved. She was glad that he walked ahead of her, which allowed her to look around so she could get her bearings without seeming to do so. Because, of course, Natalie would already know her way around this place.

She took in the high ceilings and abundant windows all around. The sweeping stairs that led up toward at least two more floors. The mix of art deco and a deep coziness that suggested this penthouse was more than just a showcase; Achilles actually *lived* here.

Valentina told herself—sternly—that there was no earthly reason that notion should make her shiver.

She was absurdly grateful when a housekeeper appeared, clucking at Achilles in what it took Valentina longer than it should have to realize was Greek. A language she could converse in, though she would never consider herself anything like fluent. Still, it took her only a very few moments to understand that whatever the danger Achilles exuded and however ruthless the swath he cut through the entire world with a single glance, this woman thought he was wonderful.

She *beamed* at him.

It would not do to let that get to her, Valentina warned herself as something warm seemed to roll its way through her, pooling in the strangest places. She should not draw any conclusions about a man who was renowned for his fierceness in all things and yet let a housekeeper treat him like family.

The woman declared she would feed him no matter if he was hungry or not, lest he get skinny and weak, and bustled back in the direction of what Valentina assumed was the kitchen.

"You're looking around as if you are lost," Achilles murmured, when Valentina didn't think she'd been looking around at all. "When you have spent more time in this penthouse over the last five years than I have."

Valentina hated the fact that she started a bit when she realized his attention was focused on her again. And that he was speaking in English, which seemed to make him sound that much more knowing.

Or possibly even mocking, unless she was very much mistaken.

"Mr. Casilieris," she said, lacing her voice with gentle reprove, "I work for you. I don't understand why you appear to be quite so interested in what you think is happening inside my head today. Especially when you are so mistaken."

"Am I?"

"Entirely." She raised her brows at him. "If I could suggest that we concentrate more on matters of business than fictional representations of what might or might not be going on inside my mind, I think we might be more productive."

"As productive as we were on the flight over?" His voice was a lazy sort of lash, as amused as it was on target.

Valentina only smiled, hoping she looked enigmatic and strategic rather than at a loss.

"Are *you* lost?" she asked him after a moment, because neither one of them had moved from the great entry that bled into the spacious living room, then soared up two stories, a quiet testament to his wealth and power.

"Careful, Miss Monette," Achilles said with a certain dark precision. "As delightful as I have found today's descent into insubordination, I have a limit. It would be in your best interests not to push me there too quickly."

Valentina had made a study out of humbly accepting all kinds of news she didn't wish to hear over the years. She bent her head, let her lips curve a bit—but not enough to be called a smile, only enough to show she was feeling...something. Then she simply stood there quietly. It was amazing how many unpleasant moments she'd managed to get through that way.

So she had no earthly idea why there was a part of her that wanted nothing more than to look Achilles straight in his dark eyes and ask him, *Or what?*

Somehow, thankfully, she refrained.

Servants came in behind them with luggage—some of which Valentina assumed must be Natalie's and thus hers—but Achilles did not appear to notice them. He kept his attention trained directly on her.

A lesser woman would have been disconcerted, Valentina thought. Someone unused to being the focus of attention, for example. Someone who hadn't spent a part of every day since she turned eighteen having cameras in her face to record every flutter of her eyelashes and rip apart every facet of whatever she happened to be wearing and how she'd done her hair. Every expression that crossed her face was a headline.

What was a cranky billionaire next to that?

"There's no need to repair to our chambers after the flight, I think," he said softly, and Valentina had that odd notion again. That he could see right through her. That he knew things he couldn't possibly know. "We can get right to it."

And there was no reason that that should feel almost...dirty. As if he was suggesting—

But, of course, that was absurd, Valentina told herself staunchly. He was Achilles Casilieris. He was renowned almost as much for his prowess in the sheets as he was for his dominance in the boardroom. In some circles, more.

He tended toward the sort of well-heeled women who were mainstays on various charity circuits. Not for him the actresses or models whom so many other men of his stature preferred. That, apparently, was not good enough for Achilles Casilieris. Valentina had found herself with some time on the plane to research it herself, after Achilles had finished the final call she'd failed entirely to set up to his liking and had sat a while, a fulminating stare fixed on her. Then he'd taken himself off to one of the jet's finely appointed staterooms, and she'd breathed a bit easier.

A bit.

She'd looked around for a good book to read, preferably a paperback romance because who didn't like hope and happiness with a bit of sex thrown in to make it spicy, but there had been nothing of the sort. Achilles apparently preferred dreary economic magazines that trumpeted out recession and doom from all quarters. Valentina had kicked off her shoes, tucked her legs beneath her on the smooth leather chair she'd claimed for the flight, and indulged herself with a descent into the tabloid and gossip sites she normally avoided. Because she knew how many lies they told about her, so why would she believe anything she read about anyone else?

Still, they were a great way to get a sense of the kind of coverage a man like Achilles suffered, which would surely tell her... something. But the answer was...not much. He was featured in shots from charity events where other celebrities gathered like cows at a trough, but was otherwise not really a tabloid staple. Possibly because he was so sullen and scowling, she thought.

His taste in bedmates, however, was clear even without being splashed across screeching front pages all over the world. Achilles tended toward women who were less celebrated for their faces and more for their actions. Which wasn't to say they weren't all beautiful, of course. That seemed to be a requirement. But they couldn't only be beautiful.

This one was a civil rights attorney of some renown. That one was a journalist who spent most of her time in terrifying war zones. This one had started a charity to benefit a specific cancer that had taken her younger sister. That one was a former Olympic athlete who had dedicated her post-competition life to running a lauded program for at-risk teenagers.

He clearly had a type. Accomplished, beautiful women who did good in the world and who also happened to be wealthy enough all on their own. The uncharitable part of her suspected that last part was because he knew a woman of independent means would not be as interested in his fortune as a woman who had nothing. No gold diggers need apply, clearly.

But the point was, she knew she was mistaken about his potentially suggestive words. Because "assistant to billionaire" was not the kind of profession that would appeal to a man like Achilles. It saved no lives. It bettered nothing.

Valentina found herself glaring at his back as he led her into a lavish office suite on the first level of his expansive penthouse. When she stood in the center of the room, awaiting further instructions, he only crooked a brow. He leaned back against the large desk that stretched across one wall and regarded her with that hot sort of focus that made everything inside her seem to shift hard to the left.

She froze. And then she could have stood there for hours, for all she knew, as surely as if he'd caught her and held her fast in his fists.

"When you are ready, Miss Monette, feel free to take your seat." His voice was razor sharp, cut through with that same rough darkness that she found crept through her limbs. Lighting her up and making her feel something like sluggish. She didn't understand it. "Though I do love being kept waiting."

More chastened than she wanted to admit, Valentina moved to one of the seats set around a table to the right of the desk, at the foot of towering bookshelves stuffed full of serious-looking books, and settled herself in it. When he continued to stare at her as if she was deliberately keeping him waiting, she reached into the bag—Natalie's bag, which she'd liberated from the bathroom when she'd left the airport with Achilles—until she found a tablet.

A few texts with her double had given her the passwords she needed and some advice.

Just write down everything he says. He likes to forget he said certain things, and it's always good to have a record. One of my jobs is to function as his memory.

Valentina had wanted to text back her thoughts on that, but had refrained. Natalie might have wanted to quit this job, but that was up to her, not the woman taking her place for a few weeks.

"Anything else?" Achilles's voice had a dark edge. "Would you like to have a snack? Perhaps a brief nap? Tell me, is there any way that I can make you more comfortable, Miss Monette, such that you might actually take it upon yourself to do a little work today?"

And Valentina didn't know what came over her. Because she

wanted to argue. She, who had made a virtue out of remaining quiet and cordial under any circumstances, wanted to fight. She didn't understand it. She knew it was Achilles. That there was something in him that made her want to do or say anything to get some kind of reaction. It didn't matter that it was madness. It was something about that look in his eyes. Something about that hard, amused mouth of his.

It was something about *him*.

But Valentina reminded herself that this was not her life.

This was not her life and this was not her job, and none of this was hers to ruin. She was the steward of Natalie's life for a little while, nothing more. She imagined that Natalie would be doing the same for her. Maybe breathing a little bit of new life into the tired old royal nonsense she'd find waiting for her at Murin Castle, but that was all. Neither one of them was out to wreck what they found.

And she'd never had any trouble whatsoever keeping to the party line. Doing her father's bidding, behaving appropriately, being exactly the princess whom everyone imagined she was. She felt that responsibility—to her people, to her bloodline, to her family's history—deeply. She'd never acted out the way so many of her friends had. She'd never fought against her own responsibilities. It wasn't that she was afraid to do any of those things, but simply that it had never occurred to her to try. Valentina had always known exactly who she was and what her life would hold, from her earliest days.

So she didn't recognize this thing in her that wanted nothing more than to cause a commotion. To stand up and throw the tablet she held at Achilles's remarkably attractive head. To kick over the chair she was sitting in and, while she was at it, that desk of his, too, all brash steel and uncompromising masculinity, just like its owner.

She wanted to do *something*. Anything. She could feel it humming through her veins, bubbling in her blood. As if something about this normal life she'd tried on for size had infected her. Changed her. When it had only been a few hours.

He's a ruthless man, something reckless inside her whispered. *He can take it.*

But this wasn't her life. She had to protect it, not destroy it, no matter what was moving in her, poking at her, tempting her to act out for the first time in her life.

So Valentina smiled up at Achilles, forced herself to remain serene the way she always did, and got to work.

It was late into the New York night when Achilles finally stopped torturing his deceitful princess.

He made her go over byzantine contracts that rendered his attorneys babbling idiots. He questioned her on clauses he only vaguely understood himself, and certainly couldn't expect her to be conversant on. He demanded she prepare memos he had no intention of sending. He questioned her about events he knew she could not possibly know anything about, and the truth was that he enjoyed himself more than he could remember enjoying anything else for quite some time.

When Demetria had bustled in with food, Achilles had waved Valentina's away.

"My assistant does not like to eat while she works," he told his housekeeper, but he'd kept his gaze on Valentina while he'd said it.

"I don't," she'd agreed merrily enough. "I consider it a weakness." She'd smiled at him. "But you go right ahead."

Point to the princess, he'd thought.

The most amazing thing was that Princess Valentina never backed down. Her ability to brazen her way through the things she didn't know, in fact, was nothing short of astounding. Impressive in the extreme. Achilles might have admired it if he hadn't been the one she was trying to fool.

"It is late," he said finally, when he thought her eyes might glaze over at last. Though he would cast himself out his own window to the Manhattan streets below before he'd admit his might, too. "And while there is always more to do, I think it is perhaps wise if we take this as a natural stopping place."

Valentina smiled at him, tucked up in that chair of hers that she had long since claimed as her own in a way he couldn't remember the real Natalie had ever done, her green eyes sparkling.

"I understand if you need a rest," she said sweetly. Too sweetly. "Sir."

Achilles had been standing at the windows, his back to the mad gleam of Manhattan. But at that, he let himself lean back, his body shifting into something...looser. More dangerous.

And much, much hotter than contracts.

"I worry my hearing has failed me. Because it sounded very much as if you were impugning my manhood."

"Only if your manhood is so fragile that you can't imagine it requires a rest," she said, and aimed a sunny smile at him as if that would take away the sting of her words. "But you are Achilles Casilieris. You have made yourself a monument to manhood, clearly. No fragility allowed."

"It is almost as if you think debating me like this is some kind of strategy," he said softly, making no attempt to ratchet back the ruthlessness in his voice. Much less do something about the fire he could feel storming through him everywhere else. "Let me warn you, again, it is only a strategy if your goal is to find yourself without a job and without a recommendation. To say nothing of the black mark I will happily put beside your name."

Valentina waved a hand in the air, airily, dismissing him. And her possible firing, black marks—all of it. Something else he very likely would have found impressive if he'd been watching her do it to someone else.

"So many threats." She shook her head. "I understand that this is how you run your business and you're very successful, but really. It's exhausting. Imagine how many more bees you could get with honey."

He didn't want to think about honey. Not when there were

only the two of them here, in this office cushioned by the night outside and the rest of the penthouse. No shared walls on these floors he owned. This late, none of the staff would be up. It was only Achilles and this princess pretending to be his assistant, and the buttery light of the few lamps they'd switched on, making the night feel thick and textured everywhere the light failed to reach.

Like inside him.

"Come here."

Valentina blinked, but her green gaze was unreadable then. She only looked at him for a moment, as if she'd forgotten that she was playing this game. And that in it, she was his subordinate.

"Come here," he said again. "Do not make me repeat myself, I beg you. You will not like my response."

She stood the way she did everything else, with an easy grace. With that offhanded elegance that did things to him he preferred not to examine. And he knew she had no desire to come any closer to him. He could feel it. Her wariness hung between them like some kind of smoke, and it ignited that need inside him. And for a moment he thought she might disobey him. That she might balk—and it was in that moment he thought she'd stay where she was, across the room, that he had understood how very much he wanted her.

In a thousand ways he shouldn't, because Achilles was a man who did not *want*. He took. Wanting was a weakness that led only to darkness—though it didn't feel like a weakness tonight. It felt like the opposite.

But he'd underestimated his princess. Her shoulders straightened almost imperceptibly. And then she glided toward him, head high like some kind of prima ballerina, her face set in the sort of pleasant expression he now knew she could summon and dispatch at will. He admired that, too.

And he'd thrown out that summons because he could. Because he wanted to. And he was experimenting with this new *wanting*, no matter how little he liked it.

Still, there was no denying the way his body responded as he watched her walk toward him. There was no denying the rich, layered tension that seemed to fill the room. And him, making his pulse a living thing as his blood seemed to heat in his veins.

Something gleamed in that green gaze of hers, but she kept coming. She didn't stop until she was directly beside him, so close that if she breathed too heavily he thought her shoulder might brush his. He shifted so that he stood slightly behind her, and jutted his chin toward the city laid out before them.

"What do you see when you look out the window?"

He felt more than saw the glance she darted at him. But then she kept her eyes on the window before them. On the ropes of light stretching out in all hectic directions possible below.

"Is that a trick question? I see Manhattan."

"I grew up in squalor." His voice was harsher than he'd intended, but Achilles did nothing to temper it. "It is common, I realize, for successful men to tell stories of their humble beginnings. Americans in particular find these stories inspiring. It allows them to fantasize that they, too, might better themselves against any odds. But the truth is more of a gray area, is it not? Beginnings are never quite so humble as they sound when rich men claim them. But me?" He felt her gaze on him then, instead of the mess of lights outside. "When I use the word *squalor*, that's an upgrade."

Her swallow was audible. Or perhaps he was paying her too close attention. Either way, he didn't back away.

"I don't know why you're telling me this."

"When you look through this window you see a city. A place filled with people going about their lives, traffic and isolation." He shifted so he could look down at her. "I see hope. I see vindication. I see all the despair and all the pain and all the loss that went into creating the man you see before you tonight. Creating this." And he moved his chin to indicate the penthouse.

And the Casilieris Company while he was at it. "And there is nothing that I wouldn't do to protect it."

And he didn't know what had happened to him while he was speaking. He'd been playing a game, and then suddenly it seemed as if the game had started to play him—and it wasn't finished. Something clutched at him, as if he was caught in the grip of some massive fist.

It was almost as if he wanted this princess, this woman who believed she was tricking him—deceiving him—to understand him.

This, too, was unbearable.

But he couldn't seem to stop.

"Do you think people become driven by accident, Miss Monette?" he asked, and he couldn't have said why that thing gripping him seemed to clench harder. Making him sound far more intense than he thought he should have felt. Risking the truth about himself he carried inside and shared with no one. But he still didn't stop. "Ambition, desire, focus and drive—do you think these things grow on trees? But then, perhaps I'm asking the wrong person. Have you not told me a thousand times that you are not personally ambitious?"

It was one of the reasons he'd kept Natalie with him for so long, when other assistants to men like him used positions like hers as springboards into their own glorious careers. But this woman was not Natalie. If he hadn't known it before, he'd have known it now, when it was a full-scale struggle to keep his damned hands to himself.

"Ambition, it seems to me, is for those who have the freedom to pursue it. And for those who do not—" and Valentina's eyes seemed to gleam at that, making Achilles wonder exactly what her ambitions were "—it is nothing more than dissatisfaction. Which is far less worthy and infinitely more destructive, I think we can agree."

He didn't know when he'd turned to face her fully. He didn't know when he'd stopped looking at the city and was looking only at her instead. But he was, and he compounded that error by reaching out his hand and tugging on the very end of her silky, coppery ponytail where it kissed her shoulder every time she moved her head.

Her lips parted, as if on a soundless breath, and Achilles felt that as if she'd caressed him. As if her hands were on his body the way he wished they were, instead of at her sides.

"Are you dissatisfied?" It was amazing how difficult it was not to use her real name then. How challenging it was to stay in this game he suddenly didn't particularly want to play. "Is that what this is?"

Her green eyes, which had been so unreadable, suddenly looked slick. Dark and glassy with some or other emotion. He couldn't tell what it was, and still, he could feel it in him like smoke, stealing through his chest and making it harder than it should have been to breathe.

"There's nothing wrong with dissatisfaction in and of itself," she told him after a moment, then another, that seemed too large for him to contain. Too dark and much too edgy to survive intact, and yet here they both were. "You see it as disloyalty, but it's not."

"How can it be anything else?"

"It is possible to be both loyal and open to the possibility that there is a life outside the one you've committed yourself to." Her green eyes searched his. "Surely there must be."

"I think you will find that there is no such possibility." His voice was harsh. He could feel it inside him, like a stain. Like need. "We must all decide who we are, every moment of every day. You either keep a vow or you do not. There is no between."

She stiffened at that, then tried to force her shoulders back down to an easier, less telling angle. Achilles watched her do it. He watched something like distress cross her lovely face, but she hid that, too. It was only the darkness in her gaze that told him he'd scored a direct hit, and he was a man who took great pride in the strikes he leveled against anyone who tried to move against him. Yet what he felt when he looked at Valentina was not pride. Not pride at all.

"Some vows are not your own," she said fiercely, her gaze locked to his. "Some are inherited. It's easy to say that you'll keep them because that's what's expected of you, but it's a great deal harder to actually *do* it."

He knew the vows she'd made. That pointless prince. Her upcoming royal wedding. He assumed that was the least of the vows she'd inherited from her father. And he still thought it was so much smoke and mirrors to hide the fact that she, like so many of her peers, was a spoiled and pampered creature who didn't like to be told what to do. Wasn't that the reason *poor little rich girl* was a saying in the first place?

He had no sympathy for the travails of a rich, pampered princess. But he couldn't seem to unwind that little silken bit of copper from around his finger, either. Much less step back and put the space between them that he should have left there from the start.

Achilles shook his head. "There is no gray area. Surely you know this. You are either who you say you are or you are not."

There was something like misery in those eyes of hers then. And this was what he'd wanted. This was why he'd been goading her. And yet now that he seemed to have succeeded, he felt the strangest thing deep in his gut. It was an unpleasant and unfamiliar sensation, and at first Achilles couldn't identify it. It was a low heat, trickling through him, making him restless. Making him as close to uncertain as he'd ever been.

In someone else, he imagined, it might be shame. But shame was not something Achilles allowed in himself. Ever.

This was a night full of things he did not allow, apparently. Because he wanted her. He wanted to punctuate this oddly emotional discussion with his mouth. His hands. The whole of his too-tight, too-interested body pressed deep into hers. He wanted to taste those sweetly lush lips of hers. He wanted to take her elegant face in his hands, tip her head back and sate himself at last. It seemed to him an age or two since he'd boarded his plane and realized his assistant was not who she was supposed to be. An agony of waiting and all that *want*, and he was not a man who agonized. Or waited. Or wanted anything, it seemed, but this princess who thought she could fool him.

What was the matter with him that some part of him wanted to let her?

He did none of the things he longed to do.

Achilles made himself do the hard thing, no matter how complicated it was. Or how complicated it felt, anyway. When really it was so simple. He let her go. He let her silky hair fall from between his fingers, and he stepped back, putting inches between them.

But that did nothing to ease the temptation.

"I think what you need is a good night's sleep," he told her, like some kind of absurd nurturer. Something he had certainly never tried to be for anyone else in the whole of his life. He would have doubted it was possible—and he refused to analyze that. "Perhaps it will clear your head and remind you of who you are. Jet lag can make that so very confusing, I know."

He thought she might have scuttled from the room at that, filled with her own shame if there was any decency in the world, but he was learning that this princess was not at all who he expected her to be. She swallowed, hard. And he could still see that darkness in her eyes. But she didn't look away from him. And she certainly didn't scuttle anywhere.

"I know exactly who I am, Mr. Casilieris," she said, very directly, and the lenses in her glasses made her eyes seem that much greener. "As I'm certain you do, too. Jet lag makes a person tired. It doesn't make them someone else entirely."

And when she turned to walk from the room then, it was with her head held high, graceful and self-contained, with no apparent second thoughts. Or anything the least bit like shame. All he could read on her as she went was that same distracting elegance that was already too far under his skin.

Achilles couldn't seem to do a thing but watch her go.

And when the sound of her footsteps had faded away, deep into the far reaches of the penthouse, he turned back to the wild gleam of Manhattan on the other side of his windows. Frenetic and frenzied. Light in all directions, as if there was nothing more to the world tonight than this utterly mad tangle of life and traffic and people and energy and it hardly mattered what he felt so high above it. It hardly mattered at all that he'd betrayed himself. That this woman who should have been nothing to him made him act like someone he barely recognized.

And her words stayed with him. *I know exactly who I am.* They echoed around and around in his head until it sounded a whole lot more like an accusation.

As if she was the one playing this game, and winning it, after all.

CHAPTER FOUR

AS THE DAYS PASSED, Valentina thought that she was getting the hang of this assistant thing—especially if she endeavored to keep a minimum distance between herself and Achilles when the night got a little too dark and close. And at all other times, for that matter.

She'd chalked up those odd, breathless moments in his office that first night to the strangeness of inhabiting someone else's life. Because it couldn't be anything else. Since then, she hadn't felt the need to say too much. She hadn't defended herself—or her version of Natalie. She'd simply tried to do the job that Natalie, apparently, did so well she was seen by other employees of the Casilieris Company as superhuman.

With every day she became more accustomed to the demands of the job. She felt less as if she really ought to have taken Achilles up on his offer of a parachute and more as if this was something she could handle. Maybe not well or like superhuman Natalie, but she could handle it all the same in her own somewhat rudimentary fashion.

What she didn't understand was why Achilles hadn't fired her already. Because it was perfectly clear to Valentina that her version of handling things in no way lived up to Achilles's standards.

And if she'd been any doubt about that, he was the first to tell her otherwise.

His corporate offices in Manhattan took up several floors at one of Midtown's most esteemed addresses. There was an office suite set aside for him, naturally enough, that sprawled across the top floor and looked out over Manhattan as if to underscore the notion that Achilles Casilieris was in every way on top of the world. Valentina was settled in the immediate outer office, guarded by two separate lines of receptionist and secretarial defense should anyone make it through security. It wasn't to protect Achilles, but to further illuminate his importance. And Natalie's, Valentina realized quickly.

Because Natalie controlled access to Achilles. She controlled his schedule. She answered his phone and his email, and was generally held to have that all-important insight into his moods.

"What kind of day is it?" the senior vice presidents would ask her as they came in for their meetings, and the fact they smiled as they said it didn't make them any less anxious to hear her answer.

Valentina quickly discovered that Natalie controlled a whole lot more than simple access. There was a steady line of people at her desk, coming to her to ask how best to approach Achilles with any number of issues, or plot how to avoid approaching him with the things they knew he'd hate. Over the course of her first week in New York City, Valentina found that almost everyone who worked for Achilles tried to run things past her first, or used her to gauge his reactions. Natalie was less the man's personal assistant, she realized, and more the hub around which his businesses revolved. More than that, she thought he knew it.

"Take that up with Natalie," he would say in the middle of a meeting, without even bothering to look over at her. Usually while cutting someone off, because even he appeared not to want to hear certain things until Natalie had assessed them first.

"Come up with those numbers and run them past Natalie,"

he would tell his managers, and sometimes he'd even sound irritated while he said such things.

"Why are you acting as if you have never worked a day in my company?" he'd demanded of one of his brand managers once. "I am not the audience for your uncertain first drafts, George. How can you not know this?"

Valentina had smiled at the man in the meeting, and then had been forced to sit through a brainstorming/therapy session with him afterward, all the while hoping that the noncommittal things she'd murmured were, at the very least, not the *opposite* of the sort of things Natalie might have said.

Not that she texted Natalie to find out. Because that might have led to a conversation Valentina didn't really want to have with her double about strange, tense moments in the darkness with her employer.

She didn't know what she was more afraid of. That Natalie had never had any kind of tension with Achilles and Valentina was messing up her entire life...or that she did. That *tension* was just what Achilles did.

Valentina concentrated on her first attempt at a normal life, complete with a normal job, instead. And whether Achilles was aware of it or not, Natalie had her fingers in everything.

Including his romantic life.

The first time Valentina had answered his phone to find an emotional woman on the other end, she'd been appalled.

"There's a crying woman on the phone," she'd told Achilles. It had taken her a day or so to realize that she wasn't only allowed to walk in and out of his office when necessary, but encouraged to do so. That particular afternoon Achilles had been sitting on the sofa in his office, his feet up on his coffee table as he'd scowled down at his laptop. He shifted that scowl to her instead, in a way that made Valentina imagine that whatever he was looking at had something to do with her—

But that was ridiculous. There was no *her* in this scenario.

There was only Natalie, and Valentina very much doubted Achilles spent his time looking up his assistant on the internet.

"Why are you telling me this?" he'd asked her shortly. "If I wanted to know who called me, I would answer my phones myself."

"She's crying about you," Valentina had said. "I assume she's calling to share her emotions with you, the person who caused them."

"And I repeat—why are you telling me this." This time it wasn't a question, and his scowl deepened. "You are my assistant. You are responsible for fielding these calls. I'm shocked you're even mentioning another crying female. I thought you stopped bringing them to my attention years ago."

Valentina had blinked at that. "Aren't you at all interested in why this woman is upset?"

"No."

"Not at all. Not the slightest bit interested." She studied his fierce face as if he was an alien. In moments like this, she thought he must have been. "You don't even know which woman I'm referring to, do you?"

"Miss Monette." He bit out that name as if the taste of it irritated him, and Valentina couldn't have said why it put her back up when it wasn't even her name. "I have a number of mistresses, none of whom call that line to manufacture emotional upsets. You are already aware of this." And he'd set his laptop aside, as if he needed to concentrate fully on Valentina before him. It had made her spine prickle, from her neck to her bottom and back up again. "Please let me know exactly what agenda it is we are pursuing today, that you expect to interrupt me in order to have a discussion about nuisance calls. When I assure you, the subject does not interest me at all. Just as it did not interest me five years ago, when you vowed to stop bothering me about them."

There was a warning in that. Valentina had heard it, plain as day. But she hadn't been able to heed it. Much less stop herself.

"To be clear, what you're telling me is that tears do not interest you," she'd said instead of beating a retreat to her desk the way she should have. She'd kept her tone even and easy, but she doubted that had fooled either one of them.

"Tears interest me least of all." She'd been sure that there was a curve in that hard mouth of his then, however small.

And what was the matter with her that she'd clung to that as if it was some kind of lifeline? As if she needed such a thing?

As if what she really wanted was his approval, when she hadn't switched places with Natalie for him. He'd had nothing to do with it. Why couldn't she seem to remember that?

"If this is a common occurrence for you, perhaps you need to have a think about your behavior," she'd pointed out. "And your aversion to tears."

There had definitely been a curve in his mouth then, and yet somehow that hadn't made Valentina any easier.

"This conversation is over," he'd said quietly. Though not gently. "Something I suggest you tell the enterprising actress on the phone."

She'd thought him hideously cold, of course. Heartless, even. But the calls kept coming. And Valentina had quickly realized what she should perhaps have known from the start—that it would be impossible for Achilles to actually be out there causing harm to so many anonymous women when he never left the office. She knew this because she spent almost every hour of every day in his company. The man literally had no time to go out there smashing hearts left and right, the way she'd be tempted to believe he did if she paid attention only to the phone calls she received, laden with accusations.

"Tell him I'm falling apart," yet another woman on the phone said on this latest morning, her voice ragged.

"Sorry, but what's your name again?" Valentina asked, as brightly as possible. "It's only that he's been working rather hard, you see. As he tends to do. Which would, of course, make it extremely difficult for him to be tearing anyone apart in any real sense."

The woman had sputtered. But Valentina had dutifully taken her name into Achilles when he next asked for his messages.

"I somewhat doubted the veracity of her claim," Valentina murmured. "Given that you were working until well after two last night."

Something she knew very well since that had meant she'd been working even longer than that.

Achilles laughed. He was at his desk today, which meant he was framed by the vertical thrust of Manhattan behind him. And still, that look in his dark gold gaze made the city disappear. "As well you should. I have no idea who this woman is. Or any of them." He shrugged. "My attorneys are knee-deep in paternity suits, and I win every one of them."

Valentino was astonished by that. Perhaps that was naive. She'd certainly had her share of admirers in her day, strange men who claimed an acquaintance or who sent rather disturbing letters to the palace—some from distant prisons in foreign countries. But she certainly never had men call up and try to pretend they had relationships with her *to* her.

Then again, would anyone have told her if they had? That sat on her a bit uneasily, though she couldn't have said why. She only knew that his gaze was like a touch, and that, too, seemed to settle on her like a weight.

"It's amazing how many unhinged women seem to think that if they claim they're dating you, you might go along with it," she said before she could think better of it.

That dark gold gaze of his lit with a gleam she couldn't name then. And it sparked something deep inside her, making her fight to draw in a breath. Making her feel unsteady in the serviceable low heels that Natalie favored. Making her wish she'd worn something more substantial than a nice jacket over another pencil skirt. Like a suit of armor. Or her very own brick wall.

"There are always unhinged women hanging about," Achilles

said in that quietly devastating way of his. "Trying to convince me that they have relationships with me that they adamantly do not. Why do you imagine that is, Miss Monette?"

She told herself he couldn't possibly know that she was one of those women, no matter how his gaze seemed to pin her where she stood. No matter the edge in his voice, or the sharp emphasis he'd put on *Miss Monette*.

Even if he suspected something was different with his assistant, he couldn't know. Because no one could know. Because Valentina herself hadn't known Natalie existed until she'd walked into that bathroom. And that meant all sorts of things, such as the fact that everything she'd been told about her childhood and her birth was a lie. Not to mention her mother.

But there was no way Achilles could know any of that.

"Perhaps it's you," she murmured in response. She smiled when his brows rose in that expression of sheer arrogance that never failed to make her feel the slightest bit dizzy. "I only mean that you're a public figure and people imagine you a certain way based on the kind of press coverage you allow. Unless you plan to actively get out there and reclaim your public narrative, I don't think there's any likelihood that it will change."

"I am not a public figure. I have never courted the public in any way."

Valentina checked a sigh. "You're a very wealthy man. Whether you like it or not, the public is fascinated by you."

Achilles studied her until she was forced to order herself not to fidget beneath the weight of that heavy, intense stare.

"I'm intrigued that you think the very existence of public fascination must create an obligation in me to cater to it," he said quietly. "It does not. In fact, it has the opposite effect. In me. But how interesting that you imagine you owe something to the faceless masses who admire you."

Valentina's lips felt numb. "No masses, faceless or otherwise, admire me, Mr. Casilieris. They have no idea I exist. I'm an assistant, nothing more."

His hard mouth didn't shift into one of those hard curves, but his dark gold eyes gleamed, and somehow that made the floor beneath her seem to tilt, then roll.

"Of course you are," he said, his voice a quiet menace that echoed in her like a warning. Like something far more dangerous than a simple warning. "My mistake."

Later that night, still feeling as off balance as if the floor really wasn't steady beneath her feet, Valentina found herself alone with Achilles long after everyone else in the office had gone home.

It had been an extraordinarily long couple of days, something Valentina might have thought was business as usual for the Casilieris Company if so many of the other employees hadn't muttered about how grueling it was. Beneath their breath and when they thought she couldn't hear them, that was. The deal that Achilles was so determined to push through had turned out to have more tangles and turns than anyone had expected—especially, it seemed, Achilles. What that meant was long hour after long hour well into the tiny hours of the night, hunched over tables and conference rooms, arguing with fleets of attorneys and representatives from the other side over take-out food from fine New York restaurants and stale coffee.

Valentina was deep into one of the contracts Achilles had slid her way, demanding a fresh set of eyes on a clause that annoyed him, when she noticed that they were the only ones there. The Casilieris Company had a significant presence all over the planet, so there were usually people coming and going at all conceivable hours to be available to different workdays in distant places. Something Valentina had witnessed herself after spending so much time in these offices since she'd arrived in New York.

But when she looked up from the dense and confusing contract language for a moment to give her ever-impending headache a break, she could see from the long conference room table where she sat straight through the glass walls that allowed her to see all the way across the office floor. And there was no one there. No bustling secretaries, no ambitious VPs putting in ostentatiously late hours where the boss could see their vigilance and commitment. No overzealous interns making busy work for themselves in the cubicles. No late-night cleaning crews, who did their jobs in the dark so as not to bother the workers by day. There wasn't a soul. Anywhere.

Something caught in her chest as she realized that it was only the two of them. Just Valentina and the man across the table from her, whom she was trying very hard not to look at too closely.

It was an extraordinarily unimportant thing to notice, she chastised herself, frowning back down at the contract. They were always alone, really. In his car, on his plane, in his penthouse. Valentina had spent more time with this man, she thought, than with any other save her father.

Her gaze rose from the contract of its own accord. Achilles sat across from her in the quiet of the otherwise empty office, his laptop cracked open before him and a pile of contracts next to the sleek machine. He looked the way he always did at the end of these long days. *Entirely too good*, something in her whispered—though she shoved that aside as best she could. It did no good to concentrate on things like that, she'd decided during her tenure with him. The man's appearance was a fact, and it was something she needed to come to terms with, but she certainly didn't have to ogle him.

But she couldn't seem to look away. She remembered that moment in his penthouse a little too clearly, the first night they'd been in New York. She remembered how close they'd stood in that window, and the things he'd told her, that dark gold gaze of his boring into her. As if he had every intention of looking directly to her soul. More than that, she remembered him reaching out and taking hold of the end of the ponytail she'd worn, that he'd looked at as if he had no idea how it had come to be attached to her.

But she'd dreamed about it almost every time she'd slept, either way.

Tonight Achilles was lounging in a pushed-back chair, his hands on top of his head as if, had he had longer hair, he'd be raking his hands through it. His jaw was dotted with stubble after a long day in the office, and it lent him the look of some kind of pirate.

Valentina told herself—sternly—that there was no need for such fanciful language when he already made her pulse heat inside her simply by being in the same room. She tried to sink down a bit farther behind the piles and piles of documents surrounding her, which she was viewing as the armor she wished she was wearing. The remains of the dinner she'd ordered them many hours before were scattered across the center of the table, and she took perhaps too much pride in the fact she'd completed so simple a task. Normal people, she was certain, ordered from take-out menus all the time, but Valentina never had before she'd taken over Natalie's life. Valentina was a princess. She'd discussed many a menu and sent requests to any number of kitchens, but she'd never ordered her own meal in her life, much less from stereotypical New Yorkers with accents and attitudes.

She felt as if she was in a movie.

Valentina decided she would take her victories where she found them. Even if they were as small and ultimately pointless as sending out for a takeaway meal.

"It's late," Achilles said, reminding her that they were all alone here. And there was something in his voice then. Or the way his gaze slammed into hers when she looked up again.

Or maybe it was in her—that catch. That little kick of something a little too much like excitement that wound around and around inside her. Making her feel...restless. Undone. Desperate for something she couldn't even name.

"And here I thought you planned to carry straight through until dawn," she said, as brightly as possible, hoping against hope he couldn't see anything on her face. Or hear it in her voice.

Achilles lowered his hand to the arms of his chair. But he didn't shift that gaze of his from hers. And she kept catching him looking at her like this. Exactly like this. Simmering. Dark and dangerous, and spun through with gold. In the cars they took together. Every morning when he walked out of his bedchamber and found her sitting in the office suite, already starting on the day's work as best she could. Across boardroom tables just like this one, no matter if they were filled with other people.

It was worse now. Here in the quiet of his empty office. So late at night it felt to Valentina as if the darkness was a part of her.

And Valentina didn't have any experience with men, but oh, the books she'd read. Love stories and romances and happy-ever-afters, and almost all of them started just like this. With a taut feeling in the belly and fire everywhere else.

Do not be absurd, she snapped at herself.

Because she was Princess Valentina of Murin. She was promised to another and had been since her birth. There wasn't space in her life for anything but that. Not even here, in this faraway place that had nothing at all to do with her real life. Not even with this man, whom she never should have met, and never would have had she not seized that moment in the London bathroom.

You can take a holiday from your life, apparently, she reminded herself. *But you still take you along with you wherever you go.*

She might have been playing Natalie Monette, but she was still *herself*. She was still the same person she'd always been. Dutiful. Mindful of what her seemingly inconsequential behavior might mean to her father, to the kingdom, to her future husband's kingdom, too. Whatever else she was—and she wasn't sure she knew anymore, not here in the presence of a man who made her head spin without seeming to try very hard—Valentina was a person who had always, always kept her vows.

Even when it was her father who had made them, not her.

"If you keep staring at me like that," Achilles said softly, a kind of ferociousness beneath his rough words that made her stomach knot, then seemed to kindle a different, deeper fire lower down, "I am not certain I'll be able to contain myself."

Valentina's mouth was dry. "I don't know what you mean."

"I think you do."

Achilles didn't move, she could see that he wasn't moving, and yet everything changed at that. He filled every room he entered—she was used to that by now—but this was something different. It was as if lightning flashed. It was if he was some kind of rolling thunder all his own. It was as if he'd called in a storm, then let it loose to fill all of the room. The office.

And Valentina, too.

"No," she whispered, her voice scratchy against all that light and rumble.

But she could feel the tumult inside her. It was fire and it was light and it threatened to burst free of the paltry cage of her skin. Surely she would burst. Surely no person could survive this. She felt it shake all through her, as if underlining her fear.

"I don't know what you mean, and I don't like what you're implying. I think perhaps we've been in this office too long. You seem to have mistaken me for one of your mistresses. Or worse, one of those desperate women who call in, hoping to convince you they ought to be one of them."

"On the contrary, Miss Monette."

And there was a starkness to Achilles's expression then. No curve on his stern mouth. No gleaming thing in the seductive gold of his dark eyes. But somehow, that only made it worse.

"You're the one who manages my mistresses. And those who pretend to that title. How could I possibly confuse you for them?" He cocked his head slightly to one side, and something yawned open inside her, as if in response. "Or perhaps you're auditioning for the role?"

"No." Her voice was no less scratchy this time, but there was more power in it. *Or more fear*, something inside her whispered. "I am most certainly not auditioning for anything like that. Or anything at all. I already have a job."

"But you told me you meant to quit." She had the strangest notion then that he was enjoying himself. "Perhaps you meant you were looking to make a lateral move. From my boardroom to my bed?"

Valentina tried to summon her outrage. She tried to tell herself that she was deeply offended on Natalie's behalf, because of course this was about her, not Valentina herself… She tried to tell herself a whole lot of things.

But she couldn't quite get there. Instead, she was awash with unhelpful little visions, red hot and wild. Images of what a "lateral move" might look like. Of what his bed might feel like. Of him.

She imagined that lean, solidly muscled form stretched over hers, the way she'd read in so many books so many times. Something almost too hot to bear melted through her then, pulling deep in her belly, and making her breath go shallow before it shivered everywhere else.

As if it was already happening.

"I know that this might come as a tremendous shock," Valentina said, trying to make herself sound something like fierce— or unmoved, anyway. Anything other than thrown and yearning. "But I have no interest in your bed. Less than no interest."

"You are correct." And something gleamed bright and hot and unholy gold in that dark gaze of his. "I am in shock."

"The next time an aspiring mistress calls the office," Valentina continued coolly, and no matter that it cost her, "I'll be certain to put her through to you for a change. You can discuss lateral moves all day long."

"What if a random caller does not appeal to me?" he asked lazily, as if this was all a game to him. She told herself it was. She told herself the fact that it was a game made it safe, but she didn't believe it. Not when all the things that moved around inside her made it hard to breathe, and made her feel anything at all but *safe*. "What if it is I who wish to alter our working relationship after all these years?"

Valentina told herself that this was clearly a test. If, as this conversation seemed to suggest, Natalie's relationship with her boss had always been strictly professional, why would he want to change that now? She'd seen how distant he kept his romantic entanglements from his work. His work was his life. His women were afterthoughts. There was no way the driven, focused man she'd come to know a bit after the close proximity of these last days would want to muddy the water in his office, with the assistant who not only knew where all the bodies were buried, but oversaw the funeral rites herself.

This had to be a test.

"I don't wish to alter a thing," she told him, very distinctly, as if there was nothing in her head but thorny contract language. And certainly nothing involving that remarkably ridged torso of his. "If you do, I think we should revisit the compensation package on offer for my resignation."

Achilles smiled as if she delighted him. But in an entirely too wicked and too hot sort of way.

"There is no package, Miss Monette," he murmured. "And there will be no resignation. When will you understand? You are here to do as I wish. Nothing more and nothing less than that. And perhaps my wishes concerning your role here have changed."

He wants you to fall apart, Valentina snapped at herself. *He wants to see if this will break you. He's poking at* Natalie *about her change in performance, not at you. He doesn't know you* exist.

Because there could be no other explanation. And it didn't matter that the look in his eyes made her shudder, down deep inside.

"Your wishes concerning my role now involve me on my back?" It cost her to keep her voice that flat. She could feel it.

"You say that as if the very idea disgusts you." And that crook in the corner of his lethal mouth deepened, even as that look in his eyes went lethal. "Surely not."

Valentina forced herself to smile. Blandly. As if her heart wasn't trying to claw its way out of her chest.

"I'm very flattered by your offer, of course," she said.

A little too sweetly to be mistaken for sincerity.

Achilles laughed then. It was an unsettling sound, too rough and too bold. It told her too much. That he knew—everything. That he knew all the things that were moving inside her, white hot and molten and too much for her to handle or tamp down or control. There was a growing, impossible fire raging in places she hardly understood, rendering her a stranger to herself.

As if he was the one in control of her body, even sitting across the table, lounging in his seat as if none of this was a matter of any concern at all.

While she felt as if she was both losing pieces of herself— and seeing her true colors for the very first time.

"Are you letting me down easy?" Achilles asked.

There was still laughter in his voice, his gaze and, somehow, dancing in the air between them despite all that fire still licking at her. She felt it roll through her, as if those big hands of his were on her skin.

And then she was suddenly incapable of thinking about anything at all but that. His hands all over her body. Touching places only she had ever seen. She had to swallow hard. Then again. And still there was that ringing in her ears.

"Do think it will work?" he asked, laughter still making his words sound a little too much like the rough, male version of honey.

"I imagine it will work beautifully, yes." She held on to that smile of hers as if her life depended on it. She rather thought it did. It was that or tip over into all that fire, and she had no idea what would become of her if she let that happen. She had no idea what would be left. "Or, of course, I could involve Human Resources in this discussion."

Achilles laughed again, and this time it was rougher. Darker and somehow hotter at the same time. Valentina felt it slide all over her, making her breasts feel heavy and her hips restless. While deep between her legs, a slick ache bloomed.

"I admire the feigned naïveté," Achilles said, and he looked like a pirate again, all dark jaw and that gleam in his gaze. It lit her up. Everywhere. "I have obviously failed to appreciate your acting talent sufficiently. I think we both know what Human Resources will tell you. To suck it up or find another position."

"That does not sound at all like something Human Resources would say," Valentina replied crisply, rather than spending even a split second thinking about *sucking.* "It sounds as if you're laboring under the delusion that this is a cult of personality, not a business."

If she expected him to look at all abashed, his grin disabused her of it. "Do you doubt it?"

"I'm not sure that is something I would brag about, Mr. Casilieris."

His gaze was hot, and she didn't think he was talking about her job or his company any longer. Had he ever been?

"Is it bragging if it's true?" he asked.

Valentina stood then, because it was the last thing she wanted to do. She could have sat there all night. She could have rung in a new dawn, fencing words with this man and dancing closer and closer to that precipice she could feel looming between them, even if she couldn't quite see it.

She could have pretended she didn't feel every moment of this deep inside her, in places she shouldn't. And then pretend further she didn't know what it meant just because she'd never experienced any of it before outside the pages of a book.

But she did know. And this wasn't her life to ruin. And so she stood, smoothing her hands down her skirt and wishing she hadn't been quite so impetuous in that London bathroom.

If you hadn't been, you wouldn't be here, something in her replied. *Is that what you want?*

And she knew that she didn't. Valentina had a whole life left to live with a man she would call husband who would never know her, not really. She had duty to look forward to, and a life-time of charity and good works, all of which would be vetted by committees and commented on by the press. She had pub-lic adulation and a marriage that would involve the mechanical creation of babies before petering off into a nice friendship, if she was lucky.

Maybe the making of the babies would be fun with her prince. What did she know? All she knew so far was that he didn't do…this. He didn't affect her the way Achilles did, loung-ing there like hard-packed danger across a conference table, his gaze too dark and the gold in it making her pulse kick at her.

She'd never felt anything like this before. She doubted she'd ever feel it again.

Valentina couldn't quite bring herself to regret it.

But she couldn't stay here tonight and blow up the rest of Natalie's life, either. That would be treating this little gift that she'd been given with nothing but contempt.

"Have I given you leave to go?" Achilles asked, with what she knew was entirely feigned astonishment. "I am clearly con-fused in some way. I keep thinking you work for me."

She didn't know how he could do that. How he could seem to loom over her when she was the one standing up and look-ing down at him.

"And because I'd like to continue working for you," Valen-tina forced herself to say in as measured a tone as she could manage, "I'm going to leave now. We can pick this up in the morning." She tapped the table with one finger. "Pick *this* up, I mean. These contracts and the deal. Not this descent into mad-ness, which I think we can chalk up to exhaustion."

Achilles only watched her for a moment. Those hands that she could picture too easily against her own flesh curled over the armrests of his chair, and her curse was that she imagined she *was* that chair. His legs were thrust out before him, long and lean. His usual suit was slightly rumpled, his tie having been tugged off and tossed aside hours earlier, so she could see the olive skin at his neck and a hint of crisp, black hair. He looked simultaneously sleepy and breathlessly, impossibly lethal—with an intensity that made that hot ache between her legs seem to swallow her whole.

And the look in his eyes made everything inside her draw tight, then pulse harder.

"Do you have a problem with that?" she asked, and she meant to sound impatient. Challenging. But she thought both of them were entirely too aware that what came out instead was rather more plaintive than planned.

As if she was really asking him if he was okay with everything that had happened here tonight. She was clearly too dazed to function.

She needed to get away from him while she still had access to what little of her brain remained in all this smoke and flame.

"Do you require my permission?" Achilles lifted his chin, and his dark eyes glittered. Valentina held her breath. "So far tonight it seems you are laboring under the impression that you give the permission, not me. You make the rules, not me. It is as if I am here for no other purpose than to serve you."

And there was no reason at all that his words, spoken in that soft, if dangerous way, should make her skin prickle. But they did. As if a man like Achilles did not have to issue threats, he was the threat. Why pile a threat on top of the threat? When the look on his face would do.

"I will see you in the morning," Valentina said, resolutely. "When I'll be happy to accept your apology."

Achilles lounged farther down in his chair, and she had the strangest notion that he was holding himself back. Keeping himself in place. Goose bumps shivered to life over her shoulders and down her arms.

His gaze never left hers.

"Go," he said, and there was no pretending it wasn't an order. "But I would not lie awake tonight anticipating the contours of my apology. It will never come."

She wanted to reply to that, but her mouth was too dry and she couldn't seem to move. Not so much as a muscle.

And as if he knew it, Achilles kept going in that same intensely quiet way.

"Tonight when you can't sleep, when you toss and turn and stare up at yet another ceiling I own, I want you to think of all the other reasons you could be wide awake in the small hours of the night. All the things that I could do to you. Or have you do to me. All the thousands of ways I will be imagining us together, just like that, under the same roof."

"That is completely inappropriate, Mr. Casilieris, and I think you know it."

But she knew full well she didn't sound nearly as outraged as she should. And only partially because her voice was a mere whisper.

"Have you never wondered how we would fit? Have you not tortured herself with images of my possession?" Achilles's hard mouth curved then, a wicked crook in one corner that she knew, somehow, would haunt her. She could feel it deep inside her like its own bright fire. "Tonight, I think, you will."

And Valentina stopped pretending there was any way out of this conversation besides the precise images he'd just mentioned, acted out all over this office. She walked stiffly around the table and gave him a wide, wide berth as she passed.

When she made it to the door of the conference room, she didn't look behind her to see if he was watching. She knew he was. She could feel it.

Fire and lightning, thunder and need.

She ran.

And heard his laughter follow behind her like the leading edge of a storm she had no hope of outwitting, no matter how fast she moved.

CHAPTER FIVE

ACHILLES ORDINARILY ENJOYED his victory parties. Reveled in them, in fact. Not for him any nod toward false humility or any pretense that he didn't deeply enjoy these games of high finance with international stakes. But tonight he couldn't seem to get his head into it, and no matter that he'd been fighting to buy out this particular iconic Manhattan hotel—which he planned to make over in his own image, the blend of European elegance and Greek timelessness that was his calling card in the few hotels scattered across the globe that he'd deemed worthy of the Casilieris name—for nearly eighteen months.

He should have been jubilant. It irritated him—deeply—that he couldn't quite get there.

His group had taken over a New York steak house renowned for its high-end clientele and specialty drinks to match to celebrate the deal he'd finally put through today after all this irritating wrangling. Ordinarily he would allow himself a few drinks to blur out his edges for a change. He would even smile and pretend he was a normal man, like all the rest, made of flesh and blood instead of dollar signs and naked ambition— an improvement by far over the monster he kept locked up tight beneath. Nights like this were his opportunity to pretend to be like anyone else, and Achilles usually indulged that impulse.

He might not have been a normal man—he'd never been a normal man—but it amused him to pretend otherwise every now and again. He was renowned for his surliness as much as his high expectations, but if that was all there was to it—to him—he never would have gotten anywhere in business. It took a little charm to truly manipulate his enemies and his opponents and even his acolytes the way he liked to do. It required that he be as easy telling a joke as he was taking over a company or using his fiercest attorneys to hammer out a deal that served him, and only him, best.

But tonight he was charmless all the way through.

He stood at the bar, nursing a drink he would have much preferred to toss back and follow with a few more of the same, his attention entirely consumed by his princess as she worked the room. As ordered.

"Make yourself useful, please," he'd told her when they'd arrived. "Try to charm these men. If you can."

He'd been deliberately insulting. He'd wanted her to imagine he had some doubt that she could pull such a thing off. He'd wanted her to feel the way he did—grouchy and irritable and outside his own skin.

She made him feel like an adolescent.

But Valentina had not seemed the least bit cowed. Much less insulted—which had only made him feel that much more raw.

"As you wish," she'd murmured in that overly obsequious voice she used when, he thought, she most wanted to get her claws into him. She'd even flashed that bland smile of hers at him, which had its usual effect—making his blood seem too hot for his own veins. "Your slightest desire is my command, of course."

And the truth was, Achilles should have known better. The kind of men he liked to manipulate best, especially when it came to high-stakes deals like the one he'd closed tonight, were not the sort of men he wanted anywhere near his princess. If the real Natalie had been here, she would have disappeared. She would have dispensed her usual round of cool greetings and even cooler congratulations, none of which encouraged anyone to cozy up to her. Then she would have sat in this corner or that, her expression blank and her attention focused entirely on one of her devices. She would have done that remarkable thing she did, that he had never thought to admire as much as perhaps he should have, which was her ability to be both in the room and invisible at the same time.

Princess Valentina, by contrast, couldn't have stayed invisible if her life depended on it. She was the furthest thing from *invisible* that Achilles had ever seen. It was as if the world was cast into darkness and she was its only light, that bright and that impossibly silvery and smooth, like her own brand of moonlight.

She moved from one group to the next, all gracious smiles. And not that bland sort of smile she used entirely too pointedly and too well, which invariably worked his last nerve, but one he'd seen in too many photographs he'd looked at much too late at night. Hunched over his laptop like some kind of obsessed troll while she slept beneath the same roof, unaware, which only made him that much more infuriated.

With her, certainly. But with himself even more.

Tonight she was the consummate hostess, as if this was her victory celebration instead of his. He could hear her airy laugh from across the room, far more potent than another woman's touch. And worse, he could see her. Slender and graceful, inhabiting a pencil skirt and well-cut jacket as if they'd been crafted specifically for her. When he knew perfectly well that those were his assistant's clothes, and they certainly weren't bespoke.

But that was Valentina's power. She made everything in her orbit seem to be only hers. Crafted specifically and especially for her.

Including him, Achilles thought—and he hated it. He was not a man a woman could put on a leash. He'd never given a woman any kind of power over him in his life, and he didn't understand how this creature who was engaged in a full-scale deception—who was running a con on him *even now*—some-how seemed to have the upper hand in a battle he was terribly afraid only he knew they were fighting.

It was unconscionable. It made him want to tear down this building—hell, the whole city—with his bare hands.

Or better yet, put them on her.

All the men around her lapped it up, of course. They stood too close. They put their hands on her elbow, or her shoulder, to emphasize a point that Achilles did not have to hear to know did not require emphasis. And certainly did not require touch.

She was moonlight over this grim, focused life of his, and he had no idea how he was going to make it through a world cast in darkness without her.

If he was appalled by that sentiment—and he was, deeply and wholly—it didn't seem to matter. He couldn't seem to turn it off.

It was far easier to critique her behavior instead.

So Achilles watched. And seethed. He catalogued every single touch, every single laugh, every single time she tilted back her pretty face and let her sleek copper hair fall behind her, catching all the light in the room. He brooded over the men who surrounded her, knowing full well that each and every one of them was imagining her naked. Hell, so was he.

But he was the only person in this room who knew what he was looking at. They thought she was Natalie Monette, his dependable assistant. He was the only one who knew who she really was.

By the time Valentina finished a full circuit of the room, Achilles was in a high, foul temper.

"Are you finished?" he asked when she came to stand by his side again, his tone a dark slap he did nothing at all to temper. "Or will you actually whore yourself out in lieu of dessert?"

He meant that to hurt. He didn't care if he was an ass. He wanted to knock her back a few steps.

But of course Valentina only shot him an arch, amused look, as if she was biting back laughter.

"That isn't very nice," she said simply.

That was all.

And yet Achilles felt that bloom of unfortunate heat inside him all over again, and this time he knew exactly what it was. He didn't like it any better than he had before, and yet there it sat, eating at him from the inside out.

It didn't matter if he told himself he didn't wish to feel shame. All Valentina had to do was look at him as if he was a misbehaving child, tell him he *wasn't being nice* when he'd built an entire life out of being the very opposite of nice and hailing that as the source of his vast power and influence—and there it was. Heavy in him, like a length of hard, cold chain.

How had he given this woman so much power over him? How had he failed to see that was what was happening while he'd imagined he was giving her the rope with which to hang herself?

This could not go on. He could not allow this to go on.

The truth was, Achilles couldn't seem to get a handle on this situation the way he'd planned to when he'd realized who she was on the plane. He'd imagined it would be an amusing sort of game to humble a high and mighty spoiled-rotten princess who had never worked a day in her life and imagined she could deceive *the* Achilles Casilieris so boldly. He'd imagined it would be entertaining—and over swiftly. He supposed he'd imagined he'd be shipping her back to her palace and her princessy life and her proper royal fiancé by the end of the first day.

But Valentina wasn't at all who he'd thought she'd be. If she was spoiled—and she had to be spoiled, by definition, he was certain of it—she hid it. No matter what he threw at her, no matter what he demanded, she simply did it. Not always well, but she did it. She didn't complain. She didn't try to weasel out of any tasks she didn't like. She didn't even make faces or let out those long-suffering sighs that so many of his support staff did when they thought he couldn't hear them.

In fact, Valentina was significantly more cheerful than any other assistant he'd ever had—including Natalie.

She was nothing like perfect, but that made it worse. If she was perfect, maybe he could have dismissed her or ignored her, despite the game she was playing. But he couldn't seem to get her out of his head.

It was that part he couldn't accept. Achilles lived a highly compartmentalized life by design, and he liked it that way. He kept his women in the smallest, most easily controlled and thus ignored space. It had been many, many years since he'd allowed sex to control his thoughts, much less his life. It was only sex, after all. And what was sex to a man who could buy the world if he so chose? It was a release, yes. Enjoyable, even.

But Achilles couldn't remember the last time he'd woken in the night, his heart pounding, the hardest part of him awake and aware. With nothing in his head but her. Yet it was a nightly occurrence since Valentina had walked onto his plane.

It was bordering on obsession.

And Achilles did not get obsessed. He did not *want*. He did not *need*. He took what interested him and then he forgot about it when the next thing came along.

And he couldn't think of a single good reason why he shouldn't do the same with her.

"Do you have something you wish to say to me?" Valentina asked, her soft, smooth voice snapping him back to this party that bored him. This victory that should have excited him, but that he only found boring now.

"I believe I said it."

"You misunderstand me," she replied, smiling. From a distance it would look as if they were discussing something as light and airy as that curve to her mouth, he thought. Achilles would have been impressed had he not been close enough to see that cool gleam in her green gaze. "I meant your apology. Are you ready to give it?"

He felt his own mouth curve then, in nothing so airy. Or light.

"Do I strike you as a man who apologizes, Miss Monette?"

he asked her, making no attempt to ease the steel in his voice. "Have I ever done so in all the time you've known me?"

"A man who cannot apologize is not quite a man, is he, Mr. Casilieris?" This time he thought her smile was meant to take away the sting of her words. To hide the insult a little. Yet it only seemed to make it worse. "I speak philosophically, of course. But surely the only people who can't bring themselves to apologize are those who fear that any admission of guilt or wrongdoing diminishes them. I think we can both agree that's the very opposite of strength."

"You must tell me if I appear diminished, then," he growled at her, and he had the satisfaction of watching that pulse in her neck go wild. "Or weak in some way."

He wasn't surprised when she excused herself and went back to working the crowd. But he was surprised he let her.

Not here, he cautioned that wild thing inside him that he'd never had to contend with before, not over a woman. And never so raw and bold. *Not now.*

Later that night, they sat in his car as it slid through the streets of Manhattan in the midst of a summer thunderstorm, and Achilles cautioned himself not to act rashly.

Again.

But Valentina sat there beside him, staring out the window with a faint smile on her face. She'd settled beside him on the wide, plush seat without a word, as if it hardly mattered to her if he spoke or not. If he berated her, if he ignored her. As if she was all alone in this car or, worse, as if her mind was far away on more interesting topics.

And he couldn't tolerate it.

Achilles could think of nothing but her, she was eating him alive like some kind of impossible acid, yet *her* mind was miles away. She didn't seem to notice or care what she did to him when he was the one who was allowing her grand deception to continue—instead of outing her the way he should have the moment he'd understood who she was.

His hands moved before he knew what he meant to do, as if they had a mind of their own.

He didn't ask. He didn't push or prod at her or fence more words, forcing some sort of temper or explosion that would lead them where he wanted her to go. He didn't stack that deck.

He simply reached across the backseat, wrapped his hand around the back of her neck and hauled her closer to him.

She came easily, as if she really was made of nothing but light. He pulled her until she was sprawled across his lap, one hand braced on his thigh and another at his side. Her body was as lithe and sweetly rounded as he'd imagined it would be, but better. Much, much better. She smelled like a dream, something soft and something sweet, and all of it warm and female and *her*. Valentina.

But all he cared about was the fact that that maddening mouth of hers was close to his.

Finally.

"What are you doing?" she breathed.

"I should think that was obvious," he growled. "And overdue."

And then, at last, he kissed her.

He wasn't gentle. He wasn't anything like tentative. He was neither soft nor kind, because it was too late for that.

He claimed her. Took her. He reminded her who he was with every slick, intense slide of his tongue. Or maybe he was reminding himself.

And he couldn't stop himself once the taste of her exploded inside him, making him reel. He wanted more. He wanted everything.

But she was still fighting him, that stubbornness of hers that made his whole body tight and needy. Not with her body, which was wrapped around him, supple and sweet, in a way that made him feel drunk. Not with her arms, which she'd sneaked around his shoulders as if she needed to hold on to him to keep herself upright.

It was that mouth of hers that had been driving him wild since the start.

He pulled his lips from hers. Then he slid his hands up to take her elegant cheekbones between his palms. He tilted her face where he wanted it, making the angle that much slicker. That much sweeter.

"Kiss me back," he demanded, pulling back farther to scowl at her, all this unaccustomed need making him impatient. And testy.

She looked stunned. And entirely too beautiful. Her green eyes were wide and dazed behind those clear glasses she wore. Her lips were parted, distractingly soft and faintly swollen already.

Achilles was hard and he was greedy and he wanted nothing more than to bury himself inside her here and now, and finally get rid of this obsession that was eating him alive.

Or indulge in it awhile.

"In case you are confused," he told her, his voice still a growl, "that was an order."

She angled herself back, just slightly. As if she was trying to sit up straighter against him. He didn't allow it. He liked her like this. Off balance and under his control, and he didn't much care if that made him a savage. He'd only ever pretended to be anything else, and only occasionally, at that.

"I *am* kissing you back," she said, and there was a certain haughtiness in her voice that delighted him. It made him grin, imagining all the many ways he could make her pay for that high-born, inbred superiority that he wanted to lap up like cream.

"Not well enough," he told her.

Her cheeks looked crisp and red, but she didn't shrink away from him. She didn't so much as blink.

"Maybe we don't have any chemistry," she theorized in that same voice, making it sound as if that was a foregone conclusion. "Not every woman in the world finds you attractive, Mr. Casilieris. Did you ever think of that?"

Achilles pulled her even more off balance, holding her over his lap and in his arms, right where he wanted her.

"No," he said starkly, and he didn't care if his greed and longing was all over his face, revealing more to her than he had ever shared with anyone. Ever. "I don't think either of those things is a problem."

Then he set his mouth to hers, and proved it.

Valentina thought she'd died and gone to a heaven she'd never dreamed of before. Wicked and wild and *better*. So very much better than anything she could have come up with in her most brilliant and dark-edged fantasies.

She had never been truly kissed before—if that was even the word to describe something so dominant and so powerful and so deeply, erotically thrilling—but she had no intention of sharing her level of inexperience with Achilles. Not when he seemed so close to some kind of edge and so hell-bent on taking her with him, toppling over the side into all of this sensation and need.

So she simply mimicked him. When he tilted his head, she did the same. She balled up her hands in his exquisitely soft shirt, up there against the hard planes of his chest tucked beneath his dark suit coat. She was aware of his hard hands on her face. She exulted in his arms like steel, holding her and caging her against him. She lost herself in that desperately cruel mouth as it moved over hers, the touch of his rough jaw, the impossible heat.

God help her, the heat.

And she was aware of that hard ridge beneath her, suddenly. She couldn't seem to keep from wriggling against it. Once, daringly. Then again when she heard that deep, wild and somehow savagely beautiful male noise he made in response.

And Valentina forgot about her vows, old and forthcoming. She forgot about faraway kingdoms and palaces and the life she'd lived there. She forgot about the promises she'd made and the ones that had been made in her name, because all of that seemed insubstantial next to the sheer, overwhelming wonder of Achilles Casilieris kissing her like a man possessed in the back of his town car.

This was her holiday. Her little escape. This was nothing but a dream, and he was, too. A fantasy of the life she might have lived had she been anyone else. Had she ever been anything like normal.

She forgot where they were. She forgot the role she was supposed to be playing. There was nothing in all the world but Achilles and the wildness he summoned up with every drag of his mouth against hers.

The car moved beneath them, but all Valentina could focus on was him. That hot possession of his mouth. The fire inside her.

And the lightning that she knew was his, the thunder storming through her, teaching her that she knew less about her body than he did. Much, much less. When he shifted so he could rub his chest against hers, she understood that he knew her nipples had pebbled into hard little points. When he laughed slightly as he rearranged her arms around his shoulders, she understood that he knew all her limbs were weighted down with the force of that greedy longing coursing through her veins.

The more he kissed her, over and over again as if time had no meaning and he could do this forever, she understood that he knew everything.

When he pulled his mouth from hers again, Valentina heard a soft, whimpering sound of protest. It took her one shuddering beat of her heart, then another, to realize she'd made it.

She couldn't process that. It was so abandoned, so thoughtless and wild—how could that be her?

"If we do not get out of this car right now," Achilles told her, his gaze a dark and breathtaking gold that slammed into her and lit her insides on fire, "we will not get out of it for some time.

Not until I've had my fill of you. Is that how you want our first time to go, *glikia mou*? In the backseat of a car?"

For a moment Valentina didn't know what he meant.

One hastily sucked-in breath later, she realized the car had come to a stop outside Achilles's building. Her cheeks flushed with a bright heat, but worse, she knew that he could see it. He saw everything—hadn't she just realized the truth of that? He watched her as she flushed, and he liked it. That deeply male curve in the corner of his mouth made that plain.

Valentina struggled to free herself from his hold then, to climb off his lap and sit back on the seat herself, and she was all too aware that he let her.

She didn't focus on that. She couldn't. That offhanded show of his innate strength made her feel…slippery, inside and outside and high between her legs. She tossed herself off his lap, her gaze tangling with his in a way that made the whole world seem to spin a little, and then she threw herself out the door. She summoned a smile from somewhere and aimed it at the doormen.

Breathe, she ordered herself. *Just breathe.*

Because she couldn't do this. This wasn't who she was. She hadn't held on to her virginity all this time to toss it aside at the very first temptation…had she?

This couldn't be who she was. It couldn't.

She'd spent her whole life practicing how to appear unruffled and serene under any and all circumstances, though she couldn't recall ever putting it to this kind of test before. She made herself breathe. She made herself smile. She sank into the familiarity of her public persona, wielding it like that armor she'd wanted, because it occurred to her it was the toughest and most resilient armor she had.

Achilles followed her into that bright and shiny elevator in the back of the gleaming lobby, using his key to close the doors behind them. He did not appear to notice or care that she was newly armored, especially while he seemed perfectly content to look so...disreputable.

His suit jacket hung open, and she was sure it had to be obvious to even the most casual observer that she'd had her hands all over his chest and his shirt. And she found it was difficult to think of that hard mouth of his as cruel now that she knew how it tasted. More, how it felt on hers, demanding and intense and—

Stop, she ordered herself. *Now.*

He leaned back against the wall as the elevator started to move, his dark gold eyes hooded and intent when they met hers. He didn't say a word. Maybe he didn't have to. Her heart was pounding so loud that Valentina was certain it would have drowned him out if he'd shouted.

But Achilles did not shout.

On the contrary, when the elevator doors shut behind them, securing them in his penthouse, he only continued to watch her in that same intense way. She moved into the great living room, aware that he followed her, silent and faintly lazy.

It made her nervous. That was what she told herself that fluttery feeling was, lodged there beneath her ribs. And lower, if she was honest. Much lower.

"I'm going to bed," she said. And then instantly wished she'd phrased that differently when she heard it echo there between them, seeming to fill up the cavernous space, beating as madly within her as her own frenzied heart. "Alone."

Achilles gave the impression of smiling without actually doing so. He thrust his hands into the pockets of his dark suit and regarded her solemnly, save for that glittering thing in his dark gaze.

"If that is what you wish, *glikia mou.*"

And that was the thing. It wasn't what she wished. It wasn't what she wanted, and especially not when he called her that Greek name that she thought meant *my sweet*. It made her want to taste that word on that mouth of his. It made her want to find out exactly how sweet he thought she was.

It made her want to really, truly be someone else so she could do all the things that trampled through her head, making her chest feel tight while the rest of her...yearned.

Her whole life had been an exercise in virtue and duty, and she'd thought that meant something. She'd thought that *said* something about who she was. Valentina had been convinced that she'd held on to her chastity all this time, long after everyone she'd known had rid themselves of theirs, as a gift to her future.

But the night all around her told her something different. It had stripped away all the lies she'd told herself—or Achilles had. All the places she'd run and hid across all these years. Because the truth was that she'd never been tested. Was it truly virtue if she'd never been the least bit tempted to give it away? Or was it only coincidence that she'd never encountered anything that had felt the least bit compelling in that regard? Was it really holding on to something if she'd never felt the least bit like getting rid of it?

Because everything tonight was different. Valentina was different—or, worse, she thought as she stared at Achilles across the little bit of space that separated them, she had never been who she'd imagined she was. She had never understood that it was possible that a body could drown out what the mind knew to be prudent.

Until now.

She had judged passion all her life and told herself it was a story that weak people told themselves and others to make their sins seem more interesting. More complicated and unavoidable. But the truth was, Valentina had never experienced passion in her life.

Not until Achilles.

"I am your assistant," she told him. Or perhaps she was telling herself. "This must never happen again. If it does, I can't work for you."

"I have already told you that I am more than happy to accommodate—"

"There will be no lateral moves," she threw at him, appalled to hear her voice shaking. "You might lie awake at night imagining what that means and what it would look like, but I don't. I won't."

"Liar."

If he had hauled off and hit her, Valentina didn't think she could have been any more surprised. Shocked. No one had ever called her a liar before, not in all her life.

Then again, chimed in a small voice deep inside, *you never used to lie, did you? Not to others and not to yourself.*

"I have no doubt that you enjoy doing as you please," she spat at him, horrified that any of this was happening and, worse, that she'd let it—when Valentina knew who she was and what she'd be going back to in a few short weeks. "No matter the consequences. But not everyone is as reckless as you."

Achilles didn't quite smirk. "And that is why one of us is a billionaire and the other is his assistant."

"And if we were having a discussion about how to make money," Valentina said from between her teeth, no sign of her trademark serenity, "I would take your advice—but this is my life."

Guilt swamped her as she said that. Because, of course, it wasn't her life. It was Natalie's. And she had the sick feeling that she had already complicated it beyond the point of return. It didn't matter that Natalie had texted her to say that she'd kissed Prince Rodolfo, far away in Murin and neck-deep in Valentina's real life, however little Valentina had thought about it since she'd left it behind. Valentina was going to marry Rodolfo. That her double had kissed him, the way Valentina probably should have, wasn't completely out of line.

But this… This thing she was doing… It was unacceptable on every level. She knew that.

Maybe Natalie has this same kind of chemistry with Ro-

dolfo, something in her suggested. *Maybe he was engaged to the wrong twin.*

Which meant, she knew—because she was that self-serving—that maybe the wrong twin had been working for Achilles all this time and all of this was inevitable.

She wasn't sure she believed that. But she couldn't seem to stop herself. Or worse, convince herself that she should.

Achilles was still watching her too closely. Once again, she had the strangest notion that he knew too much. That he could see too far inside her.

Don't be silly, she snapped at herself then. *Of course he can't. You're just looking for more ways to feel guilty.*

Because whatever else happened, there was no way Achilles Casilieris would allow the sort of deception Valentina was neck-deep in to take place under his nose if he knew about it. She was certain of that, if nothing else.

"This is what I know about life," Achilles said, his voice a silken thread in the quiet of the penthouse, and Valentina had to repress a little shiver that threatened to shake her spine apart. "You must live it. If all you do is wall yourself off, hide yourself away, what do you have at the end but wasted time?"

Her throat was dry and much too tight. "I would take your advice more seriously if I didn't know you had an ulterior motive."

"I don't believe in wasting time or in ulterior motives," he growled back at her. "And not because I want a taste of you, though I do. And I intend to have it, *glikia mou*, make no mistake. But because you have put yourself on hold. Do you think I can't see it?"

She thought she had to be reeling then. Nothing was solid. She couldn't help but put her hand out, steadying herself on the back of the nearest chair—though it didn't seem to help.

And Achilles was watching her much too closely, with far too much of that disconcerting awareness making his dark gaze shine. "Or is it that you don't know yourself?"

When she was Princess Valentina of Murin, known to the

world before her birth. Her life plotted out in its every detail. Her name literally etched in stone into the foundations of the castle where her family had ruled for generations. She had never had the opportunity to lose herself. Not in a dramatic adolescence. Not in her early twenties. She had never been beside herself at some crossroads, desperate to figure out the right path—because there had only ever been one path and she had always known exactly how to walk it, every step of the way.

"You don't know me at all," she told him, trying to sound less thrown and more outraged at the very suggestion that she was any kind of mystery to herself. She'd never had that option. "You're my employer, not my confidant. You know what I choose to show you and nothing more."

"But what you choose to show, and how you choose to show it, tells me exactly who you are." Achilles shook his head, and it seemed to Valentina that he moved closer to her when she could see he didn't. That he was exactly where he'd always been—it was just that he seemed to take over the whole world. She wasn't sure he even tried; he just did. "Or did you imagine I achieved all that I've achieved without managing to read people? Surely you cannot be so foolish."

"I was about to do something deeply foolish," she said tightly. And not exactly smartly. "But I've since come to my senses."

"No one is keeping you here." His hands were thrust deep into his pockets, and he stood where he'd stopped, a few steps into the living room from those elevator doors. His gaze was all over her, but nothing else was touching her. He wasn't even blocking her escape route back to the guest room on this floor.

And she understood then. He was giving her choice. He was putting it on her. He wasn't simply sweeping her off into all that wild sensation—when he must have known he could have. He easily could have. If he hadn't stopped in the car, what would they be doing now?

But Valentina already knew the answer to that. She could feel her surrender inside her like heat.

And she thought she hated him for it.

Or should.

"I'm going to sleep," she said. She wanted her voice to be fierce. Some kind of condemnation. But she thought she sounded more determined than resolved. "I will see you in the morning. Sir."

Achilles smiled. "I think we both know you will see me long before that. And in your dreams, *glikia mou*, I doubt I will be so chivalrous."

Valentina pressed her lips tight together and did not allow herself to respond to him. Especially because she wanted to so very, very badly—and she knew, somehow, that it would lead nowhere good. It couldn't.

Instead, she turned and headed for her room. It was an unremarkable guest room appropriate for staff, but the best thing about it was the lock on the door. Not that she thought he would try to get in.

She was far more concerned that she was the one who would try to get out.

"One of these days," he said from behind her, his voice low and intense, "you will stop running. It is a foregone conclusion, I am afraid. And then what?"

Valentina didn't say a word. But she didn't have to.

When she finally made it to her room and threw the dead bolt behind her, the sound of it echoed through the whole of the penthouse like a gong, answering Achilles eloquently without her having to open her mouth.

Telling him exactly how much of a coward she was, in case he hadn't already guessed.

CHAPTER SIX

IN THE DAYS that followed that strange night and Achilles's world-altering kiss that had left her raw and aching and wondering if she'd ever feel like herself again, Valentina found she couldn't bear the notion that she was twenty-seven years old and somehow a stranger to herself.

Her future was set in stone. She'd always known that. And she'd never fought against all that inevitability because what was the point? She could fight as much as she wanted and she'd still be Princess Valentina of Murin, only with a stain next to her name. That had always seemed to her like the very definition of futility.

But in the days that followed that kiss, it occurred to her that perhaps it wasn't the future she needed to worry about, but her past. She hadn't really allowed herself to think too closely about what it meant that Natalie had been raised by the woman who was very likely Valentina's own mother. Because, of course, there was no other explanation for the fact she and Natalie looked so much alike. Identical twins couldn't just randomly occur, and certainly not when one of them was a royal. There were too many people watching royal births too closely. Valentina had accepted the story that her mother had abandoned her, because it had always been couched in terms of Frederica's mental illness. Valentina had imagined her mother living out her days in some or other institution somewhere, protected from harm.

But the existence of Natalie suggested that Frederica was instead a completely different person from the one Valentina had imagined all this time. The woman who now called herself Erica had clearly not wasted away in a mental institution, all soothing pastels and injections and no ability to contact her own child. On the contrary, this Erica had lived a complicated life after her time in the palace that had nothing to do with any hospital—and though she'd clearly had two daughters, she'd taken only one with her when she'd gone.

Valentina didn't entirely understand how she could be quite so hurt by a betrayal that had happened so long ago and that she hadn't known about until recently. She didn't understand why it mattered so much to her. But the more she tried to tell herself that it was silly to be so bothered, the more bothered she got.

It was only when she had gone round and round and round on that almost too many times to count that Valentina accepted the fact she was going to have to do something about it.

And all these years, she'd never known how to go about looking for her mother even if she'd wanted to. She would have had to ask her father directly, the very idea of which made her shudder—even now, across an ocean or two from his throne and his great reserve and his obvious reluctance to discuss Frederica at all. Barring that, she would have had to speak to one of the high-level palace aides whose role was to serve her father in every possible way and who therefore had access to most of the family secrets. She doubted somehow that they would have told her all the things that she wanted to know—or even a few of them. And they certainly would have run any questions she had past her father first, which would have defeated the purpose of asking them.

Valentina tried to tell herself that was why she'd never asked.

But now she was tucked up in a lethally dangerous billionaire's penthouse in New York City, away from all the palace intrigue and protocol, and far too aware of the things a man like Achilles could do with only a kiss. To say nothing of his businesses. What was an old family secret to a man like Achilles?

And even though in many ways she had fewer resources at her fingertips and fewer people to ask for ancient stories and explanations, in the end, it was very simple. Because Valentina had Natalie's mobile, which had to mean she had direct access to her own story. If she dared look for it.

The Valentina who had seen her own mirror image in a bathroom in London might not have dared. But the Valentina who had lost herself in the raw fire of Achilles's kiss, on the other hand, dared all manner of things.

It was that Valentina who opened up Natalie's list of contacts, sitting there in her locked bedroom in Achilles's penthouse. She scrolled down, looking for an entry that read *Mom*. Or *Mum*. Or any variation of *Mother* she could think of.

But there was nothing.

That stymied her, but she was aware enough to realize that the sensation deep in her belly was not regret. It was relief. As if, in the end, she preferred these mysteries to what was likely to be a vicious little slap of truth.

You are such a coward, she told herself.

Because it wasn't as if her father—or Valentina herself, for that matter—had ever been in hiding. The truth was that her mother could have located her at any point over these last twenty-seven years. That she hadn't done so told Valentina all she needed to know about Frederica's maternal feelings, surely.

Well. What she *needed* to know perhaps, but there was a great deal more she *wanted* to know, and that was the trouble.

She kept scrolling until she found an entry marked *Erica*. She thought that told her a great deal about Natalie's relationship with this woman who was likely mother to them both. It spoke of a kind of distance that Valentina had certainly never contemplated when she'd thought about her own mother from time to time over the past nearly thirty years. In her head, of course, any reunion with the woman she'd imagined had been locked away in a pleasantly secure institution would be filled with love. Regret. Soft, sweet arms wrapped around her, and a thousand apologies for somehow managing to abandon and then never find her way back to a baby who lived at one of the most famous addresses in the world.

She wasn't entirely sure why the simple fact of the woman's first name in a list of contacts made it so clear that all of that was a lie. Not just a harmless fantasy to make a motherless child feel better about her fate, but something infinitely more dangerous, somehow.

Valentina wanted to shut down the mobile phone. She wanted to throw it across the small room and pretend that she'd never started down this road in the first place.

But it occurred to her that possibly, she was trying to talk herself out of doing this thing she was certain she needed to do.

Because Achilles might have imagined that he could see these mysteries in her, but what scared Valentina was that she could, too. That he'd identified a terrible weakness in her, and that meant anyone could.

Perhaps she wasn't who she thought she was. Perhaps she never had been. Perhaps, all this time, she'd imagined she'd been walking down a set path when she hadn't.

If she was honest, the very idea made her want to cry.

It had been important, she thought then, sitting cross-legged on the bed with the summer light streaming in from the windows—crucially important, even—to carry on the morning after that kiss as if nothing had changed. Because she had to pretend that nothing had. That she didn't know too much now. That she didn't think of that kiss every time she looked at Achilles. She'd gone to work, and she'd done her job, and she'd stayed as much in his presence as she ever did—and she thought that she deserved some kind of award for the acting she'd done. So cool, so composed.

So utterly unbothered by the fact she now knew how he tasted.

And she tried to convince herself that only she knew that she was absolutely full of it.

But one day bled into the next, and she'd found that her act became harder and harder to pull off, instead of easier. She couldn't understand it. It wasn't as if Achilles was doing anything, necessarily. He was Achilles, of course. There was always that look in his eyes, as if he was but waiting for her to give him a sign.

Any sign.

As if, were she to do so, he would drop everything he was doing—no matter where they were and what was happening around them—and sweep them right back into that storm of sensation that she found simmered inside her, waiting. Just waiting.

Just as he was.

It was the notion that she was the one who held the power—who could make all of that happen with a simple word or glance—that she found kept her up at night. It made her shake. It polluted her dreams and made her drift off entirely too many times while she was awake, only to be slapped back down to earth when Achilles's voice turned silken, as if he knew.

Somehow, this all made her determined to seek out the one part of her life that had never made sense, and had never fit in neatly into the tidy narrative she'd believed all her life and knew back and forth.

Today was a rare afternoon when Achilles had announced that he had no need of her assistance while he tended to his fitness in his personal gym because, he'd gritted at her, he needed to clear his head. Valentina had repaired to her bedroom to work out a few snarls in his schedule and return several calls from the usual people wanting advice on how to approach him with various bits of news he was expected to dislike intensely. She'd changed out of Natalie's usual work uniform and had gratefully pulled on a pair of jeans and a T-shirt, feeling wildly rebellious as she did so. And then a little bit embarrassed that her life was clearly so staid and old-fashioned that she found denim a personal revolution.

Many modern princesses dressed casually at times, she was well aware. Just as she was even more aware that none of them were related to her father, with his antiquated notions of propriety. And therefore none of them would have to suffer his disapproval should she find herself photographed looking "common" despite her ancient bloodline.

But she wasn't Princess Valentina here in New York, where no one cared what she wore. And maybe that was why Valentina pulled the trigger. She didn't cold-call the number that she'd found on her sister's phone—and there was something hard and painful in her chest even thinking that word, *sister*. She fed the number into a little piece of software that one of Achilles's companies had been working on, and she let it present her with information that she supposed she should have had some sort of scruple about using. But she didn't.

Valentina imagined that said something about her, too, but she couldn't quite bring herself to care about that the way she thought she ought to have.

In a push of a button, she had a billing address. Though the phone number itself was tied to the area code of a far-off city, the billing address was right here in Manhattan.

It was difficult not see that as some kind of sign.

Valentina slipped out of the penthouse then, without giving herself time to second-guess what she was about to do. She smiled her way through the lobby the way she always did, and then she set out into New York City by herself.

All by herself.

No guards. No security. Not even Achilles's brooding presence at her side. She simply walked. She made her way through the green, bright stretch of Central Park, headed toward the east side and the address Achilles's software had provided. No one spoke to her. No one called her name. No cameras snapped at her, recording her every move.

After a while, Valentina stopped paying attention to the expression on her face. She stopped worrying about her posture and whether or not her hair looked unkempt as the faint breeze teased at it. She simply…walked.

Her shoulders seemed to slip down an extra inch or two from her ears. She found herself breathing deeper, taking in the people she passed without analyzing them—without assuming they wanted something from her or were looking to photograph her supposedly "at large" in the world.

About halfway across the park it occurred to her that she'd never felt this way in her life. Alone. Free. Better yet, anonymous. She could have been anybody on the streets. There were locals all over the paths in the park, walking and talking and taking in the summer afternoon as if that was a perfectly normal pastime. To be out on their own, no one the wiser, doing exactly as they pleased.

Valentina realized that whatever happened next, this was the normal she'd spent her life looking for and dreaming about. This exact moment, walking across Central Park while summer made its cheerful noises all around her, completely and entirely on her own.

Freedom, it turned out, made her heart beat a little too fast and too hard inside her chest.

Once she made it to the east side, she headed a little bit uptown, then farther east until she found the address that had been on that billing statement. It looked like all the other buildings on the same block, not exactly dripping in luxury, but certainly no hovel. It was difficult for Valentina to determine the difference between kinds of dwellings in a place like this. Apartment buildings, huge blocks of too many people living on top of each other by choice, seemed strange to her on the face of it. But who was she to determine the difference between prosperous New Yorkers and regular ones? She had lived in a palace all her life.

And she suspected that Achilles's sprawling penthouse wasn't a far cry from a palace itself, come to that.

But once she'd located the building she wanted and its dark green awning marked with white scrollwork, she didn't know what to do. Except wait there. As if she was some kind of daring sleuth, just like in the books she'd read as a little girl, when she was just…that same old motherless child, looking for a better story to tell herself.

She chided herself for that instantly. It felt defeating. Despairing. She was anonymous and free and unremarkable, standing on a city street. Nobody in the entire world knew where she was. Nobody would know where to look and nobody was likely to find her if they tried. Valentina couldn't decide if that notion made her feel small and fragile, or vast and powerful. Maybe both at the same time.

She didn't know how long she stood there. She ignored the first few calls that buzzed at her from Natalie's mobile tucked in her pocket, but then realized that standing about speaking on her phone gave her far more of a reason to be out there in the street. Instead of simply standing there doing nothing, looking like she was doing exactly what she was doing, which was looming around as she waited for somebody to turn up.

So she did her job, out there on the street. Or Natalie's job, anyway. She fielded the usual phone calls from the office and, if she was honest, liked the fact that she had somewhere to put all her nervous energy. She was half-afraid that Achilles would call and demand that she return to his side immediately, but she suspected that she was less afraid of that happening than she was hoping that it would, so she didn't have to follow this through.

Because even now, there was a part of her that simply wanted to retreat back into what she already knew. What she'd spent her life believing.

Afternoon was bleeding into evening, and Valentina was beginning to think that she'd completely outstayed her welcome. That Erica was in one of the other places she sometimes stayed, like the one in the Caribbean Natalie had mentioned in a text. That at any moment now it was likely that one of the doormen in the surrounding buildings would call the police to make her move along at last. That they hadn't so far she regarded as some kind of miracle. She finished up the last of the calls she'd been fielding, and told herself that it had been foolish to imagine that she could simply turn up one afternoon, stand around and solve the mysteries of her childhood so easily.

But that was when she saw her.

And Valentina didn't know exactly what it was that had caught her eye. The hair was wrong, not long and coppery like her daughters' but short. Dark. And it wasn't as if Valentina had any memories of this woman, but still. There was something in the way she moved. The way she came down the block, walking quickly, a plastic bag hanging from one wrist and the other hand holding a phone to her ear.

But Valentina knew her. She knew that walk. She knew the gait and the way the woman cocked her head toward the hand holding her phone. She knew the way this woman carried herself.

She recognized her, in other words, when she shouldn't have. When, she realized, despite the fact she'd spent a whole summer afternoon waiting for this moment—she really didn't want to recognize her.

And she'd been nursing fantasies this whole time, little as she wanted to admit that, even to herself. She'd told herself all the things that she would do if this woman appeared. She'd worked out scenarios in her head.

Do you know who I am? she would ask, or demand, and this woman she had always thought of as Federica, but who went by a completely different name—the better to hide, Valentina assumed—would... Cry? Flail about? Offer excuses? She hadn't been able to decide which version she would prefer no matter how many times she'd played it out in her head.

And as this woman who was almost certainly her mother

walked toward her, not looking closely enough to see that there was anyone standing down the block a ways in front of her, much less someone who she should have assumed was the daughter she knew as Natalie, Valentina realized what she should have known already. Or maybe, deep down, she had known it—she just hadn't really wanted to admit it.

There was nothing this woman could do to fix anything or change anything or even make it better. She couldn't go back in time. She couldn't change the past. She couldn't choose Valentina instead of Natalie, if that had been the choice she'd made. Valentina wasn't even certain that was something she'd want, if she could go back in time herself, but the fact of the matter was that there was nothing to be done about it now.

And her heart beat at her and beat at her, until she thought it might beat its way straight out through her ribs, and even as it did, Valentina couldn't pretend that she didn't know that what she was feeling was grief.

Grief, thick and choking. Dark and muddy and deep.

For the childhood she'd never had, and hadn't known she'd missed until now. For the life she might have known had this woman been different. Had Valentina been different. Had her father, perhaps, not been King Geoffrey of Murin. It was all speculation, of course. It was that tearing thing in her belly and that weight on her chest, and that thick, deep mud she worried she might never find her way out of again.

And when Erica drew close to her building's green awning, coming closer to Valentina than she'd been in twenty-seven years, Valentina…said nothing. She let her hair fall forward to cover her face where she leaned against the brick wall. She pretended she was on a serious phone call while the woman who was definitely her mother—of course she was her mother; how had Valentina been tricking herself into pretending she could be anything but that?—turned into the building that Valentina had been staking out all afternoon, and was swallowed up into her own lobby.

For long moments, Valentina couldn't breathe. She wasn't sure she could think.

It was as if she didn't know who she was.

She found herself walking. She lost herself in the tumult of this sprawling mess of a bright and brash city, the noise of car horns in the street, and the blasts of conversation and laughter from the groups of strangers she passed. She made her way back to the park and wandered there as the summer afternoon took on that glassy blue that meant the hour was growing late.

She didn't cry. She hardly saw in front of her. She simply walked.

And dusk was beginning to steal in at last, making the long blocks cold in the long shadows, when she finally made it back to Achilles's building.

One of the doormen brought her up in the elevator, smiling at her as she stepped off. It made her think that perhaps she had smiled in return, though she couldn't tell. It was as if her body was not her own and her face was no longer under her control. She walked into Achilles's grand living room, and stood there. It was as if she still didn't know where she was. As if she still couldn't see. And the huge windows that let Manhattan in all around her only seemed to make her sense of dislocation worse.

"Where the hell have you been?"

That low growl came from above her. Valentina didn't have to turn and look to know that it was Achilles from on high, standing at the top of the stairs that led to his sprawling master suite.

She looked up anyway. Because somehow, the most dangerous man she'd ever met felt like an anchor.

He looked as if he'd just showered. He wore a T-shirt she could tell was soft from down two flights, stretched over his remarkable chest as if it was as enamored of him as she feared she was. Loose black trousers were slung low on his hips, and she had the giddy sense that if he did something like stretch, or breathe too heavily, she would be able to see a swathe of olive skin between the waistband and the hem of his T-shirt.

And suddenly, she wanted nothing more than to see exactly that. More than she could remember wanting anything else. Ever.

"Careful, *glikia mou*, or I will take you up on that invitation written all over your face," Achilles growled as if he was irritated…but she knew better.

Because he knew. He always knew. He could read her when no one else ever had. The masks she wore like they were second nature and the things she pretended for the whole of the rest of the world fooled everybody, but never him.

Never, ever him.

As if there was a real Valentina buried beneath the exterior she'd thought for years was the totality of who she was, and Achilles was the only one who had ever met her. Ever seen her. Ever suspected she existed and then found her, again and again, no matter how hard Valentina worked to keep her hidden away.

Her throat was dry. Her tongue felt as if it no longer fit in her own mouth.

But she couldn't bring herself to look away from him.

She thought about her mother and she thought about her childhood. She thought about the pride she'd taken in that virtue of hers that she'd clung to so fiercely all these years. Or perhaps not so fiercely, as it had been so untested. Was that virtue at all, she wondered?

Or was this virtue?

She had spent all of this time trying to differentiate herself from a woman she thought she knew, but who it turned out she didn't know at all. And for what? She was already trapped in the same life that her mother had abandoned.

Valentina was the one who hadn't left her father. She was the one who had prided herself on being perfect. She was the one who was decidedly not mentally ill, never too overwrought to do the job required of her by her blood and her father's expectations, nothing but a credit to her father in all ways. And she'd reveled in it.

More than reveled in it. It had become the cornerstone of her own self-definition.

And all of it was built on lies. The ones she told herself, and more than that, the lies that had been told to her for her entire life. By everyone.

All Valentina could think as she gazed up the stairs to the man she was only pretending was her employer was that she was done with lies. She wanted something honest. Even—especially—if it was raw.

And she didn't much care if there were consequences to that.

"You say that is if it is a threat," she said quietly. Distinctly. "Perhaps you should rethink your own version of an invitation before it gets you in trouble." She raised her brows in challenge, and knew it. Reveled in it, too. "Sir."

And when Achilles smiled then, it was with sheer masculine triumph, and everything changed.

He had thought she'd left him.

When Achilles had come out of the hard, brutal workout he'd subjected himself to that had done absolutely nothing to make his vicious need for her settle, Achilles had found her gone.

And he'd assumed that was it. The princess had finally had enough. She'd finished playing this down market game of hers and gone back to her palaces and her ball gowns and her resplendent little prince who waited for her across the seas.

He'd told himself it was for the best.

He was a man who took things for a living and made an empire out of his conquests, and he had no business whatsoever putting his commoner's hands all over a woman of her pedigree. No business doing it, and worse, he shouldn't want to.

And maybe that was why he found himself on his treadmill again while he was still sucking air from his first workout, running as if every demon he'd vanquished in his time was chasing him all over again, and gaining. Maybe that was why he'd run until he'd thought his lungs might burst, his head might explode or his knees might give out beneath him.

Then he'd run more. And even when he'd exhausted himself all over again, even when he was standing in his own shower with his head bent toward the wall as if she'd bested him personally, it hadn't helped.

The fact of the matter was that he had a taste of Valentina, and nothing else would do.

And what enraged him the most, he'd found—aside from the fact he hadn't had her the way he'd wanted her—was that he'd let her think she'd tricked him all this time. That she would go back behind her fancy gates and her moats and whatever the hell else she had in that palace of hers that he'd looked up online and thought looked exactly like the sort of fairy tale he disdained, and she would believe that she'd played him for a fool.

Achilles thought that might actually eat him alive.

And now here she stood when he thought he'd lost her. At the bottom of his stairs, looking up at him, her eyes dark with some emotion he couldn't begin to define.

But he didn't want to define it. He didn't want to talk about her feelings, and he'd die before he admitted his own, and what did any of that matter anyway? She was here and he was here, and a summer night was creeping in outside.

And the only thing he wanted to think about was sating himself on her at last.

At last and for as long as he could.

Achilles was hardly aware of moving down the stairs even as he did it.

One moment he was at the top, staring down at Valentina's upturned face with her direct challenge ringing in him like a bell, and the next he was upon her. And she was so beautiful. So exquisitely, ruinously beautiful. He couldn't seem to get past that. It was as if it wound around him and through him, changing him, making him new each time he beheld her.

He told himself he hated it, but he didn't look away.

"There is no going back," he told her sternly. "There will be no pretending this didn't happen."

Her smile was entirely too graceful and the look in her green eyes too merry by far. "Do you get that often?"

Achilles felt like a savage. An animal. Too much like that monster he kept down deep inside. And yet he didn't have it in him to mind. He reached out and indulged himself at last while his blood hammered through his veins, running his fingers over that elegant cheekbone of hers, and that single freckle that marred the perfection of her face—and somehow made her all the more beautiful.

"So many jokes," he murmured, not sure how much of the gruffness in his voice was need and how much was that thing like temper that held him fast and fierce. "Everything is so hilarious, suddenly. How much longer do you think you will be laughing, *glikia mou*?"

"I think that is up to you," Valentina replied smoothly, and she was still smiling at him in that same way, graceful and knowing. "Is that why you require so much legal documentation before you take a woman to bed? Do you make them all laugh so much that you fear your reputation as a grumpy icon would take a hit if it got out?"

It was a mark of how far gone he was that he found that amusing. If anyone else had dreamed of saying such a thing to him, he would have lost his sense of humor completely.

He felt his mouth curve. "There is only one way to find out."

And Achilles had no idea what she might do next. He wondered if that was what it was about her, if that was why this thirst for her never seemed to ebb. She was so very different from all the women he'd known before. She was completely unpredictable. He hardly knew, from one moment to the next, what she might do next.

It should have irritated him, he thought. But instead it only made him want her more.

Everything, it seemed, made him want her more. He hadn't

realized until now how pale and insubstantial his desires had been before. How little he'd wanted anything.

"There is something I must tell you." She pulled her bottom lip between her teeth after she said that, a little breathlessly, and everything in him stilled.

This was it, he thought. And Achilles didn't know if he was proud of her or sad, somehow, that this great charade was at an end. For surely that was what she planned to tell him. Surely she planned to come clean about who she really was.

And while there was a part of him that wanted to deny that what swirled between them was anything more than sex, simple and elemental, there was a far greater part of him that roared its approval that she should think it was right to identify herself before they went any further.

"You can tell me anything," he told her, perhaps more fiercely than he should. "But I don't know why you imagine I don't already know."

He was fascinated when her cheeks bloomed with that crisp, bright red that he liked a little too much. More each time he saw it, because he liked his princess a little flustered. A little off balance.

But something in him turned over, some foreboding perhaps. Because he couldn't quite imagine why it was that she should be *embarrassed* by the deception she'd practiced on him. He could think of many things he'd like her to feel for attempting to pull something like that over on him, and he had quite a few ideas about how she should pay for that, but embarrassment wasn't quite it.

"I thought you might know," she whispered. "I hope it doesn't matter."

"Everything matters or nothing does, *glikia mou.*"

He shifted so he was closer to her. He wanted to care about whatever it was she was about to tell him, but he found the demands of his body were far too loud and too imperative to ignore. He put his hands on her, curling his fingers over her delicate shoulders and then losing himself in their suppleness. And in the delicate line of her arms. And in the sweet feel of her bare skin beneath his palms as he ran them down from her shoulders to her wrists, then back again.

And he found he didn't really care what she planned to confess to him. How could it matter when he was touching her like this?

"I do not require your confession," he told her roughly. "I am not your priest."

If anything, her cheeks flared brighter.

"I'm a virgin," she blurted out, as if she had to force herself to say it.

For a moment, it was as if she'd struck him. As if she'd picked up one of the sculptures his interior designer had littered about his living room and clobbered him with it.

"I beg your pardon?"

But she was steadier then. "You heard me. I'm a virgin. I thought you knew." She swallowed, visibly, but she didn't look away from him. "Especially when I didn't know how to kiss you."

Achilles didn't know what to do with that.

Or rather, he knew exactly what to do with it, but was afraid that if he tossed his head back and let himself go the way he wanted to—roaring out his primitive take on her completely unexpected confession to the rafters—it might terrify her.

And the last thing in the world he wanted to do was terrify her.

He knew he should care that this wasn't quite the confession he'd expected. That as far as he could tell, Valentina had no intention of telling him who she was. Ever. He knew that it should bother him, and perhaps on some level it did, but the only thing he could seem to focus on was the fact that she was untouched.

Untouched.

He was the only man in all the world who had ever tasted

her. Touched her. Made her shiver, and catch her breath, and moan. That archaic word seemed to beat in place of his heart.

Virgin. Virgin. Virgin.

Until it was as if he knew nothing but that. As if her innocence shimmered between them, beckoning and sweet, and she was his for the taking.

And, oh, how Achilles liked to take the things he wanted.

"Are you sure you wish to waste such a precious gift on the likes of me?" he asked, and he heard the stark greed beneath the laziness he forced into his tone. He heard exactly how much he wanted her. He was surprised it didn't seem to scare her the way he thought it should. "After all, there is nothing particularly special about me. I have money, that's all. And as you have reminded me, I am your boss. The ethical considerations are legion."

He didn't know why he said that. Any of that. Was it to encourage her to confess her real identity to him? Was it to remind her of the role she'd chosen to play—although not today, perhaps?

Or was it to remind him?

Either way, she only lifted her chin. "You don't have to take it," she said, as if it was of no import to her one way or the other. "Certainly not if you have some objection."

She lifted one shoulder, then dropped it, and the gesture was so quintessentially royal that it should have set Achilles's teeth on edge. But instead he found it so completely her, so entirely Princess Valentina, that it only made him harder. Hotter. More determined to find his way inside her.

And soon.

"I have no objection," he assured her, and there was no pretending his tone wasn't gritty. Harsh. "Are we finished talking?"

And the nerves he'd been unable to detect before were suddenly all over her face. He doubted she knew it. But she was braver than she ought to have been, his deceitful little princess, and all she did was gaze back at him. Clear and sure, as if he couldn't see the soft, vulnerable cast to her mouth.

Or maybe, he thought, she had no idea how transparent she was.

"Yes," Valentina said softly. "I'm ready to stop talking."

And this time, as he drew her to him, he knew it wouldn't end in a kiss. He knew they weren't going to stop until he'd had her at last.

He knew that she was not only going to be his tonight, but she was going to be only his. That no one had ever touched her before, and if he did it right, no one else ever would.

Because Achilles had every intention of ruining his princess for all other men.

CHAPTER SEVEN

VALENTINA COULDN'T BELIEVE this was happening.

At last.

Achilles took her mouth, and there was a lazy quality to his kiss that made her knees feel weak. He set his mouth to hers, and then he took his time. As if he knew that inside she was a jangle of nerves and longing, anticipation and greed. As if he knew she hardly recognized herself or all the needy things that washed around inside her, making her new.

Making her his.

He kissed her for a long while, it seemed to her. He slid his arms around her, he pulled her against his chest, and then he took her mouth with a thoroughness that made a dangerous languor steal all over her. All through her. Until she wasn't sure that she would be able to stand on her own, were he to let go of her.

But he didn't let go.

Valentina thought she might have fallen off the edge of the world anyway, because everything seemed to whirl and cartwheel around, but then she realized that what he'd done was stoop down to bend a little and then pick her up. As if she was as weightless as she felt. He held her in his arms, high against his chest, and she felt her shoes fall off her feet like some kind of punctuation. And when he gazed down into her face, she thought he looked like some kind of conquering warrior of old, though she chided herself for being so fanciful.

There was nothing fanciful about Achilles.

Quite the opposite. He was fierce and masculine and ruthless beyond measure, and still, Valentina couldn't think of anywhere she would rather be—or anyone she would rather be with like this. It all felt inevitable, as if she'd been waiting her whole life for this thing she hardly understood to sweep her away, just like this.

And it had come into focus only when she'd met Achilles.

Because he was her only temptation. She had never wanted anyone else. She couldn't imagine she ever would.

"I don't know what to do," she whispered, aware on some level that he was moving. That he was carrying her up those penthouse stairs as if she weighed nothing at all. But she couldn't bring herself to look away from his dark gold gaze. And the truth was, she didn't care. He could take her anywhere. "I don't want to disappoint you."

"And how would you do that?" His voice was so deep. So lazy and, unless she was mistaken, amused, even as that gaze of his made her quiver, deep inside.

"Well," she stammered out. "Well, I don't—"

"Exactly," he said, interrupting her with that easy male confidence that she found she liked a little too much. "You don't know, but I do. So perhaps, *glikia mou*, you will allow me to demonstrate the breadth and depth of my knowledge."

And when she shuddered, he only laughed.

Achilles carried her across the top floor, all of which was part of his great master bedroom. It took up the entire top level of his penthouse, bordered on all sides by the wide patio that was also accessible from a separate staircase below. The better to maintain and protect his privacy, she thought now, which she felt personally invested in at the moment. He strode across the hardwood floor with bold-colored rugs tossed here and there, and she took in the exposed brick walls and the bright, modern works of art that hung on them. This floor was all space and silence, and in between there were more of those breathtaking windows that brightened the room with the lights from the city outside.

Achilles didn't turn on any additional light. He simply took Valentina over to the huge bed that was propped up on a sleek modern platform crafted out of a bright, hard steel, and laid her out across it as if she was something precious to him. Which made her heart clutch at her, as if she wanted to be.

And then he stood there beside the bed, his hands on his lean hips, and did nothing but gaze down at her.

Valentina pushed herself up onto her elbows. She could feel her breath moving in and out of her, and it was as if it was wired somehow to all that sensation she could feel lighting her up inside. It made her breasts feel heavier. It made her arms and legs feel somehow restless and sleepy at once.

With every breath, she could feel that bright, hot ache between her legs intensify. And this time, she knew without a shred of doubt that he was aware of every last part of it.

"Do you have anything else to confess?" he asked her, and she wondered if she imagined the dark current in his voice then. But it didn't matter. She had never wanted anyone, but she wanted him. Desperately.

She would confess anything at all if it meant she could have him.

And it wasn't until his eyes blazed, and that remarkable mouth of his kicked up in one corner, that she realized she'd spoken out loud.

"I will keep that in mind," he told her, his voice a rasp into the quiet of the room. Then he inclined his head. "Take off your clothes."

It was as if he'd plugged her into an electrical outlet. She felt zapped. Blistered, perhaps, by the sudden jolt of power. It felt as if there were something bright and hot, wrapped tight around her ribs, pressing down. And down farther.

And she couldn't bring herself to mind.

"But—by myself?" she asked, feeling a little bit light-headed at the very idea. She'd found putting on these jeans a little bit revolutionary. She couldn't imagine stripping them off in front of a man.

And not just any man. Achilles Casilieris.

Who didn't relent at all. "You heard me."

Valentina had to struggle then. She had to somehow shove her way out of all that wild electrical madness that was jangling through her body, at least enough so she could think through it. A little bit, anyway. She had to struggle to sit up all the way, and then to pull the T-shirt off her body. Her hands went to her jeans next, and she wrestled with the buttons, trying to pull the fly open. It was all made harder by the fact that her hands shook and her fingers felt entirely too thick.

And the more she struggled, the louder her breathing sounded. Until she was sure it was filling up the whole room, and more embarrassing by far, there was no possible way that Achilles couldn't hear it. Or see the flush that she could feel all over her, electric and wild. She wrestled the stiff, unyielding denim down over her hips, that bright heat that churned inside her seeming to bleed out everywhere as she did. She was sure it stained her, marking her bright hot and obvious.

She sneaked a look toward Achilles, and she didn't know what she expected to see. But she froze when her eyes met his.

That dark gold gaze of his was as hot and demanding as ever. That curve in his mouth was even deeper. And there was something in the way that he was looking at her that soothed her. As if his hands were on her already, when they were not. It was as if he was helping her undress when she suspected that it was very deliberate on his part that he was not.

Because of course it was deliberate, she realized in the next breath. He was giving her another choice. He was putting it in her hands, again. And even while part of her found that inordinately frustrating, because she wanted to be swept away by him—or more swept away, anyway—there was still a part of her that relished this. That took pride in the fact that she was choosing to give in to this particular temptation.

That she was choosing to truly offer this particular man the virtue she had always considered such a gift.

It wasn't accidental. She wasn't drunk the way many of her friends had been, nor out of her mind in some other way, or even outside herself in the storm of an explosive temper or wild sensation that had boiled over.

He wanted her to be very clear that she was choosing him.

And Valentina wanted that, too. She wanted to choose Achilles. She wanted this.

She had never wanted anything else, she was sure of it. Not with this fervor that inhabited her body and made her light up from the inside out. Not with this deep certainty.

And so what could it possibly matter that she had never undressed for a man before? She was a princess. She had dressed and undressed in rooms full of attendants her whole life. Achilles was different from her collection of royal aides, clearly. But there was no need for her to be embarrassed, she told herself then. There was no need to go red in the face and start fumbling about, as if she didn't know how to remove a pair of jeans from her own body.

Remember who you are, she chided herself.

She was Princess Valentina of Murin. It didn't matter that seeing her mother might have shaken her. It didn't change a thing. That had nothing to do with who she was, it only meant that she'd become who she was in spite of the choices her mother had made. She could choose to do with that what she liked. And she was choosing to gift her innocence, the virginity she'd clung to as a badge of honor as if that differentiated her from the mother who'd left her, to Achilles Casilieris.

Here. Now.

And there was absolutely nothing to be ashamed about.

Valentina was sure that she saw something like approval in

his dark gaze as she finished stripping her jeans from the length of her legs. And then she was sitting there in nothing but her bra and panties. She shifted up and onto her knees. Her hair fell down over her shoulders as she knelt on the bed, swirling across her bared skin and making her entirely too aware of how exposed she was.

But this time it felt sensuous. A sweet, warm sort of reminder of how much she wanted this. Him.

"Go on," he told her, a gruff command.

"That sounded a great deal like an order," Valentina murmured, even as she moved her hands around to her back to work the clasp of her bra. And it wasn't even a struggle to make her voice so airy.

"It was most definitely an order," Achilles agreed, his voice still gruff. "And I would suggest you obey me with significantly more alacrity."

"Or what?" she taunted him gently.

She eased open the silken clasp and then moved her hands around to the bra cups, holding them to her breasts when the bra would have fallen open. "Will you hold it against me in my next performance review? Oh, the horror."

"Are you defying me?"

But Achilles sounded amused, despite his gruffness. And there was something else in his voice then, she thought. A certain tension that she felt move inside her even before she understood what it was. Maybe she didn't have to understand. Her body already knew.

Between her legs, that aching thing grew fiercer. Brighter. And so did she.

"I think you can take it," she whispered.

And then she let the bra fall.

She felt the rush of cooler air over the flesh of her breasts. Her nipples puckered and stung a little as they pulled tight. But what she was concentrating on was that taut, arrested look on

Achilles's face. That savage gleam in his dark gold eyes. And the way his fierce, ruthless mouth went flat.

He muttered something in guttural Greek, using words she had never heard before, in her blue-blooded academies and rarefied circles. But she knew, somehow, exactly what he meant.

She could feel it, part of that same ache.

He reached down to grip the hem of his T-shirt, then tugged it up and over his head in a single shrug of one muscled arm. She watched him do it, not certain she was breathing any longer and not able to make herself care about that at all, and then he was moving toward the bed.

Another second and he was upon her.

He swept her up in his arms again, moving her into the center of the bed, and then he bore her down to the mattress beneath them. And Valentina found that they fit together beautifully. That she knew instinctively what to do.

She widened her legs, he fit himself between them, and she cushioned him there—that long, solid, hard-packed form of his—as if they'd been made to fit together just like this. His bare chest was a wonder. She couldn't seem to keep herself from exploring it, running her palms and her fingers over every ridge and every plane, losing herself in his hot, extraordinary male flesh. She could feel that remarkable ridge of his arousal again, pressed against her right where she ached the most, and it was almost too much.

Or maybe it really was too much, but she wanted it all the same.

She wanted him.

He set his mouth to hers again, and she could taste a kind of desperation on his wickedly clever mouth.

That wild sensation stormed through her, making her limp and wild and desperate for things she'd only ever read about before. He tangled his hands in her hair to hold her mouth to his, then he dropped his chest down against hers, bearing her down into the mattress beneath them. Making her feel glorious and alive and insane with that ache that started between her legs and bloomed out in all directions.

And then he taught her everything.

He tasted her. He moved his mouth from her lips, down the long line of her neck, learning the contours of her clavicle. Then he went lower, sending fire spinning all over her as he made his way down to one of her breasts, only to send lightning flashing all through her when he sucked her nipple deep into his mouth.

He tested the weight of her breasts in his faintly calloused palm, while he played with the nipple of the other, gently torturing her with his teeth, his tongue, his cruel lips. When she thought she couldn't take any more, he switched.

And then he went back and forth, over and over again, until her head was thrashing against the mattress, and some desperate soul was crying out his name. Over and over again, as if she might break apart at any moment.

Valentina knew, distantly, that she was the one making those sounds. But she was too far gone to care.

Achilles moved his way down her body, taking his sweet time, and Valentina sighed with every inch he explored. She shifted. She rolled. She found herself lifting her hips toward him without his having to ask.

"Good girl," he murmured, and it was astonishing how much pleasure two little words could give her.

He peeled her panties down off her hips, tugged them down the length of her legs and then threw them aside. And when he was finished with that, he slid his hands beneath her bottom as he came back over her, lifted her hips up into the air and didn't so much as glance up at her before he set his mouth to the place where she needed him most.

Maybe she screamed. Maybe she fainted. Maybe both at once.

Everything seemed to flash bright, then smooth out into a long, lethal roll of sensation that turned Valentina red hot.

Everywhere.

He licked his way into her. He teased her and he learned her and he tasted her, making even that most private part of her his. She felt herself go molten and wild, and he made a low, rough sound of pleasure, deeply masculine and deliciously savage, and that was too much.

"Oh, no," she heard herself moan. "No—"

Valentina felt more than heard him laugh against the most tender part of her, and then everything went up in flames.

She exploded. She cried out and she shook, the pleasure so intense she didn't understand how anyone could live through it, but still she shook some more. She shook until she thought she'd been made new. She shook until she didn't care either way.

And when she knew her own name again, Achilles was crawling his way over her. He no longer wore those loose black trousers of his, and there was a look of unmistakably savage male triumph stamped deep on his face.

"Beautiful," he murmured. He was on his elbows over her, pressing himself against her. His wall of a chest. That fascinatingly hard part of him below. He studied her flushed face as if he'd never seen her before. "Am I the only man who has ever tasted you?"

Valentina couldn't speak. She could only nod, mute and still shaking.

She wondered if she might shake like this forever, and she couldn't seem to work herself up into minding if she did.

"Only mine," he said with a certain quiet ferocity that only made that shaking inside her worse. Or better. "You are only and ever mine."

And that was when she felt him. That broad smooth head of his hardest part, nudging against the place where she was nothing but soft, wet heat and longing.

She sucked in a breath, and Achilles took her face in his hands.

"Mine," he said again, in the same intense way.

It sounded a great deal like a vow.

Valentina's head was spinning.

"Yours," she whispered, and he grinned then, too fierce and too elemental.

He shifted his hips and moved a little farther against her, pressing himself against that entrance again, and Valentina found her hands in fists against his chest.

"Will it hurt?" she asked before she knew she meant to speak. "Or is that just something they say in books, to make it seem more…"

But she couldn't quite finish that sentence. And Achilles's gaze was too dark and too bright at once, so intense she couldn't seem to stop shaking or spinning. And she couldn't bring herself to look away.

"It might hurt." He kept his attention on her, fierce and focused. "It might not. But either way, it will be over in a moment."

"Oh." Valentina blinked, and tried to wrap her head around that. "I suppose quick is good."

Achilles let out a bark of laughter, and she wasn't sure if she was startled or something like delighted to hear it. Both, perhaps.

And it made a knot she hadn't known was hardening inside her chest ease.

"I cannot tell if you are good for me or you will kill me," he told her then. He moved one hand, smoothing her hair back from her temple. "It will only hurt, or feel awkward, for a moment. I promise. As for the rest…"

And the smile he aimed at her then was, Valentina thought, the best thing she'd ever seen. It poured into her and through her, as bright and thick as honey, changing everything. Even the way she shook for him. Even the way she breathed.

"The rest will not be quick," Achilles told her, still braced there above her. "It will not be rushed, it will be thorough. Extremely thorough, as you know I am in all things."

She felt her breath stutter. But he was still going.

"And when I am done, *glikia mou*, we will do it again. And

again. Until we get it right. Because I am nothing if not dedicated to my craft. Do you understand me?"

"I understand," Valentina said faintly, because it was hard
to keep her voice even when the world was lost somewhere in
his commanding gaze. "I guess that's—"

But that was when he thrust his way inside her. It was a
quick, hard thrust, slick and hot and overwhelming, until he
was lodged deep inside her.

Inside her.

It was too much. It didn't hurt, necessarily, but it didn't feel
good, either. It felt…like everything. Too much of everything.
Too hard. Too long. Too thick and too deep and too—

"Breathe," Achilles ordered her.

But Valentina didn't see how that was possible. How could
she breathe when there was a person *inside* her? Even if that
person was Achilles.

Especially when that person was Achilles.

Still, she did as he bade her, because he was *inside* her and
she was beneath him and splayed open and there was nothing
else to do. She breathed in.

She let it out, and then she breathed in again. And then again.
And with each breath, she felt less overwhelmed and more…
Something else.

Achilles didn't seem particularly worried. He held himself
over her, one hand tangled in her hair as the other made its way
down the front of her body. Lazily. Easily. He played with her
breasts. He set his mouth against the crook of her neck where
it met her shoulder, teasing her with his tongue and his teeth.

And still she breathed the way he'd told her to do. In. Out.

Over and over, until she couldn't remember that she'd balked
at his smooth, intense entry. That she'd ever had a problem at
all with *hard* and *thick* and *long* and *deep*.

Until all she could feel was fire.

Experimentally, she moved her hips, trying to get a better
feel for how wide he was. How deep. How far inside her own

body. Sensation soared through her every time she moved, so she did it again. And again.

She took a little more of him in, then rocked around a little bit, playing. Testing. Seeing how much of him she could take and if it would continue to send licks of fire coursing through her every time she shifted position, no matter how minutely.

It did.

And when she started to shift against him, restlessly, as if she couldn't help herself, Achilles lifted his head and grinned down her, something wild and dark and wholly untamed in his eyes.

It thrilled her.

"Please..." Valentina whispered.

And he knew. He always knew. Exactly what she needed, right when she needed it.

Because that was when he began to move.

He taught her about pace. He taught her depth and rhythm. She'd thought she was playing with fire, but Achilles taught her that she had no idea what real fire was.

And he kept his word.

He was very, very thorough.

When she began to thrash, he dropped down to get closer. He gathered her in his arms, holding her as he thrust inside her, again and again. He made her his with every deep, possessive stroke. He made her want. He made her need.

He made her cry out his name, again and again, until it sounded to Valentina like some kind of song.

This time, when the fire took her, she thought it might have torn her into far too many pieces for her to ever recover. He lost his rhythm then, hammering into her hard and wild, as if he was as wrecked as she was—

And she held him to her as he tumbled off that edge behind her, and straight on into bliss.

Achilles had made a terrible mistake, and he was not a man who made mistakes. He didn't believe in them. He believed in opportunities—it was how he'd built this life of his. Something that had always made him proud.

But this was a mistake. She was a mistake. He couldn't kid himself. He had never wanted somebody the way that he wanted Valentina. It had made him sloppy. He had concentrated entirely too much on her. Her pleasure. Her innocence, as he relieved her of it.

He hadn't thought to guard himself against her.

He never had to guard himself against anyone. Not since he'd been a child. He'd rather fallen out of the habit—and that notion galled him.

Achilles rolled to the side of the bed and sat there, running a hand over the top of his head. He could hear Valentina behind him, breathing. And he knew what he'd see if he looked. She slept hard, his princess. After he'd finished with her the last time, he'd thought she might have fallen asleep before he'd even pulled out of her. He'd held the weight of her, sprawled there on top of him, her breath heavy and her eyes shut tight so he had no choice but to marvel at the length of her eyelashes.

And it had taken him much longer than it should have to shift her off him, lay her beside him and cover her with the sheets. Carefully.

It was that unexpected urge to protect her—from himself, he supposed, or perhaps from the uncertain elements of his ruthlessly climate-controlled bedroom—that had made him go cold. Something a little too close to the sort of panic he did not permit himself to feel, ever, had pressed down on him then. And no amount of controlling his breath or ordering himself to stop the madness seemed to help.

He rubbed a palm over his chest now, because his heart was beating much too fast, the damned traitor.

He had wanted her too much, and this was the price. This treacherous place he found himself in now, that he hardly recognized. It hadn't occurred to him to guard himself against a virgin no matter her pedigree, and this was the result.

He felt things.

He felt things—and Achilles Casilieris did not *feel*. He re-fused to *feel*. The intensity of sex was physical, nothing more. Never more than that, no matter the woman and no matter the situation and no matter how she might beg or plead—

Not that Valentina had done anything of the sort.

He stood from the bed then, because he didn't want to. He wanted to roll back toward her, pull her close again. He bit off a filthy Greek curse, beneath his breath, then moved restlessly across the floor toward the windows.

Manhattan mocked him. It lay there before him, glittering and sparkling madly, and the reason he had a penthouse in this most brash and American of cities was because he liked to stand high above the sprawl of it as if he was some kind of king. Every time he came here he was reminded how far he'd come from his painful childhood. And every time he stayed in this very room, he looked out over all the wealth and opportu-nity and untethered American dreams that made this city what it was and knew that he had succeeded.

Beyond even the wildest dreams the younger version of Achilles could have conjured up for himself.

But tonight, all he could think about was a copper-haired in-nocent who had yet to tell him her real name, who had given him all of herself with that sweet enthusiasm that had nearly killed him, and left him…yearning.

And Achilles did not yearn.

He did not yearn and he did not let himself want things he could not have, and he absolutely, positively did not indulge in pointless nostalgia for things he did not miss. But as he stood at his huge windows overlooking Manhattan, the city that seemed to laugh at his predicament tonight instead of welcoming him the way it usually did, he found himself tossed back to the part of his past he only ever used as a weapon.

Against himself.

He hardly remembered his mother. Or perhaps he had beaten

that sentimentality out of himself years ago. Either way, he knew that he had been seven or so when she had died, but it wasn't as if her presence earlier had done anything to save her children from the brute of a man whom she had married. Demetrius had been a thick, coarse sort of man, who had worked with his hands down on the docks and had thought that gave him the right to use those hands however he wished. Achilles didn't think there was anything the man had not beaten. His drinking buddies. His wife. The family dog. Achilles and his three young stepsiblings, over and over again. The fact that Achilles had not been Demetrius's own son, but the son of his mother's previous husband who had gone off to war and never returned, had perhaps made the beatings Demetrius doled out harsher—but it wasn't as if he spared his own flesh and blood from his fists.

After Achilles's mother had died under suspicious circumstances no one had ever bothered to investigate in a part of town where nothing good ever happened anyway, things went from bad to worse. Demetrius's temper worsened. He'd taken it out on the little ones, alternately kicking them around and then leaving them for seven-year-old Achilles to raise.

This had always been destined to end in failure, if not outright despair. Achilles understood that now, as an adult looking back. He understood it analytically and theoretically and, if asked, would have said exactly that. He'd been a child himself, etcetera. But where it counted, deep in those terrible feelings he'd turned off when he had still been a boy, Achilles would never understand. He carried the weight of those lives with him, wherever he went. No matter what he built, no matter what he owned, no matter how many times he won this or that corporate battle—none of that paid the ransom he owed on three lives he could never bring back.

They had been his responsibility, and he had failed. That beat in him like a tattoo. It marked him. It was the truth of him.

When it was all over—after Achilles had failed to notice a

gas leak and had woken up only when Demetrius had returned from one of his drinking binges three days later to find the little ones dead and Achilles listless and nearly unresponsive himself—everything had changed. That was the cut-and-dried version of events, and it was accurate enough. What it didn't cover was the guilt, the shame that had eaten Achilles alive. Or what it had been like to watch his siblings' tiny bodies carried out by police, or how it had felt to stand at their graves and know that he could have prevented this if he'd been stronger. Bigger. *Better.*

Achilles had been sent to live with a distant aunt who had never bothered to pretend that she planned to give him anything but a roof over his head, and nothing more. In retrospect, that, too, had been a gift. He hadn't had to bother with any healing. He hadn't had to examine what had happened and try to come to terms with it. No one had cared about him or his grief at all.

And so Achilles had waited. He had plotted. He had taken everything that resembled a feeling, shoved it down as deep inside him as it would go, and made it over into hate. It had taken him ten years to get strong enough. To hunt Demetrius down in a sketchy bar in the same bad neighborhood where he'd brutalized Achilles's mother, beaten his own children and left Achilles responsible for what had happened to them.

And that whole long decade, Achilles had told himself that it was an extermination. That he could walk up to this man who had loomed so large over the whole of his childhood and simply rid the world of his unsavory presence. Demetrius did not deserve to live. There was no doubt about that, no shred of uncertainty anywhere in Achilles's soul. Not while Achilles's mother and his stepsiblings were dead.

He'd staked out his stepfather's favorite dive bar, and this one in the sense that it was repellant, not attractive to rich hipsters from affluent neighborhoods. He'd watched a ramshackle, much grayer and more frail version of the stepfather roaring in his head stumble out into the street. And he'd been ready.

He'd gone up to Demetrius out in the dark, cold night, there in a part of the city where no one would ever dream of interfering in a scuffle on the street lest they find themselves shanked. He'd let the rage wash over him, let the sweet taint of revenge ignite in his veins. He'd expected to feel triumph and satisfaction after all these years and all he'd done to make himself strong enough to take this man down—but what he hadn't reckoned with was that the drunken old man wouldn't recognize him.

Demetrius hadn't known who he was.

And that meant that Achilles had been out there in the street, ready to beat down a defenseless old drunk who smelled of watered-down whiskey and a wasted life.

He hadn't done it. It wasn't worth it. He might have happily taken down the violent, abusive behemoth who'd terrorized him at seven, but he'd been too big himself at seventeen to find any honor in felling someone so vastly inferior to him in every way.

Especially since Demetrius hadn't the slightest idea who he'd been.

And Achilles had vowed to himself then and there that the night he stood in the street in his old neighborhood, afraid of nothing save the darkness inside him, would be the absolutely last time he let feelings rule him.

Because he had wasted years. Years that could have been spent far more wisely than planning out the extermination of an old, broken man who didn't deserve to have Achilles as an enemy. He'd walked away from Demetrius and his own squalid past and he'd never gone back.

His philosophy had served him well since. It had led him across the years, always cold and forever calculating his next, best move. Achilles was never swayed by emotion any longer, for good or ill. He never allowed it any power over him whatsoever. It had made him great, he'd often thought. It had made him who he was.

And yet Princess Valentina had somehow reached deep inside him, deep into a place that should have been black and cold and nothing but ice, and lit him on fire all over again.

"Are you brooding?" a soft voice asked from behind him, scratchy with sleep. Or with not enough sleep. "I knew I would do something wrong."

But she didn't sound insecure. Not in the least. She sounded warm, well sated. She sounded like his. She sounded like exactly who she was: the only daughter of one of Europe's last remaining powerhouse kings and the only woman Achilles had ever met who could turn him inside out.

And maybe that was what did it. The suddenly unbearable fact that she was still lying to him. He had this burning thing eating him alive from the inside out, he was cracking apart at the foundations, and she was still lying to him.

She was in his bed, teasing him in that way of hers that no one else would ever dare, and yet she lied to him. Every moment was a lie, even and especially this one. Every single moment she didn't tell him the truth about who she was and what she was doing here was more than a lie. More than a simple deception.

He was beginning to feel it as a betrayal.

"I do not brood," he said, and he could hear the gruffness in his own voice.

He heard her shift on the bed, and then he heard the sound of her feet against his floor. And he should have turned before she reached him, he knew that. He should have faced her and kept her away from him, especially when it was so dark outside and there was still so much left of the night—and he had clearly let it get to him.

But he didn't.

And in a moment she was at his back, and then she was sliding her arms around his waist with a familiarity that suggested she'd done it a thousand times before and knew how perfectly she would fit there. Then she pressed her face against the hollow of his spine.

And for a long moment she simply stood there like that, and

Achilles felt his heart careen and clatter at his ribs. He was surprised that she couldn't hear it—hell, he was surprised that the whole of Manhattan wasn't alerted.

But all she did was stand there with her mouth pressed against his skin, as if she was holding him up, and through him the whole of the world.

Achilles knew that there was any number of ways to deal with this situation immediately. Effectively. No matter what name she called herself. He could call her out. He could ignore it altogether and simply send her away. He could let the darkness in him edge over into cruelty, so she would be the one to walk away.

But the simple truth was that he didn't want to do any of them.

"I have some land," he told her instead, and he couldn't tell if he was appalled at himself or simply surprised. "Out in the West, where there's nothing to see for acres and acres in all directions except the sky."

"That sounds beautiful," she murmured.

And every syllable was an exquisite pain, because he could feel her shape her words. He could feel her mouth as she spoke, right there against the flesh of his back. And he could have understood if it was a sexual thing. If that was what raged in him then. If it took him over and made him want to do nothing more than throw her down and claim her all over again. Sex, he understood. Sex, he could handle.

But it was much worse than that.

Because it didn't feel like fire, it felt…sweet. The kind of sweetness that wrapped around him, crawling into every nook and cranny inside him he'd long ago thought he'd turned to ice. And then stayed there, blooming into something like heat, as if she could melt him that easily.

He was more than a little worried that she could.

That she already had.

"Sometimes a man wants to be able to walk for miles in any

direction and see no one," he heard himself say out loud, as if his mouth was no longer connected to the rest of him. "Not even himself."

"Or perhaps especially not himself," she said softly, her mouth against his skin having the same result as before.

Then he could feel her breathe, there behind him. There was a surprising amount of strength in the arms she still wrapped tight around his midsection. Her scent seemed to fill his head, a hint of lavender and something far softer that he knew was hers alone.

And the truth was that he wasn't done. He had never been a casual man in the modern sense, preferring mistresses who understood his needs and could cater to them over longer periods of time to one-night stands and such flashes in the pan that brought him nothing but momentary satisfaction.

He had never been casual, but this... This was nothing but trouble.

He needed to send her away. He had to fire Natalie, make sure that Valentina left, and leave no possible opening for either one of them to ever come back. This needed to be over before it really started. Before he forgot that he was who he was for a very good reason.

Demetrius had been a drunk. He'd cried and apologized when he was sober, however rarely that occurred. But Achilles was the monster. He'd gone to that bar to kill his stepfather, and he'd planned the whole thing out in every detail, coldly and dispassionately. He still didn't regret what he'd intended to do that night—but he knew perfectly well what that made him. And it was not a good man.

And that was all well and good as long as he kept the monster in him on ice, where it belonged. As long as he locked himself away, set apart.

It had never been an issue before.

He needed to get Valentina away from him, before he forgot himself completely.

"Pack your things," he told her shortly.

He shifted so he could look down at her again, drawing her around to his front and taking in the kick of those wide green eyes and that mouth he had sampled again and again and again.

And he couldn't do it.

He wanted her to know him, and even though that was the most treacherous thing of all, once it was in his head he couldn't seem to let it go. He wanted her to know him, and that meant he needed her to trust him enough to tell who she was. And that would never happen if he sent her away right now the way he should have.

And he was so used to thinking of himself as a monster. Some part of him—a large part of him—took a kind of pride in that, if he was honest. He'd worked so hard on making that monster into an impenetrable wall of wealth and judgment, taste and power.

But it turned out that all it took was a deceitful princess to make him into a man.

"I'm taking you to Montana," he told her gruffly, because he couldn't seem to stop himself.

And doomed them both.

CHAPTER EIGHT

ONE WEEK PASSED, and then another, and the six weeks Valentina had agreed to take stretched out into seven, out on Achilles's Montana ranch where the only thing on the horizon was the hint of the nearest mountain range.

His ranch was like a daydream, Valentina thought. Achilles was a rancher only in a distant sense, having hired qualified people to take care of the daily running of the place and turn its profit. Those things took place far away on some or other of his thousands of acres tucked up at the feet of the Rocky Mountains. They stayed in the sprawling ranch house, a sprawling nod toward log cabins and rustic ski lodges, the better to overlook the unspoiled land in all directions.

It was far away from everything and felt even farther than that. It was an hour drive to the nearest town, stout and quintessentially Western, as matter-of-fact as it was practical. They'd come at the height of Montana's short summer, hot during the day and cool at night, with endless blue skies stretching on up toward forever and nothing to do but soak in the quiet. The stunning silence, broken only by the wind. The sun. The exuberant moon and all those improbable, impossible stars, so many they cluttered up the sky and made it feel as if, were she to take a big enough step, Valentina could toss herself straight off the planet and into eternity.

And Valentina knew she was running out of time. Her wedding was the following week, she wasn't who she was pretending she was, and these stolen days in this faraway place of blue and gold were her last with this man. This stolen life had only ever been hers on loan.

But she would have to face that soon enough.

In Montana, as in New York, her days were filled with Achilles. He was too precise and demanding to abandon his businesses entirely, but there was something about the ranch that rendered him less overbearing. He and Valentina would put out what fires there might be in the mornings, but then, barring catastrophe, he let his employees earn their salaries the rest of the day.

While he and Valentina explored what this dreamy ranch life, so far removed from everything, had to offer. He had a huge library that she imagined would be particularly inviting in winter—not, she was forced to remind herself, that she would ever see it in a different season. A guest could sink into one of the deep leather chairs in front of the huge fireplace and read away a snowy evening or two up here in the mountains. He had an indoor pool that let the sky in through its glass ceiling, perfect for swimming in all kinds of weather. There was the hot tub, propped up on its own terrace with a sweeping view, which cried out for those cool evenings. It was a short drive or a long, pretty walk to the lake a little ways up into the mountains, so crisp and clear and cold it almost hurt.

But it was the kind of hurt that made her want more and more, no matter how it made her gasp and think she might lose herself forever in the cut of it.

Achilles was the same. Only worse.

Valentina had always thought of sex—or her virginity, anyway—as a single, solitary thing. Someday she would have sex, she'd always told herself. Someday she would get rid of her virginity. She had never really imagined that it wasn't a single, finite event.

She'd thought virginity, and therefore sex, was the actual breaching of what she still sometimes thought of as her maidenhead, as if she was an eighteenth-century heroine—and nothing more. She'd never really imagined much beyond that.

Achilles taught her otherwise.

Sex with him was threaded into life, a rich undercurrent that became as much a part of it as walking, breathing, eating. It wasn't a specific act. It was everything.

It was the touch of his hand across the dinner table, when he simply threaded their fingers together, the memory of what they'd already done together and the promise of more braided there between them. It was a sudden hot, dark look in the middle of a conversation about something innocuous or work-related, reminding her that she knew him now in so many different dimensions. It was the way his laughter seemed to rearrange her, pouring through her and making her new, every time she heard it.

It was when she stopped counting each new time he wrenched her to pieces as a separate, astonishing event. When she began to accept that he would always do that. Time passed and days rolled on, and all of these things that swirled between them only deepened. He became only more able to wreck her more easily the better he got to know her. And the better she got to know him.

As if their bodies were like the stars above them, infinite and adaptable, a great mess of joy and wonder that time only intensified.

But she knew it was running out.

And the more Achilles called her Natalie—which she thought he did more here, or perhaps she was far more sensitive to it now that she shared his bed—the more her terrible deception seemed to form into a heavy ball in the pit of her stomach, like some kind of cancerous thing that she very much thought might consume her whole.

Some part of her wished it would.

Meanwhile, the real Natalie kept calling her. Again and again, or leaving texts, but Valentina couldn't bring herself to respond to them. What would she say? How could she possibly explain what she'd done?

Much less the fact that she was still doing it and, worse, that she didn't want it to end no matter how quickly her royal wedding was approaching.

Even if she imagined that Natalie was off in Murin doing exactly the same thing with Rodolfo that Valentina was doing here, with all this wild and impossible hunger, what did that matter? They could still switch back, none the wiser. Nothing would change for Valentina. She would go on to marry the prince as she had always been meant to do, and it was highly likely that even Rodolfo himself wouldn't notice the change.

But Natalie had not been sleeping with Achilles before she'd switched places with Valentina. That meant there was no possible way that she could easily step back into the life that Valentina had gone ahead and ruined.

And was still ruining, day by day.

Still, no matter how self-righteously she railed at herself for that, she knew it wasn't what was really bothering her. It wasn't what would happen to Natalie that ate her up inside.

It was what would happen to her. And what could happen with Achilles. She found that she was markedly less sanguine about Achilles failing to notice the difference between Valentina and Natalie when they switched back again. In fact, the very notion made her feel sick.

But how could she tell him the truth? If she couldn't tell Natalie what she'd done, how could she possibly tell the man whom she'd been lying to directly all this time? He thought he was having an affair with his assistant. A woman he had vetted and worked closely with for half a decade.

What was she supposed to say, *Oh, by the way, I'm actually a princess?*

The truth was that she was still a coward. Because she didn't know if what was really holding her back was that she couldn't imagine what she would say—or if she could imagine all too well what Achilles would do. And she knew that made her the worst sort of person. Because when she worried about what he would do, she was worried about herself. Not about how she might hurt him. Not about what it would do to him to learn that she had lied to him all this time. But the fact that it was entirely likely that she would tell him, and that would be the last she'd see of him. Ever.

And Valentina couldn't quite bear for this to be over.

This was her vacation. Her holiday. Her escape—and how had it never occurred to her that if that was true, it meant she had to go back? She'd known that in a general sense, of course, but she hadn't really thought it through. She certainly hadn't thought about what it would feel like to leave Achilles and then walk back to the stifling life she'd called her own for all these years.

It was one thing to be trapped. Particularly when it was all she'd ever known. But it was something else again to see exactly how trapped she was, to leave it behind for a while, and then knowingly walk straight back into that trap, closing the cage door behind her.

Forever.

Sometimes when she lay awake at night listening to Achilles breathe in the great bed next to her, his arms thrown over her as if they were slowly becoming one person, she couldn't imagine how she was ever going to make herself do it.

But time didn't care if she felt trapped. Or torn. It marched on whether she wanted it to or not.

"Are you brooding?" a low male voice asked from behind her, jolting her out of her unpleasant thoughts. "I thought that was my job, not yours."

Valentina turned from the rail of the balcony that ambled

along the side of the master suite, where she was taking in the view and wondering how she could ever fold herself up tight and slot herself back into the life she'd left behind in Murin.

But the view behind her was even better. Achilles lounged against the open sliding glass door, naked save for a towel wrapped around his hips. He had taken her in a fury earlier, pounding into her from behind until she screamed out his name into the pillows, and he'd roared his own pleasure into the crook of her neck. Then he'd left her there on the bed, limp and still humming with all that passion, while he'd gone out for one of his long, brutal runs he always claimed cleared his head.

It had been weeks now, and he still took her breath. Now that she knew every inch of him, she found herself more in awe of him. All that sculpted perfection of his chest, the dark hair that narrowed at his lean hips, dipping down below the towel where she knew the boldest part of him waited.

She'd tasted him there, too. She'd knelt before the fireplace in that gorgeous library, her hands on his thighs as he'd sat back in one of those great leather chairs. He'd played with her hair, sifting strands of it through his fingers as she'd reached into the battered jeans he wore here on the ranch and had pulled him free.

He'd tasted of salt and man, and he'd let her play with him as she liked. He let her lick him everywhere until she learned his shape. He let her suck him in, then figure out how to make him as wild as he did when he tasted her in this same way. And she'd taken it as a personal triumph when he'd started to grip the chair. And when he'd lost himself inside her mouth, he'd groaned out that name he called her. *Glikia mou.*

Even thinking about it now made that same sweet, hot restlessness move through her all over again.

But time was her enemy. She knew that. And looking at him as he stood there in the doorway and watched her with that dark gold gaze that she could feel in every part of her, still convinced that he could see into parts of her she didn't know how to name, Valentina still didn't know what to do.

If she told him who she was, she would lose what few days with him she had left. This was Achilles Casilieris. He would never forgive her deception. Never. Her other option was never to tell him at all. She would go back to London with him in a few days as planned, slip away the way she'd always intended to do if a week or so later than agreed, and let the real Natalie pick up the pieces.

And that way, she could remember this the way she wanted to do. She could remember loving him, not losing him.

Because that was what she'd done. She understood that in the same way she finally comprehended intimacy. She'd gone and fallen in love with this man who didn't know her real name. This man she could never, ever keep.

Was it so wrong that if she couldn't keep him, she wanted to keep these sun-soaked memories intact?

"You certainly look like you're brooding." There was that lazy note to his voice that never failed to make her blood heat. It was no different now. It was that quick. It was that inevitable. "How can that be? There's nothing here but silence and sunshine. No call to brood about anything. Unless of course, it is your soul that is heavy." And she could have sworn there was something in his gaze then that dared her to come clean. Right then and there. As if, as ever, he knew what she was thinking. "Tell me, Natalie, what is it that haunts you?"

And it was moments like these that haunted her, but she couldn't tell him that. Moments like this, when she was certain that he knew. That he must know. That he was asking her to tell him the truth at last.

That he was calling her the wrong name deliberately, to see if that would goad her into coming clean.

But the mountains were too quiet and there was too much summer in the air. The Montana sky was a blue she'd never seen before, and that was what she felt in her soul. And if there was a heaviness, or a darkness, she had no doubt it would haunt her later.

Valentina wanted to live here. Now. With him. She wanted to *live*.

She had so little time left to truly *live*.

So once again, she didn't tell him. She smiled instead, wide enough to hide the fissures in her heart, and she went to him.

Because there was so little time left that she could do that. So few days left to reach out and touch him the way she did now, sliding her palms against the mouthwatering planes of his chest as if she was memorizing the heat of his skin.

As if she was memorizing everything.

"I don't know what you're talking about," she told him quietly, her attention on his skin beneath her hands. "I never do."

"I am not the mystery here," he replied, and though his voice was still so lazy, so very lazy, she didn't quite believe it. "There are enough mysteries to go around, I think."

"Solve this one, then," she dared him, going up on her toes to press her mouth to his.

Because she might not have truth and she might not have time, but she had this.

For a little while longer, she had this.

Montana was another mistake, because apparently, that was all he did now.

They spent weeks on his ranch, and Achilles made it all worse by the day. Every day he touched her, every day lost himself in her, every day he failed to get her to come clean with him. Every single day was another nail in his coffin.

And then, worse by far to his mind, it was time to leave.

Weeks in Montana, secluded from the rest of the world, and he'd gained nothing but a far deeper and more disastrous appreciation of Valentina's appeal. He hadn't exactly forced her to the light. He hadn't done anything but lose his own footing.

In all those weeks and all that sweet summer sunshine out in the American West, it had never occurred to him that she simply wouldn't tell him. He'd been so sure that he would get to her somehow. That if he had all these feelings churning around inside him, whatever was happening inside her must be far more extreme.

It had never occurred to him that he could lose that bet.

That Princess Valentina had him beat when it came to keeping herself locked up tight, no matter what.

They landed in London in a bleak drizzle that matched his mood precisely.

"You're expected at the bank in an hour," Valentina told him when they reached his Belgravia town house, standing there in his foyer looking as guileless and innocent as she ever had. Even now, when he had tasted every inch of her. Even now, when she was tearing him apart with that serene, untouchable look on her face. "And the board of directors is adamant—"

"I don't care about the bank," he muttered. "Or old men who think they can tell me what to do."

And just like that, he'd had enough.

He couldn't outright demand that Valentina tell him who she really was, because that wouldn't be her telling him of her own volition. It wouldn't be her trusting him.

It's almost as if she knows who you really are, that old familiar voice inside hissed at him. It had been years since he'd heard it, inside him or otherwise. But even though Demetrius had not been able to identify him on the streets when he'd had the chance, Achilles always knew the old man when he spoke. *Maybe she knows exactly what kind of monster you are.*

And a harsh truth slammed into him then, making him feel very nearly unsteady on his feet. He didn't know why it hadn't occurred to him before. Or maybe it had, but he'd shoved it aside out there in all that Montana sky and sunshine. Because he was Achilles Casilieris. He was one of the most sought-after bachelors in all the world. Legions of women chased after him daily, trying anything from trickery to bribery to outright lies about paternity claims to make him notice them. He was at the top of everyone's *most wanted* list.

But to Princess Valentina of Marin, he was nothing but a bit of rough.

She was slumming.

That was why she hadn't bothered to identify herself. She didn't see the point. He might as well have been the pool boy.

And he couldn't take it. He couldn't process it. There was nothing in him but fire and that raw, unquenchable need, and she was so cool. Too cool.

He needed to mess her up. He needed to do something to make all this…wildfire and feeling dissipate before it ate him alive and left nothing behind. Nothing at all.

"What are you doing?" she asked, and he took a little too much satisfaction in that appropriately uncertain note in her voice.

It was only when he saw her move that he realized he was stalking toward her, backing her up out of the gleaming foyer and into one of the town house's elegant sitting rooms. Not that the beauty of a room could do anything but fade next to Valentina.

The world did the same damned thing.

She didn't ask him a silly question like that again. And perhaps she didn't need to. He backed her up to the nearest settee, and took entirely too much pleasure in the pulse that beat out the truth of her need right there in her neck.

"Achilles…" she said hoarsely, but he wanted no more words. No more lies of omission.

No more *slumming.*

"Quiet," he ordered her.

He sank his hands into her gleaming copper hair, then dragged her mouth to his. Then he toppled her down to antique settee and followed her. She was slender and lithe and wild beneath him, rising to meet him with too much need, too much longing.

As if, in the end, this was the only place they were honest with each other.

And Achilles was furious. Furious, or something like it—something close enough that it burned in him as brightly. As lethally. He shoved her skirt up over her hips and she wrapped her legs around his waist, and she was panting already. She was gasping against his mouth. Or maybe he was breathing just as hard.

"Achilles," she said again, and there was something in her gaze then. Something darker than need.

But this was no time for sweetness. Or anything deeper. This was a claiming.

"Later," he told her, and then he took her mouth with his, tasting the words he was certain, abruptly, he didn't want to hear.

He might be nothing to her but a walk on the wild side she would look back on while she rotted away in some palatial prison, but he would make sure that she remembered him.

He had every intention of leaving his mark.

Achilles tore off his trousers, freeing himself. Then he reached down and found the gusset of her panties, ripping them off and shoving the scraps aside to fit himself to her at last.

And then he stopped thinking about marks and memories, because she was molten hot and wet. She was his. He sank into her, groaning as she encased his length like a hot, tight glove.

It was so good. It was too good.

She always was.

He moved then, and she did, too, that slick, deep slide. And they knew each other so well now. Their bodies were too attuned to each other, too hot and too certain of where this was going, and it was never, ever enough.

He reached between them and pressed his fingers in the place where she needed him most, and felt her explode into a frenzy beneath him. She raised her hips to meet each thrust. She dug her fingers into his shoulders as if she was already shaking apart.

He felt it build in her, and in him, too. Wild and mad, the way it always was.

As if they could tear apart the world this way. As if they already had.

"No one will ever make you feel the way that I do," he told her then, a dark muttering near her ear as she panted and writhed. "No one."

And he didn't know if that was some kind of endearment, or a dire warning.

But it didn't matter, because she was clenching around him then. She gasped out his name, while her body gripped him, then shook.

And he pumped himself into her, wanting nothing more than to roar her damned name. To claim her in every possible way. To show her—

But he did none of that.

And when it was over, when the storm had passed, he pulled himself away from her and climbed to his feet again. And he felt something sharp and heavy move through him as he looked down at her, still lying there half on and half off the antique settee they'd moved a few feet across the floor, because he had done exactly as he set out to do.

He'd messed her up. She looked disheveled and shaky and absolutely, delightfully ravished.

But all he could think was that he still didn't have her. That she was still going to leave him when she was done here. That she'd never had any intention of staying in the first place. It ripped at him. It made him feel something like crazy.

The last time he'd ever felt anything like it, he'd been an angry seventeen-year-old in a foul-smelling street with an old drunk who didn't know who he was. It was a kind of anguish.

It was a grief, and he refused to indulge it. He refused to admit it was ravaging him, even as he pulled his clothes back where they belonged.

And then she made it even worse. She smiled.

She sat up slowly, pushing her skirt back into place and tucking the torn shreds of her panties into one pocket. Then she gazed up at him.

Achilles was caught by that look in her soft green eyes, as surely as if she'd reached out and wrapped her delicate hands around his throat. On some level, he felt as if she had.

"I love you," she said.

They were such small words, he thought through that thing that pounded in him like fear. Like a gong. Such small, silly words that could tear a man down without any warning at all.

And there were too many things he wanted to say then. For example, how could she tell him that she loved him when she wouldn't even tell him her name?

But he shoved that aside.

"That was sex, *glikia mou*," he grated at her. "Love is something different from a whole lot of thrashing around, half-clothed."

He expected her to flinch at that, but he should have known better. This was his princess. If she was cowed at all, she didn't show it.

Instead, she only smiled wider.

"You're the expert on love as in all things, of course," she murmured, because even here, even now, she was the only person alive who had ever dared to tease him. "My mistake."

She was still smiling when she stood up, then walked around him. As if she didn't notice that he was frozen there in some kind of astonishment. Or as if she was happy enough to leave him to it as she headed toward the foyer and, presumably, the work he'd always adored that seemed to loom over him these days, demanding more time than he wanted to give.

He'd never had a life that interested him more than his empire, until Valentina.

And he didn't have Valentina.

She'd left Achilles standing there with her declaration heavy in his ears. She'd left him half fire and a heart that long ago should have turned to ice. He'd been so certain it had when he was seven and had lost everything, including his sense of himself as anything like good.

He should have known then.

But it wasn't until much later that day—after he'd quizzed his security detail and household staff to discover she'd walked out with nothing but her shoulder bag and disappeared into the gray of the London afternoon—that he'd realized that had been the way his deceitful princess said goodbye.

CHAPTER NINE

VALENTINA COULDN'T KEEP her mind on her duties now that she was back in Murin. She couldn't keep her mind focused at all, come to that. Not on her duties, not on the goings-on of the palace, not on any of the many changes that had occurred since she'd come back home.

She should have been jubilant. Or some facsimile thereof, surely. She had walked back into her well-known, well-worn trap, expecting the same old cage, only to find that the trap wasn't at all what she had imagined it was—and the cage door had been tossed wide open.

When she'd left London that day, her body had still been shivering from Achilles's touch. She hadn't wanted to go. Not with her heart too full and a little bit broken at her own temerity in telling him how she felt when she'd known she had to leave. But it was time for her to go home, and there had been no getting around that. Her wedding to Prince Rodolfo was imminent. As in, the glittering heads of Europe's ancient houses were assembling to cheer on one of their own, and she needed to be there.

The phone calls and texts that she'd been ignoring that whole time, leaving Natalie to deal with it all on her own, had grown frantic. And she couldn't blame her sister, because the wedding was a mere day away. *Your twin sister*, she'd thought, those terms still feeling too unwieldy. She'd made her way to Heathrow Airport and bought herself a ticket on a commercial plane—the first time she'd ever done anything of the sort. One more normal thing to tuck away and remember later.

"Later" meaning after tomorrow, when she would be wed to a man she hardly knew.

It had taken Valentina a bit too long to do the right thing. To do the only possible thing and tear herself away from Achilles the way she should have done a long time ago. She should never have gone with him to Montana. She should certainly never have allowed them to stay there all that time, living out a daydream that could end only one way.

She'd known that going in, and she'd done it anyway. What did that make her, exactly?

Now I am awake, she thought as she boarded the plane. *Now I am awake and that will have to be as good as* alive, *because it's all I have left.*

She hadn't known what to expect from a regular flight into the commercial airport on the island of Murin. Some part of her imagined that she would be recognized. Her face was on the cover of the Murin Air magazines in every seat back, after all. She'd had a bit of a start when she'd sat down in the remarkably uncomfortable seat, pressed up against a snoring matron on one side and a very gray-faced businessman on the other.

But no one had noticed her shocking resemblance to the princess in the picture. No one had really looked at her at all. She flashed Natalie's passport, walked on the plane without any issues and walked off again in Murin without anyone looking at her twice—even though she was quite literally the spitting image of the princess so many were flocking to Murin to see marry her Prince Charming at last.

Once at the palace, she didn't bother trying to sneak in because she knew she'd be discovered instantly—and that would hardly allow Natalie to switch back and escape, would it? So instead she'd walked up to the guard station around the back at the private family entrance, gazed politely at the guard who waited there and waited.

"But the…the princess is within," the guard had stammered. Maybe he was thrown by the fact Valentina was dressed like any other woman her age on the street. Maybe he was taken back because he'd never spoken to her directly before.

Or maybe it was because, if she was standing here in front of him, she wasn't where the royal guard thought she was. Which he'd likely assumed meant she'd sneaked out, undetected.

All things considered, she was happy to let that mystery stand.

Valentina had aimed a conspiratorial smile at the guard. "The princess can't possibly be within, given that I'm standing right here. But it can be our little secret that there was some confusion, if you like."

And then, feeling heavier than she ever had before and scarred somehow by what she'd gone through with Achilles, she'd walked back in the life she'd left so spontaneously and much too quickly in that London airport.

She'd expected to find Natalie as desperate to leave as she supposed, in retrospect, she had been. Or why else would she have suggested this switch in the first place?

But instead, she'd found a woman very much in love. With Crown Prince Rodolfo of Tissely. The man whom Valentina was supposed to marry the following day.

More than that, Natalie was pregnant.

"I don't know how it happened," Natalie had said, after Valentina had slipped into her bedroom and woken her up—by sitting on the end of the bed and pulling at Natalie's foot until she'd opened her eyes and found her double sitting there.

"Don't you?" Valentina had asked. "I was a virgin, but I had the distinct impression that you had not saved yourself for marriage all these years. Because why would you?"

Natalie had flushed a bit, but then her eyes had narrowed.

"*Was* a virgin? Is that the past tense?" She'd blinked. "Not Mr. Casilieris."

But it wasn't the time then for sisterly confessions. Mostly because Valentina hadn't the slightest idea what she could say about Achilles that wasn't…too much. Too much and too unformed and unbearable, somehow, now that it was over. Now that none of it mattered, and never could.

"I don't think that you have a job with him anymore," Valentina had said instead, keeping her voice even. "Because I don't think you want a job with him anymore. You said you were late, didn't you? You're having a prince's baby."

And when Natalie had demurred, claiming that she didn't know one way or the other and it was likely just the stress of inhabiting someone else's life, Valentina had sprung into action.

She'd made it her business to find out, one way or another. She'd assured Natalie that it was simply to put her mind at ease. But the truth was a little more complicated, she admitted to herself as she made her way through the palace.

The fact was, she was relieved. That was what had washed through her when Natalie had confessed not only her love for Rodolfo, but her suspicions that she might be carrying his child. She'd pushed it off as she'd convinced one of her most loyal maids to run out into the city and buy her a few pregnancy tests, just to be certain. She'd shoved it to the side as she'd smuggled the tests back into her rooms, and then had handed them over to Natalie so she could find out for certain.

But there was no denying it. When Natalie had emerged from the bathroom with a dazed look on her face and a positive test in one hand, Valentina finally admitted the sheer relief that coursed through her veins. It was like champagne. Fizzy and a little bit sharp, washing through her and making her feel almost silly in response.

Because if Natalie was having Rodolfo's baby, there was no possible way that Valentina could marry him. The choice—

though it had always been more of an expected duty than a choice—was taken out of her hands.

"You will marry him," Valentina had said quietly. "It is what must happen."

Natalie had looked pale. "But you... And I'm not... And you don't understand, he..."

"All of that will work out," Valentina had said with a deep certainty she very badly wanted to feel. Because it had to work out. "The important thing is that you will marry him in the morning. You will have his baby and you will be his queen when he ascends the throne. Everything else is spin and scandal, and none of that matters. Not really."

And so it was.

Once King Geoffrey had been brought into the loop and had been faced with the irrefutable evidence that his daughter had been stolen from him all those years ago—that Erica had taken Natalie and, not only that, had told Geoffrey that Valentina's twin had died at birth—he was more than on board with switching the brides at the wedding.

He'd announced to the gathered crowd that a most blessed miracle had occurred some months before. A daughter long thought dead had returned to him to take her rightful place in the kingdom, and they'd all kept it a secret to preserve everyone's privacy as they'd gotten to know each other.

Including Rodolfo, who had always been meant to be part of the family, the king had reminded the assembled crowd and the whole of the world, no matter how. And feelings had developed between Natalie and Rodolfo, where there had only ever been duty and honor between Valentina and her intended.

Valentina had seen this and stepped aside of her own volition, King Geoffrey had told the world. There had been no scandal, no sneaking around, no betrayals. Only one sister looking out for another.

The crowds ate it up. The world followed suit. It was just scandalous enough to be both believable and newsworthy. Valentina was branded as something of a Miss Lonely Hearts, it was true, but that was neither here nor there. The idea that she would sacrifice her fairy-tale wedding—and her very own Prince Charming—for her long-lost sister captured the public's imagination. She was more popular than ever, especially at home in Murin.

And this was a good thing, because now that her father had two heirs, he could marry one of his daughters off to fulfill his promises to the kingdom of Tissely, and he could prepare the other to take over Murin and keep its throne in the family.

And just like that, Valentina went from a lifetime preparing to be a princess who would marry well and support the king of a different country, to a new world in which she was meant to rule as queen in her own right.

If it was another trap, another cage, it was a far more spacious and comfortable one than any she had known before.

She knew that. There was no reason at all she should have been so unhappy.

"Your attention continues to drift, daughter," King Geoffrey said then.

Valentina snapped herself out of those thoughts in her head that did her no good and into the car where she sat with her father, en route to some or other glittering gala down at the water palace on the harbor. She couldn't even remember which charity it was this week. There was always another.

The motorcade wound down from the castle, winding its way along the hills of the beautiful capital city toward the gleaming Mediterranean Sea. Valentina normally enjoyed the view. It was pretty, first and foremost. It was home. It reminded her of so many things, of her honor and her duty and her love of her country. It renewed her commitment to her kingdom, and made her think about all the good she hoped she could do as its sovereign.

And yet these days, she wasn't thinking about Murin. All she could seem to think about was Achilles.

"I am preparing myself for the evening ahead," Valentina replied calmly enough. She aimed a perfectly composed smile at her father. "I live in fear of greeting a diplomat with the wrong name and causing an international incident."

Her father's gaze warmed, something that happened more often lately than it ever had before. Valentina chalked that up to the rediscovery of Natalie and, with it, some sense of family that had been missing before. Or too caught up in the past, perhaps.

"I have never seen you forget a name in all your life," Geoffrey said. "It's one among many reasons I expect you will make a far better queen than I have been a king. And I am aware I gave you no other choice, but I cannot regret that your education and talents will be Murin's gain, not Tissely's."

"I will confess," Valentina said then, "that stepping aside so that Natalie could marry Rodolfo is not quite the sacrifice some have made it out to be."

Her father's gaze then was so canny that it reminded her that whatever else he was, King Geoffrey of Marin was a force to be reckoned with.

"I suspected not," he said quietly. "But there is no reason not to let them think so. It only makes you more sympathetic."

His attention was caught by something on his phone then. And as he frowned down at it, Valentina looked away. Back out the window to watch the sun drip down over the red-tipped rooftops that sloped all the way to the crystal blue waters below.

She let her hand move, slowly so that her father wouldn't notice, and held it over that faint roundness low in her belly she'd started to notice only a few weeks ago.

If her father thought she was a sympathetic figure now, she thought darkly, he would be delighted when she announced to him and the rest of the world that she was going to be a mother.

A single mother. A princess destined for his throne, with child.

Her thoughts went around and around, keeping her up at night and distracting her by day. And there were never any answers or, rather, there were never any good answers. There were never any answers she liked. Shame and scandal were sure to follow anything she did, or didn't do for that matter. There was no possible way out.

And even if she somehow summoned the courage to tell her father, then tell the kingdom, and then, far more intimidating, tell Achilles—what did she think might happen then? As a princess with no path to the throne, she had been expected to marry the Crown Prince of Tissely. As the queen of Murin, by contrast, she would be expected to marry someone of equally impeccable lineage. There were only so many such men alive, Valentina had met all of them, and none of them were Achilles.

No one was Achilles. And that shouldn't have mattered to her. There were so many other things she needed to worry about, like this baby she was going to be able to hide for only so long.

But he was the only thing she could seem to think about, even so.

The gala was as expected. These things never varied much, which was both their charm and their curse. There was an endless receiving line. There were music and speeches, and extremely well-dressed people milling about complimenting each other on the same old things. A self-congratulatory trill of laughter here, a fake smile there, and so it went. Dignitaries and socialites rubbing shoulders and making money for this or that cause the way they always did.

Valentina danced with her father, as tradition dictated. She was pleased to see Rodolfo and Natalie, freshly back from their honeymoon and exuding exactly the sort of happy charm that made everyone root for them, Valentina included.

Valentina especially, she thought.

She excused herself from the crush as soon as she could, making her way out onto one of the great balconies in this water palace that took its cues from far-off Venice and overlooked the sea. Valentina stood there for a long while, helplessly reliving all the things she'd been so sure she could lock away once she came back home. Over and over—

And she thought that her memory had gotten particularly sharp—and cruel. Because when she heard a foot against the stones behind her and turned, her smile already in place the way it always was, she saw him.

But it couldn't be him, of course. She assumed it was her hormones mixing with her memory and making her conjure him up out of the night air.

"Princess Valentina," Achilles said, and his voice was low, a banked fury simmering there in every syllable. "I do not believe we have been introduced properly. You are apparently of royal blood you sought to conceal and I am the man you thought you could fool. How pleasant to finally make your acquaintance."

It occurred to her that she wasn't fantasizing at the same moment it really hit her that he was standing before her. Her heart punched at her. Her stomach sank.

And in the place she was molten for him, instantly, she ached. Oh, how she ached.

"Achilles..."

But her throat was so dry. It was in marked contrast to all that emotion that flooded her eyes at the sight of him that she couldn't seem to control.

"Are those tears, Princess?" And he laughed then. It was a dark, angry sort of sound. It was not the kind of laughter that made the world shimmer and change. And still, it was the best sound Valentina had heard in weeks. "Surely those are not tears. I cannot think of a single thing you have to cry about, Valentina. Not one. Whereas I have a number of complaints."

"Complaints?"

All she could seem to do was echo him. That and gaze at him as if she was hungry, and the truth was that she was. She couldn't believe he was here. She didn't care that he was scowling at her—her heart was kicking at her, and she thought she'd never seen anything more beautiful than Achilles Casilieris in a temper, right here in Murin.

"We can start with the fact that you lied to me about who you are," he told her. "There are numerous things to cover after that, culminating in your extremely bad decision to walk out. *Walk out.*" He repeated it with three times the fury. "On *me.*"

"Achilles." She swallowed, hard. "I don't think—"

"Let me be clear," he bit out, his dark gold gaze blazing as he interrupted her. "I am not here to beg or plead. I am Achilles Casilieris, a fact you seem to have forgotten. I do not beg. I do not plead. But I feel certain, princess, that you will do both."

He had waited weeks.

Weeks.

Having never been walked out on before—ever—Achilles had first assumed that she would return. Were not virgins forever making emotional connections with the men who divested them of their innocence? That was the reason men of great experience generally avoided virgins whenever possible. Or so he thought, at any rate. The truth was that he could hardly remember anything before Valentina.

Still, he waited. When the royal wedding happened the day after she'd left, and King Geoffrey made his announcement about his lost daughter—who, he'd realized, was his actual assistant and also, it turned out, a royal princess—Achilles had been certain it was only a matter of time before Valentina returned to London.

But she never came.

And he did not know when it had dawned on him that this was something he was going to have to do himself. The very idea enraged him, of course. That she had walked out on him at all was unthinkable. But what he couldn't seem to get his head around was the fact that she didn't seem to have seen the error of her ways, no matter how much time he gave her to open her damned eyes.

She was too beautiful and it was worse now, he thought darkly, here in her kingdom, where she was no longer pretending anything.

Tonight she was dressed like the queen she would become one day, all of that copper hair piled high on the top of her head, jewels flashing here and there. Instead of the pencil skirts he'd grown accustomed to, she wore a deep blue gown that clung to her body in a way that was both decorous and alluring at once. And if he was not mistaken, made her curves seem more voluptuous than he recalled.

She was much too beautiful for Achilles's peace of mind, and worse, she did not break down and begin the begging or the pleading, as he would have preferred. He could see that her eyes were damp, though the tears that had threatened seemed to have receded. She smoothed her hand over her belly, as if the dress had wrinkles when it was very clear that it did not, and when she looked up from that wholly unnecessary task her green eyes were as guarded as her smile was serene.

As if he was a stranger. As if he had never been so deep inside her she'd told him she couldn't breathe.

"What are you doing here?" she asked.

"That is the wrong question."

She didn't so much as blink, and that smile only deepened. "I had no idea that obscure European charities were of such interest to men of your stature, and I am certain it was not on your schedule."

"Are you questioning how I managed to score an invite?" he asked, making no particular move to keep the arrogant astonishment from his voice. "Perhaps I must introduce myself again. There is no guest list that is not improved by my presence, princess. Even yours."

Her gaze became no less guarded. Her expression did not change. But still, Achilles thought something in her steeled. And her shoulders straightened almost imperceptibly.

"I must apologize to you," she said, very distinctly.

And this was what Achilles had wanted. It was why he'd come here. He had imagined it playing out almost exactly this way.

Except there was something in her tone that rubbed him the wrong way, now that it was happening. It was that guarded look in her eyes perhaps. It was the fact that she didn't close the distance between them, but stayed where she was, one hand on the balcony railing and the other at her side. As distant as if she was on some magazine cover somewhere instead of standing there in front of him.

He didn't like this at all.

"You will have to be more specific, I am afraid," he said coolly. "I can think of a great many apologies you owe me."

Her mouth curved, though he would not call it a smile, precisely.

"I walked into a bathroom in an airport in London and saw a woman I had never met before, who could only be my twin. I could not resist switching places with her." Valentina glanced toward the open doors and the gala inside, as if it called to her more than he did, and Achilles hated that, too. Then she looked back at him, and her gaze seemed darker. "Do not mistake me. This is a good life. It is just that it's a very specific, very planned sort of life and it involves a great many spotlights. I wanted a normal one, for a change. Just for a little while. It never occurred to me that that decision could affect anyone but me. I would never have done it if I ever thought that you—"

But Achilles couldn't hear this. Because it sounded entirely too much like a postmortem. When he had traveled across Europe to find her because he couldn't bear the thought that it had already ended, or that he hadn't picked up on the fact that she was leaving him until she'd already gone.

"Do you need me to tell you that I love you, Valentina?" he demanded, his voice low and furious. "Is that what this is? Tell me what you need to hear. Tell me what it will take."

She jolted as if he'd slapped her. And he hated that, so he

took the single step that closed the distance between them, and then there was no holding himself back. Not when she was so close again—at last—after all these weeks. He reached over and wrapped his hands around her shoulders, holding her there at arm's length, like some kind of test of his self-control. He thought that showed great restraint, when all he wanted was to haul her toward him and get his mouth on her.

"I don't need anything," she threw at him in a harsh sort of whisper. "And I'm sorry you had to find out who I was after I left. I couldn't figure out how to tell you while I was still with you. I didn't want to ruin—"

She shook her head, as if distressed.

Achilles laughed. "I knew from almost the first moment you stepped on the plane in London. Did you imagine I would truly believe you were Natalie for long? When you could not perform the most basic of tasks she did daily? I knew who you were within moments after the plane reached its cruising altitude."

Her green eyes went wide with shock. Her lips parted. Even her face paled.

"You knew?"

"You have never fooled me," he told her, his voice getting a little too low. A little too hot. "Except perhaps when you claimed you loved me, then left."

Her eyes overflowed then, sending tears spilling down her perfect, elegant cheeks. And he was such a bastard that some part of him rejoiced.

Because if she cried for him, she wasn't indifferent to him. She was certainly not immune to him.

It meant that it was possible he hadn't ruined this, after all, the way he did everything else. It meant it was possible this was salvageable.

He didn't like to think about what it might mean if it wasn't.

"Achilles," she said again, more distinctly this time. "I never saw you coming—it never occurred to me that I could ever be anything but honorable, because I had never been tempted by anything in my life. Only you. The only thing I lied to you about was my name. Everything else was true. Is true." She shook her head. "But it's hopeless."

"Nothing is hopeless," he growled at her. "I have no intention of losing you. I don't lose."

"I'm not talking about a loss," she whispered fiercely, and he could feel a tremor go through her. "This isn't a game. You are a man who is used to doing everything in his own way. You are not made for protocol and diplomacy and the tedious necessities of excruciating propriety. That's not who you are." Her chin tilted up slightly. "But I'm afraid it is exactly who I am."

"I'm not a good man, *glikia mou*," he told her then, not certain what was gripping him. He only knew he couldn't let her go. "But you know this. I have always known who I am. A monster in fine clothes, rubbing shoulders with the elites who would spit on me if they could. If they did not need my money and my power."

Achilles expected a reaction. He expected her to see him at last as she had failed to see him before. The scales would fall from her eyes, perhaps. She would recoil, certainly. He had always known that it would take so very little for people to see the truth about him, lurking right there beneath his skin. Not hidden away at all.

But Valentina did not seem to realize what had happened. She continued to look at him the way she always did. There wasn't the faintest flicker of anything like revulsion, or bleak recognition, in her gaze.

If anything, her gaze seemed warmer than before, for all it was wet. And that made him all the more determined to show her what she seemed too blind to see.

"You are not hearing me, Valentina. I'm not speaking in metaphors. Do you have any idea what I have done? The lives that I have ruined?"

She smiled at that, through her tears. "I know exactly who you are," she said, with a bedrock certainty that shook him. "I worked for you. You did not wine me or dine me. You did not take me on a fancy date or try to impress me in any way. You treated me like an assistant, an underling, and believe me, there is nothing more revealing. Are you impatient? Are you demanding and often harsh? Of course." She shrugged, as if this was all so obvious it was hardly worth talking about. "You are a very powerful man. But you are not a monster."

If she'd reached over and wrenched his mangled little heart from between his ribs with her elegant hands and then held it there in front of him, it could not possibly have floored him more.

"And you will not convince me otherwise," she added, as if she could see that he was about to say something. "There's something I have to tell you. And it's entirely possible that you are not going to like it at all."

Achilles blinked. "How ominous."

She blew out a breath. "You must understand that there are no good solutions. I've had no idea how to tell you this, but our... What happened between us had consequences."

"Do you think that I don't know that?" he belted out at her, and he didn't care who heard him. He didn't care if the whole of her pretty little kingdom poured out of the party behind them to watch and listen. "Do you think that I would be here if I was unaware of the consequences?"

"I'm not talking about feelings—"

"I am," he snapped. "I have not felt anything in years. I have not wanted to feel. And thanks to you all I do now is feel. Too damned much, Valentina." She hadn't actually ripped his heart out, he reminded himself. It only felt as if she had. He forced himself to loosen his grip on her before he hurt her. "And it doesn't go anywhere. Weeks pass, and if anything grows worse."

"Achilles, please," she whispered, and the tears were falling freely again. "I never wanted to hurt you."

"I wish you had hurt me," he told her, something dark and

bitter, and yet neither of those things threaded through him. "Hurt things heal. This is far worse."

She sucked in a breath as if he'd punched her. He forged on, throwing all the doom and tumult inside him down between them.

"I have never loved anything in my life, Princess. I have wanted things and I've taken them, but love has always been for other men. Men who are not monsters by any definition. Men who have never ruined anything—not lives, not companies and certainly not perfect, virginal princesses who had no idea what they were signing up for." He shook his head. "But there is nothing either one of us can do about it now. I'm afraid the worst has already happened."

"The worst?" she echoed. "Then you know...?"

"I love you, *glikia mou,*" he told her. "There can be no other explanation, and I feel sorry for you, I really do. Because I don't think there's any going back."

"Achilles..." she whispered, and that was not a look of transported joy on her face. It wasn't close. "I'm so sorry. Everything is different now. I'm pregnant."

CHAPTER TEN

ACHILLES WENT SILENT. Stunned, if Valentina had to guess.

If that frozen astonishment in his dark gold gaze was any guide.

"And I am to be queen," she told him, pointedly. His hands were still clenched on her shoulders, and what was wrong with her that she should love that so much? That she should love any touch of his. That it should make her feel so warm and safe and wild with desire. All at once. "My father thought that he would not have an heir of his own blood, because he thought he had only one daughter. But now he has two, and Natalie has married Rodolfo. That leaves me to take the throne."

"I'm not following you," Achilles said, his voice stark. Something like frozen. "I can think of no reason that you have told me in one breath that I am to be a father and in the next you feel you must fill me in on archaic lines of succession."

"There is very strict protocol," she told him, and her voice cracked. She slid her hands over her belly. "My father will never accept—"

"You keep forgetting who I am," Achilles growled, and she didn't know if he'd heard a word she'd said. "If you are having my child, Valentina, this conversation is over. We will be married. That's an end to it."

"It's not that simple."

"On the contrary, there is nothing simpler."

She needed him to understand. This could never be. They could never happen. She was trapped just as surely as she'd ever been. Why couldn't he see that? "I am no longer just a princess. I'm the Crown Princess of Murin—"

"Princess, princess." Achilles shook his head. "Tell me something. Did you mean it when you told me that you loved me? Or did you only dare to tell me in the first place because you knew you were leaving?"

That walloped Valentina. She thought that if he hadn't been holding on to her, she would have staggered and her knees might well have given out from beneath her.

"Don't be ridiculous." But her voice was barely a whisper.

"Here's the difference between you and me, princess. I have no idea what love is. All I know is that you came into my life and you altered something in me." He let go of her shoulder and moved his hand to cover his heart, and broke hers that easily. "Here. It's changed now, and I can't change it back. And I didn't tell you these things and then leave. I accepted these things, and then came to find you."

She felt blinded. Panicked. As if all she could do was cower inside her cage—and worse, as if that was what she wanted.

"You have no idea what you're talking about," she told him instead. "You might be a successful businessman, but you know nothing about the realities of a kingdom like Murin."

"I know you better than you think. I know how desperate you are for a normal life. Isn't that why you switched places with Natalie?" His dark gaze was almost kind. "But don't you understand? Normal is the one thing you can never be, *glikia mou.*"

"You have no idea what you're talking about," she said again, and this time her voice was even softer. Fainter.

"You will never be normal, Valentina," Achilles said quietly. His fingers tightened on her shoulder. "I am not so normal myself. But together, you and I? We will be extraordinary."

"You don't know how much I wish that could happen." She didn't bother to wipe at her tears. She let them fall. "This is a cage, Achilles. I'm trapped in it, but you're not. And you shouldn't be."

He let out a breath that was too much like a sigh, and Valentina felt it shudder through her, too. Like foreboding.

"You can live in fear, or you can live the life you want, Valentina," he told her. "You cannot do both."

His dark gaze bored into her, and then he dropped his other hand, so he was no longer touching her.

And then he made it worse and stepped back.

She felt her hands move, when she hadn't meant to move at all. Reaching out for him, whether she wanted to or not.

"If you don't want to be trapped, don't be trapped," Achilles said, as if it was simple. And with that edge in his voice that made her feel something a little more pointed than simply restless. "I don't know how to love, but I will learn. I have no idea how to be a father, but I will dedicate myself to being a good one. I never thought that I'd be a husband to anyone, but I will be the husband you need. You can sit on your throne. You can rule your kingdom as you wish. I have no need to be a king. But I will be one for you." He held out his hand. "All you have to do is be brave, princess. That's all. Just be a little brave."

"It's a cage, Achilles," she told him again, her voice ragged. "It's a beautiful, beautiful cage, this life. And there's no changing it. It's been the same for untold centuries."

"Love me," he said then, like a bomb to her heart. What was left of it. "I dare you."

And the music poured out from the party within. Inside, her father ruled the way he always did, and her brand-new sister danced with the man Valentina had always imagined she would marry. Natalie had come out of nowhere and taken her rightful place in the kingdom, and the world hadn't ended when brides had been switched at a royal wedding. If anything, life had vastly improved for everyone involved. Why wasn't that the message Valentina was concentrating on?

She realized that all this time, she'd been focused on what she couldn't do. Or what she had to do. She'd been consumed with duty, honor—but none of it her choice. All of it thrust upon her by an accident of birth. If Erica had taken Valentina instead of Natalie, she would have met Achilles some time ago. They wouldn't be standing here, on this graceful balcony, overlooking the soothing Mediterranean and her father's kingdom.

Her whole life seemed to tumble around before her, year after year cracking open before her like so many fragile eggs against the stones beneath her feet. All the things she never questioned. All the certainties she simply accepted, because what was the alternative? She'd prided herself on her serenity in the face of anything that had come her way. On her ability to do what was asked of her, always. What was expected of her, no matter how unfair.

And she'd never really asked herself what she wanted to do with her life. Because it had never been a factor. Her life had been meticulously planned from the start.

But now Achilles stood before her, and she carried their baby inside her. And she knew that as much as she wanted to deny it, what he said was true. She was a coward. She'd used her duty to hide behind. She could have stayed in London, could have called off her wedding. But she hadn't.

And had she really imagined she could walk down that aisle to Rodolfo, having just left Achilles in London? Had she really intended to do that?

It was unimaginable. And yet she knew she'd meant to do exactly that.

She'd been saved from that vast mistake, and yet here she was, standing in front of the man she loved, coming up with new reasons why she couldn't have the one thing in her life she ever truly wanted.

All this time she'd been convinced that her life was the cage. That her royal blood trapped her.

But the truth was, she was the one who did that.

She was her own cage, and she always would be if she didn't do something to stop it right now. If she didn't throw open the door, step through the opening and allow herself to reach out for the man she already knew she loved.

Be brave, he'd told her, as if he knew she could do it.

As if he had no doubt at all.

"I love you," she whispered helplessly. Lost somewhere in that gaze of his, and the simple fact that he was here. Right here in front of her, his hand stretched toward her, waiting for her with a patience she would have said Achilles Casilieris did not possess.

"Marry me, *glikia mou*. And you can love me forever." His mouth crept up in one corner, and all the scars Valentina had dug into her own heart when she'd left him seemed to glow a little bit. Then knit themselves into something more like art. "I'm told that's how it goes. But you know me. I always like to push the boundaries a little bit farther."

"Farther than forever?"

And she smiled at him then, not caring if she was still crying. Or laughing. Or whatever was happening inside her that was starting to take her over.

Maybe that was what it was to be brave. Doing whatever it was not because she felt it was right, but because it didn't matter what she felt. It was right, so she had to do it.

"Three forevers," Achilles said, as if he was promising them to her, here and now. "To start."

And he was still holding out his hand.

"Breathe," he murmured, as if he could see all the tumult inside her.

Valentina took a deep breath. She remembered lying in that bed of his with all of New York gleaming around them. He'd told her to breathe then, too.

In. Out.

Until she felt a little less full, or a little more able to handle what was happening. Until she had stopped feeling overwhelmed, and had started feeling desperate with need.

And this was no different.

Valentina breathed in, then out. Then she stepped forward and slid her hand into his, as easily as if they'd been made to fit together just like that, then let him pull her close.

He shifted to take her face in his hands, tilting her head back so he could fit his mouth to hers. Though he didn't. Not yet.

"Forever starts now," Valentina whispered. "The first one, anyway."

"Indeed." Achilles's mouth was so deliriously hard, and directly over hers. "Kiss me, Valentina. It's been too long."

And Valentina did more than kiss him. She poured herself into him, pushing herself up on her toes and winding her arms around his neck, and that was just the start.

Because there was forever after forever stacked up in front of them, just waiting for them to fill it. One after the next.

Together.

CHAPTER ELEVEN

ACHILLES MADE A terrible royal consort.

He didn't know who took more pride in that, he himself or the press corps, who finally had the kind of access to him they'd always wanted, and adored it.

But he didn't much care how bad he was at being the crown princess's billionaire, as long as he had Valentina. She allowed him to be as surly as he pleased, because she somehow found that charming. She'd even supported him when he'd refused to allow her father to give him a title, because he had no wish to become a Murinese citizen.

"I thank you," he had said to Geoffrey. "But I prefer not to swear my fealty to my wife by law, and title. I prefer to do it by choice."

Their wedding had been another pageant, with all the pomp and circumstance anyone could want for Europe's favorite princess. Achilles had long since accepted the fact that the world felt it had a piece of their story. Or of Valentina, certainly.

And he was a jealous bastard, but he tried not to mind as she waved and smiled and gave them what they wanted.

Meanwhile, as she grew bigger with his child she seemed to glow more by the day, and all those dark things in him seemed to grow lighter every time she smiled at him.

So he figured it was a draw.

She told him he wasn't a monster with that same deep certainty, as if she'd been there. As if she knew. And every time she did, he was more and more tempted to believe her.

She gave birth to their son the following spring, right about the time her sister was presenting the kingdom of Tissely with a brand-new princess of their own, because the ways in which the twins were identical became more and more fascinating all the time. The world loved that, too.

But not as much as Valentina and Natalie did.

And as Achilles held the tiny little miracle that he and Valentina had made, he felt another lock fall into place inside him. Maybe they could not be normal, Valentina and him. But that only meant that the love they would lavish on this child would be no less than remarkable.

And no less than he deserved.

This child would never live in the squalor his father had. He would never want for anything. No hand would be raised against him, and no fists would ever make contact with his perfect, sweet face. His parents would not abandon him, no stepfathers would abuse him, and it was entirely possible that he would be so loved that the world might drown in the force of it. Achilles would not be at all surprised.

Achilles met his beautiful wife's gaze over their child's head, lying with her in the bed in their private wing of the hospital. The public was locked outside, waiting to meet this latest member of the royal family. But that would happen later.

Here, now, it was only the three of them. His brand-new family and the world he would build for him. The world that Valentina would give their son.

Just as she'd given it to him.

"You are mine, *glikia mou*," he said softly as her gaze met his. Fiercely. "More now than ever."

And he knew that Valentina remembered. The first vows

they'd taken, though neither of them had called it that, in his New York penthouse so long ago.

The smile she gave him then was brighter than the sun, and warmed him all the same. Their son wriggled in his arms, as if he felt it, too. His mother's brightness that had lit up a monster lost in his own darkness, and convinced him he was a man.

Not just a man, but a good one. For her.

Anything for her.

"Yours," she agreed softly.

And Achilles reckoned that three forevers would not be nearly enough with Valentina.

But he was Achilles Casilieris. Perfection was his passion.

If they needed more forever they'd have it, one way or another.

He had absolutely no doubt.

* * * * *

One Night With The
Forbidden Princess
Amanda Cinelli

Amanda Cinelli was raised in a large Irish/Italian family in the suburbs of Dublin, Ireland. Her love of romance was inspired after "borrowing" one of her mother's beloved Harlequin Modern novels at the age of twelve. Writing soon became a necessary outlet for her wildly overactive imagination. Now married with a daughter of her own, she splits her time between changing nappies, studying psychology and writing love stories.

For Zara and Mia

CHAPTER ONE

'YOU WILL RECEIVE *a marriage proposal this week.*'

Olivia's ears still rang with her father's words, even as she moved through the motions of greeting the rest of the guests at the formal luncheon. It was not every day that your father informed you that you were set to marry a stranger, after all.

But, then again, her father was a king.

And the King clearly thought that the best time to impart news of this magnitude was no less than thirty seconds before he introduced her to her intended fiancé—a complete stranger. It was a wonder that she had managed to greet their guest of honour at all before she'd hurriedly made an excuse to leave.

Princesses were generally not permitted to sneak away during royal functions. Especially when that royal function concerned a very esteemed guest of honour from a faraway kingdom. Still, Olivia found herself making her way slowly across the room in search of fresh air.

'Another glass of champagne, Your Highness?'

Olivia stopped her progress and gracefully accepted the crystal flute from the waiter's hand, noticing the way his fingers trembled slightly as he tried to balance his tray. He was quite young—fresh out of school, she would bet.

'Is this your first Royal Races?' she asked, glad of the distraction while her eyes scanned the room, plotting her escape.

'It's my first day, actually. In general,' he replied.

'You are doing a wonderful job.'

She smiled, hoping her words might help to calm his nerves somewhat. It couldn't be an easy start, balancing priceless crystal while surrounded by some of Europe's wealthiest and most famous people.

'Thank you, Princess Olivia—I mean, Your Highness. Er... thank you.' He stumbled over his words, then smiled nervously, showing a mouth full of shiny metal braces.

Olivia smiled back with genuine warmth as the boy made a wobbly attempt at a bow and moved away. She sighed, taking a small sip from her glass. She would happily have spent the rest of the afternoon chatting with the teenager simply to avoid thinking of the bombshell that had just completely taken her by surprise. As if these royal functions weren't difficult enough.

The usual array of eager guests had predictably occupied her afternoon so far, with wave after wave of polite, banal conversation. Her parents, King Fabian and Queen Aurelia of Monteverre, stood at the opposite side of the long balcony surrounded by people and bodyguards. Her own personal security team stood at strategic points around her, trying and failing to blend into the crowd in their plain black suits and crisp white shirts.

The Royal Monteverre Races were infamous around the globe for their week-long parade of upper-class style and glamour. The historic racetrack was spread out below them, and thousands of guests had gathered in their finery for a day of sport and socialising.

No one's style was more closely watched than her own. Her morning had consisted of three hours being transformed by her own personal styling team. Her naturally wavy long red hair had been ironed and pressed to perfection, and her fair skin polished and highlighted in all the right places.

The public hailed her as a stunning natural beauty, but she

knew the effort that went into upholding that image was far from natural at all. She was a public brand—a symbol for an entire country with her every single step followed closely by the whole world.

Even her older sister, Crown Princess Eleanor, was not given the same amount of attention. Perhaps it was because she was already married. The press took much more pleasure in the single siblings than they did in the 'taken' ones. And yet her younger sister had the excuse of her studies in London to avoid the limelight.

For the past five years Olivia had been very much at the centre of public attention—since taking her official role in palace life at twenty-one. She did not shy from the pressure—she had been trained for it after all. She knew to expect intense scrutiny. And yet there was nothing that could make her feel more alone than being surrounded by thousands of people who treated her like an ornament to be admired from afar.

A sudden crash jolted her out of her thoughts and she looked up with a groan of empathy to see that the young waiter seemed to have lost his balance and gone crashing into a nearby couple.

'You absolute imbecile!'

The roar came from an elderly duke, a close friend of her father, who seemed to have been the sole recipient of the tray's liquid contents. Shards of priceless crystal lay scattered across the floor in a pool of expensive champagne while the teenage server stood frozen with a mixture of embarrassment and fear.

'Have this clumsy idiot taken back to the schoolroom. Out of my sight!' the Duke spat, his eyes bulging as his equally outraged wife hurriedly tried to dry his sodden shirt with a napkin.

As Olivia watched with horror, a single bodyguard materialised from the crowd and took the boy roughly by the shoulders.

'Stop!' She moved forward suddenly, her body seeming to propel her towards the dramatic scene of its own volition.

'A princess should never concern herself with such matters.'

Her late grandmother's voice seemed to warn her from her subconscious. But she pushed the thought away, arriving by the boy's side and looking up at the burly guard with all the authority she could muster. A hush had fallen over the crowd around them.

'I think there is a better way of managing this, don't you?' She addressed the guard, then turned her attention to the elderly Duke and his wife. 'Duque L'Arosa, this young man is a friend of mine. I know he would appreciate your kindness on his first day of work.'

The Duke's eyes widened horribly, his face turning even more red as his much younger wife gripped his arm and snorted her disapproval. Olivia stood her ground, flashing her best royal smile as the guard immediately released the boy. The young waiter avoided her eyes as he hurriedly gathered his tray and rushed off in the direction of the kitchen.

Olivia became suddenly painfully aware of the quiet that surrounded her. Members of the Monteverrian nobility and various public and government figures all averted their eyes, no one daring to speak or whisper about a member of the royal family while she stood in their midst.

A strange sensation began to spread over her bare shoulders, and she instinctively turned her head and found herself pinned by the gaze of a man who stood a few feet away. He was remarkably tall—taller than most of the men in the room. Perhaps that was what had drawn her attention to him.

She tried to look away, feeling uncomfortable under his obvious scrutiny, but there was something about the way he looked at her. She was quite used to being stared at—she was a public figure after all. But his dark eyes seemed to demand her complete attention. It was quite inappropriate, she told herself. She should be annoyed. But even with the length of the room between them, having his eyes on her seemed to make her heart beat faster.

A strange quiver of anticipation jolted to life in her chest, making her want to close the gap between them just to hear how his voice sounded. She raised one brow in challenge and felt her heart thump as a sinful smile spread across his full mouth, making him appear all the more rakish and infinitely dangerous.

No man had ever looked at her that way before—as though she was a tasty snack he might like to sample. She shook her head at the ridiculous turn of her thoughts and forced herself to look away.

When she finally looked back he had vanished.

She steeled her jaw, nodding politely to the Duque and Duquesa before making a slow and graceful exit through the main doors. Her own personal team of guards made themselves known as she walked faster, all five of them closing in from their previous placements. She had never felt more frustrated at her newly heightened security than she did at that moment. There was no immediate threat—no need for the ridiculous new measures her father had put in place the week before.

'I'm feeling ill,' she announced to the men once they had exited into the empty corridor outside the racetrack's function room. 'Surely there is no need for all of you to accompany me into the bathroom?'

The men reacted predictably, coughing awkwardly before moving aside and allowing her to walk unchaperoned into the ladies' restroom. She searched the for an exit point, her eyes landing on a second door on the opposite side of the bathroom.

She smiled with triumph. Sometimes a little rebellion was necessary.

Roman Lazarov had never been particularly comfortable at high society functions. It had been sheer curiosity that had led him to accept the Sheikh of Zayarr's invitation to attend the Royal Races while he was already in Monteverre. Small European kingdoms were one of the few niche markets he had not yet entered with his security firm, as monarchies largely tended to keep to their own traditional models of operation. Old money aristocrats also tended to show a particular disdain towards new money Russians.

His fists tightened as he thought of the scene he had witnessed after only being in the room mere moments. Nothing made him feel closer to his own humble beginnings than watching a rich man treat his server badly. There was something particularly nasty about those who had been born to immense wealth. As though they believed the world should bend to their will and that those with less than them were somehow *worth* less as well. A sweeping generalisation, to be sure, but a painfully accurate one in his own experience.

The redhead had surprised him. She was clearly upper class—he could tell by the way she was dressed. Diamonds and rich yellow silk. He had noticed her the moment he'd entered the room. She had stood proud and untouchable near the centre, all alone, with her delicate fingers holding on to a champagne flute for dear life. And yet she had stepped forward for the servant and caused an obvious scene.

He should thank her, really. She had provided the perfect distraction for him to move on to his main purpose of business.

He would have liked nothing more than to stick around at the pretentious party and see if Lady Red lived up to his expectations. But really this brief detour to the races had been a mistake on his part. Time was of the essence when you had a royal palace to break into, after all...

The early summer afternoon was pleasant as Roman rounded the last bend on the dirt path, finally bringing the high walls of the palace into view. The overgrown abandoned hunting track wasn't the easiest route, but when you were about to break into the home of Monteverre's royal family you didn't usually use the front gate.

The forest was quiet but for the sounds of wildlife and the occasional creak of tree branches protesting as he methodically pulled them out of his way. Reaching the medieval stone wall, Roman looked up. It had to be at least five metres high and three metres thick—rather impressive and designed to be impossible to scale, especially when you weren't dressed for the occasion. He checked his smartwatch, zooming in on the small map that would guide him to the access point.

In another life Roman Lazarov had found pleasure in breaking the law. Bypassing even the most high-tech security system had been child's play for a hungry, hardened orphan with a taste for troublemaking. But in all his time in the seedy underworld of St Petersburg an actual palace had never made it onto his hit list.

That life was over now—replaced by a monumental self-made wealth that his young, hungry self could only have dreamed about. And yet here he was, his pulse quickening at the prospect of what lay ahead. The fact that this little exercise was completely above-board made it no less challenging. The palace had a guard of one hundred men and all he had was a digital blueprint of the castle tunnels and his own two hands.

The thought sent adrenaline running through his veins. God, but he had missed this feeling. When the Sheikh of Zayyar had first asked him for a favour, he had presumed it to be assembling a new security team for a foreign trip or something of that nature. Khal was in high demand these days, and his guard had been assembled almost entirely from Roman's security firm, The Lazarov Group. But Khal's request had intrigued him—likely as it had been meant to. The challenge had been set, and Roman was determined to enjoy it.

As for whether or not he would succeed—that question had made him laugh heartily in his oldest friend's face.

Roman Lazarov never failed at anything.

The daylight made it seem almost as though he were taking a leisurely stroll rather than performing an act of espionage. He finally reached the small metal hatch in the ground that would provide the cleanest and most ridiculously obvious point of entry. An evacuation hatch, more than likely from long-ago times of war. He had hardly believed his eyes when his team had uncovered it on an old blueprint.

Although it looked rather polished and clean for a decades-old abandoned grate, he thought to himself, sliding one finger along the sun-heated metal.

A sudden sound in the quiet made Roman go completely still, instinctively holding his breath. He felt the familiar heightened awareness that came from years of experience in the security business as he listened, scanning his surroundings. Footsteps, light and fast, were coming closer. The person was of small build—possibly a child. Still, Roman couldn't be seen or this whole exercise would be blown.

Without another thought he took five long steps, shielding himself under cover of the trees.

A shape emerged from thick bushes ten feet away. The figure was petite, slim and unmistakably female. She was fast. So damned fast he saw little more than a set of bare shapely legs and a shapeless dark hooded coat before she seemed to pirouette and disappear through the hatch in the ground without any effort at all.

Roman frowned, for a moment simply replaying the image in his head. Evidently he was not the only one who had been informed of the hidden entryway. He shook off his surprise, cursing himself for hesitating as he made quick work of reaching the hatch and lowering himself.

The iron ladder was slippery with damp and led down to a smooth, square-shaped concrete tunnel beneath. Small patches of sunlight poked through ventilation ducts at regular intervals, giving some light in the otherwise pitch-blackness.

Roman stilled, listening for the sound of the woman's footsteps. She had moved quickly, but he could hear her faint steps somewhere ahead of him in the tunnel. As he began his pursuit a half-smile touched his lips. He had come here today tasked with proving the ineptitude of this palace's security, and now he would have a genuine intruder to show as proof.

This cat burglar was about to get *very* rudely interrupted.

* * *

Olivia held her shoes tightly in one hand as she slid her hand along the wall of the tunnel for support. The ground was damp and slippery under her bare feet—a fact that should have disgusted a young woman of such gentle breeding. But then she had never really understood the whole 'delicate princess' rationale. It was at times like this, after escaping palace life for even one simple hour, that she truly felt alive.

Her sudden disappearance had likely been noticed by now, and yet she did not feel any remorse. Her attendance at the international horse racing event had been aimed at the King's esteemed guest of honour, Sheikh Khalil Al Rhas of Zayyar. The man that her father had informed her she was intended to marry.

Olivia paused for a moment, tightness overcoming her throat for the second time in a few short hours. The way he had phrased it, as her 'royal duty', still rung in her ears. She was only twenty-six, for goodness' sake. She wasn't ready for this particular duty.

She had always known it was customary for her father to hold the right to arrange or refuse the marriages of his offspring, but she had hoped the day would never come when she was called upon in such an archaic fashion. But now that day was here, and the Sheikh was set to propose to her formally any day now— before he completed his trip.

Olivia pressed her forehead briefly against the stone wall. She felt cold through and through, as if she would never be warm again.

'Drama queen.' Cressida's mocking voice sounded in her head.

Her younger sister had always been such a calm, level-headed presence in her life. It had been five years since Cress had moved away to study in England. And not a day passed that she didn't think of her. With barely a year between them, they had always been more like twins. Cress would know exactly what to say to alleviate the unbearable tension that had taken residence in her stomach today. She was sure of it.

The tunnel was a straight path along the south boundary of the palace. It seemed like an endless mile before the staircase finally appeared. Olivia climbed it in the near darkness, relying solely on memory to make her way up to the partially hidden door in the stone wall. She pressed a slim crease, sliding open a panel and stepping through easily.

The brightness of her dressing room was a welcome shock of cream and gold after the prolonged darkness. She took a moment, breathing in the clean air, before turning to slide the secret door closed.

Olivia stilled at the sound of footsteps in the tunnel below. But that was impossible. In almost fifteen years of roaming she had never seen another soul down there. She had never even told her sisters.

She stepped back down to the small landing at the top of the steps. She braced her hands on the stone balustrade to peer down into the darkness, biting the inside of her lip. Had one of the guards followed her?

The footsteps suddenly disappeared and an eerie silence filled the stone caverns. Still she held her breath. *Eight, nine, ten...* Olivia exhaled slowly, cursing her overactive imagination. The silence of the tunnel tended to play with your mind after a while—she was clearly going insane.

She turned around to move back to the doorway to her apartment—only to be blocked by a wall of muscle. Warm muscle that smelled of sandalwood and pine.

Strong hands—definitely male—appeared like chains across her chest and turned her towards the wall. Her arms were pulled behind her and she instinctively pushed her body backwards, aiming the hardness of her skull towards her assailant's nose. Even princesses were taught self-defence.

'You have some skills, I see.'

His voice was startling in the quiet darkness. A heavy accent made his threat even more worrying. This was most definitely *not* a palace guard.

Olivia hissed, turning away and trying in vain to pull against the bands of iron strength. She squinted in the darkness, trying to see his face, a uniform, an insignia—anything that might tell her who he was and why he was here. If she could remember anything from the Palace Guards' kidnapping talk it was one thing: *Don't say a thing.*

He pressed on what seemed to be a watch and turned a faint light downwards, lowering its beam to her oversized black trench coat and bare feet. She had swapped her designer blazer with someone else's coat in the cloakroom before bolting. The vintage lemon cocktail dress she wore underneath was hardly ideal for going unnoticed in public.

She turned her head and caught a brief glimpse of a hard jaw and gigantic shoulders before he plunged them into darkness once more.

'You're not exactly dressed for a quick escape,' he mused.

She almost laughed at that—almost. But being held captive by a mysterious hulk of a man had kind of dampened her infamous ability to see the bright side of every situation. As far as she could see there was nothing positive that could come of being abducted, which was the only logical solution for whoever this man was. He would recognise her any moment now and the game would be up.

Perhaps they would ransom her, she thought wildly. How much was her life worth? Hopefully not too much...the kingdom was already facing complete financial ruin as it was.

She gulped hard as she felt his hand slip just under her left armpit—a strange place to grope, indeed.

'Don't! Don't you dare touch me.' She gasped, arching her body away frantically. He tightened his hold on her slightly, barely even noticing her attempts to free herself.

'You are in no danger from me,' he gritted. 'I must ensure the same can be said of you. Stand still.'

Such was the authority in his voice that she stilled herself. She held her breath as his touch moved almost mechanically to her hip. His movements were calm and purposeful as he did the same to her other side, feeling inside the pockets of her coat and underneath to slide along the indentation of her waist.

Her mind suddenly realised that he was searching for a weapon. She sucked in a breath as strong fingers brushed her ribcage, just underneath her breasts. Of all the situations in which to become excited by a man's touch, this really wasn't it. And yet her traitorous body had begun to respond to the intensity of the situation even as her heart thumped with fear.

His breathing did not alter at all, and nor did he show any signs of noticing her response. As his hand finally moved to her thigh Olivia could take no more. She kicked out. Partly in shock at his boldness, but mostly because of the discomfort of her own reaction.

She took a deep breath. 'Do you honestly believe that I'm hiding a weapon in my underwear?'

The stranger cleared his throat. 'I have known people to hide weapons in the most ludicrous places. Women especially tend towards a certain…creativity.'

'Do *not* put your hands on me again.'

He was silent for a moment, and the only sound in the dark tunnel was that of their steady breaths mingling in the air between them.

When he spoke again his accent was more pronounced, his voice deep and intimidating. 'Tell me who you are and why you are attempting to break into the palace.'

She paused at that. So he hadn't recognised her yet. Surely if he was a kidnapper he would have come here knowing the faces of the royal family. Although it was dark, she supposed. Her choices were limited. She had no panic buttons down here—no guards within shouting distance.

She needed to get away.

She turned her head towards the door, breathing a little faster with anticipation as his shrewd gaze followed the movement and he saw the sliver of light coming through the gap.

'You managed to find a way inside, I see,' he said with surprise. 'Come on, then. Let's see what you were after, shall we?'

He held her forearm tightly, dragging her behind him up the steps and into the lavish dressing room. Her eyes adjusted quickly once again, to take in the rows and rows of her wardrobes. The room was empty, as it would be for a while, seeing as her staff presumed her to be at the races for the rest of the day.

Olivia gulped hard. She had just led an uncleared intruder right into the heart of the palace.

She took a moment to look at him for the first time in the light.

'It's you...' she breathed, realising it was the man from the racetrack.

To his credit, he also looked momentarily stunned as he took in her face in the light.

He was taller this close—almost an entire foot taller than her five feet three inches. All the self-defence classes in the world wouldn't give her a hope against such a brute. Dark hair, dark eyes and a jawline that would put Michelangelo's *David* to shame. He had a fierce beauty about him—as if he had just stepped off a battlefield somewhere—and he thrummed with vitality.

Her grandmother had always said she watched too many movies. Here she was, in very real danger, and she was romanticising her captor.

'You have taken a break from saving servants, I see.' His eyes lowered to take in the coat that covered her cocktail dress. 'You seem to be a woman of many talents.'

Olivia stayed completely silent as he spoke, knowing the more she said the more chance there was that he would put two and two together and guess her identity. She glanced to her left, searching the room for possible weapons for when the time came to run. If she could find something to kick at him, perhaps...

She looked down at her bare feet, cursing her own stupidity.

'We are in the south wing,' he mused, looking around the room. 'One of the royal apartments. How did you find out about the hidden tunnel?'

She shrugged, looking down at her feet and taking one tentative step away from him while his attention wandered.

'I saw how you slid down there. You knew exactly what you were doing. Just like you know what you are doing right now.' He grabbed her arm, stopping her progress.

She couldn't help herself then—she cursed. A filthy word in Catalan that would make her father blush if he heard her.

The stranger smiled darkly. 'We're going to get absolutely nowhere if you don't speak to me. Why are you here?' he asked again, releasing her arm and pushing her to sit down in the chair in front of her dressing table.

Exactly where she needed to be.

'I could ask you the same question,' she replied, slowly reclining backwards under the pretext of stretching her tender muscles.

'That's simple. I'm here for people like you,' he said simply, crossing his arms and staring down at her.

'People like me?' she asked breathlessly, her hand feeling blindly along the dressing table behind her for where she knew an alert button had been placed. She tried to calm her breath and prayed he would not see what she was doing. She felt a smooth round bump and pressed it quickly, holding her breath in case she needed to run.

No sirens sounded…there were no flashing lights. She moved to press it again, only to have his fingers encircle her elbow and place her hands in her lap.

'Keep your hands where I can see them.'

It was clear this wasn't going to be over any time soon.

He tilted his head to one side, looking at her in such an intense way it made her toes curl into the carpet under her feet. His eyes lowered, darkening as they swept down her legs.

The way he looked at her, the blatant male appreciation on his striking features, made something seem to uncoil in the pit of her stomach. She felt warm under his gaze and turned her face away in case she blushed.

'Whomever you think I am, I can tell you now that you are very wrong.'

His answering smile was raking, and made goosebumps break out across her arms.

The stranger bent down so that their faces were level. 'I think that, whoever you are, beautiful, you are a lot stronger and a lot more dangerous than you seem.'

CHAPTER TWO

'YOU SOUND LIKE quite the expert,' she purred, her catlike eyes seeming to glow in her pale features.

Roman frowned. 'I can tell by your eyes that you're worried about being caught in the act, and yet you mock me.'

'You're quite arrogant and you deserve some mocking, I think,' she replied sweetly.

He fought the urge to laugh at this situation. Here he was, with a thief held captive inside the palace walls, and he was enjoying their verbal sparring too much to make a decision over what to do with her.

He couldn't simply waltz up to the King's offices and present him with this gift. Problem one being that the King was out of the palace today, along with the rest of the royal family. Problem two being that the Palace Guard had no idea he would be here today. As far as they were concerned he would be just as much a criminal as the sharp-tongued redhead who sat staring at him as though she'd like to claw his eyes out.

He would have to call Khal and tell him that their plan had encountered a minor diversion. It was no matter, really. He had identified a serious security blind spot and provided the Palace Guard with an attempted burglar to boot. All in all, quite a success.

So why did the thought of handing her over make him feel so uneasy?

He had got where he was by trusting his gut, and right now his gut was telling him that something wasn't quite right here. That this woman was not all that she seemed. Something made him pause, his brain weighing the situation up piece by piece.

'You are quite possibly the most ladylike thief I have ever encountered,' he mused. 'Do you always go barefoot on a job, or was today an exception?'

'You assume that I make a habit of this?' She glared up at him.

'Correct me, then.' He held her gaze evenly until she looked away.

'You have quite an intense stare. It's making me uneasy.'

She crossed one slim leg over the other. Roman felt his throat go dry, and looked away from the expanse of creamy smooth skin below her dress.

'I'm in the business of being observant,' he said, clearing his throat. 'You might benefit from it yourself, then maybe next time you won't get caught so easily.'

'I assume you are the almighty authority on how to break into palaces?' She raised her brows, sitting straighter in her seat.

'Seeing as you arrived here first, I disagree,' he countered.

'Oh, *now* I see. You're angry that you were beaten to the punch by a woman.' She placed both feet flat on the floor, smoothing her dress over her knees. 'This whole body-searching, intimidating act has all been one big ego-stroke for you.'

'I searched you because I am not so pig-headed as to believe that you pose no threat to me simply because of your sex.' Roman shook his head in disbelief, hating himself for rising to her bait. 'Why would you assume that the fact you are a woman has anything to do with it?'

She looked away from him then. 'Because it always does.'

'I think that's far more telling of your low opinion of men

than anything else.' He raised his brows. 'Trust me, I am an expert in assessing risks. Women are not somehow physically destined to surrender to men. I have seen it first-hand. I have trained women, watched them down men twice their size without breaking a sweat.'

'You *train* women? To become…thieves?' she said with disbelief. 'Who on earth *are* you?'

Roman laughed, not bothering to correct her assumption. 'Let's just say I am the last person you wish to meet while you're on a job. Not just here, in this castle. Anywhere. I know how the criminal mind works. I have made it my business to be an expert in it.'

'So if I'm a criminal, you'll know what I am thinking right now?' Her eyes darted towards the door once more.

'I'm trying to.' Roman poised himself in case she ran. 'Just tell me what it is you're after and I can make this easier for you. Tell me your name.'

'No,' she said plainly.

Her body language was telling him that she was becoming increasingly more agitated with the situation. A flight risk if ever he'd seen one.

Even as the thought crossed his mind she jumped from the chair, her speed surprising him for a split second before he moved himself. She made it a few steps before his arms were around her waist, holding her body tightly against his as she struggled in vain.

'Please—just let me go,' she breathed.

The fear in her voice startled him, but his training had taught him not to release anyone until he had another means of restraining them.

'You are making it very difficult for me to help you here. Do you know that?' he said, holding her arms tightly to her sides and trying in vain to ignore the delicious scent of vanilla that drifted up from her hair.

'Why…? Why would you offer to help after what you think of me?'

He thought for a moment. 'Because I believe in second chances.' He spoke without thought, his answer surprising even himself. 'You always have a choice—no matter how impossible it seems.'

A strange look came over her face as their eyes locked. Her breath was coming hard and heavy against his chest but she'd stopped fighting him. Her eyes drifted away from him, settling on the distance with a mixture of resolve and deep sadness.

'I'm not who you think I am.'

Without warning a heavy weight came down behind him, followed by what he presumed to be a palace guard shouting in furious Catalan.

Roman pushed the man backwards, holding his hands up in what he hoped resembled a peaceful motion.

'I have authorisation,' he began, motioning towards the lapel of his suit jacket. 'The King knows I am here.'

Roman felt his hands being pulled behind him into handcuffs and fought the urge to laugh as he looked up into a second guard's furious face.

'You will regret this.'

He grunted at the pressure of a knee between his shoulder blades, knowing that they most likely did not speak a word of English. As his face was crushed against the carpet he looked sideways, just in time to see a pair of dainty bare feet appear by his side. Up close, he could see that a tiny hand-drawn daisy adorned each red-painted toenail.

The woman spoke in rapid-fire Catalan, her voice muted and fearful yet with a strange backbone of authority. The nearest guard nodded, uttering two words that made his body freeze.

'Si, Princesa.'

Roman crushed his face further into the carpet with disbelief and sheer dread.

He had just body-searched a damn princess.

* * *

His Majesty King Fabian of Monteverre stood up as Olivia entered the private sitting room flanked by two stony-faced members of the Royal Guard.

'Of all the days to pull one of your disappearing acts, Libby,' her father said angrily, motioning for the guards to leave them with a flick of one hand.

Her mother, elegant and perpetually silent, did not acknowledge her entry. Queen Aurelia sat poised in a high-backed chair, her eyes trained solemnly on nothing in particular.

'Where have you *been*? You were informed of the intruder hours ago,' Olivia said, breathing hard.

'And naturally you expected us to abandon the event? Honestly, Libby...' The King frowned in disbelief, reaching down to take a sip of whisky from a thick crystal tumbler.

Her father was the only one who still called her Libby. It reminded her of being five years old and being scolded for trying to sneak chocolate from the kitchens. But she was not a child any more, and she was damned tired of being treated like one.

'I was attacked,' she said slowly. 'A man held me hostage in my own dressing room. And yet I've been left to pace my apartments completely alone for the past five hours.'

'The matter has been resolved. It was a simple misunderstanding.' King Fabian avoided his daughter's eyes. 'Best to forget the whole business.'

Olivia felt all the outrage and pent-up frustration freeze in her veins as she registered her father's words. Had he actually just told her to *forget* this afternoon? She opened her mouth, then closed it, completely at a loss as to what to say in response.

'Your absence was noticed by Sheikh Khalil,' he said, scolding, his brows drawing down as they always did when he was unimpressed.

'Well, as I have just said, I was rather busy being held against my will by a dangerous intruder.' She took a deep breath, looking briefly across to her mother's uninterested blank features before returning her furious gaze to her father. 'Have I gone mad? Or are you both completely unaffected by today's events?'

'I understand it might have been...alarming...' King Fabian began solemnly.

'"Alarming" hardly covers it.' Olivia fumed. 'Why are you both so *calm*?'

The last word came out in a disbelieving whisper. She fought a distinct urge to walk over and bang her fist on her father's chest, to knock over her mother's glass, to make them both react in some way other than with this muted nothingness.

Today's events had shaken her to her core, and yet she felt as though she were intruding on their peace with her inconvenient outrage. Surely her own father should be shocked and outraged that his daughter's safety had been at risk inside their own home. Unless... Unless he wasn't shocked at all.

'What do you mean by a misunderstanding?' she asked, not bothering to hide the challenge in her voice.

'Libby...' Her father sighed, raising a hand for her to quieten.

'Please, don't "Libby" me.' She placed one hand on her hip. 'Tell me exactly what is going on. Did you know about this man?'

The King twisted his mouth in discomfort. 'Well...not directly, no.'

'Indirectly, then. You *knew* that someone would be here today? In our home.'

King Fabian strode to the window, placing one hand on the sill and looking out in silence. 'The man you met today was Roman Lazarov, founder of The Lazarov Group, an international security firm.' Her father sighed heavily. 'He is a very close friend of Sheikh Khalil and I have been assured that he is *the* authority on high-class security operations. But after the complete muddle he made today, I'm not so sure of his expert status...'

He laughed weakly, his voice trailing off as he took in her expression of horror.

'Don't look at me that way. It was a gift from Sheikh Khalil—very thoughtful of him to want to ensure your safety, I thought.'

Olivia felt a headache begin at her temples. This was all becoming too much. She closed her eyes a moment, unable to bear her father's apparent disregard for his daughter's privacy or independence.

'No, Father. In fact I find it horribly thoughtless. And intrusive, among other things.' She felt her breath coming faster, her temper rising like a caged bird set to take flight. 'This is the last straw in a long line of things I have overlooked since you began vaguely mentioning a possible marriage. I am not a piece of livestock to be insured and fenced in, for goodness' sake.'

He sighed. 'You are overreacting.'

'No, I'm really not. Did anyone consult me before all my charity events were cancelled? Was I informed when I was assigned five new bodyguards for all trips outside the palace?' She shook her head, her knuckles straining with the tightness of her fists by her sides. 'And now this. Did you even think to ask me before you sent a bloody *mercenary* into my room? I'll never feel safe there again!'

'Lazarov was simply going to *attempt* to gain entry to your rooms. To find any weaknesses in our security. Besides, you were supposed to be at the races with your fiancé.'

The tightness in her throat intensified. 'I have not yet agreed to this marriage. Until today I had no idea that you were truly serious about it! And if this is how the Sheikh shows his concern...'

She tightened her lips, willing herself to say the words. To tell her father that the whole deal was off. She didn't want this. *Any* of it.

King Fabian's voice lowered in warning. 'Olivia, these negotiations are months old—we have discussed why this is a necessary step.'

She blinked. *Months old?* 'For the kingdom, yes. I understand what we stand to gain from a political union.' She cleared her throat, her voice sounding all of a sudden smaller. 'But what about for *me*?'

Her father's brows rose imperiously. 'You will be serving your kingdom.'

'I don't see why I must get married to a complete stranger in order to serve Monteverre. I am doing good work with Mimi's Foundation—I am making a difference.'

'Your grandmother and her damned charities...' Fabian scowled darkly, draining the last of his whisky. 'You think teaching a handful of scrawny kids to read will change anything about our situation?'

'My grandmother taught me that charity is not always about money. It's important to nourish the youth as well as to do our best to help those in need. She was beloved by this kingdom.'

'Ah, yes, the eternally perfect Queen Miranda! My mother spent so much time on her charities she didn't even notice her country's economy crumbling beneath her feet.' His mouth twisted cruelly. 'Don't you *see*, you silly girl? We are facing financial ruin without this union.'

Olivia opened her mouth to protest, only to have her father's scowl stop her as he continued on his own personal rant.

'The Kingdom of Zayyar is overflowing with wealth, thanks to this man. He is an economic genius. But the civic history of his country still stands in the way of true acceptance from the west. To put it bluntly, they need our political influence and we need their money.'

'Money...' Olivia bit her lip, wanting to ask just how much she was worth, considering he was essentially trading her body for cash.

'Sheikh Khalil has the capabilities to take Monteverre back to its glory days—surely you want that for your people? What good is being able to read if they have no money to feed themselves?'

She had never heard her father speak so frankly, and his eyes were red-rimmed with half-madness. Olivia knew that Monteverre was in trouble. A series of bad leadership decisions and banking crashes had left them neck-deep in debt and with many of the younger generation emigrating to greener pastures. They were bleeding, and it appeared that this Sheikh had come offering a magic bandage. At a particular cost...

'Trusting an entire country's economic future to one man's hands? That seems a bit...reckless. Surely there is another way without the marriage—?'

'No,' he cut across her, his voice a dull bark in the silent room. 'There is no going back on this. I won't hear another word.'

Her father's eyes were dark in a way she had never seen them before, as though he hadn't truly slept in months.

'Everything you have had since birth is thanks to your position. It's not like you have an actual *career* to think of—you spend most of your time looking pretty and waving. None of that would even change. Your life would continue just as it has been—only as the Sheikha of Zayyar.' He took a breath, smiling down at her as if he had just bestowed upon her some enormous gift. 'This is your *duty*, Olivia. To Monteverre. It's not about you.'

She felt his words sink into her skin like an icy breeze, setting off goose pimples down her bare arms. Did being born a Sandoval really mean surrendering every aspect of your life to the good of the kingdom?

As the second daughter she had naïvely believed that her life would be different from her older sister's. She was not first in line to rule Monteverre—she didn't bear that crushing weight of responsibility and she had always been infinitely glad of it.

'The Sheikha of Zayyar...'

Her mother's melodic voice intruded on her thoughts, sounding absurdly serene.

'Sounds like something from a film...'

'I don't even know where Zayyar is,' Olivia said numbly, almost unable to speak past the tickle of panic spreading across her throat.

'Somewhere on the Persian Gulf,' Queen Aurelia offered, twirling the liquid in her glass. 'They have a hotel shaped like a boat sail.'

'That's Dubai.' King Fabian rolled his eyes. 'Zayyar is half-way between the desert and the Arabian Sea. Gorgeous scenery—you will love it.'

'Thank you for the sales pitch, Father.' Olivia sighed, looking across to her mother, who had once again turned to gaze into the empty fireplace.

It was customary for her mother to permanently nurse a glass of the finest cognac after midday. In Olivia's memory no one had ever questioned it or raised any concern. There had always been an unspoken understanding among the Sandoval children that their mother and father each did whatever they pleased and things would always be that way. They did not welcome personal discussions.

She looked up to the ceiling, feeling the familiar sense of exhaustion that always accompanied any meeting with her parents. For that was all they ever were. Meetings.

'Sheikh Khalil simply wanted to ensure your safety, Libby. Surely you find that romantic? I know you are prone to the sentiment.'

Her father looked down at his wife, but she had drifted off, her eyes dull and unfocused as she stared into nothingness. The look on his face changed to outright disgust and he turned away, busying himself with retrieving his jacket from a chair.

Olivia's heart broke a little for her parents' fractured marriage. She had fleeting memories of a happier time, when her parents had seemed madly in love and the Kingdom of Monteverre had been a shining beacon of prosperity and culture. Now there was nothing but cold resentment and constant worry.

'Father...' Olivia took a breath, trying to calm her rapid thoughts. 'This is all happening very fast. Perhaps if I just had some more time—'

'Why do you think the Sheikh arranged this trip? He plans

to propose formally this afternoon so that the announcement can be made public before he leaves.'

Olivia's breath caught, expanding her throat painfully. 'He... he can't do that...'

'Oh, yes, he can—and you will be grateful for his patience.'

His voice boomed across the room, the sudden anger in it startling her, making her back away a step.

He took a breath, deliberately softening his tone. 'Can't you see that you are a vital part in this? There is power in your position.'

'Power...' Olivia repeated weakly. Her shoulders drooped. Even her bones felt heavy. *Women are not always destined to surrender to men...* Those words—*his* words—had struck something deep within her.

Roman Lazarov.

She bit her lip hard. For a moment she had regretted her decision to have him captured. He had seemed to glow from within—a fiery protector and proclaimer of women's strength. Now she knew he was just like the rest of them. Here to ensure that her cage was kept good and tight. That she had no hope of freedom.

King Fabian tightened his lips, forcing a smile before shrugging into his navy dress jacket and fixing the diamond cufflinks at his wrists. He paused by her side, looking down at her.

'You will have a private lunch with Sheikh Khalil tomorrow.' He placed one hand on her shoulder, giving it a light squeeze. 'I know you will give him the answer he wants. I'm so proud of the beautiful woman you have become.'

Olivia closed her eyes, not wanting him to see the tears that glistened there. Her heart seemed to slow in her chest as she nodded her head in defeat, glad when he was gone, with the smell of cigar smoke wafting on the air in his wake. How could he be proud of the woman she was when she had no idea who she was herself?

'I can't do this,' she breathed, silently hoping her mother

would look up. That she would hold her and listen to her worries, then kiss her forehead and tell her everything would be okay.

But sadly she knew that would never happen. She had no memories of ever being in her mother's arms, and even if she had the woman who now sat like a living ghost in the sitting room was not truly her mother.

She stood still for a long time, letting the tears fall down her cheeks and stain the neckline of her dress. Eventually she wiped her face and turned away from the unbearable silence, walking through the long main corridors of the private suites.

As usual, the guards pretended not to notice her.

She took her time, idling through the gardens on her way back to her rooms. With a few deep breaths she calmed the tremor in her throat. It had been a long time since she had let a single tear fall—probably not since the day of her grandmother's funeral. Crying was a fruitless activity when her future had already been neatly packed up and arranged.

She sat heavily on a marble bench in the centre of the courtyard. This was her favourite part of the palace, where a low stone square fountain provided the perfect vantage point to sit and listen to the staff as they went about their daily duties. Here, partially concealed by bougainvillea and foliage, she had been privy to the most heart-stopping live-action dramas outside of television.

The fights, the wicked gossip, the passionate clandestine embraces. A reluctant smile touched her lips. She had seen it all.

Just in the past month it had been revealed that one of the upstairs maids had engaged in an affair with the head gardener's handsome son. Olivia had overheard the whole sordid situation developing—right up to the point when said housemaid had found out that her beau was also heavily involved with one of the palace florists. The ensuing slap had resounded across the courtyard and earned the young Romeo a speedy transfer outside the palace.

The housemaid had moved on quickly enough, accepting

a date with a palace guard. The look of delirious happiness as she'd described their first kiss to her friends had haunted Olivia for days.

She stood restlessly, leaning against the side of the fountain. Was that look the very thing she was sacrificing by agreeing to a loveless marriage?

She frowned, drawing her hand through the water and watching the ripples spread across her own solemn reflection. Love was about falling for the wrong guy, having your heart broken and then ending up with your handsome Prince Charming—not that she had ever experienced it. But she had watched enough old movies to know it was always true love's kiss at the end that gave her that butterflies feeling in her stomach. That moment when the couple swore their undying devotion and fell into each other's arms...

She wanted to feel like that. At least once in her life.

There had been a handful of kisses in her past; she was twenty-six, after all. But never more than a brief touching of lips. The kind of men who had been permitted near her just happened to be the kind of men who got aroused at the thought of their own reputations inflating with a real-life princess on their arm. Not one of the men she'd dated had ever tried to get to know her *really*.

A prickle made its way along her skin as she thought of a certain pair of grey eyes, raking their way down her body. It was madness, the way her body had seemed to thrum deep inside just from a man's gaze. It was ridiculous.

She looked down at her forearms, seeing the gooseflesh there. Why did he have to affect her so violently when no other man had managed to inspire so much as a flicker of her attraction?

She bit the inside of her cheek with frustration and turned to begin walking back to her apartments—only to find a large male frame blocking her path.

'Good evening, Printsessa.'

CHAPTER THREE

'I SEE THEY have released you... Mr Lazarov.' The Princess straightened her shoulders defensively, moving a long silken curtain of vibrant red hair away from her face as she directed her gaze upon him.

Roman ignored the strange tightening in his stomach at the way she said his name, focusing on her pale features to better read her mood.

She seemed less colourful than he remembered—as if something had stolen the fire he had witnessed earlier in the day, both at the racetrack and afterwards.

'Once they realised their mistake they were quite accommodating. I hope you were not worried for my welfare.'

'If it were my choice I would have had you detained for the night.'

She held her chin high as she delivered the blow, but Roman saw the telltale convulsive movement in her throat as she took a breath. He leaned casually against a nearby column, raising a single brow in challenge.

Far from bowing under his scrutiny, she held his gaze evenly. 'I assume you are here to make your apology?'

Roman fought the urge to laugh. 'I'm no stranger to handcuffs, Princess.' He smiled darkly. 'It would take more than five hours in a cushy palace detainment room to force me to my knees.'

Her gaze lowered a fraction and Roman gave in to his mirth, a darkly amused smile spreading across his lips.

'I don't want you to be on your...' She shook her head, exhaling hard. She crossed her arms below her chest—a gesture likely meant in defence, but all it served to do was draw his attention to the resulting swell at the neckline of her delicate yellow dress.

'Well, you are free to go,' she said, sarcasm dripping from her tone as she gestured towards the door to the main palace.

For the first time in his life Roman was at a complete loss as to what to say. How he had not recognised that she was a royal instantly, he did not know. The woman before him seemed to exude class and sophistication in every inch of her posture. She eyed him with suspicion, her brows lowering in a mixture of challenge and defence.

He should have left the moment he had been freed, and yet he had sought her out. He had told himself he needed to apologise, but right now, remembering the honest arousal in her eyes as he'd been pressed close to her... He wasn't feeling quite so apologetic.

He stood taller, hardening his voice. 'In case you are planning another escape, the tunnel has been blocked. It is no longer passable.'

'You certainly work fast,' she said quietly, leaning back against the lip of the fountain. 'I assume the Sheikh asked you to make sure my cage was good and tight?'

'Your...cage?'

She was oblivious to his confusion. 'Of course it matters to no one that I am an adult with free will. By all means let him have the run of the palace. There will be bars installed on my bedroom windows next.'

Roman raked a hand across the shadow beginning to grow

along his jaw. He allowed her to a rant a moment, before clearing his throat pointedly. 'You seem upset.'

'"Upset" does not even begin to cover it. Everything about today has been unbearable.'

Something about the faraway look in her eyes bothered him. It was as though she were on the edge of a complete meltdown, and he worried that it was his mistake that had brought her there. Perhaps there was a need for his apology after all—much as it pained him to admit it.

'Princess, I need you to understand that I am not in the habit of holding a woman against her will,' he said solemnly. 'Earlier...when I searched you...'

She looked back at him, her lashes half lowered with something dark and unspoken. 'Will you be telling your fearsome Sheikh about that, I wonder?'

'The Sheikh is not the villain you seem to think he is,' Roman said quietly, inwardly grimacing at the thought of telling his best friend how he had manhandled his future wife. 'I have never known someone as loyal and dedicated.'

'Perhaps the two of you should get married, then,' she said snidely.

'I did not expect an actual princess to be quite so...cutting.' He pressed a hand to his chest in mock injury. 'Is it any wonder I mistook you for a common thief?'

That earned him the hint of a smile from her lips. The movement lit up her eyes ever so slightly and he felt a little triumphant that he had caused it.

Roman smirked, turning to lean against the fountain, taking care to leave a good foot and a half of space between them. It had been a long time since he had been this conscious of a woman's presence.

'You seem like quite the man of mystery, Mr Lazarov,' she said, turning to look at him briefly. 'Best friends with a sheikh...founder of an international security firm.'

'You've been researching me?'

'I only found out your name twenty minutes ago,' she said honestly. 'Does the Sheikh always fly you in for such favours?'

'No, he does not.' Roman felt the corner of his mouth tilt at her mocking. It had been a long time since a woman had been so obviously unimpressed by him. 'I have my own means of transportation for such occasions.'

'Let me guess—something small and powerful with tinted windows?'

'It is black.' His lips twisted with amusement at her jibe. 'But my yacht is hardly small. No tinted windows—I much prefer the light.'

Her gaze wandered, the smile fading from her lips as she looked away from him. 'A playboy's yacht...of course.'

'These things have not magically fallen into my lap, I assure you. I have worked hard for the lifestyle I enjoy.'

'Oh, I didn't mean...' She turned her face back towards him quickly. 'I envy you, that's all.'

He raised a brow, wondering not for the first time what on earth was going on inside her head. 'There is an entire fleet of vessels moored in the harbour with the royal crest on their hulls. You're telling me you couldn't just choose one at will?'

'I spent years learning how to sail at school. But I have yet to go on a single trip by myself,' she said, looking up and meeting his eyes for a long moment. 'It's strange...' she began, before shaking her head and turning her face away. 'I've spoken more frankly with you today—a complete stranger—than I have with anyone in a long time.'

Roman did not know how to respond to that statement. He swallowed hard, looking ahead to where a group of housemaids walked and chatted their way across the second-floor balconies. When he finally looked back the Princess had moved from beside him.

He stood up, looking around him for a sign of where she had gone, only to see a glimpse of pale yellow silk disappearing through the archway that led to the royal apartments.

He took a step forward, then caught himself.

She was where she belonged—surrounded by guards and staff.

It was time for him to get back to his own life.

The afternoon sun was hot on his neck when Roman finally walked out onto the deck of his yacht the next day. In his line of work he was no stranger to going to sleep as the sun rose, but his restless night had little to do with work. Being handcuffed in a room by himself had given him far too much time with his own thoughts. A dangerous pastime for a man with a past like his.

Nursing a strong black coffee, he slid on dark sunglasses and sank down into a hammock chair. They would set sail for the *isla* soon enough, and he would be glad to see the back of this kingdom and all its upper-class pomp.

He surveyed the busy harbour of Puerto Reina, Monteverre's main port. Tourists and locals peppered the busy marble promenade that fronted the harbour—the Queen's Balcony, he had been told it was called. A glittering golden crown insignia was emblazoned over every sign in the town, as though the people might somehow otherwise forget that it was the crown that held the power.

Never had he met a man more blinded by his own power than His Majesty, King Fabian. Khal had insisted on them meeting two nights previously, so that the three men could discuss the situation of the Princess's security—Khal was notoriously meticulous when it came to bodyguards and security measures.

It had been clear from the outset that Roman would be treated like the commoner he was, so he had made the choice to leave, rather than sit and be spoken down to. His tolerance levels only stretched so far. It seemed His Majesty still harboured some ill will, as made apparent by the gap of five hours between the time he had been informed of the incident at the palace and the time at which he'd authorised Roman's release.

Roman's fists clenched by his sides. He was no stranger to dealing with self-important asses—he'd made a career of protecting arrogant fools with more money than sense. But it was hard to stay professionally disengaged when one of the asses in question was your best friend. Khal had never treated him as 'lesser'—he knew better. But he had not so much as made a phone call to apologise for his oversight.

His friend knew, more than anyone, what time locked in a room could do to him.

Roman tilted his head up to the sun and closed his eyes. He was not in a locked room right now. He was on his own very expensive yacht, which would be out in open water just as soon as it was refuelled. He exhaled slowly, visualising the clear blue waters of Isla Arista, his own private haven.

Moments passed before his visualisation was interrupted by a loud car horn. He opened one eye and sighed as he saw a sleek black limousine edging its way through the crowds on the main street, flanked by four Monteverrian policemen on Vespas.

The Sheikh of Zayyar did not simply take a taxi, he supposed dryly as he reached forward to drain the last of his coffee and then tilted his head back to the sunshine. When he finally looked up again Khal was standing a foot away, his face a mask of cool fury.

'It was nice of you to finally come to my rescue, *bratik*.' Roman raised a brow from his perch on the deckchair, but made no move to stand and greet his oldest friend.

Khal's mouth twisted. 'I was under the impression that the untouchable Roman Lazarov never *needed* help.'

'And *I* was under the impression that our friendship came before brown-nosing the King of Monteverre.' Roman spoke quietly, venom in every word.

Right now, looking at Khal in his perfectly pressed white royal robes, a good old-fashioned punching match didn't sound like the worst way to start his day. Back on the streets of St

Petersburg it was the way most fights were resolved. Fighting had sometimes been the only way not to starve.

Roman scowled, realising the hunger in his gut was doing nothing to help his already agitated mood and the dark memories of his past threatening his control.

'I was not aware that you had been held in custody until this morning.'

Khal interrupted his thoughts, frowning with genuine concern.

Roman tipped his head back, propping one foot lazily up on the low table in front of him. People generally afforded the almighty Sheikh of Zayyar a certain level of ceremony and pomp. But not him. He usually went out of his way to take Khal down a peg whenever they were alone.

'Oh, just five hours in a windowless room with my hands cuffed behind my back—no big deal.'

'I find it hard to sympathise, considering you'd held my future wife hostage like a common criminal,' Khal said simply.

'An interesting choice of words, *Your Highness*,' Roman snarled, derision in every syllable.

A silence fell between them—not the comfortable kind that came from years of close friendship. This was a silence filled with tension and frustration.

A friendship like theirs had no clear rules, different as they were.

Khal came from a long line of royalty—had been educated and privileged and born with power in his blood. Whereas Roman had fought for everything he owned, clawing his way out of the gutter he had been abandoned in as a child. Over the years he had refined his harsh manners and learned how to act like a gentleman, but underneath he would always bear the marks of his past. The darkness had branded him—quite literally—and that was something his friend had no experience of.

Khal cleared his throat loudly. 'You know, in ten years I don't think you've changed one bit.'

Roman ignored the barely veiled insult, shrugging as he put one leg casually across the table. 'I have a lot more money.'

'And an even bigger ego.' Khal frowned.

'Need I remind you that I came here as a favour? I did not *have* to dirty my hands for you, Khal. No matter what debts I may owe you.'

'Is that the only reason you came? And here I was thinking you cared for my happiness.' Khal's mouth tightened. 'Four years is a long time to hold on to your guilt, Lazarov.'

Roman shook his head, standing to pace to the railing that edged the upper deck. He had enough painful memories affecting his concentration today—he didn't need more reminders of the long line of blackness he left in his wake.

'I came here because you needed help, *bratik*. Nothing more.'

For the first time Khal looked weary as he rubbed a hand across his clean-shaven face. He sat down in the deckchair Roman had vacated and stared up at the clear sky above them.

'This whole situation is rapidly getting away from me. My trip was supposed to be simple and straightforward, tying everything up. And now I stand to lose everything I have staked.'

Roman frowned at his friend's unusual display of weakness. 'It will be fine. I will apologise to the Princess and smooth things over for you.'

Khal looked at him, realisation dawning on his dark features. 'You don't know? The Princess has disappeared, Roman. Half the Palace Guard is out searching for her.'

Roman froze with surprise. 'Disappeared? I just spoke with her last night.'

'You *spoke* with her?' Khal's voice raised an octave. 'What on earth would possess you to speak with her after what you'd put her through?'

'She had me put through far worse, trust me.'

'So this is even more your fault than I had originally thought?'

'Khal, I had the tunnel blocked, extra guards assigned. How on earth could she have just walked out of there?'

Khal shook his head. 'Clearly she wanted to get away badly enough to risk her own safety. What did you say to her?'

'We barely spoke two words. Mainly she insulted me and then she walked away.'

Both men were silent for a long moment, facing off in the midday heat.

'The girl is reckless,' Roman said darkly. 'Are you sure that you want to marry someone so...unpredictable?'

'My kingdom needs it. So it will be done.' Khal smoothed down the front of his robes. 'I have been heavy-handed with my approach so far. I worry that perhaps I have scared her off completely.'

'How so?'

'I ordered a stricter security regime. I needed to make sure she was protected adequately before her name was linked with mine. In case...'

Roman saw the haunted look in his friend's eyes and immediately stopped. How had he not realised before now?

He moved towards him, placing a hand heavily on his shoulder. 'Khal... I understand why you felt the need to ensure her security...believe me. But there *is* such a thing as smothering with safety.'

'We both know the risks for any woman who is by my side,' Khal said, standing to his feet.

The moment of weakness had passed and he was once again the formidable and controlled Sheikh of Zayyar. But Roman could still sense the heaviness in the air, the unspoken worries that he knew plagued his friend and had likely tortured him for the past four years.

Nothing would bring back his friend's wife. Her sudden death had shifted something in the easy friendship that had once bonded them together, and nothing would erase the pain of knowing that he hadn't been there in Khal's time of need.

Roman cleared his throat. 'I will go and find the Princess,' he said gruffly.

'No. Definitely not.' Khal turned back to him, crossing his arms. 'Your presence would only aggravate the situation further.'

'If it was my actions that caused her to rethink the engagement, then let me be the one to apologise and bring her back.' Roman pushed his hands into the pockets of his trousers, feeling the weight of his own error settle somewhere in his gut. 'This is *my* fault.'

'Yes. It is.' Khal raised one brow. 'And I hate not knowing if I can trust you to fix it.'

Roman's jaw clenched. Khal was like a brother to him—his *bratik*. The closest thing to a family member he had ever chosen for himself.

'You have trusted me with your life in the past. Are you telling me you don't think I'm capable of retrieving one errant little princess?'

'This is important to me, Roman.'

'I will bring her back. You have my word,' Roman said, meaning every syllable.

He would find the little siren and bring her back to her royal duty if it was the last thing he did.

This had been a terrible plan.

Olivia slumped down in her seat, tucking an errant strand of bright red hair back into her dark, wide floppy-brimmed hat. Because of the dark sunglasses she wore, and the rather plain white shift dress, thankfully so far nobody had looked at her twice.

Olivia sighed. Had she really been so naïve as to think that she could just check in to the next commercial flight without question? The realisation of what she had almost done suddenly paralysed her with fear. She had almost broken the law, for goodness' sake.

She was hyper aware of her surroundings, noticing every little movement of the people in the departures hall. Every time one of the airport security guards looked at her she unconsciously held her breath, waiting for the moment when they would realise who she was and unceremoniously haul her back to the palace. And to her father.

She didn't even know exactly what she was trying to achieve here. Honestly, had she really been so immature as to think that her father would take her more seriously just because she had attempted to run away from her engagement? In reality this little stunt had done nothing but ensure that she would have even less freedom than before.

She closed her eyes, leaning her head back against the seat and wishing that she had never come up with this stupid plan. She felt the air shift to her right, a gentle breeze bringing with it an eerily familiar scent of sandalwood and pine.

'A risky choice, hiding in plain sight,' a deeply accented male voice drawled from beside her, bringing memories of strong, muscular arms and eyes like gunmetal.

Roman Lazarov lowered himself casually into the seat beside her and lazily propped one ankle on the opposite knee.

'You really didn't think this through.'

From this angle, all she could see were powerful thighs encased in designer trousers and a pair of expensive leather shoes. She exhaled slowly, realising from the sound of his voice that he must have his face turned towards her. Watching to gauge her reaction.

He was probably congratulating himself on finding her so easily, the brute.

He cleared his throat loudly, waiting for her response.

Olivia pursed her lips and kept her eyes focused straight ahead. She wondered if, perhaps if she waited long enough, he would simply disappear into thin air.

'You have ten seconds to give up your silent act before I announce your presence to this entire airport.' He spoke low, his voice a barely contained growl.

She stiffened. 'You're bluffing.'

220 ONE NIGHT WITH THE FORBIDDEN PRINCESS

'*Look at me.*'

She turned her head at his demand, hardly realising she had obeyed until it was done. His eyes were focused on her, steel-grey and glowing, just as she remembered them. His lips, so full and perfectly moulded, seemed to quirk a little at the sides as his eyes narrowed. It took a moment for her to realise he was silently laughing at her.

'I *was* bluffing.' He smiled in triumph, showing a row of perfectly aligned white teeth.

His smile was aggressively beautiful, just like the rest of him, she thought, with more than a little frustration. She noticed the rather delicious hint of dark stubble that lined his jaw. It somehow made him appear rugged and unrefined, even in his finely tailored clothing. She felt her throat go dry and silently cursed herself.

'If you're wondering how I found you, I simply followed the enormous trail of breadcrumbs you left in your wake, Printsessa.'

'Don't call me that here,' Olivia murmured. The hum of noise in the airport was loud enough, but she didn't want to draw any more attention than was needed.

He raised one brow, but nodded.

Olivia took a sharp breath, a slight tremor audible in her throat. 'If I asked you to go, and pretend you'd never found me...'

'That will never happen.' He half smiled as he spoke the words, a small indentation appearing just left of his lips.

The man had dimples, she thought wildly. That was hardly fair, was it?

Before she could react, he had reached down and grabbed the small document she had been holding tightly in her hands. As she watched, he opened it, tilting his head to one side as he read.

After a long moment he looked up, meeting her eyes with disbelief. 'You planned to use this?'

'Initially, yes. But then I thought better of it.'

'A wise choice, considering identity fraud is a very serious crime. Even for princesses.'

Olivia remained silent, staring down at the red mark on her fingers from where she had clutched the maid's passport so hard it had almost cut off her circulation.

It had been a careless plan from the start, one borne of desperation and anger. If she had got caught... The thought tightened her throat. Fraud simply wasn't something that was in her nature, luckily. Meaning that she had come no closer than eight feet from the check-in desk before she had turned on her heel and run. Leaving her sitting on this damned chair for the past two hours, frantically wondering where to go next.

Olivia shook off the ridiculous self-pity and forced herself to get a handle on her emotions. She was emotionally and physically exhausted. Any sleep she had got last night had been plagued by dreams of being trapped in tunnels with no way out, and a man's voice calling to her from the darkness. When she had finally got up this morning it had been with the grim intent of getting as far away from Monteverre as possible, and yet here she was, less than an hour's distance from the palace and already captured.

The entire plan had been stupid and impulsive from the start. Honestly, where had she really thought she would go once she'd walked out of the palace gates? She didn't even have the right to hold her own passport, for goodness' sake. Everything in her life was planned and controlled by others. She didn't even have enough freedom to run away properly.

Roman was still looking at her intently. She could feel the heat of his gaze on the side of her face, almost as though he burned her simply by being near. He made her feel as though she were on show and he was the only person in the audience. The intensity of his presence was something she simultaneously wanted to bask in and run far away from.

'I'm not running from my title.' She spoke solemnly, knowing he could never understand.

'Then what are you running from?' His voice was low and serious, and his gaze still pinned on hers with silvery intensity.

Olivia took a deep breath, knowing this conversation had to end. He was not on her side, no matter how sympathetic he pretended to be.

'It's not safe for you to be wandering alone.' His voice took on a steely edge. 'I feel responsible for your decision to leave the palace. Perhaps you felt that yesterday reflected badly on your future husband—'

Again the 'future husband' talk. Olivia stood up, feeling her blood pressure rise with sheer frustration.

Roman's hand took hold of hers, pulling her back down to a sitting position. His voice was low, somewhere near her right ear, as he spoke in chilling warning, 'Don't make any more impulsive moves, Printsessa. I might seem gentle, but I can assure you if you run from me again I might not be quite so civilised in hauling you back where you belong.'

Her heart hammered hard in her chest, and the skin along her neck and shoulders tingled and prickled with the effects of his barely veiled threat.

'My car is parked at the door. We can do this the easy way or the hard way.'

Olivia briefly considered her options—or lack thereof. Was she really prepared to risk what might happen if she resisted? The memory of his powerful arms encircling her in her dressing room sprang to her mind. For a moment she sat completely still, wondering if the frisson of electricity that coursed through her veins was one of trepidation or one of something infinitely more dangerous.

She stood, spine straight, and began walking towards the entrance. He followed, as she'd expected, his muscular frame falling into step by her side. His hand cupped her elbow, steering her out into the daylight towards a gleaming white luxury model car with privacy-tinted windows. Not the kind of car she would have expected from a new money playboy with a taste for danger.

Her silent captor slid into the driver's seat across from her, his warm, masculine scent filling the small space. He didn't look at her as he manoeuvred the car out of the airport and through the maze of roads that led to the motorway.

She covertly glanced at him from behind the safety of her sunglasses. Strong, masculine hands handled the wheel with expert ease. She noticed the top two buttons of his black shirt lay open and his sleeves had been rolled up along forearms that practically bulged with muscle. Strange black markings encircled his skin just above his shirt cuff—tribal, perhaps, but she couldn't see more than the edge.

Of *course* he had a tattoo, she thought, biting her lip as she wondered just how many he might have. And where they might be...

'You are staring. Something you'd like to say?'

His low, accented voice jolted her and she averted her eyes, looking straight ahead, curling her fingers together in her lap. 'I was simply wondering if you will be delivering me to my father or to the Sheikh.'

'So dramatic.' He sighed. 'You make it sound like you are a shipment of goods.'

'I might as well be,' she muttered under her breath. 'It's hard not to feel like a piece of livestock. Being traded from one barbarian to another.'

His hands seemed to tighten on the wheel. 'I'd prefer if you didn't use your pity party to insult my friend in that fashion. "Barbarian" is not a term he would take lightly.'

'Mr Lazarov, at this point I can't say that I particularly care.'

'I suggest that you start caring,' Roman gritted, moving the car off the motorway and towards the mountain range that separated them from the Grand Palace.

Twenty minutes in this pampered princess's company and

he was tempted to stop the car and make her walk the rest of the way.

She was a puzzle, this fiery redhead. A spoilt, impulsive, dangerous puzzle, all wrapped up in one very tempting package. He would not feel guilty for being attracted to Khal's fiancée. A man would have to be blind not to see the raw sensual appeal in Olivia Sandoval. But, unlike her, he had his impulses under control. It was not hard to brush off attraction when he could tell that all that lay beneath her flawless skin and designer curves was a spoilt, bored little royal on the hunt for a thrill.

'Your father has asked that you be returned to the palace as soon as possible,' Roman said, noticing how her body seemed to tense at the mention of the King. 'But I feel that you and your fiancé need to speak first.'

'He is *not* my fiancé,' Olivia gritted.

'Oh, so that's what is going on here. You decided to break the engagement by running away. How very mature.'

Roman felt his jaw tighten with anger for his friend, for the future of two nations that was hanging in the balance all because of one woman.

'No, *I* haven't decided anything. That's the point!'

Roman heard the slight tremor in her voice and turned briefly to see she had her head in her hands. 'Look, if this is bridal jitters, I'm sure there's plenty of time before the wedding—'

Her head snapped up and she pinned him with the most ferocious icy blue-green gaze. 'Do you honestly think I would risk my reputation, my safety, over a little case of *bridal jitters*?'

'I only met you yesterday.' He shrugged.

It was true—he didn't know very much about her except that she had a deep-rooted mistrust of men and a mean left hook.

'This isn't something to speak about with a stranger.'

'At least you're listening...somewhat.' She sighed. 'Even if you think the worst of me.'

He said nothing, concentrating on the road as they edged around the mountain face. He could have taken the new, modern tunnel that bisected the mountain entirely. But this was a new country for him and he enjoyed the scenic routes.

Olivia lay her head back on the seat, her voice low and utterly miserable. 'How can a woman suddenly have a fiancé when she hasn't heard or even decided to accept a marriage proposal?'

'You mean… Khal didn't formally propose? This is what's upset you?'

'No. He did *not* formally propose,' she said, mocking laughter in her voice. 'I only met the Sheikh yesterday for the first time—at the races. Five minutes after my father informed me that I would be marrying him.'

CHAPTER FOUR

ROMAN FELT HIS brain stumble over her words. 'That is impossible.'

'Welcome to my life.' A deep sigh left her chest. 'Apparently Monteverre has reverted to the Middle Ages.'

'The Sheikh assured me that all the arrangements have been made. That he is simply here to make the formal announcement of your intended marriage.'

'The only arrangement that has been made is a business one. Evidently the bride was not important enough to be let in on the plans.'

She laughed once—a low, hollow sound that made Roman's gut clench.

'I'm twenty-six years old and suddenly I'm expected to tie myself to a stranger for the rest of my life.'

A tense silence fell between them and Roman took a moment to process this new information. Khal had not been honest with him. And if there was one thing that Roman Lazarov despised it was being taken for a fool. Khal had said the Princess was his future bride, leaving him with the assumption that the woman had consented to the marriage. Now, knowing that she hadn't…

Call him old-fashioned, but he believed a woman had a right to her own freedom, her own mind. Growing up on the streets, he had seen first-hand just what happened when men decided simply to assume a woman's consent.

The Princess had called Khal a barbarian, but Roman knew that was the furthest thing from the truth. He wanted to believe that this was all a misunderstanding—that Khal had been misled by the King into believing his intended bride was a willing participant in all this. However...he knew the single-minded ruthlessness that possessed the Sheikh whenever his nation's future lay in the balance.

He had said himself that this marriage was vital to Zayyar's future. Perhaps it was vital enough to overlook a reluctant bride?

They rounded a particularly sharp bend and the road began to descend towards the lush green valley that spread out below. This country had its own particular charm—there was no denying it, he thought as he took in the glittering sea in the distance.

A small lay-by had been built into the outer curve of the road—a safe place for people to stop and take photographs while stretching their legs. Making a snap decision, Roman slowed down, manoeuvring the car into a vacant spot in the deserted lay-by and bringing them to a stop.

'What are you doing?' Olivia's brows furrowed.

'I need a moment,' he said, taking the keys with him as he stood away from the car, just in case his passenger had any ideas. The lay-by was deserted, and the road far too steep for her to get anywhere on foot.

He braced his hands on the glittering granite wall and took a moment to inhale the fresh mountain air deeply. There was something about the sight of completely unspoiled nature that deeply affected him. He had spent far too much of his youth surrounded by concrete buildings and garbage-scented air.

The sea beckoned to him in the distance. His yacht was ready to leave the moment he returned—ready to sail out into the open sea, where he would be free of this troubled royal family and their tangled web.

All he had to do was drop her off at the palace and he was home free.

Why he was hesitating all of a sudden, he did not know, but something was stopping him from completing his directive without questioning it further. He heard the car's passenger door close gently and turned to see the Princess come to a stop at the wall beside him.

'This is my favourite view in all of Monteverre,' she said. There was not a hint of sadness in her voice. It was just fact, stated without emotion.

He realised that since the moment he had held her captive in the tunnel he had not seen her resort to tears once. No one, including him, would have judged her for breaking down in the face of an unknown captor. She had a backbone of steel, and yet she had not been able to follow through with her plan to use the fraudulent passport. She clearly drew the line at breaking the law, and could not blur her own moral guidelines even in apparent desperation.

'What exactly were you hoping to achieve by running?' he asked, directing his question to the side of her face as she continued to stare out at the distance.

'I don't know.' She nipped lightly at her bottom lip. 'I just needed the chance to come to a decision myself. Some time to weigh up my options. I have no idea what life is like away from my guards and my responsibilities, and yet here I am, expected to blindly trade one set of palace walls for another.'

He couldn't disagree with her logic.

'When I agreed to perform the security operation yesterday, I presumed that your marriage had already been arranged.' He ran a hand across his jaw, the memory of his handling of her raw and uncomfortable. 'Had I known the situation was not what it seemed I would not have agreed to it.'

She shrugged, defeat evident in the downward slope of her slim shoulders.

'I will take you to Khal. You can address your concerns to him directly. That is generally how adults resolve such situations.'

Olivia stared at him with disbelief. 'I am not a child. Despite being treated like one time and time again.' She braced her two hands on the wall, her perfectly manicured nails in stark contrast against the stone. 'I have no interest in pleading my case to a man I do not know. Besides, do you think I would have done this if I wasn't already completely sure that my voice will hold no weight in this situation?'

Roman pinched the bridge of his nose, a low growl forming in his chest. 'Damn it, I do not have time for this. I could have been halfway across the Mediterranean by now.'

She turned to him, one hand on her hip. 'I'm sorry that our political situation is such an inconvenience to your playboy lifestyle, Mr Lazarov.'

She took a step away, her shoulders squared with frustration, before she turned back to face him.

'You know what? I'm tired of this too. You may as well just take me to the Sheikh right now, so that I can reject his proposal in person. If his choice in friends is anything to go by, I'm sure I won't be missing out on too much.'

'You presume I *care* how you pampered royals resolve your issues?'

'You wouldn't be here if you didn't.'

'The only reason I am here is because you chose to be a coward rather than face the situation head-on.'

Hurt flashed in her eyes and he suddenly felt like the world's biggest heel.

'I don't know what to do,' she said honestly, her eyes meeting his with sudden vulnerability. 'I know that marrying the Sheikh is the right choice for my people. Despite what you might think, I *do* care about this kingdom—very much. If I didn't, I would have already said no.'

The silence that fell between them was thick and tension-filled, although the air was cooling down now, as the sun dropped lower in the sky and evening fell across the mountain.

She had accused him of tightening her cage yesterday, and today it couldn't be more true. The idea of pretending he hadn't found her in the first place was tempting…but no matter how much it would simplify his life he knew that a woman like her wasn't safe alone in the world. He knew more than anyone that there were far too many opportunistic criminals out there, just waiting for a chance at a high-class victim. Keeping rich people safe was his business, after all.

'I have never been out in public away from the Palace Guard for this length of time. It's nice…not being surrounded by an entourage.'

'You want a taste of freedom,' he said plainly, and the sudden realisation was like clouds parting to reveal blue sky after a storm.

'Isn't that what all runaways want?' She smiled sadly. 'But we both know how that has worked out for me so far.'

'I can't just let you walk away from me, Princess. You know that.'

He pondered the situation, despising his own need to problem-solve. Khal needed this marriage to go ahead. That was his directive here. There was no point returning the Princess only for her to reject the marriage completely. But maybe he could offer a solution that would benefit everyone involved.

Everyone except him, that was.

He frowned, hardly believing he was even entertaining the idea, but words escaped his mouth and he knew he had to trust his instinct. 'What if I could offer you a temporary freedom of sorts?' he asked slowly, watching as her face tipped up and her eyes regarded him with suspicion.

'I would ask what exactly you mean by "temporary".'

'I can offer you some time alone in which you can come to a decision about your marriage.'

'Or lack thereof?'

'Exactly.'

'How would you do that?' she asked. 'And, more importantly, *why* would you?'

'Don't worry about how—just trust that I am a man of my word. If I say you will be undisturbed then I mean it. But you would have your side of the bargain to hold up.'

'I'm listening.'

'All I ask is that you take time to consider all aspects of the union. I believe that you would be making a mistake in walking away from this engagement. Khal is a great man,' he said truthfully.

He was careful not to mention the small fact that she was a flight risk who would likely end up in real trouble if the situation wasn't contained. This was containment at its most extreme. He had somehow gone from holding a princess hostage to volunteering to take one on as his guest.

He waited while she visibly weighed up her options before him, worrying at her lower lip with her teeth. Her mouth was a dusky pink colour, he noticed. No lipstick or gloss, just pure silky rose flesh. She flashed him a glance and he quickly averted his gaze, looking back out at the view.

In that moment he instantly regretted his offer to salvage his friend's union. He had the sudden uncomfortable thought that perhaps he had just voluntarily offered to step out onto a tightrope with everything hanging in the balance.

But even as he began to regret his offer she nodded her head once, murmuring her acceptance.

And just like that the deal was done.

He had never gone back on a deal in the past, and he wouldn't be starting now. Self-doubt held no place in his life. He trusted his own self-control, his own loyalty to those he cared for. And so he walked her back to the car and dutifully avoided looking down at the swell of her curves as she sashayed in front of him.

'I still don't understand why you are doing this for me.' She looked up at him through long russet lashes, and he saw a smattering of freckles appearing high on her cheeks in the evening sun.

'Consider it a wedding gift,' he gritted, shutting the door with finality and steeling himself for the drive ahead.

Olivia stepped out on the deserted deck of the yacht and watched as they drew nearer and nearer to land. The evening was fast fading to pink as dusk approached. She wondered if maybe she should be worried that she had no idea where Roman was taking her, but really the destination itself didn't matter. So long as it was far enough away from the palace for her to be able to breathe again.

With every mile that had passed since they'd set sail from Puerto Reina harbour she had felt the unbearable tension begin to ease and a sense of sharp relief take its place. But her new-found sense of freedom still held an unpleasant tinge of guilt around the edges. As if a dark cloud was hovering somewhere in her peripheral vision, just waiting to spill over and wreak havoc on her fleeting sense of calm.

She was doing the right thing, wasn't she? Taking time away from the royal bubble in a controlled manner was the mature course of action. Despite what others might think, she knew she had a very important decision to make. This wasn't so simple as making the best choice for herself—putting the rest of her life first and repercussions be damned. She had been raised always to hold Monteverre in greater esteem than herself. To value the people more than she did her own family. But what happened when her own family didn't seem to value her happiness at all?

Her eyes drifted across the deck to where her slim black handbag sat atop a sun lounger. Inside that bag she held all the information she had found about the foundation that her grandmother had left in her name. Information on all of the amazing work that it had carried out since her passing ten years ago.

She wasn't quite ready to share what she had uncovered with anyone just yet.

At the moment, the bottom line was clear. Her father had said that she had no alternative but to marry the Sheikh and she had agreed with him, Going against a union arranged by the King now would have very real, very severe ramifications. Either way, her life was about to change drastically.

It was no big deal, really, she thought with a slightly panicked intake of breath. Sign her life away to a loveless marriage in order to save her kingdom or have her title stripped away for ever. No big deal at all.

She closed her eyes, breathing in the cool sea air and willing her mind to slow down. She had spent two days going around and around in circles already, and the effect made her temples feel fit to burst. Was it any wonder she had made such a rash decision to run away from it all?

She exhaled slowly, opening her eyes to find that the yacht was now sailing alongside the coast of the seemingly deserted island they had been approaching. The place looked completely wild—like something from a movie. But as they rounded an outcrop of rocks she was suddenly looking at a crescent-shaped coastline formed out of ragged black rocks and golden sand. A tall white lighthouse stood on the far coast in the distance, atop a lush green cliff. And a small marina was situated at the furthest end of the bay, in the shade of the cliffs.

She gradually felt the yacht lose speed until it began the process of mooring at the end of the long white floating dock.

Roman was still nowhere to be seen, she thought as she scanned what she could see of the upper decks. The yacht was huge, and he had disappeared almost immediately after depositing her in one of the lower deck living rooms.

She was still not quite sure why he had decided to give her this time in the first place. She doubted he felt pity for her, considering his disdain for 'pampered royals', as he had so delicately labelled her. But he had seemed genuinely surprised to hear that the marriage situation was not all that it seemed.

She was not naïve enough to believe that he was on her side, but she hoped that he understood her motivations a little more at least.

Still, she would do well to remember where his loyalties lay. He was determined to see her accept Sheikh Khal's proposal—there was no doubt in her mind about that. She imagined that Roman Lazarov was not the type of man to give up on something without putting up a good fight first.

Surprisingly, the thought of debating her future with him didn't fill her with the same dread that she had felt in her father's presence the day before. She couldn't quite explain it… He spoke to her like a person, not as someone lesser. Or, worse, as a princess. He wasn't afraid to look into her eyes as he spoke, unlike most others who met her.

He had listened to her today. She would never let him know how much that had meant to her. He was not a friend—she knew that. But maybe he didn't have to be her enemy.

As though conjured by her thoughts, Roman suddenly emerged from a door to her right, speaking to someone on the phone in a deep, throaty language she presumed to be his native Russian. He had made no move to interact with her in the hours since they had set sail from Monteverre.

He looked tired, she noticed, and yet his dark shirt and trousers barely held a single crease. She, on the other hand, was rumpled and in dire need of a shower and a full night of sleep. She smoothed the front of her dress self-consciously and turned herself to face him, shoulders held high.

He ended the call with one click and took a moment to tilt his face up to the view of the vibrant overgrown landscape around them. For a moment the harsh lines around his mouth relaxed and his eyes seemed to glow silver in the evening light. She realised with surprise that the look on his face was something very close to contentment. She'd not yet seen him with anything but hostility in his features, and she had to admit the man had very inviting lips when he wasn't smirking or insulting her.

'We still have a short drive from here,' he said, taking a quick look at his watch and motioning for the single cabin porter to take care of their luggage. 'I hope you don't get motion sickness.'

Before she could question that statement, he gestured for her to follow him down the steps onto the whitewashed boards of the marina. She practically had to run to catch up with him.

'Where are we?' she asked, her short legs struggling to keep up with his long strides.

'My very own island paradise,' he said simply, not bothering to slow down until they'd reached a dirt road at the end of the dock. Roman stopped beside a small, open-sided white Jeep and turned to face her, one hand braced lazily on the mud-spattered door frame as he held it open for her.

'Jump in, Princess.' His lips quirked.

That was a challenge if ever she'd heard one. He likely expected her to throw a fit of pique, demanding transportation that better befitted her station.

She smiled sweetly, holding up her white skirt to protect it from the worst of the dirt, and hoisted herself up into the cab without complaint. Within minutes the engine was roaring loudly and a cloud of dust flew around them as they began a steady climb up the cliffs.

'When you said you could guarantee privacy, I didn't realise you meant to maroon me on a desert island.' She forced an easy tone, trying to hide the breathlessness from her voice.

He didn't immediately respond, so she filled the silence by commenting on the views of the coast below as they drove higher and higher, weaving in and out of the treeline. As they bounced over a particularly rough stretch of terrain her shoulder was jammed hard against the window and she let out a little squeak of alarm.

She turned to see that he was smirking once more. She fought the sudden, irrational urge to punch him in the bicep.

'Judging by the transportation, am I to expect a rustic mud hut for my stay?' She gripped her seatbelt with all her might, her resolve slipping fast.

'I'm not here to act as your tour guide.' He shrugged, uninterested, his jaw tightening as he shifted gears and the terrain seemed to level out. 'I'll be sure to have your tent inspected for cockroaches, at least.'

She had never actually slept in a tent. It would be a drastic change from her usual surroundings, but she rather thought she might enjoy the novelty.

Just as she turned to say this to him she caught sight of something sparkling in the distance. The land began to slope downwards towards the lower terrain again, revealing a spectacular side view of a very large, very sleek, modern villa.

As they descended a short driveway Olivia felt her breath catch at the view that spread out before them. She could see the entire island from this vantage point. The evening sky was tinged pink and orange as the sun sank lower and lower towards the jade-green sea.

'Wow...' she breathed, her awestruck brain not quite able to form anything more eloquent after the stunning visual onslaught.

A small white-haired man appeared at the door as they stepped out of the car. He looked immediately to Roman with raised brows.

'You did not mention a guest, sir,' he said, his smile forced and pointed.

'Jorge, how many times do I have to tell you not to call me sir just because we are in company?' Roman grunted.

'It's more professional.' Jorge shrugged, trying and failing to keep his voice low.

'You are *far* from professional.' Roman smirked, clapping the other man on the shoulder with friendly familiarity. 'Ridiculously capable and efficient? Of course. But not professional in the least. That's why I hired you.'

The two men looked back to see Olivia watching the odd exchange with interest.

'Olivia, this is my right-hand man, Jorge. He travels with me to my homes as housekeeper and chef.'

Roman seemed suddenly preoccupied as he took out his phone and clicked a few buttons.

'Show her around and set her up in the white guest room.'

Olivia frowned as he began to walk away without another word. 'You mean you won't be giving me the grand tour yourself?' she called, half joking but actually quite shocked at his blatant disregard.

A harsh laugh escaped his lips as he continued to power across the hallway, away from her. 'I am not in the hospitality business. I thought you would have noticed that by now.'

And with that he disappeared through a doorway at the end of the hall, leaving her alone with his very apologetic housekeeper.

Roman ended the call with a double-click and laid his phone down hard on the marble patio table. In almost ten years of friendship he had never heard his friend curse.

Khal had been stunned at the revelation that the Princess was being strong-armed into their union by her father. But, ever practical, he had asked if there was a chance she might go ahead with it. Roman had answered truthfully—saying that he believed the Princess was just seeking a break from the heightened security measures.

'Give her time,' he had said. 'I will ensure she returns to accept your proposal.'

Khal trusted him to guard his future bride. There wasn't another person on this earth that Roman would be doing this for. He was not a personal bodyguard. He specialised in hard security. Elite risk assessments, intruder prevention, high-tech electronic systems and such. He did not have the refined people skills that were needed to work one-on-one in this kind of setting.

And yet here he was, babysitting a runaway princess on the island that he made a point to keep free of unwelcome guests.

If he had ever been a drinker now would be an excellent time for copious amounts of alcohol in which to drown his dark mood. He leaned heavily against the glass rail that lined the balcony of his master suite, looking out at the horizon where the sun had begun to dip into the Mediterranean Sea.

A sudden splash from below caught his attention and he looked down to see a creamy silhouette cutting easily across the bottom of the pool.

She had started her holiday straight away, it seemed, he thought darkly as his fist tightened on the rail.

Her head and bare shoulders broke the surface of the water as she reached the infinity ledge. Her red hair was dark and heavy on her shoulders; she hadn't bothered to tie it up. She leaned against the side of the pool, pale shoulders glistening with moisture above a bright red one-piece bathing suit. He could see the outline of long, slim legs under the water.

Roman felt the darkness inside him roar to life.

He wanted her.

He growled to himself, turning away from the tantalising view with a jaw that suddenly felt like iron. He stalked across his suite into the large white and chrome bathroom. The large floor-to-ceiling mirror showed his frustration in high definition. His pupils were dark, his nostrils flared with anger as he began unbuttoning his shirt.

It had been a while since he had been with anyone—that was all this was. His body was reacting to its recent deprivation in the most primal way possible. He had never been good at denying himself something he wanted with this kind of intensity.

A more emotionally charged person might say it had something to do with a childhood full of being denied, he thought darkly. *He* knew better. It was simply a part of him—a part of how he was put together. It was what drove him to the heights of success, always wanting more.

All he knew was that his wealth had brought along with it the delicious ability to gratify his every whim instantly. Whether it was a new car or a beautiful woman, he always got what he wanted with minimal effort.

But not her.

She was not his to think about, to look at, to covet.

He was long past his days as a thief, he thought dryly as he divested himself of the rest of his clothing and stepped under the white-hot spray of the shower, feeling the heat seep into his taut shoulder muscles and down his back.

Another man might have opted for a cold spray, but he had spent too much of his life in the cold. He had the best hot shower that money could buy and damn it, he would use it. Even if it only spurred on the heat inside him.

He was unsure whether he was angry with his friend for trusting him so blindly or angry that he did not fully trust himself. He was a sophisticated man, well capable of resisting flimsy attractions. And yet he felt a need to keep some distance between himself and the fiery-haired Olivia, with her sharp wit and unpredictable nature.

He had built his fortune on trusting his own instincts, and everything about Olivia Sandoval signalled danger.

CHAPTER FIVE

AS WAS USUAL when he stayed on Isla Arista, Roman had instructed Jorge to prepare an evening meal to be served on the terrace. The scent of aromatic rosemary chicken filled his nostrils as he stepped outside and his stomach growled in anticipation.

Olivia already sat at the table, waiting for him. He was surprised to see she had not changed after her swim; instead she was wrapped in an oversized white terrycloth robe from the pool cabana. One bare foot peeked out from where it was tucked under her. His stomach tightened at the sight of a single red-painted toenail.

'I see you are taking your holiday quite literally,' he said, taking the seat opposite her at the long marble table.

She looked down at his crisp white shirt and uncertainty flickered across her features, followed closely by embarrassment. 'Your housekeeper said it was just a quick meal. I wasn't aware that we would eat together,' she said, standing to her feet.

'Sit down,' he said and sighed.

But she vehemently shook her head, promising to be just a few minutes as she hurried away through the terrace doors at lightning speed. He fought the urge to laugh. How ironic that out of both of them it was the member of royalty who felt unfit for polite company.

True to her word, she returned less than ten minutes later. He was relieved to see that she hadn't opted for another dress, and amused that once again she wore white. The simple white linen trousers hugged her curves just as sinfully as the dress had, but thankfully she had chosen a rather sober white button-down blouse that covered her up almost to her chin.

Still, her slim shoulders were completely bare, showing off her perfect alabaster skin. He consciously lowered his gaze, to focus on filling their water glasses.

He made no move to speak. He was tired and hungry and in no mood to make her feel at ease. In fact it was better that she wasn't completely comfortable. That would make two of them.

Ever the efficient host, Jorge soon had the table filled with delicious freshly cooked dishes. Roman loaded his plate with tender chicken, garlic-roasted baby potatoes and seasonal grilled vegetables. No matter where they were in the world—New York, Moscow or this tiny remote island—his housekeeper always managed to find the freshest ingredients. He really should give him another raise...

Roman ate as he always did—until he was completely satisfied. Which usually meant two servings, at least, and then washing his meal down with a single glass of wine from his favourite regional *cantina*.

'Where on earth do you put all that food?'

Roman looked up to see Olivia watching him with open fascination, her fork still toying with the same handful of potatoes she had spooned onto her plate ten minutes previously.

'In my stomach,' he said, keeping his tone neutral. 'You had better follow suit or risk offending the chef.'

'We are not *all* graced with fast metabolisms.' She smiled tightly, putting down her fork and dabbing the corners of her mouth delicately.

'I exercise hard so that I can eat well. Good food is there to be enjoyed.' He fought annoyance as she sat back, clearly done with her food.

'The meal was wonderful—thank you.'

'If you say so, Printsessa,' he said, with just a hint of irony, considering she had barely eaten more than a child's portion. At least she didn't seem to be downing the wine to compensate for her self-imposed starvation.

'Why do you call me that?' she asked. 'I presume it's Russian? Printsessa?'

'My apologies. Do you harbour a preference for the term your subjects use? Your Highness, perhaps?'

She frowned. 'Do you enjoy mocking people for no reason?'

'I enjoy nothing of this situation, Olivia.' He exaggerated the syllables of her name with deliberate slowness and watched with satisfaction as she visibly swallowed.

'I don't understand,' she said, sitting forward, a frown forming between perfectly shaped russet brows. '*You* are the one who offered to bring me here, remember? Nobody forced you to do that. We are practically strangers, and yet you have been nothing but rude and downright hostile since the moment we met.'

'I offered to bring you here so that you would stop running away like a teenager,' he gritted. 'This is not a holiday. And I am not here to entertain a pampered royal seeking one last thrill ride before marriage.'

Her blue-green eyes narrowed with some of the fire he remembered from her dressing room the day before. 'You have made a lot of assumptions about my character in the past twenty-four hours.'

'Like it or not, right now you are in *my* charge. If I am making assumptions, it's because I can.'

'You think you know who I am? Please—enlighten me.' She sat back, crossing one slim leg over the other.

Roman watched the movement, his pulse quickening slightly as his eyes followed the curve of her thigh down to the slim silver-heeled sandals on her feet. 'I do not pretend to know who you are—nothing quite so philosophical.'

He leaned back in his chair, stretching one arm behind his neck. She followed the movement, eyelashes lowered.

'I know your type well enough,' Roman said darkly, and his mind surprised him by conjuring up an image of a familiar face. A pair of blue eyes that had haunted him for almost two decades.

His night of imprisonment must have affected him worse than he thought. The cold sweat from being handcuffed still seemed to coat his skin like dirt, even after the hot shower and plentiful meal.

Thoughts of his past were not a common occurrence these days. Thoughts of Sofiya even less common.

He cleared his throat, irritated at himself and his momentary lapse in keeping his own demons at bay. 'You are young, beautiful and privileged, frustrated with the strict rules designed to protect you. So you go out in search of adventure. A little danger to shake up the monotony.'

'So I'm just another spoilt brat looking for a bit of fun? Is that it?'

Roman shrugged noncommittally, draining the last of his wine. 'You are telling me this *isn't* about rebellion?' he asked, knowing he had hit a nerve when her eyes darted away from his to look out at the inky darkness of the sea in the distance.

'You know, insulting me and my motivation is hardly going to send me running back to accept your friend's proposal.'

'The only reason you feel insulted is because you are likely used to always hearing what you want to hear.'

Olivia sighed, leaning her head back for a moment and pinching the bridge of her nose. 'I am simply taking a brief reprieve before making one of the most important decisions of my life. No big deal, really.'

'I hate to tell you, but that's just a fancy way of saying you're running away.' He couldn't help but smirk.

'So you have me all figured out, then?' She crossed her arms over her chest, meeting his eyes head-on. 'It must be nice, being so untouchable and faultless.'

Roman shrugged. 'It is not my fault that you dislike being told the truth.'

'What I *dislike*, Mr Lazarov, is that you find it so easy to shove all my class into one pile, simply because we were born with money.' She exhaled heavily. 'In my opinion, that says far more about you than it does me.'

'Is that so?'

'Yes, *it is*. I may have been born into wealth, but that does not automatically take away the fact that I am human.' She stood up, pacing to the stone ledge of the terrace before turning back to him. 'You know nothing of my life—just as I know nothing of yours.'

Roman watched as she looked out at the distant black waves for a moment, with that same faraway look in her eyes that he had seen the night before. He almost felt guilty for goading her.

He cleared his throat loudly. 'We are getting off-track here. This is about repairing your trust in Sheikh Khal.' He sat a little straighter and laid one leg over his knee. 'Not that it will pose much difficulty. Khal is a good man.'

'I appreciate the vote of confidence,' she said, her voice rasping slightly. 'But I believe the point of this time away is for me to come to a decision alone.'

'No one knows him better than I do. Allow me to put your mind at ease.'

'You are not my friend. And I would do well to remember that. I am taking advantage of some time to clear my head—nothing more. I won't speak of this marriage business with you again.'

Roman raised a brow in question, getting to his feet and walking to stand beside her. '"Business..." An interesting word choice.'

She shrugged one slim shoulder, still looking away from him. 'It's the reality.'

'It is a very complex arrangement, from what I know—it's not just about *you*.'

* * *

It was as though he were reading straight from a script her father had written. The sudden reminder of her dilemma settled painfully like a dead weight in between Olivia's shoulders. She was so tense she could scream. She had barely slept in the past twenty-four hours, and that coupled with being in this man's presence made every nerve in her body feel completely on edge.

She felt her throat tighten. 'I may be more sheltered than your average twenty-six-year-old woman, but I know what kind of situation I am in.' She cleared her throat, steeling herself. She would *not* show weakness. 'It's *never* been about me—that's the point.'

'Are you telling me you feel you truly have no choice in the matter?' he asked, a sudden seriousness entering his eyes. 'Because a woman being forced into marriage is something I know Khal would never condone. Nor would I.'

Olivia looked up, taking in his broad stance and the furrow between his brows. Logically, she knew that his concern was for his friend, and not for the inconvenient charge he had been landed with. But for a moment she imagined what it might be like to have that kind of protectiveness completely to herself. She imagined that when a man like Roman cared for a woman he would do it fiercely—no prisoners taken. It seemed that he brought intensity into all aspects of his life.

She shook off the fanciful thoughts, suddenly hyper aware of his broad presence looming mere feet away from her. The warm headiness of his cologne teased her nostrils on the night air. His was the kind of scent that made a girl want to stand closer, to breathe it in. It was dangerous, that smell. It made her want to do dangerous things.

'Your silence doesn't exactly give me any insight.' He leaned back on the stone ledge so that he faced her, his grey eyes strangely dark and unreadable in the warm light of the outdoor lamps.

Olivia sighed, shrugging one shoulder with practised indifference. How could she tell him that the only alternative she had to this marriage was to walk away and lose everything she had grown up to value?

'I am not going to be handcuffed and frogmarched up the aisle, if that's what you mean.'

He raised a brow. 'But there would be consequences if you refused?'

She nodded once, unable to stand still in the face of his intense gaze and unwilling to discuss those consequences with a man who'd made it clear he was firmly on the opposite side. She might have escaped her father's imperious presence, but it seemed she had simply swapped one judgemental know-it-all male for another.

She suddenly felt more alone than ever. Her restless feet took her to the end of the terrace, where the stone tiles gave way to soft, spongy grass.

'I can't remember the last time I walked barefoot in the grass,' she said, more to herself than him, and she took a few tentative steps and sighed with appreciation.

One look back showed her that he was still watching her with that same unreadable expression. It was as though he were trying to categorise her, to pin down exactly what he needed to do to fix the very problem of her.

He had said the Sheikh trusted him to problem-solve. That was all she was to him—a problem. It seemed that was all she was to everyone these days, unless she shut her mouth and did what she was told.

'Olivia, come back from there.' Roman's voice boomed from behind her. 'This time of night it's—'

'You know, I think I can make that decision for myself,' she said, cutting him off mid-speech. It was rude, but she was too irritated to care. 'If I want to walk in the grass, I will. I don't need someone to manage every second of my day.'

She took a few more steps across the grass, putting some

space between herself and the surprised, strangely amused smirk that had suddenly spread across his face.

'Suit yourself,' he said quietly, looking down at the expensive watch on his wrist. 'But you're going to regret changing out of that bathing suit.'

She frowned at the cryptic statement, turning to face him. Just as she opened her mouth to question that statement the heavens seemed to open above her. Thick droplets of ice-cold rain fell hard and heavy onto her face, making her gasp as the cold spray got heavier and heavier, spreading through her clothing and down her neck and spine.

She was instantly wet through, and her mind took at least ten seconds before telling her to sprint back towards the house. After a few feet the rain suddenly stopped, and she was left looking into Roman's laughing face.

'I would have warned you about the sprinklers,' he said, crossing his arms. 'But I didn't want to manage your day too much.'

She gasped as the cool night air hit her sodden skin. She looked down at her wet clothes and, to her surprise, felt hysterical laughter bubble up her throat.

Roman frowned, also with surprise, 'What? No angry tirade about my appalling lack of consideration?'

'I'm done with being angry today.' She shook her head. 'If I don't laugh right now I might cry. And I make a point of never doing that.'

She leaned to one side, laughing once more as she began to squeeze the water from her hair. A sudden wicked urge grabbed her, and before she could stop herself she pooled the excess liquid in the palm of her hand and threw it in his direction, watching as it landed with a satisfying splash directly in his face.

'I'm sorry,' she said quickly, trying to curb her laughter as she took in his thunderous expression.

He took a step towards her and she felt her breath catch.

'You can't throw the first punch and then retreat with an

apology.' His voice was dark and silky on the night air. 'You sell yourself short. That was an excellent aim.'

'I'm not sorry, then.' She smirked, realising with a sudden jolt that she was flirting with him. And that he was flirting back.

The way he was looking at her coupled with the silent darkness of the night surrounding them made her almost imagine that this was a different moment in time entirely. That they weren't just strangers forced into each other's company by circumstance.

She imagined normal people laughed like this and poked fun at one another without fear of making a faux pas. It felt good, being normal.

'You've got quite a wild temper hidden underneath all those royal manners.' He took another step closer.

'I manage to keep it in check most of the time.'

'But not around me.' It was a statement, not a question.

'Don't flatter yourself.' She smiled nervously.

He stood little more than a foot away now, his warm scent clouding around her. She was wet and bedraggled, but she didn't want to leave just yet. She didn't want to end this—whatever it was that was passing between them. After a day filled with confrontation and being on the defensive, it was nice to lose the serious tone—even if for a brief moment.

She crossed her arms under her breasts, feeling the cold air prickle her skin into gooseflesh.

'*Khristos*, why didn't you say you were freezing?'

He reached out to touch her arm, the movement shocking them both as their eyes met in the half-darkness. It was a touch too far. They both knew it. And yet his hand stayed, gripping the soft skin just above her elbow. She shivered again, and this time it was nothing to do with the chill.

She noticed his expression darken suddenly. The air between them filled with a strange sizzling energy and his fingers flexed against her skin just a fraction.

She realised his gaze had moved below her chin. Self-consciously she looked down—and felt the air rush from her lungs in one long drawn-out breath.

Her white blouse.

She might as well be standing in front of him completely naked for all the coverage the wet piece of fabric was offering her. Of *course* tonight had to be the night when, in her haste to dress, she had decided a bra wasn't necessary. And of *course* the cool breeze had resulted in both taut peaks standing proudly to attention.

'Oh, God...'

She took in another breath, silently willing herself to laugh it off, but her mind stumbled clumsily over itself as she took in the obvious heat in his gaze. His eyes were dark and heavy-lidded as they lifted to meet hers. There was no mistaking it now. The silent strum of sensual heat that thrummed in the air between them.

It was a strange feeling—wanting to hide from the intensity of his gaze and bask in it all at the same time. He made her feel warm in places she hadn't known she could feel heat. It was as though her body was silently begging her to move towards him.

What would she do if he suddenly closed the gap between them and laid his lips hungrily on hers? Would he taste as sinfully good as he smelled?

She could suddenly think of nothing else.

What felt like hours passed, when really it was a matter of minutes. All the while his hand remained where it was, scorching her skin. Branding her.

When he finally turned his face away she fought the urge to step closer. To take the moment back. But then she followed his gaze and spied the housekeeper, quietly tidying their dinner dishes away nearby, with all the practised quietness of a professional.

She took one deliberate step away and crossed her arms over her chest, covering herself. His hand fell to his side and the haze of open lust disappeared from his features almost as quickly as it had come.

She wondered how he managed to look both furious and guilt-ridden at the same time. What would have happened if she had given in to that impulse and simply leaned forward to close the gap between them?

As though he'd heard her thoughts, a furrow appeared on his brow. He cleared his throat loudly, turning back to his house-keeper without another glance in her direction. 'Grab a towel for Miss Sandoval before she freezes.'

His cold, uncaring tone only added to the sudden chill that spread through her.

Without saying goodnight, or even looking in her direction, Roman disappeared through the terrace doors, leaving her standing alone, confused and embarrassed in her sodden clothes.

The walls of his master suite were bathed in a cold powder-blue light when Roman awoke. As usual he had not dreamed, but sleep had taken much longer than usual to claim him. And even then it had been fitful and broken at best. It was as though his entire body had thrummed with an intense nervous energy that refused to allow him any real rest.

Never one to remain in bed once his eyes had opened, Roman stood and threw on his jogging shorts.

In less than five minutes he was stretching on the steps that led to the beach. Within another ten he had completed two laps of the mile-long sandy inlet and worked up a healthy sweat. He ran barefoot on the damp sand until his chest heaved and his muscles burned with effort. And then he ran some more.

Usually a good run was enough to rid him of any thoughts strong enough to affect his sleep. A self-inflicted punishment of sorts, for those times when he knew his mind had begun to grow weak and was in need of strengthening. A weak mind had no place in his life—not when so many relied on his razor-sharp instincts to protect their homes and indeed their lives.

He prided himself on always being able to separate his personal and professional life—especially when it came to affairs with women. Lust never clouded his judgement.

The women he pursued were usually professional workaholics, just like him. Women who were sophisticated in and out of the bedroom and who weren't looking for sweet nothings to be whispered in their ear once they had scratched their mutual itch.

He had a feeling a sheltered young princess wouldn't be quite so worldly when it came to no-strings sex.

He picked up speed as he chastised himself for even entertaining the thought of a no-strings affair with Olivia. Guilt settled heavily in his chest as he thought of the night before, of the thoughts that had run through his brain as he had openly ogled his best friend's intended bride. *Stupid, weak fool.* The words flew by along with his breath as he exhausted his body with a final punishing sprint.

He had always believed that he deserved punishment for the multitude of sins he had committed in his youth. That no matter how complacent he grew in his wealth, in his power and success, there was always a darkness in him just waiting to ruin everything. It was beginning to seem that Olivia had been sent into his life to tempt that darkness to the fore. To tease him with her elegant curves and squeaky-clean nature.

He had a certain code for how he lived his life—certain people he did not betray and certain things he did not do. A rule book, of sorts, that kept him on the straight and narrow when the impulsive bastard inside him threatened to rise to the surface.

Khristos...

He exhaled hard. He had never been more tempted to break his own rules than in these past two days. Olivia reminded him of one of those perfect, luscious cakes that had always been on display behind the glass of his local bakery as a child. He had stood outside in the cold, salivating over the idea of breaking through that glass and claiming the treat for himself. But at that stage in his life his innocent boyhood self had innately known that would have been the wrong thing to do.

The Roman Lazarov of the present day did not have that luxury. Telling himself to walk away last night had been like standing in front of that bakery window all over again—hungry and frustrated, but unable to do a damn thing but fantasise about how the icing would taste in his mouth.

A delicious torture.

With his breath hard and even, he turned to the horizon and watched as the first flickers of pink and orange began to colour the dawn sky.

One of his favourite things about Isla Arista was the unspoilt view of both the sunrise and sunset from various points on the island. In those few dark months after the tragedy in Zayyar he had often spent an entire day walking here. He could completely circumnavigate the island in a few short hours because he knew the right tracks to take. It was an island of many personalities—smooth and habitable in some places, but fiercely wild and impassable in others.

He turned to begin walking back up to the villa, stopping as he spied a familiar feminine silhouette emerge from the open glass doors onto the terrace.

Olivia had been unashamedly watching Roman's progress up and down the beach with interest. It had been impossble not to stare at his broad, muscular form as he powered up and down the sand with seeming effortlessness.

She had debated hiding in her room all day, and avoiding breakfast with him altogether, but she'd decided that was something the *old* Olivia would do.

She was done with avoiding conflict and simply daydreaming of what she might say if she had the bravery in certain situations. She would sit across the table from him this morning and she would show him how completely unaffected she was by what had happened last night. Or almost happened, rather.

Aside from wanting to prove a point to herself, she had to admit that she desperately wanted to speak with him again. He was so unlike any man she had ever known. It was addictive, talking to him.

She had possibly taken slightly more time than usual in washing and preparing her hair, so that it fell in soft waves around her face. And so what if she had tried on three of the five dresses in her suitcase before committing to one?

The pale pink linen day dress was perhaps a little much for breakfast, but the way it nipped in at the waist and flowed out softly to her knees made her feel feminine and confident. And besides, she was simply taking pleasure in choosing her own outfit without a styling team surrounding her.

After twenty minutes of waiting, her stomach rumbling, with a beautiful display of fresh fruit and pastries spread out before her on the breakfast table, Jorge informed her that Mr Lazarov would be working all day and had decided it was easier to eat in his office.

She told herself that she wasn't bothered in the least as she poured herself coffee from the French press and nibbled on a piece of melon. She didn't care that he had chosen to avoid her. It was better, really. There was no one here to goad her, to push her to think about things she wanted to avoid. No all too perceptive slate-grey eyes watching her, making her skin prickle.

Eventually she gave in to the tantalising breakfast display and grabbed a large sugar-frosted croissant, smearing it liberally with butter and strawberry marmalade. The sticky sweet treat was like heaven itself as she washed it down with the fragrant gourmet coffee. Pastry was firmly on her list of *never* foods.

Regret was inevitable, and it washed over her as she self-consciously smoothed her dress against her stomach. Another result of the life she led was the constant pressure to stay slim, to stay as beautiful as possible in order to live up to her persona.

She had always harboured a soul-deep envy of her sisters and their seeming lack of pressure to play a part for the public. As the oldest, Eleanor was to be Queen one day—a position she took very seriously. She was naturally rake-thin, and always immaculately dressed, but the only media pressure *she* had to deal with was speculation on when she would start producing little heirs of her own.

Cressida was rarely, if ever, seen in the media. As a respected researcher in her field, she had somehow been allowed to study and live an almost civilian lifestyle in London, with only the barest minimum security detail.

Olivia sighed. The only skills *she* had were those best suited to what she was already doing, along with the uncanny ability to daydream herself out of any situation.

She had always adored the more dramatic movies—the ones where the heroine went through hell in order to get her happy ending. Maybe this was her punishment for refusing to adapt fully to real life?

Now, the information that lay inside that folder up in her room had the potential to change her life. To give her a little of the freedom she had longed for, for the past ten years. But, as with every choice, there would be some fall-out. And that fall-out would affect the people of her kingdom for many years to come.

Roman had said that she was spoilt and selfish. If that were true then she would have simply walked away from her place in the royal family as soon as she'd legally become an adult. Or when she had been made aware of her private inheritance three years ago.

It was her 'Get Out of Jail Free' card—a golden ticket to civilian life. But she was a royal of the realm at heart, and her father knew that. Hence why he so easily used her own loyal nature against her and made sure that she knew the consequences of her actions if she were to defy him.

She knew her father spoke the truth when he said that this marriage had the potential to solve all of Monteverre's problems.

Could she really be the person to stand in the way of that?

CHAPTER SIX

OLIVIA SAT UP quickly in the bed, feeling a sharp pain shoot through her neck. In her exhausted state she must have fallen asleep with her head propped on one arm. A quick look in the mirror showed that not only was her hair an unsightly nest, but she also bore a hot red patch on her left cheek from her uncomfortable position.

She stood up and walked to windows. A silvery moon had risen high above the bay below, casting pretty shadows all along the gardens that surrounded the villa. It was certainly past dinner time, she imagined, but still her eyes widened as the clock showed it was almost midnight.

Disorientated and groggy, she quickly ran a brush through her hair before making her way downstairs.

The villa seemed to be completely empty, and devoid of all human presence. The air was cool out on the terrace, and she half wished she had thought to take a sweater. From her vantage point she had a spectacular view of the glass-fronted villa in all its warm, glowing glory. At night, somehow the place seemed even more beautiful than it was during the day. Soft lighting warmed the space from within and made it look like a wall of glowing amber stone.

The garden was lit up with small spherical lights that appeared to float in mid-air. Tall, thick shrubbery blocked her view of the moon and its hypnotising glow on the waves. She was filled with energy, and suddenly wanted nothing more than a brisk walk along the moonlit beach.

As she made her way towards the edge of the lights she paused, briefly wondering if it was wise to venture away from the villa. The island was completely private, so she felt she was in no real danger so long as she kept to the well-lit parts. But that didn't mean that her brooding guard would take kindly to her exploring without permission...

That thought was immediately banished once she remembered how her host had effectively barricaded himself in his office for the day. She hadn't so much as caught a glimpse of him since seeing him running on the beach.

Her arms instinctively wrapped around her midriff, shielding herself from both the cool breeze and her thoughts as she made her way down the steps to the beach. Who the hell did he think he was anyway? Did he think that she would shadow him around? Begging for his attention?

She had much more pressing things on her mind than brooding Russians with ridiculously inflated egos.

The steps at the back of the house were steeper than she had anticipated. The drive up in the Jeep had not truly given her an appreciation of how high up the house was perched above the marina. She momentarily considered turning back, but stubbornness and curiosity made her keep moving. There was a safety rail on each side, and small lamps to light the way—it was not truly dangerous.

The soles of her sandals slid suddenly against the stone surface, making her gasp as she teetered forward precariously. The world seemed to shift for a split second before she clambered back, grabbing the rail for dear life.

She slid off her sandals, abandoning them on the steps. Her bare feet gave much better grip for the rest of the way down, and soon she reached the very bottom. The sand was cold and damp under her toes but the midnight air was balmy. She took a moment to stop and simply bask in the utter stillness of it all.

It reminded her of the warm nights her family had spent out on the terrace at their summer estate. The beautiful country-side manor in the southern peninsula of Monteverre was the setting of most of her fondest childhood memories. Back in the days when her grandmother had reigned over the kingdom as Queen and her father had simply been the young, handsome heir to the throne.

There had been no palace for the three young Princesses— no twenty-four-hour bodyguards. Her grandmother had ensured they were given as normal a childhood as possible, considering the circumstances.

And even as father had grown ever more reckless, and her mother had retreated into her brandy glass, Mimi had been there. Until all of a sudden she hadn't.

Olivia shivered, taking a few long strides across the sand until she reached the long whitewashed jetty of the small marina that she had arrived at. It looked different in the semi-dark, with only a few lamps illuminating the shadows. Roman's sleek yacht was a dark shadow in the distance. The moonlight glowed against its polished glass body, smooth, severe and striking— rather like the man himself, she thought.

The marina also housed a handful of other vessels. A couple of top-of-the-range speedboats—likely for sporting use—a small rescue dinghy, and the one that had caught her eye the moment she had disembarked the day before: a magnificent vintage sailboat.

In the dark, it was hard to see any of the fine detailing. She reached out, running her hand along the smooth silver letter-ing emblazoned just above the waterline.

"Sofiya",' she said out loud. 'Just who are you named after, I wonder?'

'That is none of your business.'

The deep voice boomed from behind her, startling her enough

to make her lose her footing and fall hard against the side of the boat. She fell for what seemed like minutes rather than milliseconds, before strong arms grabbed her around the waist and lifted her swiftly upright.

'Planning a midnight escape?' Roman asked, his accent both intimidating and strangely welcoming after the prolonged silence of her day.

'You...you startled me,' she breathed hard, her voice little more than a breathy whisper.

His hands were still on her waist, the heat of him seeping through the material of her dress. She reached down, covering his hands with her own for a moment before pushing them away and taking a tentative half-step back.

The loss of heat was instant. Her skin prickled with tiny bumps, as though calling his touch back.

'If you insist on sneaking around outside in the dark, I might rethink the terms of your stay here.'

'The *terms*? I assumed I had been abandoned to my own devices.'

'Fine, then. Let's get this straight. You will only leave the house in daylight hours, and you will clear it with me first.'

'You expect me to just sit around all day and go insane from my own thoughts?' She half laughed. 'This is an island—where could I even go?'

'I have learnt not to underestimate you.'

He crossed his arms and for the first time she noticed he wore only a dark-coloured sleeveless workout shirt and cut-off shorts. Her eyes took in the bulging muscles that lined his shoulders, his lean, hard biceps and strong forearms. Her gaze wandered once again to the strange black band that stretched around his left arm, just under the elbow. The design seemed intricate, but she quickly looked back up to his face, aware she had been gawking.

'Are we clear?' he asked, scowling down at her from his impressive height.

Olivia fought the urge to roll her eyes at him in all his perpetually sardonic glory. She had a feeling this was what it would be like to have a surly, unimpressed guardian angel following her every move.

In this light he certainly looked the part. The glow of the moon emphasised his harsh features, making him even more darkly attractive. But good looks and incredibly broad shoulders would never account for a severe lack of sense of humour. Did the man *ever* smile?

'Are you like this all the time or just around me?' she asked, turning on her heel and walking away from him, back towards the sand.

'Oh, you're telling me how I am now?' He fell easily into step beside her, mild amusement on his voice. 'Please enlighten me.'

'You are controlling. And rude.' She said, counting off on her fingers. 'Judgmental, intimidating, far too serious—'

'You are accusing *me* of being rude?' He clutched a hand to his chest as though mortally wounded.

Olivia stopped just short of where the wooden planks gave way to hard sand and turned to face him in the dim light of the spherical lamps that lined the small marina. 'You've just instructed me that I cannot leave the house without your permission.'

He smirked, reaching out to stop her when she made to move away with irritation.

She crossed her arms and met his eyes, determined to have this conversation like an adult.

'Olivia, closely controlled security is only required if there is a risk of the client putting themselves in danger. Unfortunately for me, in your case, that means, yes, it's needed.' He sighed. 'And I am not prepared to shadow you around this island simply to provide you with a more enjoyable experience.'

'Are you telling me I'm under house arrest just because you're determined not to spend any time alone with me?' she said with disbelief.

'I don't think it would be the best idea,' he said plainly. 'For obvious reasons.'

She watched him silently for a moment, wondering if he was actually openly referring to the chemistry between them. 'Are you really so unable to control a flimsy attraction?' she asked bravely, shocked at the words coming from her own mouth.

His eyes widened. 'I'm a grown man, Olivia. Older than you by almost a decade.'

'I fail to see what age has to do with it.'

He stepped forward, a dangerous glint in his slate-grey eyes. 'I'm not a mindless teenager who can be waylaid by a set of curves.'

'Well, then, what's the problem?' She shrugged one shoulder, fully committed to her act now, even as her insides quaked. 'I'm not about to jump your bones, and you've made it clear that you are far too mature to do anything quite so...*primal*.'

He smiled the kind of smile that screamed danger as he allowed his gaze to take her in slowly from her head down to her bare toes. 'Primal? Is that what you'd call it?'

She gulped.

He noticed.

Roman took a single step forward, closing the gap between them so that they stood almost toe to toe. 'I'd like to wager that you've never jumped anyone's bones in your life, Printsessa.'

'I'm not about to divulge that kind of information to you.' She tried her best to keep up her confident act but he'd rattled her. He knew it too.

Cursing her lack of practice in these things, she turned as nonchalantly as possible and began walking back towards the villa, hoping she'd simply seem bored or tired.

'I did not mean to offend you.' His voice drifted from behind her as she began climbing the steep steps. 'I'm sure you are perfectly capable of jumping my bones.'

'Don't flatter yourself,' she breathed, aware that she was

barely a quarter of the way up and already feeling winded from the incline.

She hadn't eaten nearly enough today to fuel this kind of exertion, and tiny spots had begun to appear at the edges of her vision. She paused, holding on to the rail for a moment as she caught her breath.

'Problem?' he asked, coming to a stop beside her.

He was barely even breathing heavily, the great brute.

She shook her head, not wanting to admit that she had been moping around the villa for most of the day and had refused Jorge's offers of lunch and dinner.

Standing up straight, she continued to climb, begging the gods of never-ending stairs to have mercy on her. Eventually she reached the top—and not a moment too soon. She caught one glimpse of the amber lights of the villa before her ears began to pop and her legs started to shake.

Roman instantly noticed the change in her demeanour. 'Was the climb *really* so tough?' he asked, half mocking.

She groaned, moving to the grass and half sitting half falling onto her rear end with an unceremonious grunt as the world tilted around her.

'You look as though you are about to be ill.' He crouched in front of her, the mocking tone completely vanished from his voice. 'Olivia?'

'I need some water,' she managed to rasp, looking up at the blurred outline of his face. 'Just a little light-headed.'

Roman took one look at Olivia's pale features and cursed under his breath. 'When did you last eat?' he asked, a mixture of anger and concern filling him as her eyes darted away from him with embarrassment.

'Just give me a moment to catch my breath.'

'No, you need a damned sandwich and some common sense,' he gritted. 'Can you walk?'

She nodded—far too quickly. Her eyes were still unfocused

and her face pale as moonlight. Still, to her stubborn credit she rose to her feet and attempted two whole steps before her legs buckled and she tipped into his waiting arms.

'This is mortifying!' she groaned, her face mashed against his chest.

Roman ignored the all too welcome sensation of having her slim figure pressed against him. With a deep breath he lifted her against his shoulder and closed the distance between them and the villa.

Once inside, he deposited her roughly onto the bench in the kitchen and set about preparing a cold meat sandwich on crusty white bread and a tall glass of ice-cold orange juice.

She sipped at the juice with gusto, and a hint of colour re-appeared in her cheeks after a moment as she nibbled on the crust of the bread.

'You eat like a rabbit,' he commented, when after five minutes she hadn't taken more than a series of tiny bites.

'I eat enough.' She shrugged.

Roman remained silent. She was watching him closely over the rim of her orange juice glass, but did not speak until the sandwich was completely gone.

'White carbs are my weakness.' She sighed. 'You've just sent me down a path of total and utter ruination in the eyes of my stylist.'

'I'm sorry its not gluten-free, but true hunger can't afford to be picky.'

'What would *you* know of true hunger?' She raised a brow. 'You eat enough to feed a small army.'

'I grew accustomed to eating as much as I could fit in once I got out of prison.' He spoke without thought, and then watched as stark realisation dawned over her delicate features. 'Old habits, I suppose.' He shrugged, instantly regretting his words.

'I never thought...' She let her voice trail off. 'I'm sorry.'

'You're sorry that I was in prison?' He leaned down, grabbing her plate and turning to deposit it in the sink. 'Don't be. I deserved every year I got. Trust me.'

'No, I'm sorry you had to experience hunger like that. I didn't think when I spoke. I was just being...snarky.'

'Don't worry about it.'

In all the years that had passed since his time in jail, he couldn't remember anyone ever commiserating with him over the hardships he must have endured. She didn't even know why he had been landed there in the first place. She knew nothing of the man he had been. No, he corrected himself, the *boy* he had been.

'You're not a bad guy,' she said quietly.

Roman looked up, unable to conceal his surprise at her words.

'I mean, obviously I've only known you a couple of days...' She shrugged her shoulders, heat lightly warming her cheeks. 'But a bad guy wouldn't have brought me here to begin with. He wouldn't be making sandwiches at one in the morning to stop me from fainting like a helpless damsel.'

'Don't paint me as some hero, Olivia.' He shook his head. 'You have no idea how far that is from the truth.'

She made to continue talking, but he'd suddenly had enough. He put a hand up, silencing her. 'I've had a long day, and I'd appreciate it if you considered what I said about obeying my rules tomorrow.'

'I'll consider it.'

She shrugged, then walked past him into the hallway and began ascending the stairs, effectively robbing him of the chance to walk away first.

'That didn't sound like a yes.' He sighed, trying and failing to avoid the delectable sight of her shapely bare calves below the hemline of her dress.

'That's because it wasn't one.'

She disappeared from his view.

* * *

Olivia shielded her eyes as her hair whipped around her. The wind was like razor blades at this altitude, but the hour-long hike had definitely been worth it. She braced herself, taking one step out onto the balcony of the lighthouse. Heights had never really been an issue for her, but then again she had never been alone on a ledge in coastal winds before.

But all fear was forgotten once she stepped out and felt the sun spread across her face, warming her through.

There was nothing but ocean ahead of her for miles. She turned and caught her breath. She could see the entire island in all its glowing emerald glory. A heavy sigh escaped her lips and she leaned her elbows against the metal railing.

The villa was little more than a pea-sized white blur from here, partially hidden in the trees far over to the north. Likely Roman was still holed up in his office there, determined to spend as little time in her company as possible.

She had almost been tempted to go and ask him to show her the lighthouse. She had walked boldly up to his office door and stood poised, ready to knock. But then she had remembered his face as he'd called her Princess. The patronising tone as he had all but called her a child in need of supervision. She had not actually agreed to his terms, so technically she wasn't breaking any promises.

The hike had been just what she'd needed to shake off the extra energy that had plagued her all morning. She had made a point of eating a good wholesome breakfast before setting off, not wanting to make the same mistake as she had the night before. Now her thighs burned from exertion and her cheeks were warm and she finally felt as if she was *doing* something. And the best part of all was that she was entirely alone.

A harsh male roar caught her by surprise and her hand almost slipped on the railing. She looked down, wide-eyed, and caught sight of Roman powering across the plane at the base of the lighthouse, angry determination in his posture as he stopped and looked up at her.

He shouted something entirely inaudible, his voice fighting against the noise of the wind and the waves below. Olivia couldn't help it—she laughed. The smile that erupted on her lips made him scowl even more as he powered ahead once more and disappeared through the door beneath her.

There were at least three storeys between them, made up of one long winding staircase, and yet it seemed like barely a minute passed before she heard him step out onto the platform behind her.

'What the hell do you think you're doing up here?' he growled.

Olivia turned to look at him over her shoulder. 'I'm enjoying the view.'

'Oh, of course. Of *course* you'd have to perch yourself fifty feet in the air. You couldn't just stand on the deck below like a normal person.'

'The door was unlocked and I've never seen the inside of a lighthouse before.' She shrugged, holding onto the railing to pull herself up. 'It's not half as quaint as I'd imagined.'

She turned to face Roman, seeing his look of cold rage turn quickly to disbelief.

'This isn't a game, Olivia,' he said darkly. 'What if you'd fallen?'

'I'm quite capable of using stairs without supervision.' She stood tall, wishing he wouldn't keep looking at her that way. 'Please, just…stop treating me like a child.'

'Well, then, stop acting like one!' He raised his voice.

She sidestepped him, neatly sliding through the doorway and starting down the steps at a rapid pace.

He followed quickly behind her.

'You are the most reckless, difficult client I have ever had.' Roman stalked behind her, his voice still holding that dark edge.

'Because I wanted to explore a little?' She paused, turning

to look back at him. 'This entire island is more secure than the royal vaults. You knew exactly where I was—as evidenced by the fact that you are *here*.'

'I was at least ten minutes behind you.'

'You are seriously overreacting, and I would like to know why.'

He met her eyes easily, his height making him tower above her even more than usual. 'I'm reacting as anyone would if they found the woman they are supposed to be protecting dangling her legs from a fifty-foot balcony.'

'It would hardly be your fault if I fell, would it?' She shrugged, turning back to continue down the steps. 'I'm sure your beloved Khal would find a replacement princess eventually.'

Strong hands encased her shoulders, effectively barring her from moving. Roman moved around her so they stood face to face.

She was almost completely level with him on the step below. The expression on his face completely took her breath away.

'Do you honestly have a death wish?' He grasped her shoulders tightly, his eyes blazing with real, deep concern.

'I... No, of course not.' She turned her face away from him, only for him to turn it right back.

His fingers were hot and hard against her cheek, and this close she was surrounded by the warm, delicious aroma of him that she had come to recognise so well.

'Your eyes tell me a different story.'

'Isn't that against the rules? Looking into my eyes?'

Was that her voice? That husky murmur? She could feel her heart hammering hard and slow in her chest. It was as though the simple act of being near him sent her vitals into chaos.

'I've always hated rules.'

His mouth tightened, and tension spread through his hands and up his arms so that they felt like bands of iron on her shoulders rather than flesh and bone.

She bit her bottom lip as shivers spread down her arms. Roman's eyes lowered to take in the movement, his pupils darkening as he pressed his lips together hard. She thought he might kiss her. He certainly looked as though he wanted to.

But she saw the moment that something changed in his eyes—something that made his mouth harden and his eyes shift away from her once more.

For one crazy moment she wondered what it might be like to lean across and kiss all that tension from his mouth. To just take a wild leap and not care about the consequences.

And then all of a sudden she was doing it.

She closed the gap between them and laid her mouth against his, feeling his shocked intake of breath as their lips connected and her breasts pressed flush against the hard, strong plane of his chest.

He was going to hell.

There were no two ways about it.

Roman felt something inside him roar to life the moment Olivia's lips gently touched his, her feather-light caresses against his mouth almost completely undoing him. His hands found their way to her hair, releasing the clasp that held it wound at the nape of her neck.

He was letting this happen.

More than that, he wanted it so badly it made him ache.

She gave just as good as she got, her hands travelling over his shoulders and down his waist. Sharp fingernails grasped his hips just above his jeans. The sensation sent pulses of heat southwards and he felt himself grow hard against his zip.

The fleeting thought of stopping the madness came and went quickly as Olivia moved against him, her abdomen in direct contact with his erection. Far from being shocked or appalled, she kissed him even harder.

Their breath mingled into one frantic cloud of white-hot need. He kissed a trail down her neck, his hands sweeping deftly to the front closures of her blouse. With each satisfying click he was treated to a delicious sliver of creamy soft skin and the smallest glimpse of white lace.

Her breasts were small and firm, perfectly rounded and straining against the lace fabric of her bra. With one hand he reached behind her, undoing the clasp.

She exhaled long and slow, biting her lip as he pulled the garment away and lowered his mouth to her breast. Her skin tasted like a smooth ripe peach, the softness unbelievable against his tongue.

As he drew one peak into his mouth she hissed out a breath. 'Roman...' she breathed in awe.

Her fingers wound through his hair, anchoring him to her as he explored one taut peak and then gave ample attention to the other.

Their position on the steps made things difficult. It would be so easy to carry her down to the landing below and take her hard and fast on the floor. He could tell she was ready for him by the way she moaned at the slightest touch. She was his for the taking...

Except, she wasn't, was she?

The thought stilled him, stopping his body mid-motion.

She wasn't his.

Roman stepped away from her as though he'd been burned. His breath escaped his nostrils in harsh bursts as his body screamed in protest. He cursed out loud, his voice echoing in the cavernous space as he realised what he had been doing. What his body was still deeply invested in doing.

Olivia fell back at an uncomfortable angle, her breasts still bared to him. She looked up, confused and flushed.

'That shouldn't have happened,' he breathed, bracing his back against the cold wall and forcing himself to look away from the tantalising curves on display.

In his peripheral vision he saw Olivia stiffen, her hands quickly moving to cover herself. A prolonged silence ensued as he turned his back and listened while she frantically tried to button up her blouse and calm her breathing. When he finally turned around it was to find her gone—back up the stairs to the top of the lighthouse.

He followed, stepping out soundlessly onto the narrow balcony alongside her.

'Olivia...' he began, exhaling on a long sigh.

'Whatever you are about to say, just *don't*,' she said, her voice tight with recrimination and something else—regret, perhaps?

'It won't happen again, between us,' he said, almost as though he were trying to convince himself along with her. 'It was a mistake, bringing you here at all. This just proves what I already knew.'

'And that is?'

'That you are incapable of controlling your impulses.'

'And *you* are the most arrogant man I have ever met.' She turned to face him. 'Are you actually trying to blame *me* for this?' she asked. 'I may have kissed you first, but at least I'm emotionally mature enough to admit it was because I wanted it.'

'Excuse me?'

'I wanted it.' She spoke slowly and deliberately, her eyes blazing emerald in the brightness of the mid-afternoon sun. 'I wanted to know how it would feel, being kissed by you. To get under that wall of stone you surround yourself with. And I may be unpractised in these things, but I know that you wanted it too.'

His mind caught on one single word she had uttered. *Unpractised.* He coughed on the sharp intake of breath that filled his lungs.

Olivia's eyes widened, her face rapidly warming with embarrassment. 'I simply meant that I'm not accustomed to making the first move,' she said quickly, her eyes wide with mortification.

'Chert voz'mi,' Roman cursed under his breath, suddenly despising his own ability to see through to the truth. 'You have never had a lover, have you?'

He watched as her shoulders tensed and she tightened her grip on the rail in front of her. She hid her face from him but he could read the signs in her body. Surprise rapidly turned to self-defence. She didn't speak, but she didn't have to. He already knew he was right.

She was a virgin.

As if there weren't enough reasons already for this attraction to be the worst kind of wrong...

He turned, bracing one hand on the balcony rail and gripping it with all his might. 'Have you any idea what kind of game you are playing?' he gritted.

'I was not playing a game.' She turned her face to him, her shoulders stiff and unyielding.

'How would you even *know* what you were doing?' he said harshly. Anger raged in him—towards her, towards himself. He felt as if he was drowning in it. 'What did you think? That you could use me as a damned test run? Lose your virginity with the rough and tumble ex-con before I sent you back to your royal fiancé's bed?'

Her eyes narrowed, her fist flying out to thump him squarely in the middle of his chest. 'How dare you?'

He grabbed her hand in his fist, stopping her movement and inadvertently pulling her closer to him.

'You are angry at me because it is the truth. You think you are attracted to me? You don't even *know* me. You're attracted to my lack of refinement, Olivia. You see me as some big, uncivilised fool who you can charm with your delicate skin and innocent eye-flutters.' He shook his head, his mouth hardening into a cruel line.

'I don't think of you that way.'

'Well, maybe you should start. I might come from the gutter, but that doesn't mean I make a habit of living like a street thug. I do not sleep with virgins or with other men's fiancées. I have morals, Olivia.'

'What? And I don't? I am not engaged. I have done nothing wrong here.'

'You are as good as spoken for,' he ground out.

She looked up at him. Eyes that moments ago had been blue-black with desire were now wide and blazing with anger. 'I will *never* be spoken for. Never again.' A tremor passed through her throat. 'I am not another man's property, to be protected and transported.'

'You are going back to the palace as soon as possible.'

'Roman, is it so hard to believe that I am just as overwhelmed as you?'

'Don't flatter yourself, Princess,' he said cruelly. 'It would take a lot more than an innocent's clumsy kisses to overwhelm *me*.'

Her face fell and he knew he had gone too far.

But she was already turning to walk out through the door. 'If you don't mind, I'd like to walk back alone.'

He made to walk after her but stopped, thinking it might be best if they both had some time to calm down.

'Fine. You can take the time to prepare your explanation. I will deliver you to your fiancé tonight.'

CHAPTER SEVEN

OLIVIA REGRETTED STEALING Roman's boat almost as soon as she had set off, but stubbornness kept her from turning back. As the wind pulled her hair around her face and the salty air filled her lungs she felt the awful tension inside her loosen a fraction.

She hated him.

Every single word that Roman had thrown at her had swum around in her head as she had hiked across the craggy woodland towards the villa. His indignant accusations. His refusal to see the truth in their situation. He seemed determined to power through any argument she had.

It was the thought of his final words that had cemented her decision to change course and hightail it for the marina. *'I will deliver you to your fiancé tonight.'*

She gripped the wheel even tighter, steering the boat as the mainland drew nearer on the horizon. The distance between Isla Arista and the small mainland town of Puerto Arista was a mere fifteen minutes, but as the small dock came into view she contemplated turning around.

What *was* it about her breaking the law when she was around this man? Once again she had proved him right by giving in to an emotional impulse without a thought for the consequences.

Still, pride kept her from doing the intelligent thing and returning with her tail between her legs. She busied herself with mooring and disembarking safely, taking pleasure in the manual work.

She had always enjoyed her national sport—there was something quite peaceful about letting her mind wander as she followed through all the steps.

This small speedboat was much more streamlined and modern than the complex sporting sailboats she was used to, so before she knew it she was climbing the limestone steps up from the dock and emerging into a busy little Spanish village. Thankfully she had worn large sunglasses and a floppy-brimmed hat on her hike, to protect her from the sun, both of which now helpfully concealed her face from possible recognition.

The streets were cobbled and sloped upwards towards the impressive white cliffs that dominated the landscape. A long row of whitewashed houses and shops lined the seafront, with terracotta roofs and vibrantly coloured windows. The village was small, and seemed almost pristine in its appearance.

It was quiet. There was none of the hustle and bustle of the coastal spots in Monteverre. It was like stepping into a well-kept secret. People smiled as they walked past, shopkeepers tipped their sunhats in her direction. No one approached her or called her name. No one cared.

It was a revelation.

After she had walked to the top of the hill and back down her stomach began to growl. The thought of returning to the island—to Roman—filled her with trepidation. Without a second thought she walked into a nearby café and eyed the delicious selection of handmade pastries and freshly cut fruit. The smell of warm butter and melted chocolate permeated the air and made her stomach flip.

Yes, this was exactly what she needed.

'Can I help you, miss?' A middle-aged man smiled jovially from behind the counter, his white apron smeared with powdered sugar.

Olivia smiled in response, really enjoying not being recognised. 'Yes—what's good here?'

'It's all good, of course.' He laughed. 'We have a special on today: three *magdalenas* for the price of two.'

Olivia looked down at the elegant golden-brown pastries and instantly felt her stomach drop.

She had no money.

With a murmured excuse she practically ran from the shop, embarrassment fuelling her as she walked swiftly down the hill back towards the marina. She stopped on the promenade, taking a seat on a bench that overlooked the small inlet.

As her breathing slowed, a heavy sadness replaced her embarrassment. She had no idea how to prepare for living in the real world. For all her thoughts of leaving her bubble and making a difference, the reality was that she had absolutely no idea how to function outside the privilege of royal life.

Her father had been right.

She had told herself that she would find a way to become the woman she wanted to be outside of her parents' expectations and royal obligations. She had believed she could fulfil the vision her grandmother had had for the foundation alone. But she didn't have a business mind—she didn't have that kind of common sense or leadership skill. She certainly didn't have the kind of innate intelligence and passion that could support her, as her siblings did.

Maybe she was delusional. Maybe her father was right and she should stick to where her strengths lay. Just another Sandoval princess, destined to stand and smile by her husband's side.

But one thing was for sure: she was *not* what Roman had accused her of being. She had not seen him as some sort of base creature to use for her own amusement. The thought that he saw her as someone capable of such cruelty…it bothered her.

She ambled towards the marina with the intention of returning and paused, watching as a familiar sailboat moored itself next to her smaller vessel. The name *Sofiya* was emblazoned across its hull.

Roman jumped down athletically onto the boards of the jetty before striding purposefully in her direction.

She turned away quickly, not quite ready for the confrontation she knew was bound to happen. He was likely furious, and he had every right to be. But she had hoped for more time to compose herself before the inevitable. Even now, the memory of his hands on her bare skin made her short of breath.

She shook off the heated thoughts, walking along the promenade at a brisk pace.

A man was walking towards her—the man from the pastry shop, she realised suddenly. He was walking quite fast and had a slightly odd expression on his face. Olivia paused, feeling suddenly very exposed on the empty promenade. As he neared her he reached into his jacket, his large hand fumbling for something in his breast pocket.

A loud growl erupted from somewhere over her left shoulder. Roman was running past her in a matter of seconds, moving to stand in front of the older man with ferocious agility and strength. His large body manoeuvred the man to the ground and he shouted to Olivia to move away. She could hear the man calling out underneath him—a strange muffled cry of one word, over and over.

Finally Roman moved from his position and the other man managed to gasp. 'Camera! Camera!'

Olivia spied the small black object that lay shattered near Roman's left knee. She rushed forward. 'Roman, it's just a camera!' She gasped, tugging at his sleeve for his to remove his body from the man. 'Roman, please stand up. He's not dangerous,' she urged, pulling at his shoulder.

Roman looked into the blue-green depths of Olivia's eyes and something inside him shifted. All at once he became aware of the man's fleshy paunch beside his knee. The roar of the waves hitting the promenade to his left. He could hear Olivia's pan-icked tone and his own fiercely ragged breathing.

Khristos, it had happened again.

He stood to his feet, looking away from where his unsus-pecting, seemingly innocent victim had stood up and shuffled away. The roaring in his ears was deafening, the hammering in his chest making him feel as though he might pass out.

Without thinking of the lack of logic in his actions, he grabbed Olivia roughly by the wrist, ignoring her protests. Eventually she gave in and allowed him to lead her down to where his sailboat lay in wait. Within moments they were on board, and he closed the door of the spacious interior saloon with a harsh exhalation of breath.

'Sit down,' he commanded, watching confusion enter into her eyes.

'Roman, what on earth—?'

'Just sit down,' he repeated harshly, his breath still raw and uneven in his chest as he fought to control the ridiculous rac-ing of his treacherous mind.

Sofiya.

His mind whirled against the onslaught of terrible memories threatening to overcome him as his sister's face broke through to his consciousness. As if in slow motion he could see the life leave her baby-blue eyes as the bullet tore through her body, silencing her scream.

He shook his head, swallowing past the dryness of fear in his throat.

Olivia moved in front of him, concern in her wide eyes as she placed her hands on his chest.

'You're shaking,' she said softly, in the kind of placating tone one used when trying to soothe a wild animal. 'Has this happened before?'

Her warm hands on his chest both irritated and calmed him. 'Don't push me, Olivia,' he warned. 'I don't want to hurt you, too.'

'You won't hurt me, Roman.'

She shook her head just a fraction, her innocent eyes so wide and confused it made him want to growl with frustration and bask in her concern all at once.

'Let me help you,' she whispered, moving her hand uncertainly to rest on his face.

The touch of her soft, feminine hands on his skin undid him completely.

He leaned forward, capturing her words roughly with his mouth, showing her just why she needed to run from him.

Her lips were soft against his, trying in vain to offer him comfort even as he plundered and deepened the kiss. He wound one hand around the back of her neck and twisted the fine silk of her hair in his hands. His rough touch anchored her to him while his other hand bunched into a tight fist by his side.

This was wrong, he told himself. He was using her in the aftermath of his own weakness, losing himself in her, and it was so wrong he hated himself. She was innocent to situations like this, he reminded himself, talking himself down from his own madness. She deserved better than this—than him.

He moved to away an inch and she looked up at him, lust clouding her vision.

'I can't keep my hands off of you,' he gritted, running his fingers down one side of her face and wincing as he noticed the small patch of blood staining the front of her dress.

Logic told him that the blood was likely from his own cut knuckles, but the sight of her pale skin next to the red smear was enough to sober him just for a moment. He tried to fish though the haze of his memory but drew up nothing but blankness.

'Roman, I need to know what happened back there.' She spoke slowly, as though afraid she might set him off again.

'I don't want to talk right now.' He shook his head, pulling himself away from the heat of her, inch by inch, even as his body screamed in protest.

It was colder without her in his arms, but safer.

'Talk to me,' she said simply.

'I'm not good at talking, Olivia.' He turned to sit heavily on the leather sofa of the saloon. 'Guns trigger something inside me. Even the *thought* of guns, apparently.' He laughed cruelly.

'There was no gun, Roman,' she said. 'No danger.'

He stood, his anger boiling over to the surface. 'You think I don't *know* that?' he asked. 'But in that moment, when my mind goes there...'

'You are powerless to stop it?' she offered helpfully.

Powerless. God, how he hated that term. Was there anything in the world more terrifying than being out of control of your own mind and body, even if only for a few moments?

Olivia moved to sit beside him, her thigh brushing his on the small settee.

'You can talk about it with me, if it helps,' she offered.

'We are not all built for flowery conversations and sharing our dreams.'

Her eyes dropped and he realised he was doing it again— being needlessly cruel.

'None of this would have happened if you hadn't run off with my damn boat,' he continued, seemingly unable to stop himself.

'You deserved it,' she said harshly.

'For trying to protect your reputation?' he said incredulously.

'I don't think my reputation has a thing to do with it, Roman. You attacked a stranger, dragged me back here like the hounds of hell were chasing you and then you kissed me like your life depended on it.'

She met his eyes without hesitation.

'I kissed you to shut you up,' he argued, turning towards the bridge that housed the control panel so they could get the hell out of here and he could find some space.

'Now who's running away?' she challenged.

'You'd prefer to wait around until local law enforcement arrives to question us both?' he said darkly. 'I didn't even stop to see if I had hurt him.'

'He was fine—just shaken. You don't remember *any* of it?'

She frowned. 'I got the chance to apologise quickly before you pulled me away.'

'If you think an apology is enough to stop him from pressing charges...'

'I told him that you were just a jealous lover.' She winced, half smiling with embarrassment.

Roman took a moment to look at her, and the situation suddenly replayed in his mind like a bad movie. He pursed his lips and then, before he knew it, dark laughter erupted from his chest.

Olivia smiled, also seeing the humour in their situation, and soon she was laughing too. She had a great laugh, he thought to himself as they both returned to silence after a moment.

'Thank you,' he said, looking deeply into her eyes for a moment.

He wasn't accustomed to thanking anyone for anything quite so personal; he made a point of not needing anyone enough to necessitate heartfelt apologies. But this woman had lied for him—protected him in a way. After he had treated her horribly.

It was a strange feeling—one he didn't want to examine too closely. For now, the ability to laugh it off was a novelty in itself.

Olivia nodded once—a graceful acceptance.

He took a step away from her, looking out at the harbour around them. It was late; the sky was already in full darkness around them. He suddenly did not want to return to the island—to the silence of the villa and the self-imposed exile he had placed himself in.

'Are you hungry?' he asked hopefully.

Simply named Faro, the small restaurant was partly built into the rocks that stood proudly at the tip of the peninsula. Olivia felt butterflies in her stomach as Roman's hand encircled hers, helping her down the steep steps to the low wooden door of the entrance.

'It doesn't look like much from the outside, but I assure you it's the best paella in all of Spain.'

'I'll take your word for it.'

She smiled, following him into a small hallway. Roman led the way down a corridor and out onto a large terrace that over-looked the coast as far as the eye could see. Warm glowing lanterns adorned the walls and brightened the space, making it seem like the terrace at the back of someone's home rather than a restaurant.

The overall effect was so welcoming she felt instantly at ease, all her tension from the afternoon leaving her shoulders as the waiter led them to a table on the very edge of the space. A man rushed over to take Roman's hand and clap him on the back. The pair began conversing in perfect English, and Roman ordered bottle of red wine.

When it came, Olivia took a sip of her wine, thanking the waiter and looking out across the bay. They were so close to the water she could see the waves crashing into the rocks below them. The after-effects of the day made her forehead tighten painfully.

Roman seemed determined to avoid the subject of their kiss entirely.

Both kisses.

She shivered at the memory of his rough handling after he had all but dragged her back to his boat. He had been com-pletely raw and out of control, and yet she had felt nothing but excitement. Maybe he was right—maybe she *was* just looking for a taste of danger. Maybe she was naïve for not fearing him.

He had made one thing clear: he did not trust her. She desper-ately wanted to ask him about the incident on the promenade—find out why a man who ran a company of armed bodyguards would have such a deep issue with guns. But maybe she was a fool for worrying about him when he'd continuously told her she was no more than a job to him.

She had told him that she was a virgin and he had made it

clear that the fact only cemented his view of her as being completely untouchable. She had never resented her own pesky innocence more than at that moment. When had he stopped being just a glowering bodyguard and become the object of all her fantasies?

She swallowed hard past the dryness in her throat as Roman sat down across from her and apologised for the interruption. After checking with her first, he ordered them both a light starter followed by the chef's special paella.

Once the waiter had taken their order they were left completely alone. The moment of uncomfortable silence was not lost on Olivia. She cleared her throat, making a show of looking up at the vaulted ceiling that partially covered the open terrace.

'You seem to know the staff quite well,' she offered.

'It's been five years, I believe, since I started coming here for lunch every day when I was overseeing building work on my island.'

'They seem to like you.'

'The chef—he is also the owner. And the waiters are his sons.' He smiled, looking over at the young men bustling around the small restaurant. 'The first day I found this place, my architect brought me for lunch. The owner, Pedro, had an argument with his oldest boy and the kid ran off, leaving him with a pile of dishes and a line of hungry guests. I rolled up my sleeves and offered to help.'

'Not many people would do that.'

'Not many princesses would do what you did at that racetrack.' Roman shrugged, sitting back as their bread and gazpacho were laid out on their table.

Olivia couldn't mask her surprise at his mention of the incident with the young waiter and the champagne. 'That afternoon seems like a lifetime ago.'

He nodded. 'Perhaps we are both destined for the sainthood?'

She smiled. 'If you are hoping to convince me that you are not entirely heartless, it's working.'

'I might not have the benevolent influence of a royal, but I'm not afraid to get my hands dirty.' He shrugged again. 'Charity isn't always about money.'

'That's...' She shook her head, frowning at the memory of her argument with her father. Of those very words that she had spoken so vehemently. And here was Roman, echoing them as though it were simply a fact.

'Is something wrong?' he asked, frowning.

She shook her head, ignoring the painful throb in her chest at hearing his words.

She took another sip of wine, clearing the fullness from her throat. 'I adore my work in the community...' Olivia sighed, unable to hide the wistfulness that crept into her voice. 'I swear it's the only time I feel like I'm doing something worthwhile with my life.'

'That sounds like a vocation,' he said, sipping from his own glass. 'And yet you don't sound fulfilled.'

She shook her head. 'This might surprise you, but princesses don't have much sway when it comes to promoting new education laws or increasing expenditure on public schooling.' She sighed again. 'Since the crackdown on my security I've missed several important events. Perhaps the children won't even have noticed. Perhaps I'm only helping *myself* by going out there, boosting my own self-importance. Maybe I'm just an egomaniac.'

'I highly doubt that,' he said, all seriousness. 'This bothers you? Your lack of power?'

'Of course it does. How would *you* feel if you had people holding you back from living your own life at every step?'

A strange look passed over his face, disappearing just as quickly.

'I can only do so much.' She shrugged. 'Potential future innovators of my kingdom are sitting in homeless shelters and all I am allowed to do lately is hold charity balls. It means absolutely *nothing.*'

'Your work means more to those children than you could ever know.'

'How can you know that?'

Roman was quiet for a long time, his hands held tight in front of him. Then, 'I've lived that life. A long time ago, now. But you never forget.' He forced a smile, draining his glass. 'I know that a stranger's kindness means more to a homeless child than you would ever believe.'

Olivia took in the tightness on his features, the guarded emotions in his dark steel-grey eyes. 'Roman, I had no idea...'

'My past is not something that I like to relive. I just want you to know that your work has value. I owe much of my success to men and women I never even knew. They received no thanks, no rewards. I never understood such selfless giving—it was not something I had grown up to feel. Never doubt such honest goodness, Olivia.'

'I am sorry that you had such a difficult upbringing.'

'I'm not. It made me who I am today. But I am not arrogant enough to forget that the world would be an awful place if it was only filled with cynical men like me.'

Olivia understood him then—a little more than before, at least. 'You're not so bad.'

He laughed. 'You don't know the half of it.'

'Tell me, then,' she said quickly. 'Tell me whatever it is you think is so awful about yourself and let me be the judge.'

'Mine is not the kind of story you tell over paella and wine.' The laughter died from his voice, making it clear that the topic was not open for further discussion.

Their main course was laid in front of them, providing a welcome distraction. The food was delicious, and yet as Olivia watched Roman eat she couldn't help but imagine him as a young boy. Thin and hungry...helpless. It was a jarring thought—one that filled her throat with emotion.

She hated to think of anyone suffering through such hardship—especially considering the luxury she had been born into.

It had never sat well with her, the enormous divide between the wealthy and the poverty-stricken. She had always felt a weight on her shoulders and an obligation to do her part.

'That was delicious,' she said, forcing a smile as the waiter came to clear their plates and replenish their wine glasses.

'I hope this meal has done something to make up for my behaviour so far,' he said, lowering his glass and looking at her. Sincerity darkened his eyes as he held her gaze. 'For some reason the idea that you see me as cold and cruel bothers me.'

'I don't think you are cold at all,' she said, in all seriousness. 'I think that's just what you prefer people to believe.'

The night had grown cold by the time they embarked at the Puerto Arista harbour and set sail for the short trip back to the island.

Olivia apologised once again for the fact that they had had to abandon his luxury speedboat, but Roman assured her it was fine. They fell into silence as he concentrated on moving the boat along the harbour safely towards open water, each of them deep in thought.

A spark in the sky behind them startled her, and she turned back just in time to see an explosion of red and blue lights erupt into the perfect black sky.

'It must be midnight,' Roman said from behind her.

She could feel him lower their speed and allow the boat to drift slightly.

'This firework display is not one to be missed, trust me.'

'There's no need to stop just for my benefit,' she said quickly.

'Consider it part two of my apology.'

He guided her to the sun deck and pulled two cushions from the built-in sofa, laying them on the cold tiled floor. It was slippery with mist, and just a little chilly, but as a cascade of golden lights began to spread across the inky black sky she knew she wouldn't have changed the night for anything.

After the final booming red spinning wheels had faded into

the air, she turned to see he was watching her intently. She took in the heat in his gaze and knew he was battling with the aftermath of that kiss just as she was. She had never wanted to be kissed again more in her life.

'We should be getting back,' he rasped, his eyes not leaving hers.

'I'm really tired of doing what I *should* do all the time.' She licked her lips, silently urging him to give in one more time to the madness between them.

'Olivia...' He shook his head a fraction, lowering his eyes from hers.

She reached out to lay her hand just under the collar of his shirt, knowing she was being brazen but needing to do *something*. To show him in definite terms what her mind was struggling to convey with words.

He took her hand in his, lowered it back to her lap. 'You're not the only one who has to live by the rules,' he said quietly. 'Sometimes they are there to stop us from getting in too deep where we don't belong.'

'I am a grown woman, Roman. If I decide to take a leap into something unknown, you'd better be sure that I've got my reasons.'

'You might *think* you know what you want—'

Olivia stood quickly, looking down at him. 'I told you that I won't be spoken for again,' she warned him, feeling her temper bubble to the surface as she alternated between wanting to hit him and wanting to beg him to take her into his arms.

'Speak, then,' he said plainly, sitting back to look up at her. 'What is it that you want?'

'It's more what I *don't* want,' she said. 'Being here—away from the bubble of royal life—being with you...' She took a breath, urging the words out, needing to say them even if he simply walked away.

Roman shook his head, not giving her a chance to continue

as he jumped to his feet and moved back downstairs to start up the engine once more.

The rest of their journey back to the island was silent and tense, unspoken words heavy in the air between them. She wanted to ask him if he still planned to take her back to the palace tomorrow. If he still believed that she should go ahead with the marriage.

The Jeep ride was bumpy, and all too quickly they were standing in the dim empty hallway of the villa. Jorge must have closed up for the night and headed off to his quarters on the opposite side of the island.

'Goodnight, Olivia.'

Roman's voice was dark and final as he made to walk away from her.

'Wait,' she said quietly. 'I've realised something.'

He turned around, crossing his arms over his chest as he waited for her to speak.

Olivia cleared her throat, suddenly feeling very much on show. 'I've realised that I don't want to walk away from my kingdom, and if marrying a stranger is the way to keep it safe then perhaps that's what needs to be done.'

She took a deep breath, wondering if that was relief or disappointment that flickered momentarily across his features. She couldn't tell in the dim hallway.

'You are quite the sacrificial lamb,' he said quietly, with not a hint of emotion in his tone. 'So you plan to return to the palace and accept the marriage?'

'I've decided to return, yes. And face the situation like an adult, at least.' She met his eyes, challenging him in the darkness. 'But I can't fully commit to the marriage knowing there is one thing I have yet to experience in life.'

'I thought you ran away because there were *many* things you hadn't experienced?' he said, sarcasm dripping from his tone.

'There is only one that truly matters to me. I cannot agree

to an arranged marriage without allowing myself to experience one of the things I truly have control over.'

His gaze was pure heat as he moistened his lips with one smooth flick of his tongue. She felt heat spread down through her veins and pool in her stomach. If a simple look could make her feel this way, she needed to know what else he could make her feel. It was suddenly the only thing she wanted.

'I want my first time with a man to be on *my* terms, with someone who wants me just as badly as I want him.'

CHAPTER EIGHT

IN HIS MIND Roman simply gathered her into his arms and carried her up to his suite as fast as his legs could take him. Surely this was far more torture than one man was expected to endure? But in reality he remained silent for a long moment, his throat dry as his mind fought to sort between loyalty and lust.

She was offering herself to him on a silver platter.

'You think you can separate sex from love?' he said softly.

'If the sex is good enough.' She shrugged one delicate shoulder, biting her lower lip gently as though embarrassed by her own words.

She couldn't even say the word without blushing and she wanted to fall into bed with him. He took one step towards her, then another, until they were almost toe to toe.

'Men like me don't make love, Olivia,' he said darkly. 'They don't make empty promises just to play into some fantasy.'

She gulped, looking up at him through hooded lashes. 'What if I don't want the fantasy?'

'I have a thousand fantasies I could tell you about,' he whispered. 'Each one more risqué and physically demanding than the last. I would have you naked in my bed quicker than you could beg me to take you. Is that what you want me to say?'

'I…' Her voice trailed off, her eyes wide with uncertainty.

Roman let one finger trace the curve of her shoulder. 'You're not ready for me, Princess,' he said cruelly. 'You need a man who is going to whisper sweet nothings in your ear and make sugar-coated promises. I'm not that man.'

Roman braced his hand on the door of his suite and laid his forehead against the wood—hard.

Loyalty be damned. He wanted nothing more than to break down every door between them and take her like the unrefined street thug that he was.

But she was a virgin. She was not his to take.

Even as his mind thought the words his fist tightened in protest.

He took another deep, rattling breath, feeling the stale air of the room fill his lungs to bursting point.

She was not his.

With more force than necessary he turned and swung open the door to the terrace, silently thanking his housekeeper for placing his guest in the opposite wing of the villa. What would Olivia think of him now? Standing out in the night air, trying desperately to calm his raging libido like a scorned youth?

He looked across to where the light shone out from her rooms.

No. He shook his head, turning to vault down the stone steps in the direction of the pool. He had made his decision, just as she had made hers. And by God he would live with it.

The night was surprisingly mild, with barely a breath of breeze blowing in from the bay. The moon was full and high in the sky, casting a silvery glow on the water of the pool.

He took no time in stripping down and diving in, shock coursing through him as the cold water encased his skin, penetrating through to his very core. The pool was deep and he pushed himself to his limit, waiting as long as possible before breaking the surface.

As the balmy air refilled his lungs he saw the unmistakable silhouette of Olivia, standing near the water's edge.

Roman stood, so that the water reached his waist, very aware that he was completely nude in the water. His heart beat slow and hard in his chest. They were silent for a long moment, his eyes never leaving hers.

'You decided to take a late-night swim,' she said, her voice strangely husky in the dim light.

'And you followed me.'

She moved to the entry steps of the pool, dipping one toe in before stepping down ankle-deep in the water.

He noticed for the first time that her legs and feet were bare, that she wore a thin robe that stopped just above her knee. He wondered if she had anything underneath. He felt an ache in his gut, so deep, and he knew right then that he would move heaven and earth to have her out of that robe and in his arms.

He moved forward in the water, closer to her with every breath.

'I decided I couldn't leave here tomorrow without knowing more about those fantasies,' she said, her voice carrying across the space between them loud and clear.

Her hands moved to the tie of her robe and Roman paused, feeling the breath freeze in his lungs as he simultaneously willed her to stop and to keep going.

'How much more?' he asked, his voice husky as it echoed off the pool walls.

'Everything,' she said, her eyes never leaving his.

Roman took another step and watched as Olivia's eyes dropped to where the water level now completely exposed him to her. Her eyes darkened as she looked, and looked, before finally dragging her gaze back up to meet his. What he saw there ignited a fire in his blood. Raw desire darkened her eyes and coloured her cheeks as she undid the tie of her robe.

The white silk slid from her skin and darkened as it touched the water, leaving nothing between them but space. He was within arm's length of her now, unconsciously moving towards her. But he stilled at the sight of her, completely nude and offered to him like the living statue of a goddess. Her skin glowed under the moonlight. Every perfect curve of her body was on display in high definition and it was a revelation.

She stood still for a moment, before modesty got the better of her and she self-consciously moved one hand to shield her most intimate parts from his hungry gaze.

Roman closed the distance between them in a single movement, encircling her waist with his hands and pulling her with him into the water. With her body partially hidden, she relaxed in his arms and pressed herself tightly against him.

'I changed my mind too,' Roman said throatily, his mouth tracing a path along the exposed curve of her neck.

Her hands refused to stay clasped at his neck, instead preferring to explore the muscles of his back and down his waist.

She bit her lip seductively, removing her nails from where they had pinched quite roughly. 'I have wanted to do that for quite a while now.'

'Oh, so we are making up for lost time?' He gathered her higher, to his chest, wrapping one of her legs around his waist before doing the same with the other and pressing her back against the wall of the pool. 'In that case...'

Olivia groaned at the sensation of having Roman's lean, hard body cradled between her thighs, and his mouth captured hers in a kiss filled with barely restrained want. She could feel the heat of his chest pressing against hers and silently prayed for him to kiss her there again. As if he'd heard her plea, he broke the kiss and began trailing a path down her neck. By the time his mouth reached her breast, her breath was coming in short bursts. His mouth, hot and sinful, captured the entire rosy peak and tortured her with slow, languorous circles.

She began writhing against him as his free hand cupped her bottom and squeezed hard. The pleasure that rocketed through her was like being shot with lightning, and suddenly it was not her mind but her body that knew exactly what she wanted and just where she wanted him.

Her hips rolled against him and she moved herself lower, startled as she felt the hardness of his erection press erotically against her skin.

'Slow down,' he whispered, nipping the skin of her ear with gentle pressure.

'I don't think I can,' she breathed, moving against him, silently urging him to move against her. To place himself against her.

She tried to be embarrassed at her wanton response, but found she was quite past caring. Roman held her hips tightly in his hands, effectively stopping her movements. She looked up to find his dark eyes trained on her face and his jaw tight with restraint.

'That is possibly the most beautiful torture I could experience,' he breathed, leaning forward to gently nip her bottom lip with his teeth. 'But I want this to be good for you.'

'It feels pretty good so far.' She licked the curve of his lower lip, her gut clenching as he pressed the full length of himself against her in one quick slide.

'Olivia... I'm so hard right now that taking you fast and furious against this wall is *not* a good idea.'

He moved again, letting the tip of his erection slide against her sensitive throbbing flesh.

'Oh...' She moaned low in her throat as he moved, making slow, aching circles over just the right spot. 'Roman...don't stop.'

She closed her eyes, tilting her head back as his mouth found her breast once more. The double effect of his touch made her heart jump into overdrive and she could feel her pulse thrumming hard, as though it tried to escape her skin.

He urged her on in a mixture of English and Russian, his low, husky words sending her soaring higher and higher until she swore she could take no more. She dug her fingernails deep into his shoulders, wanting him to stop but wanting him to keep going for ever. It was like being trapped in her own personal hurricane—being swept up into a power so much stronger than herself.

When she finally found her release Roman was right there to catch her and hold her as she fell back down to earth. Heat spread out across her body, sending electricity right down to the tips of her toes. She opened her eyes and realised she was being lifted out of the water as her skin came into contact with the cold lip of the pool.

The contact was brief, as Roman lifted himself out and gathered her up into his arms as though she weighed nothing at all. It was strange, allowing him to carry her naked across the terrace. They were completely alone on the island, so privacy was guaranteed, and as she looked up at him she realised the feeling she had was not one of nervousness but one of anticipation.

He carried her easily up the stairs to his master suite. She had barely taken in the cool grey sheets on the gigantic bed when she felt her anticipation quickly intensify to mild panic. He was advancing on her now, his perfect muscular torso glowing in the light of a single lamp as he lowered himself over her and cupped her face with one hand.

As his lips lowered to touch hers she turned her cheek, grimacing when she realised what she had done.

'Is everything okay?' he whispered from above her, one hand trailing down her shoulder in a slow, sensual path. 'Are you... rethinking this?'

'No,' she said quickly, noting his features soften with relief. 'No, I'm definitely not rethinking *any* of this.'

'Relax,' he murmured, kissing a path down between the valley of her breasts. 'This is one of those fantasies I was telling you about.'

'It is?'

She lay back, staring up at the ceiling and willing herself to calm down. His mouth was doing a very good job of distracting her. That was until she realised just where those lips were headed. She tensed, reaching down for him just as his lips began to trace a path below her navel.

'This is *my* fantasy, remember?' he said, gripping her wrists and holding them by her sides. 'And I haven't even got to the good part yet.'

'Roman...you can't honestly—'

'Do you trust me?' he asked, his eyes dark with passion as his lips pressed gentle kisses along the inside of her thigh.

Olivia watched him kiss her, watched him draw closer to the centre of her, and felt herself nod once. She did trust him. Completely.

The nerves fell away with each gentle kiss on her skin and her eyes never left him, watching as he drew his tongue slowly against the centre of her sex. Her back arched and her eyes fluttered closed for a moment. When she looked back down his eyes were on her, dark and possessive, as he moved his hands to spread her wide and kiss her even deeper.

Her head sank back against the pillows as her body was enveloped in wave after wave of hot, wet pleasure. She reached down and knitted her fingers through his hair, anchoring him to the spot that felt most intense. He growled his appreciation, sliding one finger inside her in a slow rhythm.

'Oh... Roman...' She gasped at the feeling of delicious fullness, hardly believing it when he added a second digit to join the first without breaking rhythm.

Just as she began to feel that pressure mounting once more he removed his mouth, sliding up her body in one fluid movement. He reached across to the nightstand, grabbing a small foil packet and sheathing himself with lightning speed.

'I can't wait another second. This time I want to be inside you when you come,' he rasped, his voice half demand, half question as he met her eyes in the dim glowing light.

She spread her legs wide, silently answering his question with her body.

She could feel the tension in his shoulders as he positioned himself at her entrance, slick and ready from his expert attentions. His breathing hitched as he entered her with exaggerated slowness. Olivia raised her legs to encircle his waist, showing him that she was ready. That she wanted to feel him inside her for the first time.

The feeling of fullness was so intense she almost begged him to stop. After a moment she wanted to ask if there was much more of him to go.

There was.

She breathed deep as the sensation became uncomfortable, and was vaguely aware of Roman's voice intruding on her thoughts.

'I'm hurting you,' he said, deeply concerned, and began to withdraw from her.

Olivia held him with her thighs, keeping them connected as her body adjusted to his sizeable girth. 'Now it's your turn to be patient,' she breathed.

She tested her hips once, then twice, in a slow rolling movement. What had begun as a dull sting of pressure soon gave way to a more pleasurable pulse of heat.

Roman's breath hissed from between his teeth as she moved against him, but he remained exaggeratedly still above her.

'Does that feel good for you?' Olivia asked, taking in his tense jaw and serious expression as she tightened her innermost muscles, feeling the delicious hardness of him buried inside her.

Roman lowered his face into the crook of her neck, groaning low in his throat as though he was in pain. 'Oh, yes. Oh, God, yes.'

Olivia smiled, moving against him and feeling his breathing quicken in response. Suddenly he moved over her, his body arching slowly to press more firmly against her. She looked up into his eyes and somehow knew just what he needed.

He moved her thighs high on his waist, spreading her wide so that he could thrust right to the hilt. She gasped in pleasure, her hands on his chest as he braced himself on his forearms above her. His rhythm was deep and purposeful as he moved over her. He was powerful and entirely lost in his own pleasure.

Release reached them both at the same time, crashing down in wave after wave of pleasure. Olivia closed her eyes as the last of the ripples flowed through her, feeling the mattress move as Roman lay himself down heavily beside her.

CHAPTER NINE

ROMAN LAY STILL for a long time, his brain working overtime to fight through the heavy fog that always came after orgasm. This was different—heavier, somehow. He had never experienced a climax so intense.

Thoughts of why he should not feel so relaxed threatened the edges of his consciousness but he fought them off. He would analyse the repercussions of what they had just done in the morning, for now he thoroughly intended to repeat the experience just as soon as she was able.

He turned on his side, looking down at her where she lay curled on her side. Her eyes were closed, and for a moment he wondered if she was asleep, but then her lashes fluttered open and he was pinned by that blue-green gaze. Her hair had come undone at some stage, and its long lengths were spread across his sombre grey pillows in all their vibrant red glory. If possible, it looked even redder in that moment.

He reached out, taking a strand in his hands and running his fingers along the length of it. He was suddenly overcome by the realisation that it had been her first time and he had almost taken her in the swimming pool. Thankfully his brain hadn't been too far gone to realise that she deserved an actual bed for such a delicate moment, and that they needed to use protection. He *never* forgot to take precautions.

'I hope that was…satisfactory?' He smiled, a glow of male pride in his chest as he took in the slow smile that spread across her face.

'I never even dreamed that it could be so…' she began, shaking her head. 'Earth-shattering.'

'It isn't always that way.'

He ran a finger down the valley of her breasts, watching the play of light on her flawless skin. He had only just finished making love to her and he yet he couldn't stop touching her.

'I'm glad my first time was with you,' she said softly.

Roman stilled, taking in the look of deep emotion in her eyes. Knowing his own personal warning bells should be ringing at full blast. She was not experienced enough to separate the physical side of what they had just shared from her emotional reaction. And yet even as he told himself to remind her of his rules he found that he himself was having a hard time abiding by them.

He fought the urge to lean in, to kiss her mouth and lay a trail of kisses down her neck. He frowned. Such actions were dangerously close to tenderness. He was not a tender lover— to a virgin or not.

But he cared what she thought of him, that she'd enjoyed her first time—that was entirely normal, wasn't it?

Maybe that was the problem. He had nothing to compare it to, having steered clear of virgins up to now. He had never enjoyed the idea of being a woman's first, of having that much pressure on the act. But now, knowing he was the only one to have touched her, been inside her, heard her scream out in her orgasm…

He wanted more.

It was a dangerous madness, feeling like this. He had always prided himself on remaining detached and aloof from the women he chose to spend time with. They knew he wasn't in it for commitment. They got what they needed and left his bed satisfied as a result.

Olivia sighed deeply and moved so that she lay against his side. Her hand stroked up the inside of his wrist to his elbow and he looked down to see her curiously tracing the thick black band of ink that encircled his forearm.

He didn't think of the tattoo often—it was usually covered up and out of sight. But every now and then he found himself looking at it, thinking of the man who'd branded him, of the *life* that had branded him. And yet he had never had it removed.

'It's a gang tattoo,' he offered, not knowing why he suddenly felt the urge to explain. 'Not my own personal choice of design.'

Her lips formed a delicate little O as her fingers stilled over him. 'From your time in prison?' she asked quietly.

'Long before prison.'

A silence fell between them. Roman wondered if perhaps she was regretting her choice of lover after his revelation, but after a moment she sat up on her elbow, pinning him with her gaze.

'This gang—did they use guns a lot? Is that where your fear stems from?'

Roman frowned, laying his head back against the pillows as he remembered the events of the day before in painful detail. 'No. That's not where it comes from.'

She seemed suddenly self-conscious. 'I'm sorry if this isn't exactly pillow-talk material. I know you are probably the kind of guy who doesn't like to talk afterwards.'

'I don't,' he said honestly. 'But I can compromise.' He turned smoothly onto his side, so that they were face to face. 'You can ask me *one* question about my past and I will answer it—truthfully.'

Her eyelashes lowered momentarily. 'Who is Sofiya?'

Roman was silent for a moment. Then, 'Sofiya was my little sister,' he said. 'She died a long time ago.'

'Oh, I'm sorry.' Olivia's brow deepened into a frown. 'She must have been very young.'

'Sixteen.' He shrugged. 'It's in the past. Almost twenty years ago.'

'Grief doesn't care about time.' The corners of her lips tilted down sadly. 'My grandmother was buried ten years ago and I still visit her grave often.'

'I have never visited Sofiya's resting place,' Roman said, surprised at how easily the words spilled from him. 'Her parents despised me.'

Olivia sat up slightly. '*Her* parents? Not yours?'

'We were both abandoned by our birth mother at a very young age. Sofiya was a tiny blonde cherub with big blue eyes. She was adopted very quickly. I was not.'

'Oh...' She sat up slightly, looking down at him with concern.

He hated the feeling of being so vulnerable, and yet somehow he was unable to stop the words from coming once they'd started. 'Unlike my sister, I wasn't the most appealing child. I always had too much to say. It became a part of me to cause as much trouble as I could manage.'

He frowned, remembering the uncontrollable rage that had filled him as a child. He had broken toys, furniture—even bones on a few occasions.

'I was fuelled by anger and hatred. I was kept at the orphanage until I grew too big to contain. After I ran away for the third time they stopped trying to bring me back.'

'That is when you became homeless?'

Roman nodded. But the truth was he had never known a home. The only difference was that once he'd left the orphanage he'd had the added struggle of finding a safe place to sleep at night.

'I can't imagine how that was for a young boy.'

'I was thirteen—practically a man.' A low, harsh laugh escaped his lips as he thought of his gangly young self, so cocky and self-assured. 'When the local thugs saw the size of me they asked me to run errands. I didn't mind that they were criminals. They took me in…gave me a warm bed. One of the guys even bought me shoes.'

His chest tightened at the memory. He had worn those shoes until his feet had burst out of them. Then he had gone out and stolen himself a brand-new pair.

'I was thin and fast. They used me to climb through windows and vents and such on jobs. I felt very important.'

Olivia was quiet as he spoke on, telling her of his ascent into the criminal gangs of St Petersburg. To her credit, she did not react in any way other than to ask a question or to clarify a point. She just listened.

She listened when he told her of Alexi—the father of 'the brotherhood', as he'd called it. She nodded as he told her how, when he had grown broader and stronger, he had advanced to being a part of the main crew. They'd held up banks, intercepted cash in transit and generally just taken whatever they wanted. More than once he felt the old shame seep in, threatening to silence him, but she urged him on.

'This Alexi guy…he sounds dangerous,' she said softly, tracing a small circle on his chest as she watched him.

Roman thought for a moment of the man who had simultaneously given him everything and then torn his life to pieces.

'I wanted nothing more than for Alexi to be proud of me. He was the only dominant male figure I had ever known. It made me feel needed, validated—I don't know.' He shook his head, uncomfortable with the conversation all of a sudden. He didn't like to think of Alexi, of the hold he had once had on him.

'I think that was only natural. You were easily groomed—an easy target. You were vulnerable and he exploited that.'

'I never truly relaxed into the so-called brotherhood, and Alexi could see that. I had seen how quickly some of their drunken brawls escalated and I made a point to always stay sober. More than once he questioned my loyalty using violence.'

'Is *that* where your issue with guns stems from?' she asked quietly.

Roman frowned, realising he had gone off on a tangent. How had he kept on speaking for this length of time? Usually talking of the brotherhood and its fearless leader was enough to send him into silence for days, but something about Olivia had kept him talking...opening up.

Unwelcome memories assaulted his brain. Memories of the last night he had seen Alexi. Of the blood and the outrage and that pair of terrified, lifeless, baby-blue eyes.

Suddenly he couldn't talk any more. He stood up, walking to the terrace doors to look out at the night beyond. He shivered, feeling a cold that was not actually in the air but inside him. Ingrained in him.

Olivia bit her bottom lip hard as Roman remained completely silent by the doors and then watched as he walked into the bathroom, shutting the door behind him with finality. She had pushed too hard—her curiosity had been too overbearing. He was likely already planning the best way to tell her to leave.

He had made it perfectly clear that he was a one-night-only, no-snuggling type of guy—and here she was, initiating a psychotherapy session.

She lay back, throwing one arm across her face in mortification. She had just made love with this physically gifted specimen of a man and still she kept digging deeper, wanting more from him than he had warned her to expect. Trying to peek under his armour.

She angrily swung her legs over the side of the bed and stood, feeling her inner muscles throb with just the barest hint of exertion. She didn't feel too different, she thought with a frown. A little sore, perhaps, but not monumentally transformed as she had expected.

Still, it had been...utterly perfect.

Maybe it was best that it ended this way. She would arrange

to have a helicopter pick her up in the morning and that would be it. No awkward morning-after encounter, no hurt feelings. They both knew what this was, that it could be nothing more. She was completely fine with that.

But still some small naïve part of her made her linger for a moment outside the bathroom door until she heard the shower turned on. He couldn't have sent a clearer signal if he'd shouted the words *Go away!* at the top of his lungs.

The night was over.

She returned to her bedroom in darkness, not bothering to turn on any lights as she slipped in between the cool white covers and let stillness wash over her. Her mind raced, thoughts of what tomorrow might bring seeping through to her consciousness as the afterglow of her one experience of lovemaking dimmed.

Was one night of perfect lovemaking with a man of her choosing really enough to carry her through a lifetime of a loveless marriage?

As her exhausted brain admitted defeat and she drifted into half-sleep, she imagined what her wedding day might look like. Only in her mind the man at the top of the aisle was Roman. Devastating in a dark tuxedo as he took her hand and professed his eternal love for her.

All of a sudden her dream shifted to their wedding night, becoming infinitely more erotic. She sighed as he leaned in and pressed his lips to hers, the scent of him so familiar and overwhelming it was as if she could actually feel the heat of his skin pressing against her.

'You are so beautiful...'

His voice rasped near her ear, sending shivers down her spine and even lower.

Her eyes snapped open. 'Roman?'

He was draped across her, the scent of his shower fresh and warm on the air as his mouth laid a trail of kisses down the side of her neck.

'You left without giving me a chance to say goodbye,' he said, a dark glint in his eye as he moved lower to take one of her breasts into his mouth.

'You were the one who left.' She exhaled on a slow hiss as his teeth grazed her skin. 'I thought you were a one-night-only kind of guy.'

A wicked smile spread over his dark features as he poised himself over her, one hand snaking a path down her abdomen to slip between her thighs.

'The night isn't over yet, Princess.'

His kisses became more heated as his fingers took her higher and higher towards climax. Before she could completely shatter, he turned onto his back and urged her to straddle him.

'You will still be tender… I don't want to hurt you,' he rasped, his breath coming hard and fast, evidence of his arousal.

Olivia moved over him so that her breasts grazed the smattering of dark hair on his chest. She was clumsy at first, uncertain in her own movements as she poised her body over the sizeable length of him. He was rock-hard and already sheathed, waiting for her. She took a moment to slide the tip of him against her most sensitive spot, enjoying the sensation of molten heat that spread through her.

She repeated the motion a few times, wondering if he would grow impatient and take over himself. He didn't. Even as his rigid jaw showed the extent of his control he remained still, allowing her this moment of exploration.

'I'm not quite sure if I'll be any good at this,' she said uncertainly, lifting herself so that he was poised at her entrance.

'I'm right here, holding you.' He ran his large hands down her back, cupping her buttocks with possession as he guided her.

Her body stretched around him as she took him deep inside her in one smooth movement. The barest hint of discomfort faded quickly to an impatient need to roll her hips, to ride him and increase the delicious pressure she could feel with each movement.

'Is that...good?' she asked, her breath coming faster as arousal pooled and tightened inside her.

'You are driving me insane in the best possible way,' he groaned, his eyes never leaving hers. 'Don't come yet. Not until I'm right there with you.'

Olivia tried to slow down, to control her movements and somehow hold off the mounting climax that seemed ready to shatter her entire being at any second. He held her gaze, his hands gripping her hips as he began thrusting upwards slowly, in time with her.

Their rhythm was so smooth, so gentle, and yet somehow it was filled with a barely restrained madness as they both rose closer and closer to climax. Roman's breath fanned hard and fast against her cheek as she leaned forward, her breasts crushed against his chest. His hands moved up her back to hold her close, a deep primal groan escaping his lips as he slowed down even further and moved deeper inside her.

Olivia gasped at the overwhelming intensity of being so absolutely cocooned in his strength, and then the intense friction tipped her over the edge and she fell headlong into an orgasm that seemed to ripple through every inch of her body.

As she fell she felt a tightening in her throat, and prayed he wouldn't see the sheen of moisture in her eyes as she watched him lose control entirely beneath her.

Roman kissed her neck, growling something deeply erotic in his native tongue as the muscles of his abdomen began to ripple with the force of his own orgasm.

Afterwards, as she listened to his breathing deepen with sleep, she wondered if she had ever felt closer to another human being in her entire life.

The thought made her feel sad and grateful all at once. She had got her wish, without a doubt. He had made her first time the most sensual, real experience of her life.

His long, hard body was partly covered, but she still let her gaze sweep over him in the darkness, lingering on his features.

His face was transformed in sleep, the hard lines of his mouth completely relaxed. It made him seem younger...more carefree. It dawned on her that she had never seen him look at peace. Here, in sleep, Roman the great and powerful master of security, was completely vulnerable.

The thought of returning to the palace, to her own empty bed, was suddenly inconceivable. And even worse was the thought of sleeping alongside another man.

Marrying another man.

Her throat tightened painfully with the force of her emotion. Roman would not offer her any more than this night—she knew that. He was not the marrying kind, no matter what she suddenly hoped. He was not even the relationship kind.

But as she lay staring up at the play of shadows on the ceiling she knew one thing with more certainty than she had ever known anything in her life.

She would not marry the Sheikh.

When she awoke the bed was empty beside her in the early-morning light. Ignoring the sting of loss, she grabbed a white robe and stepped out onto the terrace, taking a moment simply to breathe and take in the gorgeous view of the bay spread out below.

Her hair was a nest of tangles, and she was in dire need of a shower, but for once she had no formal breakfast to attend, no official functions. She could stand here all morning if she chose, enjoying the last few hours of her freedom.

Roman would expect her to leave today, and that was perfectly understandable.

She thought of his revelations last night, the deep, dark secrets he'd shared, and wondered if he would regret sharing so much now that their night together was done.

He had told her only briefly of his life in St Petersburg. Of the orphan who had been abandoned to sleep in cold gutters, but she remembered every word in vivid detail. Every little piece of the puzzle he had revealed that made him what he was.

Roman had lived through hell itself. It was no wonder he seemed harsh. The world had hardened him from the moment he was born. He shouldn't have had a chance—and yet he had risen from his old life, determined and hungry for better. He had created his own empire without a single care for his social class or his chequered past.

He was the master of his own destiny.

Here, in the rosy glow of dawn, she felt utterly transformed simply by having known him. She laughed at her own thoughts. Romantic, indeed, or maybe simply foolish. Perhaps all virgins felt this way about their first lover?

How would he react to the news once he found out that her marriage was not going ahead? She imagined he would be frustrated with her—with himself. He would blame it all on their brief affair.

But, truly, Olivia wasn't sure her decision was completely down to their night together. On some level she had known she was not destined for a loveless marriage from the moment her father had thrust the idea upon her.

No amount of loyalty to Monteverre would outweigh the value she needed to feel in herself. Roman had made her see that, somehow.

She told herself that it didn't bother her that he was completely unaffected by their time together. She was not going to read anything into last night, and nor would she expect anything more from their liaison. He had made it very clear that he was not the kind of guy who slept with the same woman twice.

CHAPTER TEN

ROMAN HAD TOLD Jorge to take the day off, to ensure them some privacy, wanting as little intrusion as possible so that he could deal with the aftermath of their night together.

Olivia arrived down to breakfast dressed in pink. The dress had the kind of high waist and flowing, knee-length bell-shaped skirt that made her appear like something straight from a vintage movie.

She was breathtaking.

Her eyes were shuttered and her smile forced as she sat at the table across from him. The silence was heavy and uncomfortable, and his mind scrambled to find something to break the tension. In the end he accepted that there was simply nothing to say.

To his amazement, Olivia demolished two full plates of fresh fruit and a cream-drizzled pastry. She moaned as she devoured her last bite of pastry, looking up to find his eyes trained on her.

'I was hungry,' she said, a light blush on her cheeks.

'I've seen prison inmates eat with more decorum,' he found himself saying playfully. 'One night with me and you've completely forgotten how to behave like a princess.'

Her eyes widened at his mention of last night, as though he

had broken some unwritten rule by acknowledging that it had happened.

She sat back in her seat, a smile crossing her lips as she met his eyes boldly. 'Whatever will my subjects think?'

Roman raised a brow. 'That you've been taken down the path to ruin by a disreputable mongrel.'

'Mongrel?' She looked both amused and shocked.

'You come from a world where breeding is everything, after all.'

'Have we suddenly become *Lady and the Tramp*?' She laughed.

'I have no idea what that is,' he said honestly, smiling at the look of horrified surprise on her face.

'I can't believe you've never seen such a classic. It's wonderful—the lady dog comes from a fancy home and gets lost, and the tramp dog saves her?'

'You are likening me to a tramp dog?' He raised one brow in disbelief. 'I'm flattered.'

'*You* likened yourself to a mongrel—not me!' she exclaimed. 'It's not *my* fault that my brain associates everything with movies.'

'Film and television were not a regular part of my childhood,' he said, disliking where this conversation was headed. 'But let me guess: they all live happily ever after at the end?'

'Yes, exactly.' She smiled.

'That's why I don't waste my time on movies. It's not reality.'

'Well, of *course* it's not reality.' She laughed. 'That's what makes them an escape.'

Roman stood, gathering their plates and placing them less than gently into the sink. 'You spend far too much of your time escaping real life—you know that?' he said, knowing he had hit a nerve when he looked up and saw both of her hands balled into fists on the tabletop.

'You're being cruel now, and I have no idea why.'

'This is not cruelty, Olivia,' he said calmly. 'You have no idea what true cruelty is. What true hardship is, even. You dislike it when people put real life in front of you—that's your problem.'

She shook her head slowly. 'I have no idea why you're being like this right now. We were just talking about a movie.'

'Life is not like the movies, and the sooner you realise it the better!' He raised his voice, surprising himself with the force of his outburst.

Olivia stood, closing the distance between them. 'I may not have known the kind of hardship that you have experienced in your life, but that does not negate the fact that I have feelings too.'

'I thought it was clear that last night was not about feelings,' he said stiffly.

'And yet here you stand, shouting at me, when I was perfectly prepared to leave here on good terms.' She shook her head. 'It's probably best that I wait outside until my helicopter arrives.'

'You are leaving?' he said, the words tasting like sawdust in his mouth.

'I called the palace first thing this morning. They are sending someone to get me.' She nodded, moving to the table to pick up her coffee cup before returning to place it in the sink.

Even with her perfect posture and impeccably coiffed hair she seemed quite at ease, clearing up after herself. Far from a domesticated goddess, but still not too far above herself to consider leaving the mess for him to clean.

He thought of their conversations the evening before, of her talk of charity work. She was not the pampered royal he'd accused her of being and it was high time he admitted it to himself.

It was easy to place her in that box—to see her as stuck up and untouchable. It made her less real. But here she was, the woman who had shattered something inside him with her lovemaking last night, all too real.

And all too ready to leave him.

He knew then why he was being cruel. He simply wasn't

ready to give this up. To give *her* up. Not yet. And yet he knew it had already gone on too long as it was.

He was the worst kind of bastard, he thought darkly. Khal had trusted him with this—had entrusted him with the care of the woman he hoped to spend the rest of his life with. Whether the union was cold and political or not, it did not matter. He had rationalised his actions simply because their passion had been mutual. He had got lost in the novelty of feeling so utterly out of control.

Olivia deserved more than this. She deserved more than a brief fling with a man like him. And that was all he could offer her. Once the passion wore off he would only end up hurting her when he left. Roman Lazarov did not *do* relationships. He did not make declarations of love and commitment or plan lifetimes together.

In the past he had never been good at returning the things he had stolen. He refused to repeat his mistakes. And yet the idea of Khal knowing what had happened made him balk. Not for himself, but for Olivia. She deserved his protection.

'I'm coming with you,' he said, surprising himself.

Olivia turned around, her eyes wide with confusion. 'There is no need to escort me home, noble as it seems.'

'This is not about being noble—it's about being honest with Khal.'

Guilt entered her expression at the mention of the Sheikh's name. His gut churned at the realisation that by rights he should be displaying the same emotions himself, seeing as he had spent the past twelve hours in bed with the woman his best friend hoped to marry.

'Do you honestly want us to tell him about last night?' she said with disbelief.

'I will speak to him alone. There is no need for you to see him.' He found himself saying the words—words he had meant to protect her—and yet he could tell by the dark look on her face that they had come out wrong. As usual.

'You presume that I need you to explain on my behalf.' Her gaze seemed to darken as he took a step closer to her. She stood tall. 'I am quite capable of speaking for myself.'

'Clearly you are not. Otherwise none of this would have happened.' Roman shook his head, anger at the whole ridiculous situation coursing through him.

'Feeling some remorse, I see.' She pursed her lips.

'*One* of us should. Do you simply plan to go back and accept his proposal with the heat from my bed barely gone from your skin?'

'Is that actually what you think of me? Do you even know me at *all*?' She was completely still, unnaturally still, like the eerily calm glass of the ocean before a hurricane.

'I'm trying to—God help me. But you're not making it very easy.'

'And just what will you tell him? Seeing as you've got this covered.'

'Whatever needs to be said. Bottom line: he needs to know that we have slept together. I cannot let your marriage go ahead with him in the dark.'

'*Bottom line?*' Olivia's eyes widened. 'You know that telling him will essentially be ending the engagement before it can even happen? Why the sudden change of heart? Two days ago you were doing everything in your power to make this union go ahead.'

'Do I truly need to explain to you what has changed?'

Olivia's eyes darkened. 'Yes. You do.'

And there it was. The gauntlet, large and heavy, hanging in the tension-charged air between them.

'You spent the night with me, Olivia,' he said. 'I took your virginity.'

'That does not qualify as an explanation.' She bit one side of her lip, taking a few paces away from him before turning back. 'You said it yourself—it was just sex.'

Roman met the unmistakable challenge in her blue-green

eyes. He had not lied when he'd told her that sex was not always so intense.

'Sex is never "just sex" when it is one person's first time,' he said quietly, knowing he was being a complete coward.

'I think that is up to me to decide.'

'You wouldn't need to decide anything if I had done the right thing and walked away last night.'

'How utterly male of you to think that.' She rolled her eyes. 'Spending the night in your bed was *my* choice too, Roman. I wanted it just as much. I wanted *you*.' Olivia took a step towards him, the sunlight glowing on her Titian waves. 'You did not *take* my virginity. You can't take something that is given freely. I took last night just as much as you did.'

She looked so beautiful at that moment—all strength and feminine power. Hadn't he told her she needed to let this woman be free?

The unmistakable sound of helicopter blades in the distance intruded on the moment. Roman looked out of the windows and sure enough a scarlet-coloured chopper was coming in from the coast, the gold crest of Monteverre emblazoned along its side.

I wanted you.

Her words echoed in his mind as he analysed his own motivation for wanting to tell Khal of their night together. He knew that telling his friend would stop the engagement, knowing Khal as he did. He still wanted her. He was not fool enough to deny the fact. One night was just not enough when it came to Olivia. She was the best and the worst thing that he had ever stolen in his life, and the bastard in him wanted to keep her here until they were both truly done with each other.

Was he really that selfish? To manipulate her situation and push Khal out of the picture simply so that he could get her out of his system?

He ran one hand through the short crop of his hair, trying to make sense of his own thoughts.

'What if I told you that I plan to refuse the marriage?'

Her voice was quiet from behind him, strangely uncertain after the power of her speech moments before.

'You said yourself that your loyalty to your country is important.'

'Yes, but that was before I realised how it felt to take control of my own life for once.' She bit her bottom lip. 'Being with you…it's made me realise that I can have more. That I want more.'

'I can't give you what you want,' he said plainly, panicking at the look of open emotion on her face. 'If you plan on placing your entire future on the hope of something more between us then you are more naïve than I originally thought.'

She flinched at his harsh words and he felt like the worst kind of bastard. Hearing her speak of their time together so tenderly did strange things to his chest. As if with every word she uttered, bands grew tighter around his lungs. And it made him want to lash out with words to make her stop. To make her see him for what he was.

It was ridiculous, and immature, and yet he could no more stop himself from reacting that way than he could stop his brain from seeing guns where they didn't exist.

Olivia fought the tightness in her throat, refusing to let him see how deeply his words had cut. She met his gaze evenly. 'I will be returning to the palace alone. I trust that you will respect my privacy when it comes to last night. I should at least have the right to that from you.'

'I never said I didn't respect you,' he said harshly.

'Good. We have an understanding.'

She kept her voice even, walking over to the terrace doors to watch as the helicopter finished its landing and a familiar assistant exited the door, making her way towards the villa.

'This is goodbye, then,' she said, not wanting to turn to look at him but knowing she would regret it for ever if she didn't.

She felt anger, hot and heavy, burning in her chest. 'Thank you for allowing me to be one of the many women in your bed.'

His eyes narrowed, a cynical snarl appearing on his lips. 'Indeed. I will always have the pleasure of knowing that when it comes to you I was the first.'

'You are using the past tense already—how honest of you.'

'I have been nothing but honest with you about the kind of man I am,' he said harshly.

'Last night... I just thought that things seemed different somehow. That *we* seemed different.' She spoke calmly, trying and failing to hide the hint of insecurity in her voice.

'Everything seems different in the heat of passion, Printsessa.'

The silence that followed might only have lasted a matter of seconds, but to Olivia it felt like an eternity. In her mind she willed him to say more. Even a hint that he felt something more would be enough. Had she truly imagined that last night was momentous for them both?

And then he turned from her. Every step that he took across the kitchen seemed to hammer into her heart. Dampening down any flicker of hope she might have had.

She listened as his footsteps echoed across the marble tiles. Did he pause for just a split second in the doorway or did she imagine it? For a moment she thought he had taken a breath, preparing to speak. But then his steps kept going, out into the hallway, echoing as he moved further and further away from her.

She let out a breath that she hadn't even realised she'd been holding. The air shuddered through a gap in her teeth, like a balloon deflating and making a spectacular nosedive towards the ground. It was the ultimate heartbreak...knowing she had been just another woman in his bed.

She wanted to be *the* woman. The *only* woman.

But hadn't he made it abundantly clear that he would never be that kind of man? Was she really such a clichéd, naïve little virgin that she had fallen head over heels in love with him and expected him to do the same?

Typical that there wasn't a drop of vodka on the damned boat when he needed it.

Roman threw the empty bottle down hard on the glass bar-top, feeling it crack and shatter in his hand as it hit the surface.

'Chert voz'mi!'

He held his hand over the sink as the first drops of blood began to fall. The cuts were not deep, just surface wounds.

'*Damn* whoever is in charge of stocking the damned bar.'

'That would be me, sir.'

Roman turned to see Jorge in the open doorway, the man's face filled with concern.

'I came to see if you want me to close up the house.'

'Do whatever you like. I won't staying around long enough to check.'

'I see that Olivia has left us,' Jorge said tentatively.

Roman lowered his voice. 'I do not want to speak about Olivia. I want to relax and enjoy the rest of my vacation on my damned boat—alone.'

'With vodka?' Jorge added.

'Yes. With vodka. Is there a problem with that?' Roman spat. 'I am a grown man and you are not my father.'

'No. No, I am not,' Jorge said, a hint of sadness in his voice. 'But you have made it clear in the past that you at least see me as a friend of sorts.'

Roman grunted, wrapping a strip of linen carelessly around his injured hand.

'Can I speak frankly with you?' Jorge asked.

'You always do.'

The older man half smiled, crossing his arms and taking a deep breath before speaking. 'I think that you are hurting right now.'

'Believe me, I've had worse in my lifetime. I'll heal.'

'I'm not talking about the cuts on your hands.'

'Neither am I.'

'The Roman I know would never concede defeat so easily. You are not the kind of stupid man who would let pride stand in the way of what he wants.'

'Just because I want something, it doesn't mean I should have it. I have learnt that lesson in the past, Jorge. She is meant for a better man than me. A *good* man.'

'She loves you.'

'No. She is in love with the *idea* of love and nothing more.'

'I watched her get into that helicopter and, believe me, I know a heartbroken woman when I see one.'

'Well, that's not my fault. I did not hide from her the man that I am.'

'The man that you are would never come railing into his liquor cabinet unless he was deeply hurt by something. Or someone.'

'Jorge, you really must add psychoanalysis to your list of skills.'

'Tell me I'm wrong,' the other man said. 'Tell me she doesn't mean anything to you and I will fill that bar with vodka and send you on your way.'

'She is nothing to me,' he said the words, willing himself to believe them. Willing himself to ignore the burning pit of anger in his stomach.

'So if Khal marries her you will stand by his side and wish them well? I can see it now. You can visit them each summer in Zayyar. If you are lucky, their children might even call you Uncle.'

Roman's eyes snapped up to meet the gaze of his all too knowing housekeeper.

'*There.* That's all the reaction I needed to see.'

'Just because I feel the marriage is the wrong choice for both of them, it doesn't mean there is something deeper going on. I know Khal, and I know he would not be happy with a woman

318 ONE NIGHT WITH THE FORBIDDEN PRINCESS

like Olivia. She is too adventurous, too unpredictable. She wants to see the world, to be surprised by life. Not trade one palace prison for another.'

'And have you said any of this to the woman herself?'

Roman sat down on the bar stool, pulling the linen tighter on his hand and feeling the sting of pain that came with it. Jorge was right. He had not told Olivia how he felt about the marriage. Not honestly. He had spent half his time with her trying to convince her to marry Khal, and the other half trying to make her forget.

Was it really surprising that she had run from him again at the first chance? From the start he had handled her badly.

Women like Olivia were out of his league. She was too open, too caring and kind-hearted for a cold, unfeeling bastard like him. She deserved love. She deserved the happy-ever-after that she craved. And if he couldn't give it to her himself then he would make damned sure that she had a decent chance of finding it elsewhere.

'Shall I have the boat readied for departure?' Jorge asked hopefully.

Roman nodded once, watching as his housekeeper practically skipped from the room. He really should give that man a raise, he thought darkly as he moved to look out at the waves crashing against the lighthouse in the distance.

The marriage would not go ahead—not if he had anything to do with it.

CHAPTER ELEVEN

THE FIRST THING that Roman noticed as he entered the Sheikh's penthouse hotel suite was the utter stillness of the place. A single palace guard welcomed him inside before returning to his post outside the doorway. There was no butler to accept his coat or announce his presence—in fact no one at all roamed the halls as he passed through from room to room.

He had almost given up when finally he reached a large dining room that looked out over the lush green mountainscape of Monteverre's famous rolling hills. Khal stood alone at the head of the long dining table, his back turned as he stared out at the view.

Roman cleared his throat, feeling as though he had interrupted a moment of quiet meditation and wishing he had called ahead of his arrival.

'Roman. Now, this *is* a surprise,' Khal said, surprise filtering into his dark features as recognition dawned.

But Roman had not missed the mask of dark stillness that had been on his friend's face. That look bothered him deeply, and yet he knew that if he asked his concern would be met with a stone wall.

They were much alike, he and Khal.

'I need to speak with you,' Roman started, finding the words much more difficult than he had anticipated.

Truthfully, he was unsure where to begin. He had come here, all guns blazing, ready to rock the boat and make sure this ridiculous marriage did not go ahead. But how exactly did he tell his best friend that he had not only broken a rather important promise, but that he had done it in the worst way possible? He had promised to bring the Princess back to Monteverre to take her place as Khal's future wife, and instead...

Well, instead he had found himself consumed by a passion and a need so intense it had bordered on obsession.

He had not stopped thinking of Olivia in the few hours they had been apart. Memories of her assaulted him at every turn. If he closed his eyes he could almost smell the warm vanilla scent of her hair as it had lain spread across his pillows. He could almost hear her throaty laughter. She consumed him like no other woman ever had.

In fact, it was a mark of the strength of his feelings for her that he chose *not* to fight for her.

He was not here to lay claim to her.

He was here to set her free.

Khal sat heavily in one of the high-backed chairs, putting his feet up on the marble tabletop and surveying Roman with one raised brow. 'By all means, speak.'

'The Princess is the wrong choice for your bride.' He met Khal's gaze purposefully, making sure that there was no mistaking the seriousness of his tone.

'You sound quite sure.'

'I am. And I would like you to take my concern into account. There are things more important in life than politics.'

'Such as friendship, perhaps?' the Sheikh suggested, a strange hint of cynicism in his voice.

'I was thinking more along the lines of personal happiness.'

'I'm touched, Roman. Truly.'

'I'm trying to do the right thing here. To stop you from making a mistake that will last the rest of your life.'

'If you were doing the right thing you would be telling me the truth. You see, you need not worry about my personal happiness at all, Lazarov. Princess Olivia has already made her refusal of marriage to me quite clear.'

Roman felt his chest tighten painfully. 'Olivia? She came to you?'

'Not long before you, actually. Strangely, when she spoke of you she bore the same look on her face as you do right now when I mention her name.'

Hot guilt burned low in his stomach as his friend stood up and met his eyes with a cold detached evenness he had never witnessed before.

'I'm trying to control my temper here, Roman, because I don't want to jump to conclusions. But I'm struggling. Three months of planning. The future of two kingdoms hanging in the balance. And after a few days with you she's ready to give everything up.'

Roman remained silent for a moment, taking in the glint of barely controlled temper visible in his oldest friend's eyes. He knew he should walk away before things became any more heated. Olivia had already refused the marriage—he had no reason to be here.

But something held him rooted to the spot. In his mind all he could picture was King Fabian, planning Olivia's life for months before informing her of her impending engagement. Using an innocent woman as a pawn in his own political games. The man was cold enough to practically sell his own daughter to the highest bidder—as though she were a commodity rather than his own flesh and blood. It made the proud, possessive street thug inside him roar to life and demand justice.

'Tell me something,' he said calmly. 'In your three months

of planning did you ever think to speak to the woman herself to see if she *wanted* a political marriage?'

He watched Khal's mouth harden into a tight line as they stood toe to toe in the utterly silent dining room. There were no onlookers here, no palace guards or servants. They did not need to maintain any level of propriety. Right now they were just two men.

'I will ask *you* this question, because I deemed it inappropriate to ask the lady herself.' Khal's voice was a low whisper. 'Did you sleep with her, Roman?'

'Yes. I did,' Roman said the words harshly, feeling the air crackle with tension between them. 'And I am not going to apologise. Not to you, or to her damned father, or anybody.'

'Well, I'm glad to see you showing some remorse.'

'She is a *person*, Khal,' Roman spat. 'Not mine or yours. She can make her own damned choices—which you would know if you had ever bothered to treat her as such.'

'Right now this has nothing to do with her and *everything* to do with you,' Khal snarled, taking a step forward and jamming one finger hard against Roman's shoulder. 'You just couldn't control yourself—admit it. You wanted a woman and so you had her. Does the Princess *know* that she is just another notch on your bedpost? Or perhaps you are both just as selfish and impulsive as each other?'

Roman surged forward. Their noses were now mere inches apart. 'She is *nothing* like me,' he said coldly. 'She is kind and giving and she deserves more in a man than either of us could ever offer her.'

He paused, watching the anger drain from Khal's face as his brows furrowed with surprise. With a deep, shuddering breath he stepped away, turning to face the window.

A long moment of deathly silence passed before he heard Khal exhale slow and hard behind him, a slight whistle escaping his lips. 'I don't believe this... You are in love with her.'

Roman braced one hand on the window ledge, looking out

and seeing nothing. 'Don't be a fool. You said it yourself—women have only ever served one purpose for me.'

Khal's low whistle of laughter sounded across the room. 'I never thought I'd see this day. Roman Lazarov—brought to the edge of his infamous personal control by love.'

Roman shook his head, turning to take in the look of amused wonderment on the Sheikh's dark features. 'I am not prone to the sentiment. I simply believe Olivia has been treated poorly and I want to see it made right.'

'You poor, naïve fool. Sadly, love is not something we can choose to feel or not to feel. Trust me—I know.'

'I am not like you, Khal. I am not made for family life.' He took a deep breath, knowing it was finally time to say out loud the words that he had wanted to say for a long time. 'Look at my history with protecting the women I care for. My sister, your wife... I break things. I always have. I am simply not the kind of man she needs me to be.'

The mention of his late wife was usually enough to put an end to any conversation, but Khal surprised him, standing and placing a hand heavily on his shoulder.

'It was not your fault that Priya was killed. I have told you this time and time again. Just as it was not your fault that So-fiya was killed. You cannot take on the blame for everything that goes wrong around you.'

'What about Zayyar?' Roman said, shaking his head. 'This marriage was part of your great plan and now it's all gone to crap.'

'Perhaps not,' Khal said cryptically. 'I am not completely out of options just yet. Once Olivia ran away, the King and I discussed a possible fallback plan.'

Roman was silent for a moment. 'The youngest Princess?'

Khal shrugged. 'If she is willing, so be it. If not, I will retreat and regroup—as always.'

Roman nodded, glad that all hope was not lost for the two nations.

* * *

Olivia stood in her dressing room and placed the elegant emerald tiara upon her head for the last time. She met her own eyes in the mirror with a mixture of sadness and excitement, knowing that after tonight everything would change.

And yet everything had already changed for her.

Would anyone notice that everything inside her had undergone a massive transformation in the past few days?

With sudden momentous clarity she realised that for the first time in her life she truly didn't care. From tomorrow she would be giving up her right to succeed to the throne voluntarily, and making the leap into actually leading Mimi's Foundation. She was done with being a pretty face who smiled and waved. The time had come for her to use her own two hands to make the difference she craved.

Perhaps once all of this was over she might appreciate this moment more—the sudden power she felt as she left her suite and began to descend the grand staircase on the way to take her life back into her own hands. But at that moment she felt neither powerful nor relieved.

She had given her virginity and her heart to a man who had repeatedly warned her that he would treasure neither. She knew now that romantic souls could not simply choose to behave otherwise. She could not switch off the part of herself that yearned to feel loved, no matter how much she willed herself to.

A lifetime of training had taught her how to relax her facial muscles into a polite mask of indifference, even while emotions threatened her composure. Harsh decisions would likely need to be made, and comfort zones abandoned. But for the first time in her twenty-six years she was not worried about the unknown.

Olivia couldn't recall the grand palace ballroom ever looking more beautiful. As she descended the long staircase into the crowd of guests below she reminded herself to smile and hold herself tall and proud.

Perhaps one day in the far future she might look back on this night and yearn for a moment like this. But even as the tug of uncertainty threatened she pushed it away. She had made her decision and the time had come to put herself first.

The Sheikh had not been half as forbidding as she had anticipated—in fact he had seemed more pensive than anything as she had carefully outlined her reasons for refusing his proposal. His gaze had seemed knowing as he had enquired about Roman's treatment of her, but perhaps that was just her own sense of guilt.

She had her own reasons for keeping her affair with Roman private. She wanted to treasure her time with him, not have it sullied by the judgement of others. Either way, she had taken her power back and it felt great. The marriage would not be going ahead.

But she was not naïve enough to think that the hardest part was over.

Even as the thought crossed her mind she looked up to see her father watching her from across the ballroom. They had not yet formally met, but by now she assumed he would have spoken with the Sheikh. He would know that she had refused the proposal and he would be planning his punishment for her supposed betrayal.

Let him plan, she thought with a solemn shake of her head. He had no control over her. Not any more.

A commotion near the entrance caught her eye and she looked up to the top of the staircase to see a man pushing past the guards to descend the steps with ease. Two Royal Zayyari guards in crisp white and purple uniforms flanked him, holding off the Monteverre palace guards with ease and forcing them to stand down.

Roman.

Her mind went completely blank as the man she loved advanced towards her, his powerful frame accentuated by a perfectly tailored tuxedo.

'What are you doing here?' she blurted, so taken off balance by his appearance that it made her insides shake.

'It's good to see you too, *milaya moya*.'

His voice was like a balm to her soul. She hadn't realised how much her silly lovesick heart had yearned to hear it again. Just one more time. It had barely been twenty-four hours since she had left Isla Arista, and yet it felt like a lifetime since she had stood in front of him. Since she had looked into his slate-grey eyes as he had broken her heart with all the practice of a pro.

He opened his mouth to speak, but was cut off by the booming voice of her father as he advanced upon them from the other side of the room.

'Guards! Get this criminal out of my palace this instant!' King Fabian was livid, his cheeks a bright puce as he came to a stop a few steps away from where Roman stood.

The ballroom seemed to have become very quiet all of a sudden, and Olivia was thankful that the room was only half full as the guests had only just started to arrive.

'King Fabian—I was hoping I would see you tonight.' Roman's eyes narrowed, his shoulders straightening with sudden purpose.

Olivia reached out as Roman took a step towards her father, her hand on his arm stilling his movements. 'This is my fight, not yours,' she said, steeling herself as she turned to her father.

'The Sheikh has said that you refused his proposal after your little trip with this thug,' King Fabian spat. 'Judging by the lovesick puppy expression on his face, I can take a good guess as to why.'

Roman snarled, but remained dutifully silent.

'Father, I had planned to have this conversation at a better time,' she said, looking around to see that the palace guards had descended to herd the guests to the other side of the room, offering the royal family some privacy.

'There is nothing you can say to save yourself now, girl.' Her father shook his head sadly. 'I hope he's worth giving up your place in this family.'

'He has nothing to do with me giving up my place,' she said, as Roman frowned. 'Well, he does—but not in the way that you think.'

She took a deep breath, facing her father head-on.

'By giving up my right to succeed to the throne I am free of your control. That's worth more to me than being a princess ever could be.'

Roman reached out to touch her arm, 'Olivia, you don't have to do this.'

'I do. You see, my father has made more life-altering decisions on my behalf than this one.' She looked back at her father, noting his gaze darken. 'Such as when I inherited sole ownership of my grandmother's foundation ten years ago and he had me sign away my rights to him. At sixteen years old I didn't understand the repercussions. But now I do. And I know that by stepping out from under your thumb I'll get to take control of my own destiny for once and truly start helping people.'

'You can't do that.' King Fabian laughed cruelly. 'You can't simply walk away from this life.'

'I already have, Father,' she said sadly. 'I've been in contact with external advisors over the past few months to discuss the legalities. Once I relinquish any claim I have to the throne the foundation goes back into my name alone. Just as Mimi wished it to be.'

She hated it that her own father could look at her with such open disgust simply because she had chosen to go against his wishes.

Her own personal happiness did not matter to him.

Roman's eyes had widened as he listened to the exchange but he did not speak for her again. Nor did he attempt to interrupt as Olivia finished her conversation with her father and simply turned and walked away.

He took a moment to stand toe to toe with His Majesty, King Fabian. The urge to say everything he wished to say was so intense it consumed him. But Olivia had handled the situation with all the style and grace of the Princess she truly was. There was nothing he could add that wouldn't ruin it.

And so he walked away, following the woman he loved and ignoring the slew of vulgar curses in Catalan shouted in his wake.

He followed her in the direction of the outer terrace, instructing the two Zayyari guards Khal had lent him to stand sentry by the doors and make sure they were undisturbed.

Olivia stood with her back to him, staring out at where the moonlight shone across the ornamental pond in the gardens.

He moved to her side, reaching out his hand, needing to touch her. She flinched away and something inside him flinched too, with the hurt of that small movement.

'You're angry with me...of course you are,' he said softly, silently urging her to turn to look at him.

She didn't speak. Instead she wrapped her arms around herself defensively and stared resolutely ahead.

'I came here because I wanted to save you,' he said. 'I never even entertained the possibility that you were completely capable of saving yourself.'

'I'm glad I surprised you,' she said, irony dripping from her words as she turned to face him.

'Olivia...' he breathed. 'I came here to make sure that the marriage would not go ahead. I told myself that I was doing it for *you*, to save you from making a mistake that would last a lifetime. But I know now that I was only lying to myself.'

He braced one hand on the balustrade beside her, making sure to keep some space between them.

'I have never told anyone the things that I told you about my past.' He looked away for a moment, out at the darkness of the water. 'Something about you makes me want to tell you everything. To confide in you and trust you, even though I have spent a lifetime trusting no one. It scared me to death, to be quite honest.'

'Oh, Roman…' she said softly, reaching out her hand to touch him.

He raised his hand, holding her off. 'Wait just another moment. I've been thinking all evening about what I would say when I got here, you see.' He inhaled sharply, felt the adrenaline coursing through him. 'I've spent years—decades—blaming myself for my sister's murder at the hands of a man I trusted. She was shot right in front of me by Alexi, to teach me a lesson.'

Olivia's hands covered her mouth and tears filled her eyes. This was all going wrong, he thought. He hadn't meant to upset her—he just needed her to understand.

He stepped forward, taking her hands in his and kissing her knuckles gently. 'No, please don't cry. Anything but that.' He looked deeply into her eyes. 'I'm telling you this because I want you to understand why I'm such a cold, unlovable bastard. That monster wanted me to see love as a weakness. So he could break me down and make me easier to control. I have unknowingly let that lesson stick to me like tar for the past twenty years. I let that man's actions shape me, even from beyond the grave.'

'You are so brave to have overcome that…' She shook her head. 'To have become what you are now…'

'My success is nothing so long as I am alone,' he said simply, taking a breath and steeling himself for possible rejection.

She was utterly breathtaking, her long fiery hair backlit by the glow of the lights in the garden. The dress she wore was utter perfection in emerald silk, but truly she could have worn rags and he would have found her breathtaking. She was beautiful, it was true. But knowing her as he did now…knowing what lay below that surface beauty… It was infinitely more spectacular.

'I came here to tell you that I love you, Olivia,' he said softly, watching as his words resonated. 'I didn't know how much I needed you until I thought of seeing you on another man's arm.

Any other man. Of watching you become his wife and have his children… I cannot bear the thought of you marrying anyone… other than me.'

Olivia's heart thumped wildly in her chest as she looked into the solemn, emotion-filled eyes of the man she loved. 'Is that a proposal?' she breathed.

'I hadn't planned on laying it all out like that so quickly,' he said uncertainly. 'I understand if I've done too much. If I've been too cold for you to ever trust me or feel the same way.'

She shook her head, a small smile forming on her lips. 'I trusted you from the moment you offered to take me away with you.'

'Foolish girl.' He smiled, uncertainty still in his eyes.

'But love…?' she said, taking a step closer and running her hand over the lapel of his suit jacket. 'That didn't come until I truly knew you. Knew the man you are underneath all the bravado and the ice. Then I fell in love with you so deeply it took my breath away.'

He finally took her into his arms. His mouth was hot and demanding on hers as his hands held her tightly against him. His embrace filled her with warmth and strength. When he finally pulled away she groaned with protest, never wanting the moment to end.

'Are you sure you want to marry me? Even though I am no longer a princess?' She let a smile seep into her words as he tipped her back in his arms.

Roman shrugged. 'I suppose it's okay to settle for a simple philanthropist as my wife.' He sighed, sweeping his hands down her sides. 'If you're okay with the fact that *I* don't run an entire kingdom?'

She pretended to consider her options for a long moment, until his hands began to move lower on her hips and he pulled her hard against him in mock warning, with playfulness and a joy that mirrored her own in his eyes.

'I love you, Roman Lazarov,' she said solemnly. 'And nothing would make me happier than becoming your wife.'

The kiss that sealed their engagement was one filled with passion and promises. Olivia sighed with soul-deep contentment as she looked up into the face of the man she loved. The man she had chosen for herself.

Her own destiny.

* * * * *

At His Majesty's Convenience

Convenience

Jennifer Lewis

Books by Jennifer Lewis

Desire

The Boss's Demand #1812
Seduced for the Inheritance #1830
Black Sheep Billionaire #1847
Prince of Midtown #1891
*Millionaire's Secret Seduction #1925
*In the Argentine's Bed #1931
*The Heir's Scandalous Affair #1938
The Maverick's Virgin Mistress #1977
The Desert Prince #1993
Bachelor's Bought Bride #2012
†The Prince's Pregnant Bride #2082
†At His Majesty's Convenience #2093

*The Hardcastle Progeny
†Royal Rebels

JENNIFER LEWIS

has been dreaming up stories for as long as she can remember and is thrilled to be able to share them with readers. She has lived on both sides of the Atlantic and worked in media and the arts before she grew bold enough to put pen to paper. Happily settled in England with her family, she would love to hear from readers at jen@jenlewis.com. Visit her website at www.jenlewis.com.

Dear Reader,

I've always been attracted to amnesia stories. In fact, the first book I ever wrote—which will never see the harsh light of day!—featured a hero with amnesia. I've written about twenty books since that first brave attempt, but I've always wanted to return to the theme of amnesia and explore it in a new story. There's something so fascinating about someone waking up and having to interact with the world around them without the familiar filter of experience and memory that governs so much of what we do.

In this story, Andi's amnesia allows the characters to step out of their accustomed roles, as monarch/boss and loyal admin, and see each other with fresh eyes. On the other hand, Andi's memory loss gives her no choice but to trust Jake and what he tells her about their relationship, so things get very complicated when her memory returns and she realizes he's taken liberties with the truth.

I hope you enjoy Jake and Andi's romantic (mis)adventures!

Jen

Dedication:

For Lulu, a gracious lady and a powerful communicator
who's encouraged me to slow down
and see the big picture.

Acknowledgments:

More thanks to the lovely people who read this book
while I was writing it: Anne, Cynthia, Jerri, Leeanne,
my agent Andrea and my editor Charles.

CHAPTER ONE

HE WON'T EVER forgive you.

Andi Blake watched her boss from the far end of the grand dining room. Dressed in a black dinner jacket, dark hair slicked back, he looked calm, composed and strikingly handsome as usual, while he scanned the printed guest list she'd placed on the sideboard.

Then again, maybe he wouldn't care at all. Nothing rattled Jake Mondragon, which was why he'd transitioned easily from life as a successful Manhattan investor to his new role as king of the mountainous nation of Ruthenia.

Would her departure cause even a single furrow in his majestic brow? Her heart squeezed. Probably not.

Her sweating palms closed around the increasingly crumpled envelope containing her letter of resignation. The letter made it official, not just an idle threat or even a joke.

Do it now, before you lose your nerve.

Her breath caught in her throat. It didn't seem possible to just walk up to him and say, "Jake, I'm leaving." But if she didn't she'd soon be making arrangements for his wedding.

She'd put up with a lot of things in the three years since she'd moved from their lofty office in Manhattan to this rambling

Ruthenian palace, but she could not stand to see him marry another woman.

You deserve to have a life. Claim it.

She squared her shoulders and set out across the room, past the long table elegantly set for fifty of his closest friends.

Jake glanced up. Her blood heated—as always—when his dark eyes fixed on hers. "Andi, could you put me next to Maxi Rivenshnell instead of Alia Kronstadt? I sat next to Alia last night at the Hollernsterns and I don't want Maxi to feel neglected."

Andi froze. How could it have become her job to cultivate his romances with these women? Ruthenia's powerful families were jostling and shoving for the chance to see their daughter crowned queen, and no one cared if little Andi from Pittsburgh got trampled in the stampede.

Least of all Jake.

"Why don't I just put you between them?" She tried to keep her tone even. Right now she wanted to throw her carefully typed letter at him. "That way you can kiss up to both of them at once."

Jake glanced up with a raised brow. She never spoke to him like this, so no wonder he looked surprised.

She straightened her shoulders and thrust the letter out at him. "My resignation. I'll be leaving as soon as the party's over."

Jake's gaze didn't waver. "Is this some kind of joke?"

Andi flinched. She'd known he wouldn't believe her. "I'm totally serious. I'll do my job tonight. I'd never leave you in the lurch in the middle of an event, but I'm leaving first thing tomorrow." She couldn't believe how calm she sounded. "I apologize for not giving two weeks' notice, but I've worked day and night for the last three years in a strange country without even a week's vacation so I hope you can excuse it. The Independence Day celebrations are well under way and everything's been delegated. I'm sure you won't miss me at all." She squeezed the last words out right as she ran out of gumption.

"Not miss you? The Independence Day celebrations are the biggest event in the history of Ruthenia—well, since the 1502 civil war, at least. We can't possibly manage without you, even for a day."

Andi swallowed. He didn't care about her at all, just about the big day coming up. Wasn't it always like this? He was all business, all the time. After six years working together he barely knew anything about her. Which wasn't fair, since she knew almost everything about him. She'd eaten, slept and breathed Jake Mondragon for the past six years and in the process fallen utterly and totally in love with him.

Shame he didn't even notice she was female.

He peered down at her, concern in his brown eyes. "I told you to take some vacation. Didn't I suggest you go back home for a few weeks last summer?"

Home? Where was home anymore? She'd given up her apartment in Manhattan when she moved here. Her parents both worked long hours and had moved to a different suburb since she left high school, so if she went to see them she'd just end up hanging around their house—probably pining for Jake.

Well, no more. She was going to find a new home and start over. She had an interview for a promising job as an event planner scheduled for next week in Manhattan, and that was a perfect next step to going out on her own.

"I don't want to be a personal assistant for the rest of my life and I'm turning twenty-seven soon so it's time to kick-start my career."

"We can change your title. How about…" His dark eyes narrowed. She couldn't help a slight quickening in her pulse. "Chief executive officer."

"Very funny. Except that I'd still be doing all the same things."

"No one else could do them as well as you."

"I'm sure you'll manage." The palace had a staff of nearly thirty including daytime employees. She was hardly leaving him in the lurch. And she couldn't possibly stand to be here for Independence Day next week. The press had made a big deal of how important it was for him to choose a bride; the future of the monarchy depended on it. He'd jokingly given their third Independence Day as his deadline when he'd assumed the crown three years ago.

Now everyone expected him to act on it. Being a man of his word, Andi knew he would. Maxi, Alia, Carina, there were plenty to choose from, and she couldn't bear to see him with any of them.

Jake put down the guest list, but made no move to take her letter of resignation. "I know you've been working hard. Life in a royal palace is a bit of a twenty-four-hour party, but you do get to set your own hours and you've never been shy about asking for good compensation."

"I'm very well paid and I know it." She did pride herself on asking for raises regularly. She knew Jake respected that, which was probably half the reason she'd done it. As a result she had a nice little nest egg put aside to fund her new start. "But it's time for me to move on."

Why was she even so crazy about him? He'd never shown the slightest glimmer of interest in her.

Her dander rose still higher as Jake glanced at his watch. "The guests will be here any minute and I need to return a call from New York. We'll talk later and figure something out." He reached out and clapped her on the arm, as if she was an old baseball buddy. "We'll make you happy."

He turned and left the room, leaving her holding her letter of resignation between trembling fingers.

Once the door had closed behind him, she let out a growl of frustration. Of course he thought he could talk her down and turn everything around. Isn't that exactly what he was known for? And he even imagined he could make her "happy."

That kind of arrogance should be unforgivable.

Except that his endless confidence and can-do attitude were possibly what she admired and adored most in him.

The only way he could make her happy was to sweep her off her feet into a passionate embrace and tell her he loved her and wanted to marry her.

Except that kings didn't marry secretaries from Pittsburgh. Even kings of funny little countries like Ruthenia.

"The vol-au-vents are done, cook's wondering where to send them."

Andi started at the sound of the events assistant coming through another doorway behind her.

"Why don't you have someone bring them up for the first guests? And the celery stalks with the cheese filling." She tucked the letter behind her back.

Livia nodded, her red curls bobbing about the collar of her white shirt, like it was just another evening.

Which of course it was, except that it was Andi's last evening here.

"So did they ask you in for an interview?" Livia leaned in with a conspiratorial whisper.

"I cannot confirm or deny anything of that nature."

"How are you going to manage an interview in New York when you're imprisoned in a Ruthenian palace?"

Andi tapped the side of her nose. She hadn't told anyone she was leaving. That would feel too much like a betrayal of Jake. Let them just wake up to find her gone.

Livia put her hands on her hips. "Hey, you can't just take off back to New York without me. I told you about that job."

"You didn't say you wanted it."

"I said I thought it sounded fantastic."

"Then you should apply." She wanted to get away. This conversation was not productive and she didn't trust Livia to keep her secrets.

Livia narrowed her eyes. "Maybe I will."

Andi forced a smile. "Save a vol-au-vent for me, won't you?"

Livia raised a brow and disappeared back through the door.

Who would be in charge of choosing the menus and how the food should be served? The cook, probably, though she had quite a temper when she felt pressured. Perhaps Livia? She wasn't the most organized person in the palace and she'd been skipped over for promotion a few times. Probably why she wanted to leave.

Either way, it wasn't her problem and Jake would soon find someone to replace her. Her heart clenched at the thought, but she drew in a steadying breath and marched out into the hallway toward the foyer. She could hear the hum of voices as the first guests took off their luxurious coats and handed them to the footmen to reveal slinky evening gowns and glittering jewels.

Andi smoothed the front of her black slacks. It wasn't appropriate for a member of staff to get decked out like a guest.

All eyes turned to the grand staircase as Jake descended to greet the ladies with a kiss on each cheek. Andi tried to ignore the jealousy flaring in her chest. How ridiculous. One of these girls was going to marry him and she had no business being bothered in any way.

"Could you fetch me a tissue?" asked Maxi Rivenshnell. The willowy brunette cast her question in Andi's direction, without actually bothering to meet her gaze.

"Of course." She reached into her pocket and withdrew a folded tissue from the packet she kept on her. Maxi snatched it from her fingers and tucked it into the top of her long satin gloves without a word of thanks.

She didn't exist for these people. She was simply there to serve them, like the large staff serving each of their aristocratic households.

A waiter appeared with a tray of champagne glasses and she helped to distribute them amongst the guests, then ushered people into the green drawing room where a fire blazed in a stone fireplace carved with the family crest.

Jake strolled and chatted with ease as the room filled with well-dressed Ruthenians. Several of them had only recently returned after decades of exile in places like London, Monaco and Rome, ready to enjoy Ruthenia's promised renaissance after decades of failed socialism.

So far the promise was coming true. The rich were getting richer, and—thanks to Jake's innovative business ideas—everyone else was, as well. Even the staunch anti-monarchists who'd opposed his arrival with protests in the streets now had to admit that Jake Mondragon knew what he was doing.

He'd uncovered markets for their esoteric agricultural products, and encouraged multinational firms to take advantage of Ruthenia's strategic location in central Europe and its vastly underemployed workforce. The country's GDP had risen nearly 400% in just three years, making eyeballs pop all across the globe.

Andi stiffened as Jake's bold laugh carried through the air. She'd miss that sound. Was she really leaving? A sudden flash of panic almost made her reconsider.

Then she followed the laugh to its source and her heart seized as she saw Jake with his arm around yet another Ruthenian damsel—Carina Teitelhaus—whose blond hair hung in a silky sheet almost to her waist.

Andi tugged her gaze away and busied herself with picking up a dropped napkin. She would not miss seeing him draped over other women one bit. He joked that he was just trying to butter up their powerful parents and get them to invest in the country, but right now that seemed like one more example of how people were pawns to him rather than living beings with feelings.

He'd marry one of them just because it was part of his job. And she couldn't bear to see that.

She needed to leave tonight, before he could use his well-practiced tongue to... Thoughts of his tongue sent an involuntary shiver through her.

Which was exactly why she needed to get out of here. And she wasn't going to give him a chance to talk her out of it.

Jake pushed his dessert plate forward. He'd had all the sticky sweetness he could stand for one night. With Maxi on one side and Alia on the other, each vying to tug his attention from the other, he felt exhausted. Andi knew he liked to have at least one decent conversationalist seated next to him, yet she'd followed through on her threat to stick him between two of the most troublesome vixens in Ruthenia.

Speaking of which, where was Andi?

He glanced around the dining room. The flickering light from the candles along the table and walls created deep shadows, but he didn't see her. Usually she hovered close by in case he needed something.

He summoned one of the servers. "Ulrike, have you seen Andi?"

The quiet girl shook her head. "Would you like me to find her, sir?"

"No, thanks, I'll find her myself." At least he would as soon as he could extricate himself from yet another eight-course meal. He couldn't risk offending either of his bejeweled dinner companions with an early departure since their darling daddies were the richest and most powerful men in the region. Once things were settled, he wouldn't have to worry so much about currying their favor, but while the economy was growing and changing and finding its feet in the world, he needed their flowing capital to oil its wheels.

He could see how men in former eras had found it practical to marry more than one woman. They were both pretty—Maxi a sultry brunette with impressive cleavage and Alia a graceful blonde with a velvet voice—but to be completely honest he didn't want to marry either of them.

Carina Teitelhaus shot him a loaded glance from across the table. Her father owned a large factory complex with a lot of potential for expansion. And she didn't hesitate to remind him of that.

Ruthenia's noblewomen were becoming increasingly aggressive in pursuing the role of queen. Lately he felt as if he were juggling a bevy of flaming torches and the work of keeping them all in the air was wearing on his nerves. He'd committed to choosing a bride before Independence Day next week. At the time he'd made that statement the deadline had seemed impossibly far off and none of them were sure Ruthenia itself would even still be in existence.

Now it was right upon them, along with the necessity of choosing his wife or breaking his promise. Everyone in the room was painfully aware of each glance, every smile or laugh he dispensed in any direction. The dining table was a battlefield, with salvos firing over the silver.

Usually he could count on Andi to soothe any ruffled feathers with careful seating placements and subtly coordinated private trysts. Tonight, though, contrary to her promise, she'd left him in the lurch.

"Do excuse me, ladies." He rose to his feet, avoiding all mascara-laden glances, and strode for the door.

Andi's absence worried him. What if she really did leave? She was the anchor that kept the palace floating peacefully in the choppy seas of a changing Ruthenia. He could give her any task and just assume it was done, without a word of prompting. Her tact and thoughtfulness were exemplary, and her organizational skills were unmatched. He couldn't imagine life without her.

After a short walk over the recently installed plum-colored carpets of the west hallway, he glanced into her ever-tidy office—and found it dark and empty. He frowned. She was often there in the evenings, which coincided with business hours in the U.S. and could be a busy time.

Her laptop was on the desk, as usual. That was a good sign.

Jake headed up the west staircase to the second floor, where most of the bedrooms were located. Andi had a large "family" bedroom rather than one of the pokey servants' quarters on the third floor. She was family, dammit. And that meant she couldn't pick up and leave whenever she felt like it.

A nasty feeling gripped his gut as he approached her closed door. He knocked on the polished wood and listened for movement on the other side.

Nothing.

He tried the handle and to his surprise the door swung open. Curiosity tickling his nerves, he stepped inside and switched on the light. Andi's large room was neat and free of clutter—much like her desk. It looked like a hotel room, with no personal touches added to the rather extravagant palace décor. The sight of two black suitcases—open and packed—stopped him in his tracks.

She really was leaving.

Adrenaline surged through him. At least she hadn't gone yet, or the bags would be gone, too. The room smelled faintly of that subtle scent she sometimes wore, almost as if she was in the room with him.

He glanced around. Could she be hiding from him?

He strode across the room and tugged open the doors of the massive armoire. His breath stopped for a second and he half expected to see her crouched inside.

Which of course she wasn't. Her clothes were gone, though, leaving only empty hangers on the rod.

Anger warred with deep disappointment that she intended to abandon him like this. Did their six years together mean nothing to her?

She couldn't leave without her suitcases. Perhaps he should take them somewhere she couldn't find them. His room, for example.

Unfamiliar guilt pricked him. He didn't even like the idea of her knowing he'd entered her room uninvited, let alone taken her possessions hostage. Andi was a stickler for honesty and had kept him aboveboard more times than he cared to remember. Taking her bags just felt wrong.

She'd said she'd leave as soon as the party was over. A woman of her word, she'd be sure to wait until the last guest was gone. As long as he found her before then, everything would be fine. He switched off the light and left the room as he'd found it.

He scanned the east hall as he headed for the stairs, a sense of foreboding growing inside him. The packed bags were an ominous sign, but he couldn't really believe she'd abandon Ruthenia—and him.

"Jake, darling, we were wondering what happened to you," Maxi called to him from the bottom of the stairs. "Colonel Von Deiter has volunteered to play piano while we dance." She stretched out her long arm, as if inviting him to share the first dance with her.

Since coming to Ruthenia he sometimes felt he'd stepped into a schnitzel-flavored Jane Austen story, where people waltzed around ballrooms and gossiped behind fans. He was happier in a business meeting than on a dance floor, and right now he'd much rather be dictating a letter to Andi than twirling Maxi over the parquet.

"Have you seen Andi, my assistant?"

"The little girl who wears her hair in a bun?"

Jake frowned. He wasn't sure exactly how old Andi was—mid-twenties, maybe?—but it seemed a bit rude for someone of twenty-two to call her a little girl. "She's about five foot seven," he said, with an arched brow. "And yes, she always wears her hair in a bun."

Come to think of it, he'd literally never seen her hair down, which was pretty odd after six years. A sudden violent urge to see Andi with her hair unleashed swept through him. "I've looked all over the palace for her, but she's vanished into thin air."

Maxi shrugged. "Do come dance, darling."

His friend Fritz appeared behind her. "Come on, Jake. Can't let the ladies down. Just a twirl or two. I'm sure Andi has better things to do than wait on you hand and foot."

"She doesn't wait on me hand and foot. She's a valued executive."

Fritz laughed. "Is that why she's always hovering around taking care of your every need?"

Jake stiffened. He never took Andi for granted. He knew just how dependent on her he was. Did she feel that he didn't care?

Frowning, he descended the stairs and took Maxi's offered hand. He was the host, after all. Two waltzes and a polka later he managed to slip out into the hallway.

"Any idea where Andi is?" he asked the first person he saw, who happened to be the night butler.

He shrugged in typical Ruthenian style. "Haven't seen her in hours. Maybe she went to bed?"

Unlikely. Andi never left a party until the last guest had rolled down the drive. But then she'd never quit before, either. He was halfway up the stairs before he realized he was heading for her bedroom again.

Jake stared at her closed door. Was she in there? And if not, were her bags still there?

He knocked, but heard no movement from inside. After checking that the corridor was deserted, he knelt and peered through the keyhole. It was empty—no key on the inside—which suggested she was out. On the other hand, the pitch darkness on the other side meant he couldn't see a thing.

He slipped in—didn't she know better than to leave her door unlocked?—and switched on the light. The suitcases were still there. Closer inspection revealed that one of them had been partially unpacked, as if an item was removed. Still, there were no clues as to Andi's whereabouts.

Frustration pricked his muscles. How could she just disappear like this?

At the foot of the stairs, Fritz accosted him, martini in hand.

"When are you going to choose your bride, Jake? We're all getting impatient."

Jake growled. "Why is everyone so mad for me to get married?"

"Because there are precious few kings left in the world and you're up for grabs. The rest of us are waiting to see who's left. None of the girls dare even kiss us anymore, let alone do anything more rakish, in case they're making themselves ineligible for a coronet. They're all fighting for the chance to be called Your Majesty."

"Then they're all nuts. If anyone calls *me* 'Your Majesty,' I'll fire 'em."

Fritz shoved him. "All bluster. And don't deny you have some of the loveliest women in the world to choose from."

"I wish the loveliest women in the world would take off for the night. I'm ready to turn in." Or rather, ready to find and corner Andi.

Fritz cocked his head. "Party pooper. All right. I'll round up the troops and march 'em out for you."

"You're a pal."

Jake watched the last chauffeured Mercedes disappear down the long driveway from the east patio. He needed some air to clear his head before tackling Andi—and watching from here ensured that she couldn't leave without him seeing her.

Could he really stand to marry Maxi or Alia or any of these empty-headed, too-rich, spoiled brats? He'd been surrounded by their kind of women all his life, even in New York. Just the circle he'd been born into. You'd think a king would have more choices than the average Joe, but that was apparently not the case.

Something moving in the darkness caught his eye. He squinted, trying to make out what was crossing the lawn. An animal? Ruthenia had quite large deer that he was supposed to enjoy hunting.

But this creature was lighter, more upright, and moved with a kind of mystical grace. He stepped forward, peering into the gloom of a typical moonlit but cloudy night. The figure whirled and twirled on the lawn, pale fabric flowing around it.

A ghost? His back stiffened. The palace was nearly three hundred years old and built over a far more ancient structure. Tales of sieges and beheadings and people imprisoned in the dungeons rattled around the old stone walls.

Long, pale arms extended sideways as the figure twirled again. A female ghost.

Curiosity goaded him across the patio and down the stone stairs onto the lawn. He walked silently across the damp grass, eyes fixed on the strange apparition. As he drew closer he heard singing—soft and sweet—almost lost in the low breeze and the rustling of the trees.

Entranced, he moved nearer, enjoying the figure's graceful movements and the silver magic of her voice.

He stopped dead when he realized she was singing in English.

"Andi?"

Despite the hair streaming over her shoulders and the long, diaphanous dress, he recognized his assistant of six years, arms raised to the moon, swaying and singing in the night.

He strode forward faster. "Are you okay?"

She stopped and stared at him and the singing ceased. Her eyes shone bright in the darkness.

"What are you doing out here?" He walked right up to her, partly to prove to himself that she was real and not a figment of his imagination. His chest swelled with relief. At least now he'd found her and they could have that talk he'd been rehearsing in his head all night.

"Why don't we go inside?" He reached out for her hand, almost expecting his own to pass through it. She still looked so spectral, smiling in the cloud-veiled moonlight.

But the hand that seized his felt warm. Awareness snapped

through him as her fingers closed around his. Her hair was longer than he'd imagined. Almost to the peaks of her nipples, which jutted out from the soft dress. He swallowed. He'd never noticed what…luxurious breasts Andi had. They were usually hidden under tailored suits and crisp blouses.

He struggled to get back on task. "We need to talk."

Andi's grip tightened on his, but she didn't move. Her face looked different. Transfixed, somehow. Her eyes sparkling and her lips glossy and parted. Was she drunk?

"You must be cold." On instinct he reached out to touch her upper arm, which was bare in the floaty evening gown she wore. As he drew closer, her free arm suddenly wrapped around his waist with force.

Jake stilled as she lifted her face to his. She smelled of that same soft scent she always wore, not a trace of alcohol, just flowers and sweetness. He groped for words, but failed to find any as her lips rose toward his.

Next thing he knew he was kissing her full—and hard—on the mouth.

CHAPTER TWO

JAKE LET HIS arms wind around her waist. The movement was as instinctive as breathing. Their mouths melted together and her soft body pressed against his. Desire flared inside him, hot and unexpected, as the kiss deepened. His fingers ached to explore the lush curves she'd kept hidden for so long.

But this was Andi—his faithful and long-suffering assistant, not some bejeweled floozy who just wanted to lock lips with a monarch.

He pulled back from the kiss with great difficulty, unwinding himself from the surprisingly powerful grip of her slim arms. A momentary frown flashed across her lovely face—why had he never noticed she was so pretty?—then vanished again as a smile filled her soft eyes and broadened her mouth.

She lifted a hand and stroked his cheek. "You're beautiful."

Shocked, Jake struggled for a response. "*You're* beautiful. I'm handsome." He lifted a brow, as if to assure himself they were both kidding.

She giggled—in a most un-Andi-like way—and tossed her head, which sent her hair tumbling over her shoulders in a shimmering cascade. She twirled again, and the soft dress draped her form, allowing him a tantalizing view of her figure. He'd certainly never seen her in this dress before. Floor-length and daringly see-through, it was far dressier and more festive than her usual attire.

"Happiness is glorious joy," she sang, as she turned to face him again.

"Huh?" Jake frowned.

"Mysterious moonlight and wonderful wishes." Another silver peal of laughter left her lips—which looked quite different than he remembered, bare of their usual apricot lipstick and kissed to ruby fullness.

Unless she'd suddenly turned to poetry—very bad poetry at that—she must be intoxicated. He didn't smell anything on her breath, though. And didn't she always insist she was allergic to alcohol? He couldn't remember ever seeing her with a real drink.

Drugs?

He peered at her eyes. Yes, her pupils were dilated. Still, Andi experimenting with illegal substances? It seemed impossible.

"Did you take something?"

"Steal? I'd never steal from you. You're my true love." She gazed at him as she spoke the words, eyes clear and blue as a summer sky.

Jake groped for words. "I meant, did you take any pills?"

You're my true love? She was obviously tripping on something. He'd better get her inside before she tried to fly from the parapets or walk on the water in the moat. "Let's go inside."

He wrapped his arm around her, and she squeezed against him and giggled again. This was not the Andi he knew. Perhaps the stress of threatening to leave had encouraged her to take some kind of tranquilizer. He had no idea how those things worked, but couldn't come up with any other explanation for her odd behavior.

"You smell good." She pressed her face against him, almost tripping him.

Jake's eyes widened, but he managed to keep walking. Her

body bumping against his was not helping his own sanity. Now she'd slid an arm around his waist and her fingers fondled him as they walked. His blood was heating in a most uncomfortable way.

Maybe he could bring both of them back down to earth.

"It was cold of you to seat me between Maxi and Alia."

"Who?" She marched gaily along over the lawn, still clinging to him. No reaction to the names.

"Maxi and Alia. Both of them fighting over me was a bit much to take on top of the cook's roulade."

"Pretty names. We haven't met. You must introduce me sometime." She pulled her arm from his waist and took off skipping across the damp lawn.

Jake paused and stared for a moment, then strode after her.

Since he didn't particularly want any of the other staff to see Andi in this compromising state, Jake hustled her into his private chambers and locked the door. That was the accepted signal that he was off duty for the night and not to be disturbed.

Andi made herself quite at home, curling up on one of the sofas, with a languid arm draping along the back. "Happiness is as happiness does," she said dreamily.

Jake resisted the urge to pour himself a whisky. "Listen, what you said about leaving. I saw your bags—"

"Leave? I would never leave you, my love." Her face rested in a peaceful smile.

Jake swallowed. "So you're staying."

"Of course. Forever and ever and ever." Her eyes sparkled.

"Ah. That's settled then." He moved to the liquor cabinet, deciding to have that whisky after all. "I am relieved. The thought of managing without you was quite frightening."

Andi had risen from the sofa and was now waltzing around the room by herself, singing, "Someday my prince will come." She twirled, sweeping her pale evening dress about her like smoke. "Some day I'll love someone." Her radiant smile was almost infectious.

Almost. Jake took a swig of his drink. Did she really think they were having some kind of relationship outside their well-established professional one? As much as the idea appealed right this second, he knew it would really mess things up once she snapped out of whatever chemical induced trance she was in.

He'd better remind her of that. "We've worked together a long time."

She stopped twirling for a moment, and frowned. "I don't think I do work."

"You're a lady of leisure?"

She glanced down at her evening gown. "Yes." She frowned; then her expression brightened. "I must be. Otherwise why would I be dressed like this?"

Had she temporarily forgotten that she was his assistant? "Why are you dressed like that?" She'd certainly never worn anything so festive before.

"It's pretty, isn't it?" She looked up at him. "Do you like it?"

"Very much." He allowed his eyes to soak up the vision of it draped over her gorgeous body. Desire licked through him in tiny, tormenting flames.

Andi reached out and tugged at his shirt. Even that made his synapses flash and his groin tighten.

"Why don't you come sit with me." She stroked the sofa cushion next to her.

"I'm not sure that's a good idea." His voice came out gruff.

"Why not?"

"It's late. We should get to bed." The image of her in his bed flooded his brain, especially as it was right there in the next room. But caution tightened his muscles.

"Oh, don't be silly—" She frowned. "How odd." She glanced up at him. "I can't think of your name right now."

Jake was about to tell her, but something made him stop. "You don't know my name?"

She looked up for a few moments, as if searching her brain. "No, I don't seem to know it."

Panic tightened his chest. "What's your name?"

She looked toward the ceiling, scrunched up her brow and clenched her fists. When she finally looked back at him, her expression had changed from glee to confusion. "I'm not sure."

"I think we should call for a doctor." He pulled his phone out.

"A doctor? What for? I feel fine."

He hesitated. "Let me look at you. Did you bump your head?"

She shrugged. "I don't think so."

He put his phone back in his pocket and touched her temples with his thumbs. Her eyes sparkled as she looked up at him and her scent was a torment. He worked his fingers gently back into her hair—which was soft and luxurious to touch. "Hey, I feel a lump."

"Ouch!"

"You have a bruise." He touched it gently. A big goose egg. That explained a whole lot. "We're definitely calling the doctor. You could have a concussion." He dialed the number. "Listen, sorry it's so late, Gustav, but Andi's taken a fall and bumped her head. She's not talking too much sense and I think you should look at her."

Gustav replied that he'd be there in the ten minutes it took to drive from the town, and to keep her awake until he got there.

After letting the staff know to expect Gustav, Jake sat down on the sofa opposite her. It made sense to find out just how much of her memory had vanished. "How old are you?" Odd that he didn't know that.

"Over twenty-one." She laughed. Then frowned. "Other than that, I'm not too sure. How old do I look?"

Jake smiled. "I'd be a damned fool if I answered a question like that from a woman." He decided he'd be better off following the lawyer's strategy of only asking questions he knew the answer to. It was pretty embarrassing that he really didn't know how old she was. "How long have you lived here?"

She stared at him, mouth slightly open, then looked away. "Why are you asking me these silly questions? I've lived here a long time. With you."

Her gaze—innocent yet needy—ate into him. She stroked the sofa arm with her fingers and his skin tingled in response. She seemed to have lost her memory, and, in its absence, assumed they were a couple.

Jake sucked in a long breath. They'd never had any kind of flirtation, even a playful one. She always seemed so business-like and uninterested in such trivial matters. He'd never really looked at her that way, either. Much simpler to keep business and pleasure separate, especially when a really good assistant was so hard to find and keep.

Right now he was seeing a different aspect of Andi—alarming, and intriguing.

She rose and walked a few steps to his sofa, then sank down next to him. Her warm thigh settled against his, causing his skin to sizzle even through their layers of clothing. He stiffened. Was it fair to offer a man this kind of temptation?

At least it was keeping her awake.

Her fingers reached up to his black bow tie and tugged at one end. The knot came apart and the silk ribbons fell to his starched shirtfront.

"Much better." She giggled again, then pulled the tie out from his collar and undid the top button of his shirt. Jake watched, barely breathing, trying to suppress the heaving tide of arousal surging inside him.

After all, it would be rude to push her away, wouldn't it? Especially in her delicate and mysterious condition.

When her fingers roamed into his hair, causing his groin to ache uncomfortably, he had to take action. He stood up rapidly. "The doctor will be here any minute. Can I get you a glass of water?"

"I'm not thirsty." Her hurt look sent a pang to his heart.

"Still, it's good to keep hydrated." He busied himself with

filling a glass at the bar, and took care not to accidentally brush her fingertips as he handed it to her. Her cheeks and lips were flushed with pink, which made her look aroused and appealing at the same time.

She took the glass and sipped cautiously. Then looked up at him with a slight frown. "I do feel odd."

Jake let out a sigh of relief. This seemed more like the real Andi than the one spouting loopy epithets. "You'll probably feel better in the morning, but it can't hurt to have the doctor take a look."

Alarm filled him as tears welled in her eyes. "It's just so strange not being able to remember anything. How could I not even know my own name?" A fat tear rolled down her soft cheek.

Disturbing that he now knew how soft her cheek was.

"Your name is Andi Blake."

"Andi." She said it softly. Then frowned again. "Is that short for something?"

Jake froze. Was it? He had no idea. He didn't remember ever calling her anything else, but it had been six long years since he'd seen her résumé and frankly he couldn't remember the details. "Nope. Just Andi. It's a pretty name."

He regretted the lame comment, something you might say to a six-year-old. But then he didn't have experience in dealing with amnesiacs, so maybe it wasn't all that inappropriate.

"Oh." She seemed to mull that over. She wiped her eyes. "At least I know my own name now." Then she bit her lip. "Though it doesn't sound at all familiar." Tears glistened in her eyes. "What if my memory doesn't come back?"

"Don't worry about that, I'm sure—" A knock on the door announced the arrival of the doctor, and Jake released a sigh of relief. "Please send him in."

Andi's tearful trembling subsided as the doctor checked her over, peering into her eyes with a light, checking her pulse and breathing, and taking her temperature.

As the local doctor, he'd been to the palace before and knew Andi. She showed no sign of recognizing or remembering him. His questions revealed that while she remembered general concepts, like how to tie a knot, she recalled nothing about her own life.

"Andi, would you excuse us a moment?" The doctor ushered Jake out into the hallway. "Is she exhibiting mood changes?"

"Big time. She's not like herself at all. She seemed happy—silly even—when I first found her. Just now she was crying. I think the reality of what's going on is setting in."

"Sounds like a pretty textbook case of temporary memory loss, if there is such a thing." The older man snapped his briefcase closed. "Lots of emotion. Mood swings. Loss of long-term memory. I've never seen it before, myself, but in most cases the memory eventually starts to come back."

"When? How long will she be like this?"

The doctor gave a Ruthenian shrug. "Could be days, could be weeks. There's a slim possibility she won't ever recall everything. She's certainly had a good bump to her head, but no signs of concussion or other injury. Do you have any idea what happened?"

Jake shook his head. "I found her out dancing on the lawn. I didn't see anything happen at all."

"Make sure she gets plenty of sleep, and encourage her with questions to bring back her memory." The doctor hoisted his bag onto his shoulder. "Call me anytime, of course."

"Thanks." Jake frowned. "Can we keep this amnesia thing between us? I think Andi would be embarrassed if people knew what was going on. She's a very private person."

The doctor's brow furrowed even more than usual. "Of course." *Your Highness.* The unspoken words hovered in the air. Jake sensed slight disapproval at his request for secrecy, but he knew the physician would honor it. "Please keep me posted on her progress."

Jake went back into his suite and locked the door. Andi was

sitting on the sofa and her mood seemed to have brightened. Her tears were gone, and a smile hovered in her eyes as she looked up at him. "Will I live?"

"Without a doubt. It's late. How about some sleep?"

"I'm not at all sleepy." She draped herself over the sofa, eyes heavy-lidded with desire. "I'd rather play."

Jake's eyes widened. Could this really be the same Andi he'd worked with all these years? It was shocking to imagine that this flirtatious person had been lurking inside her the whole time. Unless it was just a mood swing caused by her condition.

She rose from the sofa and swept toward him, then threw her arms around his waist. "I do love you."

Gulp. Jake patted her cautiously on the back. This could last for days. Or weeks. Or longer.

His skin tingled as her lips pressed against his cheek. "I'm so glad we're together." Her soft breath heated his skin as she breathed the words in his ear.

And this was the woman who'd announced, only a few hours before, that she was leaving for good, that night.

At least that was off the agenda for now.

His phone rang and he tensed. What now? "Excuse me." He extricated himself from her embrace and pulled it from his pocket.

A glance at the number revealed the caller was Maxi. She'd formed a new habit of calling him at bizarre times like the crack of dawn or during his morning workout. This call in the wee hours was a new and even more unappealing attempt to monopolize his time.

Still, maybe there was some kind of emergency.

"Hi, Maxi."

"Jake, are you still awake?" Her breathy voice grated on his nerves.

"I am now." He glanced at Andi, who was twirling around the room doing the dance of the seven veils, or something. "What do you want?"

"So impatient. I just wanted to chat. About you and me."

He shoved a hand through his hair. Maxi was definitely not The One. In fact she could be voted Least Likely to be Queen of Ruthenia, since she was firmly in his "keep your enemies closer" circle. He'd been drawing her in and inviting her confidence on purpose. Not because he loved her, or was even attracted to her. He'd found evidence that her family was involved in weapons dealing and possibly worse, but he didn't have enough proof to do anything about it yet.

None of the other girls dealt in arms or drugs, as far as he knew, but they were all empty-headed and silly. Right now he was more attracted to his own assistant than to any of Ruthenia's pampered beauties.

An idea crept into his brain.

Since Andi seemed to assume they were a couple, why not make it a reality? He had to marry someone. He could announce to the press tomorrow that his chosen bride was his own assistant.

A chill of sangfroid crept over him. Could he really arrange his own marriage so easily? Andi was agreeable, intelligent and practical, perfectly suited to life in the spotlight. She'd worked just outside it for years and knew the whole routine of palace life perfectly. Apart from her presumably humble origins—he really didn't know anything about her origins, but since he'd never met her parents at a ball, he was guessing—she'd be the ideal royal wife.

They'd known each other for years and he could simply announce that they'd been involved for a long time but kept their relationship secret.

The announcement would send the long-fingernailed wolves away from his door for good. He and Andi could marry, produce an heir and a spare or two, and live a long, productive life in the service of the citizens of Ruthenia—wasn't that what was really important?

Andi had wandered into the bedroom and a quick glance revealed that she now lay sprawled on his bed.

Heat surged through him like a shot of brandy.

Her dress draped over her, displaying her inviting curves like an ice-cream sundae with whipped cream on top. Her gaze beckoned him, along with her finger. His muscles itched to join her on the bed and enjoy discovering more of Andi's wickedly intriguing sensual side.

"Maxi, I have to go. Have a good night."

"I can think of a way to have a much better night."

Jake's flesh crawled. "Sleep knits up the raveled sleeve of care."

"Is that Moby?"

"Shakespeare. Goodnight, Maxi."

"When are you going to choose your wife?" Jake flinched at the blunt question, and the shrill voice that asked it. "Daddy wants to know. He's not sure whether to contribute funds for the new hydroelectric project."

Jake stiffened. This is what it all boiled down to. Money and power. Well, he didn't want to build Ruthenia with ill-gotten gains from the black market, and he'd rather share his life with a hardworking woman than one who thought she could buy her way into a monarchy. "I've already chosen my wife."

"What do you mean?" she gasped.

He moved across the room, away from the bedroom where Andi now sprawled enticingly on the bed. She was humming again, and wouldn't hear him. "I intend to marry Andi Blake, my longtime assistant."

"You're joking."

"Not in the slightest. She and I have had a close relationship for six years. We intend to enjoy each other's company for many more."

Already his pronouncement had an official ring to it. Marriage to Andi was a perfectly natural and practical course of action. He was confident Andi would agree, especially since she seemed to have romantic feelings toward him.

"People are going to be very, very..." She paused, apparently struggling for words.

"Happy for us. Yes. Of course you'll be invited to the wedding." He couldn't help a tiny smile sneaking across his mouth. Maxi had clearly intended to be the featured host of the event.

"Invited to the wedding?" Her growl made him pull the phone away from his ear. "You're impossible!"

The dial tone made a satisfying noise. And now he wouldn't have to even make an announcement. Maxi would do all the legwork for him.

All he had to do was tell Andi.

CHAPTER THREE

MORNING SUNLIGHT STREAMED through the gap between heavy brocade curtains. Hot and uncomfortable, Andi looked down to find herself wearing a long evening dress under the covers. Weirdest thing, she had no idea why.

She sat bolt upright. Where was she?

His room. She remembered the soft touch of his lips on her cheek. Her skin heated at the memory. "Good night, Andi," he'd said. So she was Andi.

Andi.

Who was Andi? She racked her brain, but the racks were empty. She couldn't even remember the name of the handsome man who'd put her to bed, though she knew they were close.

How could her whole reality just slip away? Her heart pounded and she climbed out of bed. Her chiffon-y dress was horribly wrinkled and had made an uncomfortable nightgown, leaving lines printed on her skin.

She moved to the window and pulled one of the heavy drapes aside. The view that greeted her was familiar—rolling green hills dotted with grazing sheep, rising to fir-covered mountains. The village in the middle distance, with its steep clay-tiled roofs and high church steeple.

Looking down she saw the long rectangular fishpond in the walled courtyard. She didn't recall seeing it from this angle before.

But then she didn't recall much.

Andi what? She pressed a hand to her forehead. Blake, he'd said. How could even her own last name sound alien and unfamiliar?

She walked to the door and cautiously pulled it open. She caught her breath at the sight of him, standing in front of the mirror, buttoning his collar. Thick black-brown hair swept back from the most handsome face she'd ever seen. Warm, dark eyes reflected in the glass. Mouth set in a serious but good-humored line. Heat flooded her body and she stood rooted to the spot.

He turned. "Morning, Andi. How are you feeling?"

His expression looked rather guarded.

"Okay. I think. I... I can't seem to remember much." Had she slept with him last night? Her fully dressed state seemed to suggest not. Her body was sending all kinds of strange signals, though—pulsing and throbbing and tingling in mysterious places—so she couldn't tell.

"What can you remember?" He didn't look surprised at her announcement. Did he know what was going on?

"Why can't I remember?"

He took a few steps toward her and put his hand on her arm. Arousal flashed through her at his touch. "You bumped your head. The doctor says you're not concussed."

"How long have I been like this?" Fear twisted in her stomach.

"Just since last night. The doc said your memory will come back soon. A few weeks at most."

"Oh." Andi frowned, feeling ridiculously vulnerable, standing there in her wrinkled dress with no idea of who or where she was. Except that she was very—very—attracted to this man. "What should I do in the meantime?"

"Don't worry about a thing. I'll take care of you." He stroked her cheek. The reassuring touch of his fingers made her breath catch and sent tingles of arousal cascading through her.

She frowned. How should she put a question like this? "Are we...intimate?"

His gaze flickered slightly, making her stomach tighten. Had she said the wrong thing? She felt sure there must be something between them. She remembered kissing him last night, and the memory of the kiss made her head grow light.

"Yes, Andi. We're going to be married." He looked down at her hands, gathering them in his.

"Oh." She managed a smile. "What a relief that I have you to take care of me until my memory comes back." If it did come back. "It's embarrassing to ask, but how long have we been together?"

"Oh, years." He met her gaze again.

"It seems impossible, but I don't remember your name."

"Jake." He looked slightly flustered, and why wouldn't he? "Jake Mondragon."

"Jake Mondragon." She smiled dreamily, allowing herself to relax in his sturdy presence. And his face was kind, despite the proud, sculpted features. Totally gorgeous, too. She was very lucky. "So I'm going to be Andi Mondragon."

Jake's eyes widened. "Uh, yes. Yes, you are."

Why did he seem surprised by the idea? It was hardly an odd one if they'd been together for years. "Or was I going to keep my original surname?" Curiosity pricked her.

He smiled. "I don't think we'd discussed whether you would change it or not."

"Oh." Funny they hadn't talked about that. After all, what would the children be called? "How long have we been engaged?"

He lifted his chin slightly. "Just since yesterday. We haven't even told anyone yet."

Yesterday? Her eyes widened. "How odd that I would lose my memory on the same day. I can't even remember the proposal."

She watched his Adam's apple move as he swallowed. He must be upset that she couldn't even remember such a momentous and important moment. "I'm sure it will come back eventually."

An odd sensation started forming in the pit of her stomach. Something felt...off. How could she have forgotten her own fiancé? It was disorienting to know less about her own life than someone else did. "I think I should lay low for a few days. I don't really want to see anyone until I know who I am."

Jake grimaced. "I'm afraid that's going to be hard. The media will probably want an interview."

"About my memory?"

"About our engagement."

"Why would we tell the media?"

Jake hesitated for a moment. "Since I'm the king of this country, everything I do is news."

Andi's mouth fell open. "You're the king?" She was pretty sure she wasn't some kind of royal princess or aristocrat. She certainly didn't feel like one. But maybe that explained the long evening gown. She glanced down at its crumpled folds. "How did we meet?"

Jake's lids lowered slightly. "You're my longtime assistant. We just decided to marry."

She blinked. That explained all the sizzling and tingling in her body—she'd been intimate with this man for a long time. How bizarre that she had to hear about her own life from someone else. From the man she'd apparently dated for years and planned to marry.

Then again, if she'd been seeing this man for years, why did his mere presence send shivers of arousal tingling over her skin and zapping through her insides?

A deep breath didn't help clear the odd mix of confusion and emptiness in her brain. She hoped her memory would return before she did anything to embarrass him. "I guess I should get changed. I feel silly asking this, but where are my clothes?"

Jake froze for a moment, brow furrowed. "You wait here. I'll bring some for you."

"It's okay, I don't want to put you to any trouble. If you'll just tell me where they are." She hated feeling so helpless.

"It's no trouble at all. Just relax on the sofa for a bit. I'll be right back."

She shrugged. "I suppose you probably know what I like to wear better than I do. Still, I could come with you. I need to figure out where everything is."

"Better that you get dressed first. I'll be right back."

He left the room abruptly, leaving Andi uneasy. Why was he so anxious for her to stay here? Like he didn't want anyone to see her. Maybe he didn't want people to know about her loss of memory.

She glanced around the room, already feeling alone and worried without him. Did he have to leave? As the king, you'd think he'd just call for a servant to bring her clothes.

Or did things not work that way anymore? When your memory had taken flight it was hard to distinguish between fairy tales and ordinary life.

She lay back on the sofa and tried to relax. She was engaged to a handsome and caring man that she was fiercely attracted to. Maybe her real life was a fairy tale?

Jake strode along the corridor, hoping he wouldn't run into anyone—which was an unfamiliar feeling for him. Usually he prided himself on being up-front and open, but right now he didn't want anyone to know Andi had been about to leave.

That felt...personal.

He was confident she'd keep it to herself until she'd squared things with him. She'd proved over the years that she was the soul of discretion and confided in no one.

Her job was her life. At least it had been until she decided she'd had enough of it. Hurt flared inside him that she could even consider abandoning him and Ruthenia, especially now he'd realized she was the ideal wife for him. This odd memory loss would give him a chance to turn things around and keep her here for good.

He reached her door and slipped into the room with a sense of relief. Her packed suitcases still sat on the floor next to the bed. He closed the door and began to unpack, hanging the clothes back in the closet and placing some items in the large dresser. He intended to make it look as if she'd never thought of leaving.

Some things startled him. A lacy pink nightgown. A pair of black stockings and garters. When had she had occasion to wear these? He didn't think she had been on a single date since they'd moved to Ruthenia.

Guilt speared him at the thought. She was so busy working she had no life at all outside of her job. Why had he assumed that would be enough for her?

He placed her toiletries back in the bathroom. Handling her shampoo bottle and deodorant felt oddly intimate, like he was peeking into her private life. She had a lot of different lipsticks and he tried to arrange them upright on the bathroom shelf, though really he had no idea how she kept them.

She looked a lot prettier without all that lipstick on. Maybe he should just ditch them and she'd be none the wiser?

No. These were her possessions and that would be wrong.

He arranged her eyeliner pencils and powders and bottles of makeup on the shelf, too. Did all women have so much of this stuff? She had a ridiculous assortment of hair products, too—gels and sprays and mousses—which was funny since her hair was almost always tied back in a bun.

It took a full twenty minutes to get her bags unpacked and rearranged in some sort of convincing order. He shoved the bags under the bed and stood back to admire his handiwork.

Too perfect. He pulled a pair of panty hose from a drawer and draped them over the bed. Better.

He was about to leave when he remembered he was supposed

to bring her back something to wear. Hmm. Mischief tickled his insides. What would he like to see her in? Not one of those stiff, bright suits she always wore.

He pulled a pair of jeans from one of the drawers. He'd never seen her in those, so why not? A blue long-sleeved T-shirt seemed to match, and he pulled some rather fetching black lace underwear—tags still attached—from the drawer.

He removed the tags. Why not let her think she wore stuff like this every day?

He rolled the items in a soft blue-and-gray sweater and set off down the corridor again, glancing left and right, glad that the palace was still quiet at this hour.

Andi's uncharacteristically anxious face greeted him as he returned to his rooms. She seemed quite different from last night, when she was spouting garbled poetry and dancing around the room. Now she sat curled up on the sofa, clutching her knees.

"How are you feeling?" Her rigid posture made him want to soothe and relax her.

"Nervous. It's odd not knowing anything about myself or my life. More than odd. Scary."

Jake tried to ignore the trickle of guilt that slid down his spine. He had no intention of telling her the truth about her plans to leave. And come to think of it, he hadn't seen any tickets or itineraries in her room. Maybe her plans weren't all that firm, anyway. "Don't worry. It'll all come back eventually. In the meantime, we'll just carry on as usual. Does that sound okay?"

She nodded.

"I brought some clothes." He set them down on the sofa beside him.

She unrolled the sweater and her eyes widened briefly at the sight of the lacy bra and panties. "Thanks."

She glanced up at him, and then at the pile of clothes again. He resisted a powerful urge to see her slip into that sexy underwear. "You can change in the bedroom if you want some privacy. There are fresh towels in the bathroom if you'd like to take a shower."

Andi closed the bedroom door behind her. If Jake was her fiancé, why did the thought of changing in front of him make her want to blush crimson? She'd probably done it numerous times in the past. This whole situation was so weird. Her own fiancé felt—not like a stranger, but not like an intimate companion, either.

Must be pretty uncomfortable for Jake, too, though he didn't seem too flustered. Maybe he was just the sort to take things in stride. He had a reassuring air of composure, which was probably a good thing in a king.

Andi slipped out of her crumpled evening gown and climbed into a luxurious marble shower that could accommodate about six people. Unlike the scenery outside the window, and even the dressing room/sitting area, which felt at least somewhat familiar, everything in the bathroom suite seemed totally strange, like she'd literally never been there before. Maybe the memory was selective like that in its recall.

The warm water soothed and caressed her and she dried off feeling fresher.

She managed to arrange her hair into some semblance of order using a black comb, and applied some rather masculine-scented deodorant. They obviously didn't share this bathroom as there were no girly items in here at all. Unease pricked her skin again. No real reason for it though. Probably plenty of engaged couples slept in separate rooms. And one would expect extra attention to propriety in a royal household.

The black underwear he'd brought made her want to blush again. Why? It was her own, so why did it feel too racy for her? The bra fit perfectly, and the panties, while very low-cut, were comfortable, too. She was glad to quickly cover them with the practical jeans and blue T-shirt. No socks or shoes? Well, she could go retrieve those herself. She tied the soft sweater around her shoulders and stepped outside.

Jake's mouth broadened into a smile at the sight of her. "You look great." His dark eyes shone with approval.

She shrugged. Something about the ensemble felt funny. Too casual, maybe. It didn't seem right to wear jeans in a royal palace.

"You didn't bring any shoes." She pointed to her bare feet.

"Maybe I wanted to admire your pretty toes."

Heat flared inside her as his gaze slid down her legs to the toes in question. She giggled, feeling suddenly lighthearted. "My toes would still like to find some shoes to hide in. Why wasn't I wearing any last night? I looked in the bedroom and the dressing room, but I didn't see any."

"I don't know." Jake's expression turned more serious. "You were twirling barefoot on the lawn when I found you."

Andi's skin prickled with unease again. "So we decided to get engaged, and then I lost my memory?"

Jake nodded. His guarded expression didn't offer much reassurance.

He took a step toward her. "Don't worry, we'll get through this together." He slid his arms around her waist. Heat rippled in her belly. His scent stirred emotions and sensations and she softened into his embrace. She wondered if he was going to say he loved her, but he simply kissed her softly on the mouth.

Pleasure crept over her. "I guess I'm lucky it happened right here, and that I'm not wandering around some strange place with no idea who I am like those stories you see on the news."

"It is fortunate, isn't it?" He kissed her again. This time both their eyes slid closed and the kiss deepened. Colors swirled and sparkled behind Andi's eyelids and sensation crashed through her, quickening her pulse and making her breath come in unsteady gasps. Her fingers itched to touch the skin under his starched shirt.

She stepped back, blinking, once they managed to pull apart. Were their kisses always this intense?

Jake smiled, relaxed and calm. Apparently this was all par for the course. Andi patted her hair, wishing she could feel half as composed as he looked. Terror snapped through her at the prospect of facing strangers and trying to pretend everything was normal. "Can we keep our engagement a secret for now?"

Jake's eyes widened for a second. "Why?"

"Just so I don't have to answer a lot of questions when I don't even know who I am."

He frowned. "I'm afraid it's too late. I told someone on the phone last night."

"Who?" Not that she'd even know the name.

"Maxi Rivenshnell. She's a...friend of the family."

Andi paused. The name had a nasty ring to it. Maybe it was the way he pronounced it, like something that tasted bad. "Maybe she won't tell anyone."

"I suspect she'll tell everyone." He turned and strode across the room. Shoved a hand through his dark hair. Then he turned and approached her. "But nothing's going to stop me buying you a ring today, and you're going to choose it. First, let me summon your shoes."

Jake parked his Mercedes in his usual reserved spot in the town's main square. No need for chauffeurs and armed escorts in tiny Ruthenia. He rushed around the car to help Andi out, but she was already on her feet and closing the door by the time he got there.

She'd devoured her breakfast of fruit and pastries in the privacy of his suite. At least he knew what she liked to eat. Despite obvious confusion over little things like how to find her way around, she seemed healthy and relatively calm, which was a huge relief.

Of course her reluctance to announce their engagement was

a slight hitch in his plans to unload his unwanted admirers, but word would get out soon enough. Ruthenia had more than its share of gossiping busybodies, and for once they'd be working in his favor.

He took her arm and guided her across the main square. Morning sunlight illuminated the old stone facades of the shops and glinted off the slate tiles of the church steeple. Pigeons gathered near the fountain, where a little girl tossed bread crumbs at them and two dogs barked a happy greeting as their owners stopped for a chat.

"The local town," murmured Andi.

"Does it look familiar?"

"A little. Like I've seen it in a dream rather than in real life. It's so pretty."

"It is lovely. You and I saw it together for the first time three years ago."

She paused. "You didn't grow up here?"

"No, I grew up in the States, like you. I didn't come here until the socialist government collapsed in a heap of corruption scandals and people started agitating for the return of the royal family. At first I thought they were nuts, then I realized I could probably help put the country back on its feet." He looked at her, her clear blue eyes wide, soaking in everything he said. "I couldn't have done it without you."

His chest tightened as he spoke the words. All true. Andi's quiet confidence and brisk efficiency made almost anything possible. The prospect of carrying on without her by his side was unthinkable.

"Was I good at being your assistant?" Her serious gaze touched him. "I don't remember anything about my job."

"Exemplary. You've been far more than my assistant. My right-hand woman is a better description."

She looked pleased. "I guess that's a good thing, since we're getting married."

"Absolutely." Jake swallowed. How would she react when her memory returned and she realized they were never romantically involved? He drew in a breath. She wasn't in love with him. Still, she was sensible enough to see that marriage between them would be in the best interests of Ruthenia.

And that kiss had been surprisingly spicy. In fact, he couldn't remember experiencing anything like it in his fairly substantial kissing experience.

Maybe it was the element of the forbidden. He'd never considered kissing his assistant and it still felt...wrong. Probably because it was wrong of him to let her think they'd been a couple. But once a ring was on her finger, they really would be engaged and everything would be on the up and up.

At least until her memory came back.

"The jeweler is down this street." He led her along a narrow cobbled alley barely wide enough for a cart. The kind of street he'd have to fold in his wing mirrors to drive down without scraping the ancient walls on either side. Thick handblown glass squares glazed the bowed window of the shop, giving a distorted view of the luxurious trinkets inside.

Despite its old-world ambience—or maybe because of it—this jeweler was one of the finest in Europe and had recently regained its international reputation as part of Jake's Rediscover Ruthenia campaign. He'd bought quite a few pieces here—gifts for foreign diplomats and wealthy Ruthenian acquaintances. Why had it never occurred to him to buy something lovely for Andi?

He opened the heavy wood door and ushered her in, unable to resist brushing her waist with his fingers as he coaxed her through. The formally attired proprietor rushed forward to greet them. "Welcome, sir." Jake was grateful the man remembered his aversion to pompous titles. "How can we assist you today? A custom commission, perhaps?"

Jake hesitated. Andi might well like a ring designed to her

exact specifications—but he needed a ring on her finger right now to make an honest man of him. He certainly didn't want her memory coming back before the setting was tooled. "I suspect you have something lovely in the shop already."

He took Andi's hand in his. It was warm, and he squeezed it to calm her nerves. "We're looking for an engagement ring."

The elderly jeweler's eyes opened wide. His gaze slid to Andi, then back again. He seemed unsure what to make of the situation. Perhaps he'd been following the local gossip columns and was already designing one with Maxi or Alia in mind. "Should I be offering you my congratulations?"

"Most certainly." Jake slid his arm around Andi.

"Wonderful." The jeweler bowed his head slightly in Andi's direction. "My best wishes for you both. And in time for Independence Day, too." A smile creased his wrinkled face. "The whole nation will be overjoyed. I do think a custom creation would be most appropriate. Perhaps with the family crest?"

"Why don't we take a look at what you have in stock?" He tightened his arm around Andi's waist, then loosened it, suddenly aware of how intent he was to hold on to her. Not that she was resisting. She leaned into him, perhaps seeking reassurance he was happy to provide.

A large tray of sparkling rings appeared from a deep wooden cabinet. Jake glanced at Andi and saw her eyes widen.

"See if anything appeals to you." He spoke softly, suddenly feeling the intimacy of the moment. The first step in their journey through life as a married couple. The rings were nearly all diamonds, some single and some triple, with a large stone flanked by two smaller stones. A few more had clusters of diamonds and there was a large sapphire and a square cut ruby.

Andi drew in a long breath, then reached for a small single diamond in a carved platinum band. She held it for a moment, then extended her fingers to try it on. "Wow, this feels weird.

Like you should be doing it, or something." She glanced shyly at him.

Jake swallowed. He took the ring from her—the diamond was too small, anyway—and gingerly slid it onto her slender finger. His skin tingled as he touched hers and a flutter of something stirred in his chest. The ring fit well and looked pretty on her hand.

"What do you think?" She turned her hand, and the stone sparkled in the light.

"Nice." He didn't want to criticize, if that was her choice.

The jeweler frowned. "It's a fine ring, but for the royal family, perhaps something a bit more...extravagant?" He lifted a dramatic large stone flanked by several smaller stones. The kind of ring that would make people's eyes pop. Jake had to admit it was more appropriate under the circumstances.

Andi allowed the older man to slide her choice off her finger and push the big sparkler onto it. His face creased into a satisfied smile as it slid perfectly into place. "Lovely. Much more suitable for a royal bride, if you don't mind my saying."

She tilted her hand to the side and studied the ring. Despite the large size of the stones it also looked elegant on her graceful hands. Jake wondered how he'd never noticed what pretty hands she had. He'd been watching them type his letters and organize his files for years.

"It's a bit over the top...." She paused, still staring at it. "But it is pretty." She looked up at Jake. "What do you think?"

"Very nice." He intended to buy her many more trinkets and baubles to enjoy. It was worth it to see the sunny smile on her face, and they were supporting the local economy. "Let's buy it and go get a hot chocolate to celebrate."

She hesitated for a moment more, studying the ring on her finger. When she looked up, confusion darkened the summerblue of her eyes. She seemed like she wanted to say something, but hesitated in front of the jeweler. The shop owner tactfully excused himself and disappeared through a low door into a back room.

"I guess he trusts us alone with the merchandise." Jake grinned. "There must be a million dollars worth of rocks on this tray."

"I'd imagine a crown inspires a certain amount of trust." She looked up at him, eyes sparkling. "I'm still getting used to the idea that you're a king."

"Me, too. I'm not sure I'll ever be completely used to it, but at least it's starting to feel like a suit that fits. How does the ring feel?"

Andi studied the ring again. "It is lovely, but it's just so... big."

"He's right, though. It makes sense to go dramatic. Do you want people muttering that I'm a cheapskate?" He raised a brow.

Andi chuckled. "I guess you have a good point." Then she frowned. "Are people going to be shocked that you're marrying your assistant?" She bit her lip for a moment. "I mean... did they know that we're...intimate?"

Jake inhaled. "We kept it all pretty private."

"Did anyone know?" Her serious expression tugged at him.

"A few people may have guessed something." Who knew what people might imagine, even if there had never been anything to guess? "But on the whole, we were discreet so it'll be a surprise."

Andi's shoulders tightened a bit. "I hope they won't be too upset that you're not marrying someone more...important."

"No one's more important than you, Andi. I'd be lost without you." It was a relief to say something honest, even if he meant it in a business sense, rather than a romantic one.

"I guess I should get the fancy one. If they're going to talk, let's give them something to talk about."

"That's the attitude." Jake rang the bell on the counter and the jeweler appeared again like Rumpelstiltskin. "We'll take it."

The old man beamed. "An excellent choice. I wish you both a lifetime of happiness."

Me, too, thought Jake. He'd need to think on his feet when Andi snapped out of this thing.

CHAPTER FOUR

ANDI BLINKED AS they stepped out of the dark shop into bright morning sunlight that reflected off everything from the gray cobbles to the white-crested mountain peaks that loomed over the town. The cold air whipped at her skin and she drew her warm coat about her. Out in the open she felt violently self-conscious about the huge ring on her finger, and gratefully tucked it into her coat pocket.

"The coffeehouse is just up the road." Jake took her arm. "You may not remember, but they have the best hot chocolate in the known world and you love it."

Andi's muscles tightened at the reminder that he knew more about her than she did. "Do you go there often?" It seemed odd for a king to frequent a local café. Then again she had no idea what was normal. Very strange how she remembered things like old fairy tales but not her own life.

"Of course. Got to support the local businesses."

He certainly was thoughtful. That cozy feeling of being protected and cared for warmed her as he slid his arm through hers again. How lucky she was! No doubt her memory would come back soon and—

A moped skidded past them on the narrow street. Its rider, a man in a black leather jacket, stopped and leaped off, camera in hand. "Your Highness, is it true you are engaged?" he asked, in a French accent.

Jake paused. "It is true." Andi stared in surprise at his polite demeanor.

"May I take your picture?"

Jake took Andi's hands in his. "What do you say, Andi? He's just doing his job."

Andi cringed inwardly. She didn't want anyone seeing her in her confused state, let alone photographing her. She also didn't want to make a fuss in front of a stranger. That might give the game away.

She swallowed. "Okay, I guess." She pushed a lock of hair self-consciously off her face. She hadn't had time to style it—not that she even remembered what style she usually wore—but Jake had assured her it looked lovely.

The man took about fifty pictures from different angles through a long, scary-looking lens that would probably show every pore on her face. Jake was obviously used to the attention and remained calm and pleasant. He even adjusted them into several dignified romantic poses as if they were at a professional shoot.

Almost as if he'd planned this encounter.

She fought the urge to frown, which certainly wouldn't be a good idea for the pictures. How did the photographer know they were engaged when it had only happened last night?

Jake managed to politely disengage them from the impromptu photo session and continue down the road. He smiled and nodded at passersby, all of whom seemed quite comfortable rubbing shoulders with their monarch. But when they reached the main square she saw two more reporters, a woman with a tiny microphone clipped to her jacket and a tall man with a notepad. They greeted Jake with warm smiles and asked if congratulations were in order.

Andi tried to maintain a pleasant expression while unease gnawed at her gut.

"How does it feel to marry a king?" asked the woman, in soft Ruthenian tones.

"I'm not sure yet," admitted Andi. "Since we're not married. I'll have to let you know after the ceremony."

"When will that be?" asked the man. Andi glanced at Jake.

"We'll make an announcement when we have all the details sorted out. A royal wedding isn't something you rush into."

"Of course." The reporter was a middle-aged woman with soft blond hair. "And you've kept your promise of choosing your bride before Ruthenia's third Independence Day next week."

"The people of Ruthenia know I'm a man of my word."

Andi only just managed not to frown. He'd become engaged to her at the last minute because of some promise he made? That was awfully convenient. The knot in the pit of her stomach tightened.

The woman asked if she could see Andi's ring. Andi pulled it out and was alarmed to see it looked even bigger and brighter out here in daylight. The camera flashed several times before she could hide her hand back in her pocket again.

When Jake finally excused them, her heart was pounding and her face flushed. She let out a silent sigh of relief as he guided her into the warm and inviting coffee shop. She removed her coat and hung it on a row of iron hooks that looked hundreds of years old.

"I'm glad they didn't ask any questions I couldn't answer."

"The paparazzi are polite here." Jake took her hand and led her to a secluded table. "They know I can have them clapped in irons if they're not."

She glanced up to see if he was kidding and was relieved to see a sparkle of humor in his eye.

"The press has been helpful in letting the world know about my efforts to bring the country into the twenty-first century. It pays to keep them happy."

"How could they know about our engagement already? Did that girl you spoke to phone them?" Andi sat in the plush upholstered chair. A small fire snapped and sizzled nearby. The coffee shop had dark wood paneling and varied antique tables and chairs clustered around the low-ceilinged space that looked unchanged since the 1720s—which it probably was.

"I doubt it. They seem to know everything. It's a bit spooky at first, but you get used to it. Maybe they saw us inside the jeweler's?"

"Or maybe he tipped them off." Andi gingerly pulled her be-ringed hand from her pocket to take a menu from the elegantly attired waiter.

"Old Gregor is the soul of discretion." Jake studied his menu. Andi wondered for a second how he knew to trust Old Gregor. Had he commissioned gems for other women? But he said they'd been dating for years.

She cursed the hot little flame of jealousy that had flickered to life inside her. Why were they suddenly engaged after years of dating? Was it somehow precipitated by this promise he'd made, or had she previously refused?

For a moment Andi was hyperaware of people at tables all around them, sipping their drinks and eating. Could they tell she was missing a huge part of her life?

He shrugged. "It's their job. We live in the public eye." He reached across the table and took her hand. His strong fingers closed around hers. She squeezed his hand back and enjoyed the sense of reassurance she got from him. "You'll get used to it again."

"I suppose I will." She glanced warily about the interior of the intimate coffeehouse. "It's so unnerving not to even know what's normal. Then you can't figure out what's odd and unusual."

"It would certainly be odd for us to sit here without drinking hot chocolate." He summoned the waiter and ordered a pot of hot chocolate and a dish of cream. "And, just so you know, the waffles with summer berries are your favorite."

"Did we eat here together a lot?" The place didn't look especially familiar.

"Yes. We often brought business associates and visitors from the States here, since it's so quaint and unchanged. Now that we're engaged…" He stroked her hand inside his and fixed his dark eyes on hers. "It's just the two of us."

Andi's insides fluttered as his gaze crept right under her skin. If only she could remember what their relationship was like. It didn't sound as if they ate out unless in company, which was a bit odd. A secret affair.

It must be strange and unsettling for him to have her behaving like a different person.

Then again, he didn't seem rattled by the situation. His handsome face had an expression of calm contentment. The chiseled features were steady as the mountains outside and it was hard to imagine him getting upset or bothered by anything. Jake was obviously the kind of man who took things in stride. Her hand felt totally comfortable in his, as if he was promising her that he'd take care of her and make sure only good things happened.

Why did it feel so bizarre that such a gorgeous and successful man was all hers?

Well, of course she had to share him with a small nation, but after the lights went out he was hers alone. Hope and excitement rose through her, along with a curl of desire that matched the steam rising off the hot chocolate.

Jake kept his gaze on her face as the waiter poured the fragrant liquid into two wide round cups and then dropped a dollop of thick whipped cream on top of each one. When the waiter moved away, Jake lifted her hand to his lips and kissed it. Sensual excitement flashed through her body at the soft touch of his mouth on her skin, a promise of what would come when they were alone together.

Andi fought the urge to glance around to see if anyone had witnessed the intimate moment. She drew in a deep breath and forced herself to display the kind of cool that Jake possessed naturally. She'd better get used to being in the public eye, since she'd be spending the rest of her life in it.

If she really was marrying Jake. The idea still seemed too far-fetched and outrageous to truly believe. He gently let go of her hand and she moved it quickly to her cup and covered her confusion with a sip. The rich and delicious chocolate slid down her throat and heated her insides. Perfect.

Everything was perfect. Too perfect.

So why couldn't she escape the niggling feeling that when she got her memory back she'd discover something was horribly wrong?

Andi grew increasingly nervous as they drove back to the palace. None of the other staff knew about their engagement—at least as far as she knew. How would they react?

She climbed out of the car on shaky legs. Did she have a best friend here in whom she confided? Or was that person Jake? Tears hovered very close to the surface, but she tried hard to put on a brave face as they approached the grand doorway up a flight of wide steps.

"Good morning, sir." A black-attired man opened the door before they even reached it. "And may I offer you congratulations."

Andi cringed. They all knew already? Word spread around this tiny country like a plague.

"Congratulations, Andi. I'm not sure whether it's appropriate to tell you that, as usual, the mail is in your office."

She didn't even know she had an office, let alone where it was. She gulped, realizing that she'd be expected to do her job, regardless of whether or not she could remember how.

Either that or tell everyone that her mind had been wiped blank, and she couldn't face that. "Thanks," she managed.

She kept her hand buried deep in the pocket of her wool coat as they crossed the marble-floored entrance hall. Faces looked vaguely familiar, but she couldn't remember names or if they were friends as well as coworkers. Jake stopped to answer some questions about a phone call they'd received, and Andi hesitated, unsure which direction to walk in, or where to even hang her coat. Worse yet, a girl with lots of red hair rushed up to her, wide-eyed. "Why am I the last to know everything?"

Andi managed a casual shrug.

The redhead leaned in and lowered her voice. "I see you decided not to leave after all?"

Andi's eyes widened. "Leave?" She glanced up to see if Jake had heard, but he was still deep in conversation several yards away.

"Stop acting innocent. I saw the suitcases you bought in town. Still, obviously something better than a new job came up."

"I don't know what you're talking about." Truer words were never spoken. Anxiety churned the hot chocolate in her stomach. Suitcases? A new job? That was odd. She needed to get to her room and see if she could find something to jog her memory.

If only she knew where her room was.

She remembered the way back to Jake's suite, and was tempted to head that way without him just to get away from the inquisitive redhead. Then again, he was apparently her boss, so that might look odd.

The ring practically burned her finger, still hidden deep inside her coat. "Let me take that for you." An older man with neat white hair crossed the floor. Andi stared. "Your coat," he continued, demonstrating the hanger in his hand. "I wonder if it's premature to call you Your Majesty?" he asked with a kind expression.

"Probably." She managed a smile while shrugging the coat off. She looked up at Jake and their eyes met. He must have seen the plea in her face as he detached himself from his questioner and strode to her side. "Let's head for my office."

As soon as they were on the stairs, she whispered that she

didn't know where her room was. He frowned for a second, then smiled. "We'll go there right now."

The hallway was empty. "I don't even know anyone's name. It's the most awkward feeling. People must think I'm so rude."

"That was Walter. Worked here back when it was a hotel and always the first to know every bit of gossip. He probably spread the word."

"This building was a hotel?"

"For a while. It had a few different lives while my family was in exile in the States. It took a lot of work to get it looking like this, and you were in charge of most of it."

Andi bit her lip, walking along carpet she may even have selected. Jake pointed to the third polished wood door in a long hallway, only a few yards from his. "That's yours. It wasn't locked when I came to get your clothes."

She tried the handle and it swung open. A neat, hotel-like room greeted her, with heavy brocade curtains and a small double bed. The dark wood furniture looked antique and impressive. She cringed at the sight of a pair of panty hose draped over the bed.

"Um, maybe I should spend a little time alone here. See if anything jogs my memory."

"Sure." Jake stroked her back softly. Her skin heated under her T-shirt as he turned her toward him and lowered his face to hers. All worries and fears drifted way for a few seconds as she lost herself in his soft and gentle kiss.

"Don't worry about anything." He pointed to a dresser. "Your phone's right there and you've always told me I'm programmed in as number one." He winked. "I'll head for my office to deal with this electrical supply situation that's cropped up. Call me if you need anything, and even if you don't."

Her fingers felt cold as he released them from his, but she couldn't help a sigh of relief as she closed the door behind him and found herself alone in the room. At last she could... fall apart.

Part of her wanted to run to the bed and collapse on it, sobbing. But another, apparently more influential, part wanted to pull open the drawers and search for signs of who she was. She tucked the stray panty hose back into their drawer, wondering if she'd taken them out when she was dressing in her evening gown. She wasn't wearing any when she'd woken up in the morning.

The drawer was rather disorganized, as if everything was just shoved in there without much thought. What did this tell her about herself? She frowned and pulled open the drawer above it. Three carelessly folded blouses and some socks gave no further encouragement about her organizational skills.

The closet door was slightly ajar and she pulled it open. An array of colorful suits hung from the hangers, along with several solid-colored dresses and skirts. At least it didn't look as messy as her drawers. She pushed some hangers apart and pulled down one of the suits. A medium blue, it was tailored but otherwise quite plain. She tried to smooth out a horizontal crease that ran just below the lapels. Another crease across the skirt made her frown. Why would a suit hanging in a closet have creases running across it?

She pulled out another suit and saw that it too had lines running through the middle. A forest-green dress also showed signs of having been folded recently, and a navy skirt and... She stopped and frowned. All the items in the closet had crease marks running across them. Not deep, sharp creases, but soft ones, as if they'd been folded only for a short time. What could that mean?

After she hung the suit back in the closet, she walked into the attached bathroom. A floral smell hovered in the air and felt reassuringly familiar. Her favorite scent? She recognized it—which meant it was a memory. Cheered, she examined the cosmetics arranged on a low shelf. There were a lot of lipsticks. She pulled one open and applied it. A rather garish orangey-pink that didn't do her complexion any favors. She put it back on the shelf and wiped her lips with a tissue.

She found the bottle of scent and removed the cap. Warmth suffused her as she sprayed some on her wrists and inhaled the familiar smell. Relief also swept through her that at least something around here felt familiar.

The scent...and Jake.

Excitement mixed with apprehension tickled her insides. How odd that they'd become engaged and she'd lost her memory in the same night. She couldn't help wondering if the two things were related.

Jake was lovely, though. He'd been so sweet and encouraging with her since she'd lost her memory. She was lucky to be engaged to such a kind and capable man. A bit odd that he was a king, but that was just one facet of him. Just a job, really. No doubt she wasn't bothered by his royal status or she wouldn't have become romantically involved with him in the first place.

She picked up her hand and looked at her big diamond ring. It was beautiful and fit her perfectly. She'd feel comfortable wearing it once she got used to it.

Once she got used to any of this.

A knock on the door made her jump. "It's me, Livia."

Andi gulped. Apparently she was supposed to know who Livia was. So far no one seemed to know about her memory except Jake and the doctor, but that was bound to change unless it came back soon. She smoothed her hair and went to open the door.

It was the same red-haired girl from downstairs. The one who'd talked about her leaving. She had a huge grin on her freckled face. "You are a dark horse."

Andi shrugged casually, as if admitting it, even though she didn't know exactly whether Livia referred to the engagement or her memory loss.

"You never breathed a word. How long have the two of you

been…?" Her conspiratorial whisper sounded deafening in the quiet hallway.

"Come in." Andi ushered her into the room. Livia glanced around. Andi got the idea that she hadn't been here before, so they probably weren't the closest of friends, but maybe she could learn something from her. She managed a smile. "We didn't really want anyone to know. Not until we were sure."

Livia seemed satisfied with that answer. "How romantic. And after working together all these years. I never suspected a thing!"

"I hardly believe it myself."

"So the suitcases were for your honeymoon." Livia grinned and shook her head. "Where are you going?"

"Not sure yet." Jake hadn't said anything about a honeymoon. Surely they had to have a wedding first.

"This time make sure I'm not the last person in the palace to know. I know you're always insisting that it's part of your job to keep mum about things, but I can't believe I had to learn about your engagement on the radio."

"What did they say?"

"That you and Jake were out ring shopping in town this morning, and you told reporters you were getting married. Hey, let's see the rock!" She reached out and grabbed Andi's hand. "Wow. That's some ring. I wouldn't go on the New York City subway in that."

So Livia had come from New York, as well? That meant they'd probably known each other at least three years. Andi felt awful that she didn't even remember her.

Livia sighed. "And just imagine what your wedding dress will be like. You could probably get anyone in the world to design it for you. Some people have all the luck."

Andi was sorely tempted to point out that she had the bad luck to not even know who she was, but a gut instinct told her not to confide in Livia. She sensed an undercurrent of jealousy or resentment that made her reluctant to trust her.

"Oh, there are the suitcases, under your bed." Livia pointed. Andi could see the edges of two black rolling cases.

"You're very obsessed with those."

"I thought you were going to take off and leave us. At least to do that interview."

Andi frowned. Had she planned a job interview somewhere?

"I was even starting to think that if we both went back to New York we could share an apartment or something. Guess I was wrong." She widened her eyes, which fell again to Andi's hand.

"You were. I'll be staying here." She smiled, and conviction filled her voice. How nice it was to be sure of something.

"I bet you will."

A million questions bounced around Andi's brain, as many about Jake and life at the palace as about herself. But she couldn't think of any way to ask them without giving the game away, and she wasn't ready to do that yet. On the other hand, at least Livia could help her find her way to her own office. That would be one less problem for her to bother Jake with.

"Why don't you walk to my office with me?"

Livia looked curious. Andi worried that she'd made a misstep. She had no idea what Livia did at the palace, and her clothing, dark pants and a blue long-sleeved peasant shirt, didn't offer any clues. "Sure."

They set out, Andi lagging a fraction behind so that Livia could lead the way without realizing it. They went along the hallway in the opposite direction from Jake's suite, and up a flight of stairs to the third floor. At the top of the stairs a blond man hurried up to them. "Goodness, Andi. Congratulations."

"Thanks." She blushed, mostly because she had no idea who he was. Luckily it was an appropriate response.

"Cook wanted me to ask you whether we should do duck or goose on Thursday for the Finnish ambassador."

"Whichever she prefers would be fine." She froze for an agonizing second while it occurred to her that Cook might be a he.

His eyes widened. "I'll let her know. I suspect you have a lot on your plate right now, what with, well, you know." He smiled. "We're all very happy for you, Andi."

She forced another smile. He'd looked surprised by her lack of decisiveness. She must usually be a very take-charge person. At least the engagement gave her an excuse to be out to lunch—literally and figuratively. She was "preoccupied."

They reached a door halfway down a corridor on the third floor, and Livia hesitated. Andi swallowed, then reached out a hand and tried the door. The handle turned but didn't open it. "Oh no. I forgot my key! You go on with what you're doing and I'll go back and get it. See you later."

Livia waved a cheery goodbye and Andi heaved a sigh. She counted the doors along the hallway so she could find her way here alone next time. Back in her room she searched high and low for the key. When she found a black handbag at the bottom of her closet, her heart leapt.

She'd already discovered that the phone in her bedroom was for business only. Not a single personal number was stored in it. She'd called each one with hope in her heart, only to find herself talking to another bank or supplier. She must have another phone somewhere.

Eager to see her wallet and find out some more about herself, she dove into the bag with her hands. A neat, small wallet contained very few clues. A New York driver's license, with an 81st Street address, about to expire. A Ruthenian driver's license ornamented with a crest featuring two large birds. A Visa credit card from an American bank, and a MasterCard from a European one.

She seemed to be living a double life—half American and half Ruthenian. But that wasn't unusual among expats. She probably kept her accounts open, figuring she'd go back sooner or later.

The bag did contain a keychain containing two keys—her bedroom and office? Other than that there was a small packet of tissues and two lipsticks. No phone. Disappointment dripped through her. Maybe she just had no life.

Except Jake.

She glanced at the business phone on the dresser and her nerves sizzled with anticipation at the thought of calling him. She felt a lot safer in his large, calm presence.

But she didn't want to be a bother. She'd wait until she really needed him.

Keys and phone in the pocket of her jeans, she set off back for the locked office. Her instincts proved correct and the smaller key opened the door. Like her bedroom, her office was neat and featureless, no photos or mementos on the desk. She'd be worried that she was the world's dullest person, except that apparently she was intriguing enough for a king to want to marry her.

She opened a silver laptop on the desk. Surely this would reveal a wealth of new information about her life—her work, anyway. But the first screen asked her to enter her password.

Andi growled with frustration. She felt like she was looking for the password to her own life and it was always just out of reach. Password, password. She racked her brain for familiar words. *Blue,* she typed in. The screen was blue. Nothing happened. *Jake?* Nothing doing. *Love?*

Nada. Apparently her computer, like her memory, was off-limits for now.

Irritation crackled through her veins. She pulled open the drawers in the antique desk and was disappointed to find nothing but a dull collection of pens, paper clips, empty notebooks. The entire office revealed nothing about her. Almost as if every trace of her individuality had been stripped away.

The way you might do if you were leaving a job.

A pang of alarm flashed through her at the thought. Had she stripped her office bare in preparation for abandoning it? She could see how getting engaged to Jake could mean her leaving her job as his assistant, or at least changing it dramatically. But surely Jake would have mentioned it?

She picked up her phone and punched in his number. Feelings of helplessness and anxiety rose inside her as she heard it ring, but she fought them back.

"Hi, Andi. How are you doing?"

A smile rose to her lips at the sound of his deep, resonant voice. "Confused," she admitted. "I'm in my office and feeling more lost than ever."

"I'll meet you there."

She blew out a long breath as she put the phone back in her pocket. It was embarrassing to feel lost without Jake at her side, but wonderful that she could call him to it at any moment. She glanced at the ring on her finger. The big diamond sparkled in the sunlight, casting little shards of light over her skin, a symbol of his lifelong commitment to her.

At least she knew what it felt like to be loved.

She flew to the door at the sound of a knock. A huge smile spread over her face at the sight of him, tall and gorgeous, with a twinkle in his dark eyes.

"I missed you," he murmured, voice low and seductive.

"Come in." Her belly sizzled with arousal and her nipples tightened just at the sight of him. "Do you always knock on my office door?" It seemed oddly formal if they'd worked together and dated for years.

A shadow of hesitation crossed his face for a split second. "I suppose I do. Would you prefer me to barge right in?"

"I don't know." She giggled. Nothing seemed to matter all that much now that Jake was here. "I guess it depends on if I'm trying to keep secrets from you."

"Are you?" His brow arched.

"I have no idea." She laughed again. "Hopefully if I do, they're not very dark ones."

"Dark secrets sound rather intriguing." He moved toward

her and lifted his hand to cup her cheek. Her skin heated under his palm. "I might have fun uncovering them."

Their lips met, hot and fast, and his tongue in her mouth drove all thoughts away. She pressed herself against him and felt his arms close around her. *Much better.* Wrapping herself up in Jake was the best medicine for anything that ailed her.

His suit hid the hard muscle beneath it, but that didn't stop her fingers from exploring his broad back and enjoying the thickness of his toned biceps. Her fingertips were creeping into his waistband when a sharp knock on the door made them jump apart.

She blushed. "Do we get carried away like that often?"

Jake shot her a crooked smile. "Why not?"

A glance at the door sent her cheer scattering. "I won't recognize the person."

"I'll help you out."

She drew in a deep breath as she approached the door. "Who is it?"

"Domino." A male voice. "Just wanted to take a peek at Jake's calendar for tomorrow."

She glanced back at Jake and whispered, "I have no idea where your calendar is."

"You can peek at it in my head, Dom." Jake's voice boomed across the room.

A compact, dark-haired man in a gray suit flung the door open and entered. "Sorry, Mr. Mondragon, I didn't know you were in here. I just wondered if there was a set time for the Malaysian High Commission's arrival."

Andi listened while Jake rattled off a few planned events for the following day and tried to keep them filed in her brain in case anyone else asked her. It couldn't hurt to practice using her memory again. Still, she didn't truly breathe again until Domino backed out with a slight bow.

"I feel like the world's most incompetent assistant. Is the calendar on the computer?"

"Yup."

"It's password protected and I don't know the password. Do you know it?"

Jake looked thoughtful. "No."

"Any ideas what it might be?"

"None whatsoever. I guess there are some dark secrets between us." He lifted a brow playfully. "Maybe you have it written down somewhere."

"That's another thing." She frowned, apprehension twisting her gut as she prepared to tell him. "There's nothing personal in here at all. It's all business all the time, as if all the personal effects had been removed."

Jake blinked and his gaze swept the room. A furrow deepened between his brows; then he shrugged. "I'm not much for personal knickknacks in the office, either. Why don't we take a break and go stroll around the palace? Then at least you'll know where everything is."

Andi was a bit alarmed by the brusque way he changed the subject. One question burned in her mind. "Am I still your assistant? I mean, now that we're engaged."

"Yes, of course." Jake looked startled for a second. "I'd be lost without you arranging my life."

"Then prepare to get lost, since I can't arrange my own computer desktop right now." Tears loomed again. Apparently they'd never been very far away. "I still don't remember anything at all."

Jake took her into his arms again. His scent, familiar and enticing, wrapped around her as his embrace gave her strength. "The doctor said it would take time for your memory to return. Come on, let's go for that walk. There's no point getting upset over something you can't control."

The palace was so large that probably no one knew exactly how many rooms it had or how to get to all of them. As Jake explained, it had been the home of several dynasties of Ruthenian royals, all of whom had left their own stylistic stamp, so the building had everything from fortified turrets to elegant rows of French windows opening out onto a terrace for alfresco dancing.

As they walked about, on the pretext of discussing the decor, everyone stopped to offer their congratulations on their engagement. Some people hid their surprise, but Andi could tell it was a startling occurrence. Could they really have not noticed a romance occurring—over several years—right beneath their noses?

CHAPTER FIVE

"JAKE, CONGRATULATIONS ON your engagement." The silvery tones emerging from his phone dripped with acid. Jake glanced across his suite to where Andi reclined on the sofa looking through a tourist brochure about Ruthenia.

"Thanks, Carina." Lucky thing she couldn't see how happy he was not to be marrying her.

"Quite a surprise." Her tone was cool. "I had no idea you were involved with your assistant."

"You know how these things are. It seemed…unprofessional, but you can't halt the course of true love." He'd already explained the same to three other would-be queens, so it rolled naturally off his tongue.

"Indeed." She cleared her throat. "Daddy accuses you of toying with my affections, but I assured him that I'm a big girl and that he should still fund the new industrial development."

These veiled threats were becoming familiar, too.

"I do hope he will. We look forward to entertaining you both at the palace again soon." He was smiling when he hung up the phone. Right now everything was going as smoothly as could be expected. He was now officially off the hook for choosing the next queen of Ruthenia. No one had actually pulled support from any key projects or threatened to fund a revolution.

It was probably a plus that he hadn't offended one Ruthenian big shot by choosing the daughter of another. Selecting his American assistant as his bride had left all the local families equally offended—or mollified. And so far things were working out nicely.

He couldn't understand why he'd never plotted this tidy solution together with Andi, before she lost her memory. Choosing his wife now seemed like an agenda item he'd neatly checked off.

"Why don't you join me on the sofa?" Her come-hither stare and soft tones beckoned to him.

Blood rushed to his nether regions and he stiffened. Of course there were some aspects of their engagement that should remain off-limits until Andi's memory came back. It was one thing to pretend to love your assistant, it was quite another thing to actually make love to her.

"That dinner was delicious, but I find I'm still hungry." Andi's blue eyes sparkled. She curled her legs under her and stretched one arm sensually along the top of sofa.

Her voice called to a part of him that wasn't at all practical. Jake was struck by a cruel vision of the black lacy underwear beneath her jeans and T-shirt. *She'll be angry if you sleep with her under false pretenses.*

But were they really false? He did intend to marry her.

Which was funny, as he'd never planned to marry anyone. His parents' long and arduous union—all duty and no joy—had put him off the whole institution from an early age. They'd married because they were a "suitable" match, his father the son of the exiled monarch and his mother the daughter of a prominent noble, also in exile. They'd soon discovered they had nothing in common but blue Ruthenian blood, yet they'd held up the charade for five decades in the hope they'd one day inhabit this palace and put the Ruthenian crest on their stationery again.

They were both gone by the time the "new regime" crumbled and Ruthenia decided it wanted its monarchy back. Jake had assumed the mantle of political duty, but it didn't seem fair or reasonable to expect him to take it into his bedroom, as well.

He'd much rather take Andi into his bedroom. Her lips looked so inviting in that sensual half smile. And he could just imagine how those long legs would feel wrapped around his waist....

But that was a really bad idea. When she got her memory back she'd likely be pretty steamed about the whole scenario he'd cooked up. She'd be downright furious if he took advantage of her affections, as well. Much better if they kept their hands to themselves until they could talk things over sensibly.

"Do you want me to walk you back to your room?" His voice sounded tight.

"Why? I'm not going to sleep there, am I?" She raised a brow. She seemed far more relaxed, bolder, than he'd seen her so far. She was obviously feeling comfortable, even if her memory still showed no signs of returning.

"I think you should. It's a question of propriety."

She giggled. "You are joking."

"No." He felt a bit offended. "It's a royal thing."

"So, we've never...?" She rose from the sofa in an athletic leap and strode across the room. "I don't remember the details about my own life, but I remember general stuff and I'm pretty sure that it's totally normal for dating couples to...sleep together. So I don't believe that we've been dating for years and never done more than kiss."

Jake shrugged. She had a point. If only she knew he was trying to protect her. "Okay, I admit we may have been...intimate. But now that we're engaged and it's all official and formal, I think we should play by the rules."

"Whose rules?" She raised her hand and stroked his cheek with her fingers.

His groin tightened and he cleared his throat. "Those official, hundreds-of-years-old rules that the king should keep his hands off his future bride until after the wedding."

Her mouth lifted into a wicked smile. "These hands?" She picked up his hands and placed them squarely on her hips. Heat rose in his blood as he took in the curves beneath his palms. She wriggled her hips slightly, sending shock waves of desire pulsing through him.

I'm in full control of my hands and my mind. The thought did nothing to reassure him, especially when one of his hands started to wander toward her backside. Andi pressed her lips to his and her familiar scent filled his senses. Next thing he knew his hands were straying up and down her back, enjoying the soft curves under his palms.

His pants grew tight as Andi pressed her chest against his. He could just imagine what those deliciously firm breasts must look like in her lacy bra. If he coaxed her out of her T-shirt—which would not be difficult—he could find out right away.

But that might lead to other things.

In fact, he was one hundred percent sure that it would.

He pulled back from the kiss with considerable effort. "Don't you have some…embroidery to do or something?"

"Embroidery?" Laughter sparkled in her clear blue eyes. "Do I really embroider stuff?"

He chuckled. "Not that I know of, but does a man really know what his fiancée gets up to in the privacy of her room?"

"I guess that depends how much time he spends there." She raised a brow. "Maybe we should go to my room?"

Jake froze. That seemed like a really bad idea. Which underlined what a bad idea all this kissing and cuddling was. Much better to keep things professional, with just enough hint of romance to keep the people around them convinced. At least until Andi came back to her senses.

He flinched as Andi's fingers crept beneath the waistband of his pants. He'd grown rock hard and the thought of pushing her away was downright painful. Her soft cheek nuzzled against his and his fingers wandered into her hair. She looked so different with her hair loose, much less formal and more inviting.

Her cool fingers slid under his shirt and skated up his spine. Jake arched into the sensation, pulling her tighter into his embrace. Her breathing was faster and her pink lips flushed and parted. He couldn't resist sticking his tongue into her mouth and she responded in kind, until they were kissing hard and fast again.

"Still think I should go to my room?" She rasped the question when they came up for air.

"Definitely not." He had to take this woman to bed, whether it was a good idea or not.

He reached under her T-shirt and cupped her breast, enjoying the sensation of skin and scratchy lace under his fingers. He could feel her heartbeat pounding, like his own, as anticipation built toward boiling point.

"Let's go into the bedroom." He disentangled himself from her with some effort and led her into the other room. The plain white bedcovers looked like an enticing playground and he couldn't wait to spread her out on them and uncover her step by step.

He swept her off her feet—eliciting a shriek of delight—and laid her gently on the bed.

Suddenly horizontal, Andi looked up at Jake with alarm. Her entire body pulsed and tingled with sensation. About to reach for the buttons of his shirt, her fingers stopped in midair. Their eyes met, his dark with fierce desire that made her insides tremble.

Everything about this situation felt new and different.

Jake's hands showed no hesitation as he unzipped her jeans and slid them off. Heat snapped in her veins, deepening the sense of unease creeping over her.

"What's the matter?" Jake paused and studied her face.

"I don't know. It just feels strange."

"Go with it." He lifted the hem of her T-shirt and eased it off over her head. Her nipples stood to attention inside her lacy bra, which was now exposed to view along with its matching panties. Jake's devouring gaze raked her body and Andi felt both very desirable and very, very nervous.

Jake unbuttoned his own shirt and shrugged it off, revealing a thickly muscled chest with a line of dark hair running down to his belt buckle. His powerful biceps flexed as he undid the belt and the button of his pants.

Andi's hesitation flew away. "Wait, let me do that." She rose to the edge of the bed and unzipped his pants as excitement and arousal replaced her apprehension. She pushed them down to reveal dark boxers and powerful hair-roughened thighs.

Both in their underwear, they stretched out on the cool white sheets, skin to skin. She touched his chest with a tentative finger, enjoying the warmth of his body. She traced the curve of his pec and traveled lower, to where his arousal was dramatically evident against the dark fabric of his shorts.

Jake's taut belly contracted as she trailed over it then paused.

She looked up at his face. The naked desire in his eyes further unraveled her inhibitions. She let her hands roam lower, tugging at his boxers until they slid down and his erection sprang free. She gasped, and he chuckled. Then she pulled the soft fabric down over his strong legs until he was totally naked.

"You're gorgeous," she breathed. Then she blushed, realizing that must sound silly when she'd seen him naked many times before.

"You're far more gorgeous." His slightly callused fingers tickled her skin as he ran his hand along her side, from her bra to her panties.

"But you're not seeing me as if it was the first time."

"Yes, I am," he murmured. Then he looked up. "At least that's what it feels like." Excitement danced in his dark eyes. "I could never grow tired of looking at you."

Andi swallowed. If Jake's feelings for her were anything like the intense roar of passion pulsing in her veins right now, she could understand how this could feel new and fresh even after several years.

He slid his arm behind her back and tugged her closer. Her belly flipped as it touched his, and her breasts bumped against his chest.

"Time to unwrap this present," he breathed. He propped himself on one elbow and deftly undid the clasp on her bra, releasing her breasts. She felt his breathing quicken as he tugged the lacy fabric off over her arms and lowered his mouth to one tight pink nipple.

Andi arched her back and let out a little moan as Jake flicked his tongue over the delicate skin. The sound of her own voice in the still night air startled her, and quickened her pulse further. She pushed her fingers into his thick hair and enjoyed the silky sensations roaming through her body as he licked and sucked.

"Kiss me," she begged, when she couldn't take the almost painful pleasure anymore. He responded by pressing his lips to hers with passion and kissing the last of her breath away.

Arms wrapped around him, she held Jake close. His warm masculine scent filled her senses and the heat of his skin against hers only increased her desire. Fingers trembling with anticipation, she took hold of his erection. Jake released a low moan as she ran her fingers over the hard surface, then tightened them around the shaft, enjoying the throb of pleasure that issued through him.

Had she really done this before? She couldn't believe it. Again that odd sensation of unfamiliarity almost dampened her pleasure. Everything she did was like taking a step into the dark and hoping the floor would still be there under her foot when she put it down. Where would these strange and intense sensations and urges lead her?

Jake's mouth crushed over hers once more and her doubts crumbled beneath the fierce desire to feel him inside her.

Working together they eased off her panties and he climbed over her. The inviting weight of him pressed against her chest for a moment; then he lifted himself up with his powerful arms and entered her slowly.

Too slowly.

She found herself writhing and arching to encourage him deeper. Her insides ached to hold him and her whole body burned hot and anxious with an urgent need to join with him. Her fingers dug into his back as he finally sank all the way in and she released a deep moan of pleasure into his ear.

Jake layered hot kisses along her neck and cheek as he moved over her, drawing her deeper into the mysterious ocean of pleasure that felt so strange and so good at the same time. They rolled on the bed, exploring each other from different angles and deepening the connection between them. Her hands wandered over his body, enjoying the hard muscle, squeezing and stroking him as he moved inside her.

She loved riding on top of him, changing the rhythm from slow to fast and back again as the sensations inside her built toward a dangerous crescendo. Jake was over her again when she felt herself suddenly lose control of her muscles and even her mind as a huge wave of release swept her far out of herself. She drifted in limbo as pulses of sheer pleasure rose through her again and again. Then she seemed to wash back up in Jake's arms, exhausted and utterly at peace.

"That was…" She couldn't seem to find the words. Any words, really.

"Awesome."

Jake's unroyal response made her laugh. "Exactly." Then she frowned. "Is it always like this when we…make love?"

She could swear she felt him flinch slightly. "Yup. It is."

"I guess that's good." She smiled. She must be one of the luckiest people on earth, to have a loving relationship—with really hot sex—with this ridiculously handsome man who just happened to be a king.

She stretched, still feeling delicious pulses of pleasure tickling her insides. She couldn't help wondering how she'd arrived at this juncture. How did she find herself engaged to a gorgeous monarch? Maybe she was from some kind of upper-crust family herself. It was so odd not knowing anything about yourself. She opened her eyes and peered at Jake.

"Will you tell me some things about myself?"

His sleepy gaze grew wider and a smile tilted his mouth. "Like what?"

"My background, the kind of things I like to do, that sort of stuff."

He frowned, still smiling that half smile. "Hmm, it's hard to know where to start."

Adrenaline buzzed through her at the prospect of nailing down a few details. "How about at the beginning. Did I grow up in New York?"

"No. You moved there after college." He kissed her cheek softly. "You came to work for me right after you graduated."

"What did I study in college?"

"Hmm. I can't remember exactly. I think it was something to do with literature. Or maybe French. You spoke French fluently even though you'd never been to France. I remember that."

"Oh." It wasn't so odd that he didn't know what she'd majored in. That was before she met him. "Where did I go to college?"

Jake hesitated, and frowned. "Was it U Penn? Somewhere in Pennsylvania. I'm pretty sure of that."

"You don't remember where I went to college? You're almost as bad as I am. Where did I grow up?"

Jake licked his lips. His eyes showed a mild trace of alarm. "Pennsylvania, definitely. Philly, maybe. Or was it Pittsburgh?"

"We've never been there together?" An odd knot of tension was forming in her stomach. She propped herself up in bed on one elbow.

"No, our relationship has always been pretty under wraps. The whole professional thing."

"So you haven't met my family." Again, unease niggled somewhere deep inside her.

"No. You have parents and a sister somewhere, though. You get together with them for holidays."

"In Pennsylvania?"

"I think so. You usually took the train."

"Oh." How odd that she couldn't remember anything about them. Or Pennsylvania. And it was a little disturbing that Jake seemed to know so little about her. Did they never talk about her past? "What's my sister's name?"

Jake pursed his lips for a moment. "I don't know."

"I guess I didn't talk about her that much." Maybe she and her sister weren't close. What a shame. Maybe she'd try to improve their relationship once she got her memory back. "What about my parents? Do you know their names or where they live? We could get in touch with them and see if they could jog my memory back into existence."

Jake's brow had furrowed. "I suppose we should be able to find that information somewhere."

"It's probably on my computer if I could just figure out the password."

"We'll worry about that in the morning." Jake pulled her closer to him. "Right now let's just enjoy each other."

Andi let out a sigh and sank back into his arms. "You're right. Why get stressed out over something I can't control?"

But even in his soothing embrace, there wasn't a single second when she didn't ache to recover her memory—and her history. How could you really go forward, or even live in the moment, if you don't know who you are?

After breakfast, Jake left Andi in her office to look over her files. She seemed anxious that she wasn't able to do her job since she didn't remember the details of palace life, let alone any specific events. He mused that he should have been concerned, too, since a key purpose of this whole engagement was to keep her at his side running the show, but somehow the palace was managing to tick along. And he was enjoying her company far more than he'd imagined.

How could he have worked with her for six years and not even know where her family lived? As far as he knew she was born behind the desk in his Manhattan office. And he cringed at not knowing her sister's name. For all he could remember she just referred to her as "my sister."

He strode to his current office, intent on mining it for the information he should know simply on the basis of their long acquaintance. They spent all day together—did they usually talk about nothing but work?

Andi was always excellent about keeping them focused so no time was wasted. She managed their affairs with such efficiency that there was little downtime for chin-wagging, especially since they'd moved to Ruthenia and tackled challenges higher than the legendary Althaus mountains that loomed over the palace. He'd always appreciated her professional approach to her job and to life in general.

But now he was beginning to realize he'd missed out on enjoying her company all this time. She was much more complex than he'd realized, more vulnerable and intriguing—and not just because of her missing memory. He'd never seen her as a person with emotions, with needs, before, because she'd done such an excellent job hiding that aspect of herself.

And he'd never realized she was so tempting. She'd hidden that, too.

He closed his office door and walked through to the cabinets in the file room, where the personnel files from New York were stored. Thanks to Andi's relentless organization he quickly laid his hands on her file, and the résumé she'd submitted when she applied for the job as his admin back when he was simply a venture capitalist.

A quick scan revealed that she'd graduated from Drexel University in Pennsylvania—right state, at least—with a degree in business administration and a ridiculously long list of clubs and activities to her name. Apart from some temping in Manhattan, her first job was with him. She'd graduated from North Hills Senior High School in Pittsburgh—ha, right again, maybe he wasn't so bad after all. He had to congratulate himself on being able to pick such a promising employee despite her lack of relevant work experience.

But that didn't solve his current problem of finding out about her past and helping her recover her memory.

Wait. Did he even want her to recover her memory? If she did, she'd surely remember that their relationship had been strictly professional and the whole engagement his invention.

Discomfort rose in his chest, threatening to overwhelm the sense of satisfaction—of happiness, dammit—that had suffused his body and mind since their overnight encounter.

Andi was sensational between the sheets. He'd never have dreamed that his quiet, prim assistant hid so much passion and energy beneath her suited exterior. She even looked different, like she'd forgotten to put on the mask of no-nonsense propriety she usually painted on with makeup and pinned into place with a spritz of hair spray. The real Andi—the one without the mask—was soft and sexy and downright irresistible.

Desire stirred inside him again, tightening his muscles. Blood rushed to his groin as he thought about her in his arms that morning, scented with passion as well as her usual floral fragrance. He put the résumé back in its file.

Maybe her memory wouldn't come back and they could start over from the night he'd found her dancing outside, freed of the inhibitions and anxieties built by a lifetime of experience. He couldn't help believing that the woman who'd shared his bed was the real Andi, and that she'd been hiding inside all this time, waiting for a chance to be free.

Andi let out a cry of sheer joy. She'd finally cracked the password on her computer. A cryptic penciled list in the drawer seemed like a meaningless string of words—until she started typing them in one by one.

Queen had proved to be the key that unlocked her hard drive, and possibly her whole life. Funny! She must have picked it because she knew she soon would be queen.

That thought stopped her cold for a second. Queen Andi. Didn't quite sound right. Still, she'd get used to it. And maybe Andi was short for a more majestic name, like Andromeda or something.

Her heart raced as the computer opened her account and laid a screen full of icons out before her. Yikes. So many different files, some with the names of countries, some of companies. She didn't know where to start. A sound issued from the machine, and she noticed that the email icon announced the presence of fifty-three messages. She clicked on it with a growing sense of anticipation, and scrolled back to the last one she had opened. Eticket confirmation.

Frowning, she opened the email, which revealed an itinerary for Andi Louise Blake—apparently she wasn't really named Andromeda—to travel from Munich to New York. The date listed was…yesterday.

Her blood slowed in her veins and her breathing grew shallow.

Obviously she hadn't gone on the trip, and if it was a business-related one, surely Jake would have mentioned it. Munich—the nearest international airport, perhaps?—to New York, where she used to live…

She had been planning to leave.

Head spinning, she sat back in her chair. Why would she leave, if she was in love and about to get engaged?

She should just ask Jake about this. Why get all worked up when it could be a business trip that just got canceled at the last moment, maybe due to her loss of memory, or their engagement?

Andi glanced down at her ring with a growing sense of unease. She never had figured out why her clothes were creased as if they'd been packed. She must have changed her mind and unpacked at some point, but when? And why did Jake not know about her plans to take off?

Had she issued an ultimatum and forced him into proposing to her?

She swallowed, then started to chew on a nail. Her stomach curled up into a tight ball. Maybe she should see what else was going on in her email before she spoke to Jake.

It was hard to read with so much nervous energy leaping through her system. Her eyes kept jumping around on the screen. Most of the emails were business related—responses to invitations, scheduling questions, orders for supplies and that kind of thing.

Then one titled What's going on? from a Lizzie Blake caught her eye. Blake—the same last name as her. What *was* going on? She clicked on it with her heart in her mouth.

Andi, I know you told me not to email personal stuff to this account, but I've tried calling you and you won't call back. We saw a news story on TV yesterday saying that you're going to marry Jake Mondragon, your boss. Is this true? How come you didn't tell us? I thought you were getting ready to quit from the way you've been talking lately. Mom is pretty upset that you'd keep something like this from us. I remember you saying years ago that your boss was hot, but you never mentioned dating him, let alone getting engaged. Anyway, get in touch ASAP and let me know if I need to find a dress for a royal wedding. XX Sis.

Andi sat back, blinking. She had a sister called Lizzie. Who knew absolutely nothing about her relationship to Jake. And who'd been calling her but not getting through. She *must* have another phone somewhere that she used for personal calls.

She scanned the rest of the emails, but nothing else looked truly personal.

Where would she keep another phone? Brain ticking fast, she hurried back to her bedroom, glad she didn't run into anyone in the hallway—especially Jake.

A pang of guilt and hurt stung her heart. She was avoiding him. Only this morning they'd lain in each others arms and she'd enjoyed such contentment and bliss that she hadn't even minded about her memory being gone.

Now she was racked with suspicion and doubt. She locked her bedroom door behind her and started to go through the closet and drawers again. Finally, in the pocket of a black pair of pants she found a small silver phone. The pants showed signs of being recently worn—slightly creased across the hips and behind the knees—so maybe she had them on just before she lost her memory.

She flipped the phone open and pulled up recent messages. There were three from Lizzie and one from her mom, who sounded noticeably upset. Her voice, with its hint of tears, struck a sharp and painful chord deep inside her. On instinct Andi hit the button to dial the number.

"Andi!"

"Mom?" Her voice shook slightly. "Is it really you?"

"Of course it's me. Who else would be answering my phone?" A bright laugh rang in her ear. "What the heck is going on over there?"

Andi drew in a steadying breath. "I don't really know, to be honest. I lost my memory."

"What?"

"Jake found me dancing around outside and I couldn't remember anything at all. I didn't even remember you or Lizzie until I saw her email and found the messages on my phone."

"Oh, my gosh, that sounds terrifying. Are you okay?"

"More or less. It's been strange and kind of scary, but I'm not sick or injured or anything."

"That's a blessing. Has your memory come back?"

Andi blinked. A blurry vision of a face—an energetic woman with short light brown hair and bright blue eyes filled her brain. "I think it's coming back right now. Do you have blue eyes?"

"Of course I do. That's where you got them from. You forgot my eye color?"

"I forgot you even existed. I didn't know my own name." Other images suddenly crowded her brain: a man with gray hair and a warm smile, a blonde with long curls and a loud laugh. "But it's coming back now that I hear your voice." Excitement crackled through her veins. Finally she had an identity, a past. The details crashed back into her brain one after the other— her childhood home, her school, her old dog Timmy...

"Are you really engaged to your boss?" Her mom's voice tugged her back to the present.

Andi froze. That part she didn't remember. "He says we got engaged right before I lost my memory. I don't remember it."

"Do you love him?" The voice on the phone was suddenly sharp.

"Oh, yes. I've always loved him." The conviction rang through her whole body. "I've loved him for years."

"You never said a thing. I had no idea you were even involved with him."

Andi blinked rapidly. The memories flooding her brain were curiously devoid of any romantic images of her and Jake. She had plenty of memories of working with him, but as she mentally flipped through them looking for signs of their relationship a strange and awful truth dawned on her. "That's because I wasn't involved with him."

CHAPTER SIX

HER MOM'S CONFUSED and anxious reaction prompted Andi to make excuses and hang up the phone. She needed someone who could answer questions, not just ask them. Instinct told her to call her sister, Lizzie.

"Your Majesty!" Her sister's now-familiar voice made her jump.

"Lizzie, you wouldn't believe what's been going on."

"You're right. I don't, so you'll have to break it down into tiny pieces for me. Are you really marrying your boss?"

Andi bit her lip. "I don't know. It's the weirdest thing, I lost my memory and ever since then we've been engaged. But my memory's coming back now—since I found your phone messages and spoke to Mom—and I don't remember anything at all about being engaged to him."

"You never even told me you were dating him."

"I don't remember anything about that, either. I do recall being seriously attracted to him for, oh, years and years, but not that anything actually came of it. Now suddenly I seem to be engaged to him and I have no idea what's going on."

"How does he explain the situation?"

Andi blew out. "I don't know. I haven't spoken to him about

it yet. My memory only just started coming back and he doesn't know yet."

"Do you remember him asking you to marry him?"

She thought for a second. "No. I don't remember everything, though. There's a gap." She raised a hand to her head where she could still feel a slight bump. "I must have fallen and banged my head, or something." She paused, remembering the etickets she'd seen on her computer. "Did I say anything about coming back to the States?"

"For Christmas, you mean?"

Andi wondered how much to reveal, then decided things were so complicated already that she might as well be truthful. "For good. I think I was planning to leave here. I had tickets back to New York."

"And you don't remember why?"

I do.

The realization was seeping back into her, almost like blood rushing to her brain. She had intended to leave. She wanted to go because she was tired of adoring Jake while he flirted with other women in the name of business.

Because she loved him and knew she could never have him.

A sharp pain rose in her middle around the area of her heart. How had six years of yearning turned—overnight—into a fantasy engagement?

It didn't add up. There was a missing piece to the puzzle and she had no idea what it was.

"So are you marrying him, or what?" Lizzie's amused voice roused her from her panicked thoughts.

Her eyes fell on the big ring, flashing in the afternoon sunlight pouring through the large office window. "Yes." Then she frowned. "At least I think so."

"Well, I saw it in the *National Enquirer,* so it must be true, right?" Lizzie's voice was bright with laughter. "There's a picture of you with a rock on your finger the size of my Mini Cooper. Is that thing real?"

Andi stared at the glittering stones. She was pretty sure it was a real diamond, but was it a real engagement ring? "Sure. It's from a jeweler here in town. Jake bought it for me yesterday."

"Sounds pretty official to me. Is he good in bed?"

Andi's mouth fell open.

"Come on, I'd tell you. Or do royal romances not involve any sex?"

Her teasing voice brought a smile to Andi's lips. "He's amazing."

"Ha. I had a feeling. I've seen pictures of him and he's seriously handsome. I love the dark flashing eyes. Is he romantic?"

"Very." She could almost feel his arms around her right now, holding and steadying her. "He's been so sweet with me since I lost my memory. We've managed to keep it a secret so far. You and Mom and the doctor he called are the only other people who know."

"Why keep it a secret?"

"I guess because I felt so vulnerable. Like everyone around me knows more about me than I do. I didn't want anyone to know. It's all coming back now, though. Not all the tiny details yet, like work stuff I have to do, but the bigger things like who I know and where I'm from and…"

How much I've always loved Jake.

Were they really going to be married and live happily ever after? It seemed too much to hope for.

"So you're going to be a queen. Will I have to curtsy to you?"

"Gosh, I hope not." Andi laughed. "What a strange idea. I can't quite see myself with a crown on."

"You'd better get used to the idea. Can I be your maid of honor? Or maybe they don't have them in Ruthenia."

"I have no idea. I've never planned a wedding here and apparently I haven't paid close enough attention at the few I've attended." Images of Jake's other would-be brides crowded her mind. Alia and Maxi and Carlotta and Liesel…there were so

many of them. Rich and beautiful and fawning all over him.
Why, out of all the glamorous and powerful women available
to him, had Jake chosen her?

It was time to track him down and ask some questions.

After promising to call Lizzie back and tell her the details, Andi
went into the bathroom and looked in the mirror. Her cosmetics were strung out along a shelf, which was not how she used
to keep them. She also remembered that she nearly always
tied her rather wispy hair up in a bun and slicked it down with
gel—she was always experimenting with different brands as
the Ruthenian climate was surprisingly humid. Now her hair
lay loose around her shoulders, and her face looked oddly col-
orless without the lipstick and blush she usually donned.

A glance in her closet reminded her she was a hard-core
suit wearer. She felt it was important to project a professional
image, and she liked bright colors as they seemed assertive and
positive. Right now she had on a rather uncharacteristic pastel
yellow blouse and a pair of slacks and her hair wafted around
her shoulders. People must have noticed the difference.

Part of her felt embarrassed that she'd been walking around
the palace looking like a paler, less polished version of herself.
And part of her wondered whether Jake actually preferred the
less made-up look. He'd chosen the super-casual jeans and T-
shirt she'd worn all the previous day. She blushed as she remembered he'd also chosen the racy lingerie. A glance in her
underwear drawer confirmed that cotton briefs and no-nonsense bras were more her style.

Still, if Jake liked lacy lingerie and jeans, she could adjust.
She couldn't resist smoothing just a hint of blush on her cheeks.
They were a bit pale with shock. But she used a clear gloss instead of lipstick and left her hair loose—maybe it didn't look
so bad after all.

With a deep breath, she set off for his office. Her pulse rate
roared like a runaway truck by the time she finally plucked up

the courage to peek around the open door. Jake was in conversation with a man she instantly remembered as the minister of economics. Jake looked up when she entered the doorway, and an expression flickered across his face—shock?—almost as if he suddenly knew her memory was back.

Andi struggled not to fidget as the conversation continued for another couple of minutes—something urgent to do with trade tariffs. Her nerves were jumping and her palms sweating.

In his dark suit, with his usual air of unhurried calm, Jake seemed perfectly poised and in control of any situation. She, on the other hand, had no idea what their situation really was. She could remember nearly everything about her life—except a romance with Jake.

He finally closed the door behind the economics minister and turned to her. Again she could see in his face that he knew something was different.

"My memory is coming back." She floated the words out, as if on a string, wondering what his response would be. Would he take her in his arms with a cry of joy?

Jake didn't move an inch. "That's great." He seemed to be waiting for her to reveal more.

"It started when I saw an email from my sister. Then I phoned my mom. That jogged something in my brain and the memories started bubbling up."

"What a relief." His voice was oddly flat. He still made no move toward her.

Andi's eyes dropped to her ring, which seemed to sting the skin underneath it. "It's strange, I remember working with you for years, but I don't..." Her voice cracked as fear rose in her chest. "I don't remember anything about us." She faltered. "I mean us being...romantically involved."

Jake stepped up to her and took her hand. Her heart surged with relief and she was about to smile, but his deadly serious demeanor stopped her. "I'll be completely honest with you."

"About what?" Her pulse picked up and a sense of dread swelled inside her.

"We weren't involved. Our relationship was strictly professional until two days ago."

"We weren't dating? Not even in secret?" Her heart hammered against her ribs.

"No."

Andi swallowed hard and her rib cage tightened around her chest. The ostentatious ring suddenly seemed to weigh down her hand and drain her strength. "So, the engagement is fake?" Her voice came out as a rasping whisper, filled with every ounce of apprehension and terror she felt. "It was all pretend?"

Jake tilted his head. "No."

Andi wanted to shake him. "Could you be more explicit?"

He frowned. "It's hard to explain. You were going to leave, and I didn't want you to. I was under pressure to choose a bride, and then you lost your memory. Things fell into place and I realized you're the ideal woman to be my wife."

She blinked, trying to make sense of his words. "So we are engaged?"

"Absolutely." His dark eyes looked earnest.

Then a cold sensation crept over her. "But you're not in love with me."

He swallowed. "Love is something that grows over time. I'm confident that we'll enjoy a happy and successful marriage. The important thing is to provide stability for Ruthenia, and as a team we can do just that."

Andi struggled for breath. The man of her dreams, whom she'd fantasized about and mooned over for six long years, wanted to marry her.

Because she'd be a key member of his team.

A cold laugh flew from her lips. "Wouldn't it have been easier to just offer me a higher salary?"

He raised a brow. "I tried that."

"And I said no? Wait. Now I remember saying no. You were

so sure you could talk me around, just like you always do." Her vision blurred as tears rose to her eyes. "And you really thought I'd go along with this crazy plan?"

"You're sensible and practical. I knew you'd see the sense in it."

"In spending my life with a husband who doesn't love me? You never even noticed I was female." A flashback to their lovemaking filled her brain. He'd noticed it then. But maybe he'd just pretended she was one of the glamorous socialites that usually buzzed around him. He'd had no shortage of girlfriends in the time she'd worked for him.

"My parents married because their families were both ex-iled Ruthenian nobles. They were married nearly fifty years."

His parents had died before she met him. She knew little about them except that they were part of New York society. "Were they happy?"

He hesitated. "Of course."

"You don't sound convinced. Did they love each other?"

"It was a successful marriage, and they achieved their life-long goal of producing an heir who'd be ready to take the throne of Ruthenia when the time came."

"Lucky thing you were cooperative. It would be a shame to throw away fifty years of your life and have your son insist he was going to be a pro skateboarder. Did you really think I'd just go along with your plan?"

"Yes."

His calm expression exasperated her. He still thought she was going to go along with his scheme. He obviously didn't care about her feelings at all. "We slept together." Her body still siz-zled and hummed with sensual energy from that amazing night.

The passion they'd shared might have been fake on his side, but on hers it was painfully real.

"I didn't intend for that to happen." His expression turned grim. "I understand that you must be furious with me for tak-ing advantage of your situation."

"You're right. I am." Devastated would have been a better word. Their lovemaking wasn't the fruit of a long-term and loving romance, at least not for him. On her side she'd probably had enough romance in her head to last a lifetime.

He must have found it hilarious that she fell into his arms so easily. "Didn't you think it was wrong to sleep with an employee?"

His eyes narrowed. "Yes. I didn't intend to sleep with you until I'd explained the situation."

"Until you'd explained to me that you needed a wife and I was handy?" She still couldn't quite believe he took her so totally for granted.

Obviously he had no respect for her feelings and wishes. A chill swept through her and she hugged herself.

"You were confused after losing your memory. I didn't want to complicate matters when I knew you were in no state to make an important decision."

"So you just made it for me."

He drew in a breath. "You know me well enough to trust my judgment."

She struggled to check her anger. "I trust your judgment perfectly in matters of business, but not where my personal life is concerned. You already knew I intended to leave because I wasn't feeling fulfilled."

No need to say she couldn't stand to see him marry another woman. He'd assume she was thrilled that he'd made a cold-hearted and clinical decision to marry her. "It's downright arrogant of you to assume I'd marry you."

"I know you're capable of rising to any challenge."

"But what if I don't want to?" Her voice rose a little and she struggled to check tears. A romance with Jake was such a heartfelt wish. Suddenly it had become a duty.

No doubt sex with her was supposed to seal the pact in some way.

What a shame she'd enjoyed it so much. Right now she

wanted to chastise her body for still craving his touch. She should hate him for what he'd done when she needed his help the most.

Jake still stood there, calm and regal, chin lifted high.

A sinister thought crept over her. If he could plan something so outrageous as marriage to a woman who didn't know who she was, perhaps he contrived to put her in such a vulnerable position.

"Were you responsible for me losing my memory?" If he'd gone this far in his deception, who knew what he could be capable of?

"No." His answer was decisive.

She wanted to believe him—and hated herself for it.

"Then what did happen?" So many pieces were still missing.

"I don't know how you lost your memory. I found you outside dancing around on the grass in the moonlight."

Andi blushed. Had she done anything embarrassing? She couldn't remember a single thing about that night. Though now that he mentioned it, she did remember telling him she was going to leave. A cold sensation slithered through her. She was leaving to protect her heart.

Right now her heart was being flayed open. Jake's desire to keep her had nothing to do with him wanting her as his fiancée, or even his friend, and everything to do with keeping his office running smoothly.

And he'd seduced her into his bed on the pretext that they'd been dating for years.

Her insides still hummed with sense memories that would probably torment her forever. She'd thought they were making love—and her whole spirit had soared with the joy of it—but he was just cementing a deal.

On instinct she pulled the big ring from her finger. It wedged a bit over the knuckle, but she managed to get it off. "Take this back."

His eyes widened. "Oh, no. You must wear it."

"I don't have to do anything." She shoved it forward. "It's not real."

"I assure you those stones are genuine and worth a large sum of money."

Andi's mouth fell open, then closed shut. How could he not understand a word she was saying? She walked to his desk and put the ring down on the polished surface. It looked odd there, sparkling away amongst the piles of papers.

"I don't intend to wear or own any kind of engagement ring unless I'm actually engaged. And since we're not really engaged or even involved, I don't want anything to do with it." Tears threatened in her voice. She crossed her arms, and hoped it would hide the way her hands were shaking.

"But we are engaged." Jake's words, spoken softly, crept into her brain and heart. "I really do want to marry you."

Andi blinked, trying to catch her breath. How could a dream come true in such a horrible, distorted way?

The odd expression in his eyes almost made her consider it. There was something like...yearning in their dark depths.

Then again, she was obviously good at dreaming stuff up.

Now that her memory was back she knew—in the depths of her aching soul—that she'd loved Jake for years, pined for him and hoped that one day he'd see her as something other than an efficient assistant. She'd adored him in silence, occasionally allowing herself to fantasize that things might one day be different if she waited patiently for him to notice her. Their time as an engaged couple was the fulfillment of all secret hopes—and now she'd woken to find herself living a mockery of her cherished dreams.

Anger flared inside her, hot and ugly. "You honestly think I would continue with this charade that you sprung on me when I was at my most vulnerable? To let people think that we love each other when we're nothing more than boss and assistant, as always?"

"We'll be equals, of course, like any couple."

He said it simply, like he really believed it. But then Jake could convince anyone of anything. She'd watched him in action for too long. "I'm not sure that many couples are equals, especially royal ones." She'd be the official wife, sensibly dressed and courteous as always. The one who got left behind with her embroidery—not that she did embroidery—while he was out having affairs with other women.

"I need to leave, and right now." If she continued with this pretense for even another hour, she'd get sucked into hoping their official engagement might turn into true romance. Even with every shred of evidence pointing to that being impossible and hopeless, she'd already proven herself to be that kind of softheaded, dreaming fool.

"The story's gone around the world already."

She steadied herself with a breath. All her relatives knew, probably all her old friends. Everyone she'd ever known, maybe. "You'll just have to explain that it was all a big lie. Or a joke." Her voice cracked on the last word. It did feel like a cruel joke at her expense. She'd never experienced such feelings of happiness and contentment as during the last couple of days as Jake's fiancée. Their night of lovemaking had raised the bar of pure bliss so high that she'd likely never know anything like that again.

"I'm going to pack my bags." She turned for the door. Her whole body was shaking.

Jake caught hold of her arm and she tried to wrench it away, but his grip was too strong. "The people of Ruthenia are counting on you. I'm counting on you."

His words pierced her soul for a second, but she summoned her strength. "I'm sure the people of Ruthenia can find something else to count on. Television game shows, perhaps."

"We're going to be on television tonight. To talk about celebrating our engagement during the Independence Day celebrations."

Andi froze. "Independence Day. That's what this is all about, isn't it?" She turned and stared at his face. A memory of Jake's public promise to choose a wife formed in her mind. "You committed to picking a bride before Ruthenia's third Independence Day." She squinted at him, looking for signs of emotion in his face. "Your deadline had come right up on you and you had to pick someone or you'd be a liar. And there I was, clueless as a newborn babe and ripe for duping."

"Andi, we've been partners for years. It's not that big a leap."

"From the office to a lifetime commitment? I think that's a leap. You can't just get a plane ticket and leave a marriage." She lifted her chin as anger and hurt flashed over her. "Though apparently I can't just get a plane ticket and leave my job with you, either." Fury bubbled up inside her. "Do you think you can control everything and everyone?"

"I'm not trying to control you, just to make you see sense. We're a great team."

"I've never been into team sports. When I marry, it will be for love." Her heart ached at the thought that she'd loved Jake almost since the day she met him.

Though right now she hated him for tricking her into a relationship that meant nothing to him.

"Think it over, Andi. Be sensible."

"I am sensible. That's why I know this would never work."

Jake's expression grew impenetrable. "Stay until after Independence Day, at least."

"You think I'll change my mind? Or maybe you think I'll just be guilt-tripped into marrying you by seeing all those smiling Ruthenian faces. What if people don't like the idea of you marrying your lowly assistant? They'd probably rather see you marry some Ruthenian blue blood with twelve names."

"They'll all know I made the right choice."

His words hung in the air. *The right choice.*

Impossible.

Still, his quiet conviction both irked and intrigued her.

She stared hard at his chiseled face. "You really do want to marry me?"

He took her hands in his. Her skin tingled and sizzled, and she cursed the instant effect he always had on her. "I do want to marry you."

Those accursed hopes and dreams flared up inside her like embers under a breath.

He doesn't love you. Don't get carried away.

Still, maybe something could come of this crazy situation. Could she live with herself if she didn't at least try to make it work?

She inhaled a shaky breath. "If I agree to stay until Independence Day, then decide it won't work, you'll let me go?"

His expression clouded. "Yes."

She wasn't sure she believed him. Jake didn't often admit, or experience, defeat. But she could always sneak away this time.

Or stay here for the rest of her life.

Her heart thumped and her stomach felt queasy. "I can't really believe this is happening. We'll sleep in separate rooms?"

"If you prefer." His cool reply sounded like a challenge. He probably intended to seduce her again. She silently determined not to let him.

"Independence Day is three days away." Could she stand to be Jake's unloved but practical fiancée for seventy-two hours? She really didn't want to let everyone down and ruin the Independence Day celebrations. She could look at it as her job, as long as there was no kissing or sex involved.

And then there was that insane hope that they really could live happily ever after.

Jake picked up the ring from among the papers on his desk. "You'll need this."

Andi eyed it suspiciously. Putting the ring back on would mean agreeing to his terms. Clearly he expected her to, and why wouldn't he? She'd always done everything he asked in the past.

He picked up her hand without asking permission. Her skin

heated instantly at his touch and she made the mistake of look-ing up into his face. His dark gaze dared her to refuse him—and she knew in that instant that she couldn't.

Why did he still have so much power over her?

She was disoriented right now. Confused. Her memory slip-ping and sliding back into her head while she tried to take in the strange new reality of Jake wanting to marry her.

Wanting to *marry* her.

It should be a dream come true—so why did it feel more like a waking nightmare?

CHAPTER SEVEN

THE FOLLOWING AFTERNOON, Andi adjusted the collar of her new and fabulously expensive dress. Fit for a queen. The rack of designer clothes had arrived with a coordinator from Ruthenia's most snooty bespoke tailor to help her choose the right look and make any necessary alterations.

She'd tried not to tremble when the seamstress stuck pins in around her waist and bust. Now the freshly sewn green fabric draped over her like a second skin of luxurious silk.

But did she look like a future queen? She'd be paraded on TV as one tonight. RTV was setting up cameras in the ballroom to interview her and Jake. She'd tried to beg off and delay any public appearances until after she'd made her decision, but endless calls from the television station had hounded her into it and at this point she'd appear snooty and uncooperative if she said no again.

"Earrings." A representative from the jeweler where they'd bought the ring opened a case filled with sparkly gems. Andi hadn't even noticed her come in, but then people were coming and going in a constant scurry, preparing for the evening shoot. The earrings blurred into a big shiny mass.

"You choose." Andi didn't even want to look at them. Better to let these professionals decide whether she looked like a future queen or not.

She certainly didn't feel like one.

Was it her job to act this part? It felt more like her patriotic duty. Which was silly since she was American, not Ruthenian. At least until she married Jake.

If she married Jake.

She tried to keep her breathing steady as the girl clipped big emeralds to her ears and murmured, "Perfect." The seamstress nodded her approval and beckoned across the room.

A middle-aged woman with a blond pompadour and a rat-tail comb approached with a gleam in her eye. She picked up a strand of Andi's limp hair between her thumb and finger and winced slightly. "Don't worry. We can fix it."

Thirty minutes later her hair hung around her shoulders in plump curls that everyone assured her looked "lovely." The woman staring back at her from the mirror, wide-eyed and pale beneath her carefully applied makeup, didn't even look like her. She'd barely managed to remember who she was, and now she was being turned into someone else.

"Andi, can you come in for a moment? They want to check the lighting."

She steadied herself and walked—slowly in her long, rather heavy dress—toward the formal library where the cameras were set up.

Jake was nowhere to be seen.

It's your job, she told herself. Just be professional. Being a monarch's fiancée definitely felt more like a career assignment than a romantic dream come true.

Strangers' hands shuffled her into place under blistering hot lights that made her blink. More powder was dotted on her nose and fingers fluffed her curls. Out of the corner of her eye she could see the local news anchor going over some notes with a producer. What kind of questions would they ask?

I won't lie.

She promised herself that. This whole situation was so confusing already; she had no intention of making it worse by having to keep track of stories. She'd try to be tactful and diplomatic, of course.

Just part of the job.

A sudden hush fell over the room and all eyes turned to the door. His majesty. Jake strode in, a calm smile on his face. Andi's heartbeat quickened under her designer gown. Fear as well as the familiar desire. Would she manage to act the role of fiancée well enough to please him?

She cursed herself for wanting to make him happy. He hadn't given her feelings any thought when he'd tricked her into wearing his ring.

Their eyes met and a jolt of energy surged through her. *I really do want to marry you.* His words echoed in her brain, tormenting and enticing. How could she not at least give it a shot?

A producer settled them both on the ornate gilt-edged sofa under the lights, in full view of three cameras. Andi felt Jake's hand close around hers, his skin warm. She almost wished he wouldn't touch her, as she didn't want him to know she was shaking and that her palms were sweating.

No aspect of her job had ever made her so terrified. She'd greeted foreign dignitaries and handled major international incidents without so much as a raised pulse. Why did every move she made now feel like a matter of life and death?

Silence descended as the interviewer moved toward them, microphone clipped to her blue suit. Andi's heart pounded.

I won't lie.

But Jake didn't have to know that.

"Your Majesty, thank you so much for agreeing to this interview." Jake murmured an assent. "And for allowing us to meet your fiancée." The journalist smiled at Andi.

She tried not to shrink into the sofa. Yesterday morning she'd been totally comfortable and happy as Jake's fiancée. It had felt as natural as breathing. But now everything was different and she'd been dropped into the middle of a movie set—with no script.

The reporter turned her lipsticked smile to Andi. "You're living every young girl's dream."

"Yes," she stammered. *Except in the dream the prince actually loves you.* "I still can't believe it."

No lies told so far.

"Was the proposal very romantic?"

Andi grew hyperconscious of Jake's hand wrapped around hers. She drew in a breath. "I was so stunned I don't remember a word of it."

The reporter laughed, and so did Jake. Andi managed a smile.

"I guess the important part is that you said yes." The reporter turned to Jake. "Perhaps you could tell us about the moment."

Andi stared at Jake. Would he make something up? He'd lied to her when he'd told her they were engaged. Unless a king could become engaged simply by an act of will.

"It was a private moment between myself and Andi." He turned to look at her. Then continued in a low voice. "I'm very happy that she's agreed to be my wife."

Until Independence Day. He was obviously confident he'd convince her to stay after that, but as she sat here under the lights with people staring at her and analyzing every move she made, she became increasingly sure she'd couldn't handle this.

It would have been different if Jake wanted to marry her for the right reasons and she could look forward to true intimacy and companionship, at least when they were alone together.

But she'd never been enough for him before, and she was painfully sure that she wouldn't be enough for him now—ring or no ring.

"What a lovely ring." Andi's hand flinched slightly under the reporter's gaze. "A fitting symbol for a royal romance."

Yes. All flash and pomp. "Thanks. We bought it right here in town. The local village has such skilled craftspeople."

"I think it's charming that you chose the work of a Ruthenian artisan, when you could so easily have bought something from New York or Paris."

"Both Andi and I are proud of Ruthenia's fine old-world craftsmanship. It's one of the few places where attention to detail is more important than turning a quick profit. Some people might see our steady and deliberate approach to things as a hindrance in the modern world of business, but I see them as strengths that will secure our future."

Andi maintained a tight smile. He was turning their engagement interview into a promotional video for Ruthenia. Something she would have heartily approved of only a few days ago, but now made her heart contract with pain.

With his "steady and deliberate" approach to marriage, he expected her to devote her life to Ruthenia and fulfill the role of royal wife, whether he loved her or not.

Andi startled when she realized the reporter was staring right at her. She'd obviously just asked a question, but Andi was so caught up in her depressing ruminations that she hadn't even heard it. Jake squeezed her hand and jumped in. "Andi will be making all the wedding arrangements. In our years of working together she's proved that she can pull off the most elaborate and complicated occasions."

He went on to talk about Ruthenian wedding traditions and how they'd be sure to observe and celebrate them.

What about my family traditions? Andi remembered her cousin Lu's wedding two summers ago. A big, fat Greek wedding in every sense of the word. What if she wanted to celebrate her mom's Greek heritage as well as Jake's Ruthenian roots?

Not a chance. Just one more example of how her life would slide into a faded shadow of Jake's.

But only if she let it.

Resolve kicked through her on a surge of adrenaline. She didn't have to do anything she didn't want to. "Of course, we'll also honor our American roots and bring those into our planning. I have ancestors from several different countries and we'll enjoy bringing aspects of that heritage into our wedding."

The reporter's eyes widened. Jake was so big on being all Ruthenian all the time, trying to prove that despite his New York upbringing, every cell in his blue blood was Ruthenian to the nucleus. Right now she couldn't resist knocking that. If he wanted a Ruthenian bride there was no shortage of volunteers.

But he'd chosen an American one. She smiled up at him sweetly. His dark eyes flashed with surprise. "Of course. Andi's right. Our American background and experience have enriched our lives and we'll certainly be welcoming many American friends to the wedding."

Andi felt his arm slide around her shoulders. She tried not to shiver at the feel of his thick muscle through her dress. "And now, if you don't mind, we have a lot to do to prepare for the Independence Day celebrations this week. Our third Independence Day marks a turning point for our nation, with our gross national product up and unemployment now at a fifty-year low. We hope everyone will join us in a toast to Ruthenia's future."

He circled his arm around her back, a gesture both protective and possessive. Andi cursed the way it stirred sensation in her belly and emotion in her heart. The reporter frowned slightly at being summarily dismissed, but made some polite goodbye noises and shook their hands.

Andi let out a long, audible sigh once the cameras finally turned off.

Jake escorted her from the room, and it wasn't until they were in the corridor outside that he loosened his grip on her arm slightly. "Nice point about our American heritage."

She wasn't sure if he was kidding or not. "I thought so." She smiled. "I'm kind of surprised you decided to pick an American wife. I was sure you'd marry a Ruthenian so you could have some ultra-Ruthenian heirs."

An odd expression crossed his face for a second. Had he forgotten about the whole royal heir thing? This engagement scenario seemed rather by-the-seat-of-the-pants; maybe he didn't think it through enough. Did he really want a Heinz 57 American girl from Pittsburgh to be the mother of Ruthenia's future king?

"Being Ruthenian is more a state of mind than a DNA trait." He kept his arm around her shoulders as they marched along the hall.

"Kind of like being king?" She arched a brow. "Though I suppose that does require the right DNA or there'd be other claimants. The only way most Ruthenians can claim the throne is by marrying you. I guess I should be honored."

Jake turned to stare at her. She never usually talked back to him. Of course she didn't—he was her boss. Maybe once he discovered the real, off-hours Andi had a bit more spunk to her he'd lose all interest in hoisting her up onto his royal pedestal.

"I don't expect you to be honored." Humor sparkled in Jake's dark eyes. Did nothing rile him? "Just to think about the advantages of the situation."

"The glorious future of Ruthenia," she quipped.

"Exactly."

"What if I miss Philly cheesesteak?"

"The cook can prepare some."

"No way. She's from San Francisco. She'd put bean sprouts in it."

"We'll import it."

"It'd go cold on the plane."

"We'll fly there to get some."

"Is that fiscally responsible?"

He laughed. "See? You're a woman after my own heart."

"Cold and calculating?" She raised a brow.

"I prefer to think of it as shrewd and pragmatic." He pulled his arm from around her to reach into his pocket and she noticed they were at the door to his suite. She stiffened. She did not want to go in there and wind up in his bed again. Especially if it was the result of some shrewd and pragmatic seduction on his part.

The intimacy they'd shared left her feeling tender and raw. Probably because she'd always loved him and the act of making love only intensified everything she'd already felt. Now that she knew he didn't love her—that it was a mechanical act for him—she couldn't bear to be that close to him again.

"I guess I'll head for my room." She glanced down at her ridiculously over-the-top interview dress. "Am I supposed to give this dress to someone?"

"You're supposed to wear it to the state dinner tonight."

State dinner? She didn't remember planning any dinner. In fact she remembered deliberately not planning anything for the first few days after she intended to leave. "Maybe my memory isn't fully back yet, but I…" It was embarrassing to admit she still wasn't in full control of her faculties.

"Don't worry, you had nothing to do with it. I pulled the whole thing together to butter up all the people cheesed off by our engagement."

"That's a daring use of dairy metaphors."

Jake grinned. "Thanks. I'm a man of many talents."

If only I weren't so vividly aware of that. She sure as heck wished she'd never slept with him. That was going to be very hard to forget.

"So let me guess, all your recently jilted admirers, and their rich and influential daddies, will be gathered around the table in the grand dining room to whisper rude remarks about me." Her stomach clenched at the prospect.

"They'll do no such thing." Jake had entered the suite and obviously expected her to follow. He'd totally ignored her comment about heading for her room. "They wouldn't dare."

That's what you think. Powerful people could afford to be blissfully ignorant about what others thought, since no one would dare say anything to their face. She, on the other hand, was more likely to get a realistic picture of their true feelings since people didn't bother to try to impress a mere assistant.

But would they act differently now they thought she was engaged to Jake?

She glanced down at her perfectly tailored dress. It might be interesting to see how they behaved now the tables were turned and she was the one about to marry a king.

And it would certainly be educational to see how Jake behaved in their midst now that he was officially engaged to her.

"You look stunning." Jake's low voice jolted her from her anxious thoughts. His gaze heated her skin right through the green silk as it raked over her from head to toe, lingering for just a split second longer where the bodice cupped her breasts.

"Thanks. I guess almost anyone can look good when they have a crowd of professionals available to take charge."

"You're very beautiful." His dark eyes met hers. "Without any help from anyone."

Her face heated and she hoped they'd put on enough powder to hide it. Did he mean it or was he just saying that to mollify her? She didn't really believe anything he said anymore.

On the other hand, maybe he'd come to see her in a new light since he started considering her as wife material. She did feel pretty gorgeous under his smoldering stare.

"Flattery will get you everywhere." A sudden vision of herself in his bed—which was less than forty feet away—filled her mind. "Okay, maybe not everywhere. How long do we have until dinner?" She wasn't sure hanging around in his suite was a good idea. It might be better to spend time in more neutral territory.

"About half an hour."

"And who arranged this dinner if I didn't?" Curiosity goaded her to ask the question. The palace seemed to be running pretty well without her input, which should make her feel less guilty about leaving, but it irked her somewhat, too.

"Livia. She's been really helpful the last few days. Really stepped into your shoes."

"Oh." Andi stiffened. Why did it bother her that Livia might be after her job? She was planning to leave it, after all. Still, now that she remembered more of her past, she knew Livia had always felt somewhat competitive toward her, and resentful that Andi was hand in glove with Jake while she did the more routine work like ordering supplies and writing place cards.

She couldn't help wondering if Livia might now be resentful that Jake planned to marry her—talk about the ultimate promotion.

If you were into that sort of thing.

"Champagne?" Jake gestured to a bottle chilling in a silver bucket of ice. He must have had it brought here during the interview.

"No thanks." Better to keep her head. She had a feeling she'd need it. "But you go ahead."

"I couldn't possibly drink alone. And it's a 1907 Heidiseck."

"Are you sure it's not past its sell-by date?"

He chuckled. "It was recovered from a ship that was wrecked on its way to deliver champagne to the Russian Imperial family. It's been brought up from the bottom of the sea and tastes sublime even after decades of being lost."

"Very appropriate, considering the history of Ruthenia."

"That's what the friend who gave it to me thought. Won't you join me in a toast to our future?" His flirtatious glance tickled her insides.

She took a deep breath and tried to remain calm. "Not until I've figured out whether I want us to have a future."

Jake tilted his head. "You're very stubborn all of a sudden."

"That's because we're discussing the rest of my life, not just some seating placements or even a corporate merger."

"I like that about you. A lot of women would jump at the chance to marry me just to be queen."

Or just because you're embarrassingly attractive and shockingly wealthy. She tried to ignore those enticements herself.

Jake lifted a brow. "That doesn't mean much to you, does it?"

"I've never had the slightest desire to be called Your Majesty."

"Me, either." He grinned. "But if I can learn to put up with it, I'm sure you could handle it, too."

"Did you always know you'd be king one day?" She'd wondered this, but never dared ask him.

"My parents talked about it, but I thought they were nuts. I planned to be a king of Wall Street instead."

"And now you're doing both. I bet your parents would be very proud. It's a shame they weren't alive to see you take the throne." She knew they'd died in a small plane accident.

"If they were alive they'd be ruling here themselves, which would have been just fine with me."

"You don't like being king?" She couldn't resist asking.

"I like it fine, but it's a job for life. There's no getting bored and quitting. Sometimes I wonder what I would have done if I'd had more freedom."

"You were brave to take on the responsibility. Not everyone would have, especially with the state Ruthenia was in when you first arrived."

"I do feel a real sense of duty toward Ruthenia. I always have, it was spooned into me along with my baby food. I couldn't turn my back on Ruthenia for anything."

She didn't feel the same way. In fact she could leave and never look back—couldn't she? She hadn't been raised to smile and wave at people or wear an ermine robe, but she had always felt a strong sense of commitment to her job—and her boss.

Who stood in front of her tall and proud, handsome features picked out by the light of a wall sconce. She admired him for stepping up to the responsibilities of getting Ruthenia back on its feet, and committing himself to help the country and its people for the rest of his life.

She should be touched and honored that he wanted her help in that enterprise, regardless of whether he loved her.

Still, she wasn't made of stone. Something she became vividly aware of when Jake reached for her hand and drew it to his lips. Her skin heated under his mouth and she struggled to keep her breathing steady.

He's just trying to seduce you into going along with his plan. It doesn't mean he really loves you—or even desires you.

Her body responded to him like a flipped switch, but then it always had, even back when he saw her as nothing more than an efficient employee. Heat flared in her belly and her fingertips itched to reach out and touch his skin.

But she'd resisted six long years and she could do it now.

She pulled her hand back with some difficulty. Her skin hummed where his lips had just touched it. A quick glance up was a mistake—his dark eyes fixed on hers with a smoldering expression that took her breath away.

But she knew he was an accomplished actor. You had to be to pull off international diplomacy, especially when it involved placating all the outrageous characters he dealt with in Ruthenia.

"You're very suspicious." His eyes twinkled.

"Of course I am. I woke up from amnesia to find myself engaged to my boss. That kind of thing makes a girl wary."

"You know you can trust me." His steady gaze showed total confidence.

"I thought I could trust you." She raised a brow. "Over the last day I've learned I can't trust you. You used me to your advantage, without consulting me."

His expression darkened. "I couldn't consult with you because you didn't know who you were."

"You could have waited until my memory came back and we could discuss it calmly." *Instead you decided to convince me between the sheets.* He'd undermined all her inhibitions and drawn her into the most intense and powerful intimacy.

Too bad it had worked so well.

"Time was of the essence. Independence Day is coming right up."

"And you couldn't disappoint the people of Ruthenia."

"Exactly. I knew you'd understand."

She did. The people of Ruthenia and his own reputation were far more important than her feelings.

Did he even know she had feelings?

She had three days to put him to the test.

CHAPTER EIGHT

ANDI WOULD HAVE liked to sweep into the dining room and smile confidently at the gathered Ruthenian dignitaries and their snooty daughters, then take her place at the head of the table.

But it didn't work like that.

The toe of her pointed shoe caught in the hem of her dress on her way into the anteroom and she pitched through the doorway headfirst. Jake, walking behind her, flung his arms around her waist and pulled her back onto her feet before she fell on her face into the Aubusson carpet. It was not an auspicious entrance into high society.

Her face heated, especially when she saw the looks of undisguised glee on Maxi's and Alia's faces.

Jake laughed it off and used the occasion to steal a kiss in front of the gathered audience. She was too flustered to attempt resistance, which would have looked rude and strange anyway, since as far as everyone knew they were madly in love.

The kiss only deepened her blush and stirred the mix of arousal and anguish roiling in her gut.

"Congratulations!" A portly older man with medals on his jacket stepped forward and bowed low to Andi. She swallowed. This was the Grand Duke of Machen. He didn't have any marriageable daughters left, so he was one of the few non-hostile entities in the room. He turned to Jake. "We're all thrilled that you've finally chosen a bride to continue the royal line."

The royal line? Andi's muscles tightened. As Jake's wife she'd be expected to produce the future king or queen. Which meant that even if it were a marriage of convenience, there would be some sex involved. She'd already learned that making love with Jake touched something powerful and tender deep inside her. Not something she could do as a matter of routine. Could he really expect that of her? It was different with men. They could turn off their emotions and just enjoy the pure physical sensations.

If only she could do that.

A glance around the room revealed that not everyone was as thrilled as the grand duke. Maxi's father Anton Rivenshnell looked grim—salt-and-pepper brows lowered threateningly over his beady gray eyes. Maxi herself had abandoned her usual winning smile in favor of a less-flattering pout.

"I suppose an American bride seemed a natural choice when you spent your entire life in America," growled Rivenshnell, his dark suit stretched across an ample belly. "Though this is naturally a disappointment for the women of Ruthenia."

Jake seemed to grow about a foot taller, which, considering his already impressive height of six-one, made him a little scary. "Andi has demonstrated her commitment to Ruthenia over the last three years, living and working by my side. She is one of the women of Ruthenia."

Ha. Andi couldn't help loving his spirited defense of her. "I've never been so happy as I am here." The honest truth. She wasn't going to lie. "I've spent every day enjoying the people and the beautiful countryside, and I've come to love Ruthenia as my home."

"And you fell in love with your boss, too." The grand duke's laugh bellowed across the room.

"Yes." She managed a shaky smile. Again, it was the truth—

but no need for Jake to know that. As far as he was concerned she was just fulfilling her part of the arrangement.

Andi felt very self-conscious as they were ushered into the dining room by a rather smug Livia. This was the first time she'd attended one of these affairs as a guest, not one of the staff members hovering along the walls ready to serve the diners and tend to Jake's needs. Livia shot her at least three meaningful glances, though she couldn't actually tell what they meant.

At least she managed not to fall on her face on her way to the end of the table, where she was seated far, far away from Jake, probably in between two daddies of rejected girls.

Jake was seated between Alia and Maxi, just as she'd sat him before she lost her memory. Then she'd done it as a joke, to torment him with his two most ardent admirers and hopefully put him off both of them. Now he must have planned it himself, for reasons she could only guess at.

Did he intend to have affairs with each of them now that he was no longer on the hook to make one his queen? Surely quiet little Andi wouldn't object.

The very thought made her seethe. Still, she didn't remember Jake ever cheating on one of his many girlfriends. On the other hand, he rarely dated the same one for long enough to get the chance. As soon as a girl showed signs of getting serious, he brought an abrupt end to things.

Andi had rather liked that about him. He never continued with a relationship just because it was there. He was often blunt and funny about the reasons he no longer saw a future with a particular girl. And it always gave her fresh hope that one day he'd be hers.

And now he was. At least in theory.

Irritation flickered through her at the sight of Alia brushing his hand with her long, manicured fingers. Jake smiled at the elegant blonde and spoke softly to her before turning to Maxi. The sultry brunette immediately lit up and eased her impressive cleavage toward him. Jealousy raged in Andi's gut and she cursed herself for caring.

"Your parents must be delighted." The gruff voice startled Andi, who realized she was staring.

"Oh, yes." She tried to smile at the white-haired man by her side. Up close she could see he was probably too old to have a jilted daughter, so that was a plus.

Her parents would be happy if she married Jake. At least she imagined so. How would they feel if she refused to marry him?

"Have they visited Ruthenia before?"

"Not yet. But I'm sure they'll love it here."

"I imagine they'll move here." His blue eyes twinkled with... was it warmth or malice?

"They have their own lives back in Pittsburgh, so I don't think they'll be leaving."

"But they must! Their daughter is to be the queen. It would be tragic for a family to endure such separation."

"It's quite common in the U.S. for families to live hundreds or even thousands of miles apart."

"In Ruthenia that would be unthinkable."

"I know." She shrugged. Was he also implying that having such a coldhearted and independent American as their queen was unthinkable? "But they have jobs they enjoy and friends where they live. I'm sure they'll come visit often."

"They've *never* visited you here? How long have you been here?"

"Three years, but it's an expensive trip and..." He was making her feel bad, and she had a feeling that's exactly what he intended. "Have you ever visited the States?" She smiled brightly. Every time she looked up, someone was peeking at her out of the corner of their eye. Including Livia. She was beginning to feel under siege.

Jake shot her a warm glance from the far end of the table. Even from that distance he could make her heart beat faster.

He looked totally in his element, relaxed, jovial and quite at home in the lap of luxury, surrounded by Ruthenian nobles.

Whereas she felt like a scullery maid who'd wandered into the ballroom—which wasn't a million miles from the truth. In all her dreams of herself and Jake living happily ever after, they lived happily in a fantasy world of her own creation. While life in the Ruthenian royal palace was definitely someone's fantasy world, it wasn't hers, and Jake was clearly making a terrible mistake if he thought this could work.

Jake beamed with satisfaction as staff poured the coffee. Andi looked radiant at the far end of the table, resplendent in her regal gown and with her hair arranged in shiny curls that fell about her shoulders. Ruthenia's haughty beauties disappeared into the drapery with her around. He'd tried to reassure them that his marriage was a love match and not a deliberate insult to them and their families. He couldn't afford to lose the support of Ruthenia's most powerful businessmen. Noses were definitely bent out of shape, but no one had declared war—yet.

A love match. He'd used the term several times now, though never within earshot of Andi. He couldn't say something so blatantly untrue right in front of her—at least not now that she had her memory back. He knew nothing of love. Raised by a succession of nannies while his parents traveled, he'd been groomed for duty and honor and not for family life and intimate relationships. Love seemed like something that happened in poems but not in real life, and he didn't want to promise anything to Andi that he couldn't deliver.

He was hotly attracted to her and admired all her fine qualities, and that was almost as good. Many people married for love and ended up divorced or miserable. It was much more sensible to go into a lifetime commitment with a clear head and a solid strategy.

Andi seemed concerned about the lack of love between them once her memory returned and she knew they hadn't been in-

volved. His most important task over the next two days was
to convince her they were meant to be together, and surely the
best way to do that was to woo her back into his bed. The warm
affection they'd shared stirred something in his chest. Maybe
it wasn't the kind of love that inspired songs and sonnets, but
he ached to enjoy it again.

It took some time for the guests to filter out the front door,
and he kept half an eye on Andi the whole time in case she
should decide to slip away. She looked tense, keeping up her
end of every conversation but looking around often as if checking for escape routes. He'd been so busy rebuilding the relationships he'd worked hard to cement in the past three years by
dancing with different girls that he hadn't danced with Andi.
There was plenty of time for him to catch up with her after
the guests left.

He kissed Alia on the cheek and ignored the subtle squeeze
she gave his arm. He slapped her father on the back and promised to call him to go over some business details. So far, so
good. Now where was Andi? She'd managed to slip away as
the Kronstadts made their exit.

Irritation and worry stirred in his gut along with a powerful desire to see her right now. He strode up the stairs from
the foyer and intercepted her in the hallway outside her room.

He slid his arms around her waist from behind—just as
he'd done when she dove unceremoniously into their company
earlier. A smile spread across his mouth at the feel of her soft
warm body in his arms, and he couldn't wait to spend the night
together.

But she stiffened. "I'm tired, Jake."

"Me, too." He squeezed her gently. "We can sleep in each
other's arms."

"I don't think that's a good idea." She unlocked her door and
he followed her in, arms still wrapped around her. Her delicious
scent filled his senses. He twirled her around until they were
face-to-face—and noticed her face looked sad.

"What's going on, Andi? You did a fantastic job this evening."

Her mouth flattened. "We should close the door, for privacy."

"Sure." That was a promising start. He turned and pushed it shut. "Why do you look unhappy?"

"Because I can't do this. I don't fit in here. I feel like an intruder."

"That's ridiculous. You fit in here as well as I do."

"I don't. I felt out of place and people kept going on about me being American. They obviously don't like the idea of you marrying a foreigner."

"Monarchs nearly always marry foreigners. That's how the British royal family ended up being German." He grinned. "They used to import brides from whichever country they needed to curry diplomatic favor with. It's a time-honored tradition."

"I don't think marrying me will get you too far with the White House."

"Oh, I disagree." He stroked her soft cheek with his thumb. "I'm sure any sensible administration would admire you as much as I do."

Her eyes softened for a moment and a tiny flush rose to her pale cheeks. But she wouldn't meet his gaze.

He placed his hands on either side of her waist. She had a lovely figure, a slender hourglass that the dress emphasized in a way her stiff suits never could. The tailored bodice presented her cleavage in a dangerously enticing way, and a single diamond sparkled on a fine chain between her small, plump breasts.

A flame of desire licked through him. "You were the loveliest woman in that room tonight."

"You're sweet." There was no hint of sparkle or a smile in her eyes. She didn't seem to believe him.

"You know I'm not sweet." He lifted a brow. "So you'd better believe me. Every minute I danced with those other girls, I wished I was dancing with you."

* * *

But you weren't.

He'd danced with those women because it was good for the nation's economy to keep their families on his side. Maybe he'd desired them, too, but that wasn't why he twirled them around the floor. Andi knew that business would always come first with Jake. She's always known that, and admired it. But now that she contemplated the prospect of spending the rest of her life with a man who didn't love her, it seemed like a mistake.

Mostly because she loved him so much.

The press of his strong fingers around her waist was a cruel torment. Her nipples had thickened against the silk of her bodice, aching for his touch. The skin of her cheek still hummed where he'd brushed his thumb over it.

She even loved him for the fact that he'd marry a woman he didn't love just for the sake of his country. That kind of commitment was impressive.

Unless you were the woman he didn't love, and had to watch from the sidelines, or even under the spotlight, while he gave his heart and soul to Ruthenia and its people.

His presence dominated her room, with its neat, impersonal decor. He was larger than life, bolder, better-looking and more engaging than any man she'd ever met. Wasn't it enough that he wanted to marry her?

Why did she think she was so special she deserved more than he offered? Maybe it was the independent-minded American in her who wanted everything. It wasn't enough to be queen and have a handsome and hardworking husband—she had to have the fairy-tale romance, as well.

Jake leaned in and kissed her softly on the mouth. Her breath caught at the bottom of her lungs as his warm, masculine scent—soap and rich fabrics with a hint of male musk—tormented her senses. Her lips stung with arousal as he pulled back a few inches and hovered there, his dark gaze fixed to hers.

Her fingers wanted to roam under his jacket and explore the

muscles of his back and she struggled to keep them still at her sides. If she let him seduce her she was saying "yes" to everything he offered.

Including sex without love.

Yes, they'd had sex once already, but at the time she'd been under the delusion that he loved her and had proposed to her out of genuine emotion. Which was very different from the business arrangement he'd presented to her earlier.

His lips lowered over hers again, but she pulled back, heart thumping. "Stop, Jake. I'm not ready."

His eyes darkened. "Why not?"

"It's all happening too fast. I still barely know who I am. I can't think straight with you kissing me."

"Maybe I don't want you to think straight." A gleam shone in his seductive dark eyes.

"That's what I'm worried about." She tugged herself from his embrace, and almost to her surprise, he let her go. "I don't want to rush into this and realize a year or so from now that it was a huge mistake."

"I'll make sure you never regret it."

"I think that's quite arrogant of you." She tilted her chin. She'd never spoken to him like this before and it scared her a little. How would he react? "You seem to think you know exactly what I feel, and how I'll react."

"I know you very well after six years together." His warm gaze and proud, handsome face were dangerous—both familiar and alluring.

"But those were six years together in a professional relationship, not a marriage." For a start, he'd never barged into her room with his arms wrapped around her waist.

"I don't really see the difference." He looked down at her, slightly supercilious.

Indignation surged inside her, battling with the infuriating desire to kiss his sensual mouth. "That's the problem. It is different. As your assistant I have to follow certain rules of

behavior, to always be polite and not express my opinion unless it's directly relevant to our work. To be on my best behavior and keep my emotions to myself. Maybe I'm not really the
person you think I am at all." Her voice rose and she sounded
a little hysterical.

Which was probably good, since he seemed to think she
was some kind of well-mannered automaton who could easily
approach the rest of her life as a kind of well-paid job with excellent benefits and perks.

"So the real Andi is very different from the one I know?"

She let out a long sigh. "Yes." She frowned. Who was the real
Andi and what did she want? For so long she'd wanted Jake—
while knowing in her heart that he would never be hers—that
it was hard to think straight. "I don't know. But that's why we
need to take it slow. You don't want to marry me and then find
out I'm not the faithful and loyal helpmeet you imagine."

"I'd love to get to know your wild side." His eyes narrowed
and a half smile tilted his mouth.

"I'm not sure I have one."

"You do." His smile widened, showing a hint of white teeth.
"I've seen it."

Her face heated. "I still can't believe you slept with me under
false pretenses." Her body stirred just at the memory of being
stretched against him, skin to skin.

"They weren't false. We really are engaged."

She crossed her arms over her chest, and tried to ignore the
tingling in her nipples. "I beg to differ. You hadn't asked the real
me to marry you. You just assumed that I would. Not the same
thing at all."

"But you seemed so happy about it." His expression was
sweetly boyish for a moment, which tugged at a place deep inside her. "I thought you truly wanted us to be together."

I did.

She blinked, trying to make sense of it all. Jake's sturdy
masculine presence wasn't helping one bit. She was painfully

aware of the thickly muscled body under his elegant evening suit and how good it would feel pressed against hers.

He picked up her hand and kissed it. A knightly gesture no doubt intended to steal her heart. She shivered slightly as his lips pressed against the back of her hand, soft yet insistent.

During the nightmare of not knowing who she was, the one source of relief and happiness was Jake. He'd been the rock she could lean on and draw strength from while everything else around her was confusing and mysterious. She had been happy then, at least during the moments that the rest of the world fell away and they were alone together, lost in each other.

Could that happen again?

"I think we should spend some time together away from the palace." Getting out of their everyday work environment would be an interesting test of their relationship. They really hadn't spent leisure time together. Of course Jake didn't exactly have free time, unless you counted junkets with investors and state dinners. She didn't either, since she'd always devoted every minute to her job. She never went on the staff trips to the local nightclub or their weekend jaunts to Munich or Salzburg. As Jake's assistant she'd always felt herself too needed—or so she'd told herself—to disappear for more than an hour or two.

Jake stroked her hand, now held between both of his. She struggled to keep herself steady and not sink into his arms. "Is there someplace near here that you've always wanted to go?"

He tilted his head and his gaze grew distant. "The mountains."

"The ones you can see out the window?"

"Yes. I've always wanted to climb up and look down on the town and the palace." He shrugged. "There's never time."

"There isn't time right now, either." She sighed. "I don't suppose you really can get away from the palace right before Independence Day." Her request for time alone seemed silly and petty now that she thought about it. He had a lot of work to do and people would be arriving from all over the world in the run-up to the celebrations.

"Then we'll have to make time." He squeezed her hand.

An odd sensation filled her chest. He was willing to drop everything on a whim to get away with her? "But who will greet the arriving guests? We'd be gone for hours." There was a large group of Ruthenian expats arriving from Chicago, including three prominent businessmen and their families who had been invited to stay at the palace.

"I'm sure the staff can manage. Livia's proving very capable."

A slight frisson of anxiety trickled through her. Why did the idea of Livia quietly taking over her job make her so uncomfortable? Surely it was ideal.

"And how would we get there?"

"My car." Amusement twinkled in his eyes. "I can still drive, you know, even though I rarely get the chance."

"No driver or attendant?"

"Not even a footman. And we'll leave our PDAs behind, too. No sense being halfway up a mountain texting people about trade tariffs."

Andi laughed. He really was prepared to drop everything just to make her happy. Selfish of her to want that, but it felt really good. And the mountains had always called to her. Right now the slopes below the snow-covered peaks were lush with grass and wildflowers. "We'd better bring a picnic."

"Of course. Let the kitchen know what you want and tell them to pack it in something we can carry easily."

Andi blinked. This would be a test for her of how she could handle the transformation from staff to employer.

Or as Jake's wife was she just a high-level member of staff? The situation was confusing.

She pulled her hand gently from his grasp. "When should we go?"

"Tomorrow morning. I've learned to seize the moment

around here. If we wait any longer we'll get sucked into the Independence Day activities."

"I guess we should call it an early night." She hoped he'd take a hint and leave.

"But the morning is still so far off." A mischievous twinkle lit Jake's eyes.

"It's after midnight."

"One of my favorite times of day. Maybe we should go dance around on the lawn outside." His gaze swept over her elegant dress—and sent heat sizzling through the defenseless body underneath it. "You're dressed for it."

"I don't think so. I might lose my memory again." *Or just my heart.*

She did not want anything sensual to happen between them until she'd had a chance to wrap her mind around the whole situation and make some tough decisions. Jake's touch had a very dangerous effect on her common sense, and this was the rest of her life at stake here.

"Just a stroll in the moonlight?" He took a step toward her. Her nipples thickened under her bodice and heat curled low in her belly.

"No." She'd better get him out of here and away from her while she still could. It wasn't easy saying no to something you'd dreamed of for six long years. "We'll be doing plenty of walking tomorrow. Conserve your energy."

"What makes you think I need to?" He lifted a brow. Humor sparkled in his eyes.

Andi's insides wobbled. Was he really so attracted to her? It was hard to believe that he'd gone from not noticing her at all, to trying every trick in the book to lure her into his bed.

Then again, he was known for his ability to close a deal by any means necessary.

It was more important right now to learn whether he could respect her wishes, or not. This was a crucial test.

"Goodnight, Jake." She walked to the door and opened it.

"I'll see you in the morning." Her pulse quickened, wondering if he'd protest and refuse to leave.

"Goodnight, Andi." He strolled to the doorway and brushed a soft kiss across her lips. No hands, thank goodness, though her body craved his touch. He pulled back and stepped into the hallway.

Her relief was mingled with odd regret that she wouldn't be spending the night in his strong arms.

He'd passed her test.

Then he turned to face her. "I have a bet for you."

"A bet? I'm not the gambling type."

"I didn't think you were." His mouth tilted into a wry smile. "But I bet you that tomorrow night you'll sleep in my bed— with me."

Her belly quivered under the force of his intense gaze, but she held herself steady. "What are the odds, I wonder?"

"I wouldn't advise betting against me." He crossed his arms over his powerful chest.

"Normally, neither would I." She couldn't help smiling. His confidence was rather adorable. "But I think it's important to keep a clear head in this situation."

"I completely agree." He flashed his infuriating pearly grin.

His arrogance alone made her determined to resist. Apparently she'd be the one with a test to pass tomorrow.

CHAPTER NINE

ANDI WATCHED AS two footmen loaded their picnic lunch—impractically packed in two large baskets—into the trunk of Jake's black BMW sedan. The cook had acted as if Andi was already mistress of the house. No questioning of her ideas or complaining that they were low on certain ingredients, as she usually did.

Livia managed to pass on a couple of comments from the staff gossip—including that everyone knew Jake had slept alone the previous night. Andi blushed. Of course everyone knew everything in the palace, especially the maids. Livia obviously wasn't intimidated by Andi's new status and she made it clear that Jake would have had company in bed if she were in Andi's shoes.

In the old days it would be expected for her to wait until the wedding night. Now it was quite the opposite. People would wonder what was wrong if she persisted in sleeping alone.

She'd dressed in those jeans Jake liked and a pale pink shirt she'd bought on a whim, then decided it wasn't professional enough. Her hair was in a ponytail—not as formal as the bun—and she'd forgone all makeup except blush and lip gloss.

Apparently she wanted him to find her attractive.

This whole situation was very confusing. She wanted him to want her—but only for the right reasons.

Jake strode down the steps, talking on his phone. He'd abandoned his usual tailored suit for a pair of dark jeans and a white shirt, sleeves rolled up over tanned arms. He smiled when he saw her, and her stomach gave a little dip.

Pulling the phone from his ear he switched it off and handed it to one of the footmen. "Kirk, please hold this hostage until I get back. I don't want any interruptions." He turned to Andi. "Did you leave yours behind, too?"

"It's on my desk. I can handle the challenge of being incommunicado all afternoon."

"What if you need to call for help?" asked Kirk.

"We're quite capable of helping ourselves." Jake held the passenger door open for Andi. She climbed in, anticipation jangling her nerves. She couldn't remember being anywhere all alone with Jake. She felt safe with him though. He'd be a match for any wolves or bears or whatever mythical creatures stalked the mountains of Ruthenia.

He climbed in and closed the door. In the close quarters of the car he seemed bigger than usual, and his enticing male scent stirred her senses. His big hand on the stick shift made her belly shimmy a little. "How do you get so tanned?"

"Tennis. We should play it sometime."

Of course. He played with any guests who showed an interest, and invariably won. He was far too naturally competitive to be diplomatic while playing a sport.

"I haven't played since college."

"I bet you were good." He shot her a glance.

"I wasn't too bad." Her nerves tingled with excitement at the prospect of playing with him. There was something they had in common. Of course he'd beat her, but she'd enjoy the challenge of taking even a single point off him. "We'll have to give it a try."

If I stay.

They pulled out of the large wrought-iron gates at the end of the palace driveway and past the old stone gatehouse. Andi waved to the guards, who nodded and smiled. Somehow living here as Jake's...partner didn't feel all that odd right now.

It felt downright possible.

"Do you know which roads to take to get to the foot of the mountain?"

"I know which roads to take to get halfway up the mountain, and that's where we're headed."

"Don't like climbing?"

"I love it, but why not climb the high part?"

Andi laughed. "That sounds like a good approach to life in general."

"I think so."

They drove through the ancient village, where some of the buildings must be a thousand years old, with their sloping tile roofs and festoons of chimneys. The road widened as they left the village and headed through a swathe of meadows filled with grazing cows. The sun was rising into the middle of an almost cloudless sky and the whole landscape looked like a 1950s Technicolor movie. She almost expected Julie Andrews to come running down a hillside and burst into song.

"What would you have done if you were born to be king of somewhere really awful?"

Jake laughed. "Everywhere has its merits."

"Antarctica."

"Too many emperors there already—the kind with flippers. But I see your point. Still, a lot of people said Ruthenia was too badly broken to be fixed. Years of decline during and after the fall of communism, no work ethic, low morale and motivation. And it's turned on its head in three short years since independence. You just have to believe."

"And work hard."

"No denying that. But when you have concrete goals and a good road map, almost anything is doable."

The sunlight pouring through the windshield played off his chiseled features. His bone structure alone contained enough determination for a small, landlocked nation.

He'd been totally up-front about his goals and road map where she was concerned. The goal was obviously a long and successful marriage that would help him as a monarch, and the road map apparently included seducing her into his bed tonight.

She was not going to let him do that. Her judgment was already clouded enough by his sturdy, masculine presence in the car next to her.

The car started to climb steadily, as the road wound around the base of the mountain. It looked much bigger from here, the snow-capped peak now invisible above a band of conifers that ringed the mountain's middle like a vast green belt. The road petered out into a steep farm track past a group of cottages, then finally ended at a field gate about a mile farther on.

"We're on our own from here." Jake climbed out and popped the trunk. "And since we don't have sherpas, we'd better eat lunch close by. These baskets look like they were designed for royal picnics in the nineteenth century."

"They probably were." Andi touched the soft leather buckles on the big, wicker rectangles. She and Jake carried one together through the gate and into the field. Distant sheep ignored them as they spread their blanket under a tree and unpacked the feast.

Jake took the lid off the first dish. "Cabbage rolls, very traditional." He grinned. She had a feeling he'd appreciate her picking a Ruthenian dish. The spicy meat wrapped in soft boiled cabbage was as Ruthenian as you could get, and there was a jar of the hot dipping pickle and onion sauce served with it at Ruthenian inns. Jake picked up a perfectly wrapped cabbage roll and took a bite. "Ah. New Yorkers have no idea what they're missing out on. We really should market this for the States."

"Do you ever stop thinking about business?" She raised a brow.

"Truthfully? No. But then you know that already." His eyes twinkled as he took another bite.

At least he was honest. Andi reached into another dish and pulled out one of the tiny phyllo pastry wraps filled with soft, fresh goat cheese. This one came with a dish of tangy beetroot sauce. She spooned the sauce onto her pastry and took a bite. Like many things in Ruthenia it was surprising and wonderful. "These would definitely be a big hit. Perhaps a Ruthenian restaurant in Midtown."

"To give the Russian Tea Room a run for its money?" Jake nodded and took a phyllo wrap. "I like the way you think. You can't deny that we're a good team."

Her heart contracted a little. "Yes." A good team. They were that. But was that enough? She wanted more. She wanted... magic.

The midday sun sparkled on the roofs of the town far below them. "Why didn't they build the castle up here? It would have been easier to defend."

"It would also have been really hard getting a cartloads of supplies up and down that steep track."

"I guess the peasants would have had to carry everything."

"And maybe they would have staged a revolt." Jake grinned, and reached for a spicy Ruthenian meatball. "Easier to build on the flat and put a town nearby."

"As an imported peasant I have to agree."

Jake laughed. "You're the king's fiancée. That hardly makes you a peasant."

"Don't think I'll forget my humble peasant origins." She teased and sipped some of the sweet bottled cider they'd bought. "I'm the first person in my family to go to college, after all."

"Are you really? What do your parents do?"

Andi swallowed. So odd that they hadn't talked about her past or her family before now. Jake had never been interested. "My dad works at a tire dealership and my mom runs the cafeteria at a local elementary school."

Jake nodded and sipped his cider. Was he shocked? Maybe he'd assumed her dad was a lawyer and her mom a socialite.

Discomfort prickled inside her. "Your ancestors would probably be scandalized that you're even thinking of marrying someone like me."

"I bet the old Ruthenian kings married the miller's daughter or a pretty shepherd girl from time to time."

"Maybe if they could spin straw into gold," Andi teased. "Otherwise they probably just had affairs with them and married girls who came with large estates and strategically located castles."

He laughed. "You're probably right. But you can spin straw into gold, can't you?"

"I find that spinning straw into freshly minted Euros is more practical these days." She bit off a crunchy mouthful of freshly baked Ruthenian pretzel, fragrant with poppy seeds. "Gold makes people suspicious."

Jake smiled. Andi really did make gold, at least in his life. "If only people knew that you're the dark secret behind the salvation of the Ruthenian economy. Sitting up there in your office at your spinning wheel."

"They probably figure I must have mysterious powers. Otherwise why wouldn't you marry a Ruthenian glamour girl?"

"Those Ruthenian ladies are all a handful. None of them grew up in Ruthenia, either. I'd like to know what they're doing in those Swiss finishing schools to produce such a bunch of spoiled, self-indulgent princesses. They're far too much like hard work, and you'd certainly never catch them doing any real work." And none of them had Andi's cute, slightly freckled nose.

She looked pleased. "They can't all be like that."

"The ones who aren't are off pursuing careers somewhere—probably in the U.S.—and aren't hanging around the palace trying to curry favor with me."

"You could have staged a campaign to invite all Ruthenian expats to come back and compete for your hand."

Jake shuddered at the thought. "Why would I want to do that when you're right here?" He took a bite of a pretzel. "You've already passed every possible kind of test life in Ruthenia has thrown at you and proved yourself a star."

She blushed slightly. "I wouldn't say that."

"I would." His chest filled with pride that Andi had managed the big shift in lifestyle with such grace and ease. She'd eased the transition for him in so many ways that he'd probably never even know. No one could deny they were a powerful team. "Let's drink to us."

She took a glass with a slightly shaky hand. "To us."

"And the future of Ruthenia." Which would be a very bright one, at least for him, with the lovely Andi at his side. He'd seen another side of her since her memory came back—a feistier, more independent Andi than the one who'd worked so tirelessly as his assistant. He liked her all the more for being strong enough to stand up to him.

And the chemistry between them...if that's what it was. He couldn't put it into words, but the very air now seemed to crackle with energy when they got a little too close. He hoped she felt it, too—and suspected she did. Her cheeks colored sometimes just when he looked at her, and there was a new sparkle in her lovely blue eyes—or maybe it had always been there and he'd just never noticed it before?

Obviously he'd been walking through life with blinkers on where Andi was concerned. Thank heavens he'd finally realized what he'd been missing out on all these years.

After they'd finished eating they packed the baskets back in the car and set off up the grassy slopes on foot. The meadows grew steeper as they climbed, and the view more magnificent. They could see over the ancient forest on the far side of the town, and to the hills beyond, with villages scattered in the valleys, church steeples rising up from their midst. Jake's heart swelled at the sight of his beautiful country, so resilient and hopeful.

"Thank you for bringing us up here." He wanted to touch her, to hold her and kiss her and share the joy that pulsed through him, but Andi managed to remain out of reach.

After about an hour of steady climbing, they reached a small round tower, almost hidden in a grove of trees.

"Yikes. I wonder if the witch still has Rapunzel imprisoned in there." Andi peered up at the gray stones, mottled with moss and lichens.

"It's a lookout post," he replied. "I've seen it on the old maps. They would watch for soldiers approaching in the distance, then signal down to the palace—which was a fortified castle back then—with a flag that let them know what was happening. Let's go inside."

He strode ahead into the arched doorway. Andi followed, rather more hesitant.

"There was probably a door, but it's gone," she said as she peered up into the tower. Any ceiling or upper floors were also gone, and the stone walls circled a perfect patch of blue sky. "It would make a great play fort for kids."

"We'll have to refurbish it for ours." Jake smiled. He'd never given much thought to having children, but the prospect of sharing family life with Andi stirred something unexpected and warm inside him.

Andi's eyes widened.

"Have I shocked you?"

"Maybe. It's all just a bit...sudden."

Jake shrugged. His changed relationship with Andi felt surprisingly natural, as if it had been in the cards the whole time without him knowing it, almost in the same way he was destined to return to Ruthenia.

But one thing still pricked at him. She'd been planning to take off—to abandon him and Ruthenia in search of...what? "Why were you going to leave?"

She startled slightly. "I already told you. I didn't see any future in my job and I felt it was time to move on."

He frowned. He couldn't help but feel there was more to it than that. "What were you going to do, back in the States?" He walked toward her. Sunlight pouring through the open roof illuminated her hair with a golden halo and cast sunbeams over her slender form.

"Um, I was thinking of starting my own business."

Shock and hurt surprised him. Her leaving still felt like a personal betrayal. "Intriguing. What kind of business?" She could start her business here.

"Event planning. I intended to find a job at an event-planning company, then gradually branch out on my own."

"You've certainly got the experience for it."

"I know." She lifted her chin. "I must have planned hundreds of events over the last six years."

She wanted to be independent, in charge of her own destiny. He admired that. "As queen you'll have significant responsibilities. You'll be an important person in your own right. People will request your presence for events I can't attend." He knew she'd find it fulfilling.

"It's hardly the same." She lifted her chin. "I'd still be working for you."

"Working *with* me." He took a step toward her. "As equals." Another step. She hadn't moved. He reached out and took her hand. His skin hummed as their fingers met.

"You shouldn't," she breathed, tensing at his touch. "I really was planning to leave, and I still might."

His chest tightened, though he didn't really believe her. "You'll have a wonderful life here. You already know that. You'll never be bored and you can run all the businesses you want, as well as being queen." He stroked her hand with his thumb. Her skin was so soft.

"I still don't believe that staying is the right thing to do."

"I'll convince you." Pride mingled with emotion coursed through him as he raised her hand to his mouth and pressed his lips to her palm.

She gasped slightly and tried to pull her hand back, but he held it fast.

Her lips quivered slightly as his moved closer. Her delicious scent tormented his senses. He eased toward her until their chests were almost touching. She still hadn't moved. He could see in her darkening gaze that she felt the same fierce attraction he did. She wanted him every bit as much as he wanted her, despite her foolish worries and reservations. He'd just have to prove to her that her future should be right here, with him.

His lips closed over hers in a single swipe that drew them together. She arched into him, and he felt her nipples tighten inside her blouse as her fingertips clutched at his crisp shirt. She kissed him back hard, running her fingers into his hair and down his collar.

Jake sighed, reveling in the glorious sensation of holding Andi tight in his arms and kissing her doubts away.

She shuddered as his hand slid over her backside and down her thigh. Her knees buckled slightly as he touched her breast with his other hand, squeezing gently through her soft blouse.

No denying the energy between them. It had a life force of its own and drew them closer and bound them more tightly together every time they touched.

She shivered as his hand roamed under her blouse and his fingers brushed her taut nipple through her bra. At the same time his tongue flicked hers in a way that made her gasp.

Jake grimaced. He'd grown painfully hard. The sheer pleasure of kissing Andi was rather undermined by the powerful urge to strip off her clothes and make mad, passionate love to her right here, right now.

But he didn't want to drive her away. He'd already pushed too far too fast and he needed to let her come to him—to leave her wanting more.

He eased his mouth from hers and left her blinking in the half light of the tower as he pulled back. "Let's not get carried away. It's not too comfortable in here."

When he took things further, he needed to be sure she'd say yes. It was a delicate dance and he didn't entirely want her to know how much power she had over him. She could use it against him. The last nights alone had been painful and he had no intention of prolonging the torment by coming on too strong. He couldn't risk losing her now.

They walked a little higher up the mountain, then decided they'd scaled lofty enough heights for one day and turned for home. A bit out of character for him. Normally if he started something he had to take it as far as it could go.

In the car on the way back he realized he was going to forfeit his bet. Yes, he could seduce her on a whim—her reaction in the tower proved that. But he no longer wanted to. He wanted her heart and mind entwined with his, not just her body, so winning a bet seemed meaningless in the grand scheme of things.

It was a sign of maturity to forfeit a battle in order to win the war. He kissed her good-night with chaste tenderness, and watched her walk away to her own room with regret and desire singing in his blood.

Andi couldn't help a tiny twinge of guilt when she awoke in the morning and remembered that she'd made him lose his bet.

The kiss in the tower had shocked and scared her. How easily she fell into his arms, panting and moaning and letting him know just how easily her control evaporated around him. If he hadn't broken off the kiss she'd probably have made love to him right there on the moss-covered stones.

All that talk about their children and her future as queen had mingled with his powerful touch to throw her into a swoon of excitement, and at that point she might have agreed to anything just to feel his body against hers.

Not good.

She needed to think with her head, and not with her heart. Or any other parts of her body. Jake was still Jake—all business, all about Ruthenia, practical and not personal. He'd never for one instant hinted that he loved her. He was too much of a gentleman to lie about something like that.

She shivered, despite the morning sun. Why did she have to be so crazy about him?

It was the last day before the Independence Day celebrations turned Ruthenia into a countrywide party. She knew they'd both be flat-out busy today making last-minute plans and it should be easy to avoid him.

At least until tonight.

A tiny ray of pride shone through her anxiety. She'd managed to resist him after all, which meant she could still be clearheaded about her choice to stay or go. After the kiss in the tower she hadn't been so sure.

She showered and dressed, hoping she could manage not to be alone with him too much today. Her schedule—so recently abandoned—was packed with things to organize for the festivities. Plans made long before his crazy idea of marrying her, and which she couldn't really trust to anyone else.

Or that she didn't want to.

"Hey, Andi." A voice through the door made her jump. Not Jake's voice. Livia's. "Want me to take over for you so you can spend the day with His Majesty?"

"Not at all. I have everything covered." She hurried to the door and pulled it open, glad she'd painted on her usual business face. "I'll run through the guest list and make sure plans are in place to receive all the dignitaries arriving today. If you could check the menus and make any adjustments based on availability, I'd appreciate that."

A smile pulled at Livia's mouth. "You don't have to do all this stuff anymore, you know."

"This is the biggest occasion in Ruthenia's history—since independence, anyway, and I intend to pull my weight." And keep as busy and as far away from Jake as possible.

"I can handle it." Livia crossed her arms.

"I'm sure you have plenty of other things to handle." Would

Livia offer to handle Jake, as well? Andi felt sure she'd be happy to take charge of his very personal needs, if requested. A twinge of jealousy tweaked her. "I have some phone calls to make."

She spent the day running from her office to the various meeting rooms and dining rooms, making last-minute changes to travel schedules and setting up tours of the local area for the visitors. Around lunchtime, visitors started to trickle in, arriving in their diplomatic cars and in hired limos, and she welcomed them to the palace.

Of course she welcomed them as Jake's fiancée, and the congratulations rang painfully in her ears as guest after guest remarked on how happy they were for the royal couple.

Jake looked rather pleased and proud, but then maybe he always looked like that. Twice he managed to slide his arm around her in situations where it would have been embarrassing to resist. Once in front of the French ambassador, and another time while greeting the Taiwanese cultural attaché. She cursed the way her skin hummed and sizzled under his touch, even through her tailored suit.

The big ring glittered on her finger, like a sign saying, Property of the Palace.

But Jake didn't own her. She hadn't agreed to marry him, simply to stay until after the celebrations.

At least that's what she tried to tell herself.

Feelings of foreboding and guilt, that she'd let down the entire country as well as Jake, gathered in her chest like a storm. Could she really leave?

If it meant escaping a lifetime of heartache, yes.

CHAPTER TEN

THIS WAS IT, his last chance. Jake eyed Andi from the far end of the long table, over the sparkling crystal and polished plates of the state dinner. Tomorrow was Independence Day and he could feel in his gut that he still hadn't convinced her to stay.

Why was she so stubborn?

She knew how many women would give a limb to be in her position, but she didn't seem to value the role of queen at all. Andi wasn't interested in wearing inherited diamonds or dressing up in silk and lace. She didn't care about dining with international luminaries or being called Your Majesty. She cared about people, regardless of whether they were important or not.

All of which only made him like her more.

And then there was that face. Curious and intelligent, with that active mouth and slightly upturned nose. Those sharp blue eyes that never missed anything.

And her slim but strong body, which beckoned him from beneath her fitted golden dress. Tonight he would claim her and sleep with her in his arms, assured that she'd never leave him.

He danced with her three times—heat crackling through his veins—while the jazz quartet played in the ballroom. In between, while dancing with other women, he barely took his eyes off her.

"I'm afraid Andi and I must retire," he announced, after the shortest decent amount of time. He didn't want to give her a chance to escape. "We've got a big day tomorrow, so I'm sure you'll excuse us."

He strode toward her and took her arm, then swept her out of the ballroom. She stiffened once they exited the soft lighting and sensual music, and entered the gilt-trimmed hallway.

"I'm exhausted," she murmured, avoiding his gaze.

"No, you're not." Not yet. He slid his hand along her back and saw the way her nipples peaked under the fine silk of her gown. A flush spread from her cheeks to her neck.

Desire flashed through him at this fresh confirmation that she wanted him as badly as he wanted her.

And he was going to make sure neither of them was disappointed.

"You're coming with me." He tightened his arm around her waist and marched her along the hallway.

"You can't make me." She whispered while her flushed cheeks and dark, dilated pupils argued with her words.

"I'm not going to make you do anything." Her hand felt hot in his, and desire whipped around them, distinct and intoxicating. It had been building all day. All week. For the past six years—though he'd been too wrapped up in business to notice it until now.

He opened the door to his suite and tugged her inside. Then closed and locked it. Her mouth opened in protest, lips red, and he kissed her words away.

She struggled slightly—a token resistance he'd expected— before she softened and her arms closed around him as he knew they would. Once again he felt her fingertips press into the muscle of his back—claiming him—and he grew hard as steel against her.

Andi's soft body felt like a balm to his aching soul. Her mouth tasted like honey and sunshine, and her skin was warm and soothing. His fingers roamed into the silk of her hair and down over her gentle curves.

She writhed, and a gentle sigh slid from her lips as he cupped her breast. He could feel the connection between them, invisible and powerful, and he knew she could feel it, too, when she let down her resistance.

Her dress came off easily, via a simple zipper concealed behind a row of false buttons. Pleasure rippled through his muscles as the luxurious fabric pulled away, revealing soft lace and even softer skin.

Groaning, he settled her onto the bed and pressed a line of kisses over her chin and neck, then down between her breasts and over her belly, which twitched as he roamed lower, burying his face in the lace of her panties.

He felt her fingertips in his hair and heard her low moan as he sucked her through the delicate fabric and enjoyed the heat of her arousal. Her legs wrapped around his shoulders, pulling him closer into her and he licked her to a state of silky wetness before slipping the delicate lingerie down over her smooth thighs.

"You're so beautiful." He murmured the words as his eyes feasted on her lush nakedness. All wide, blue-eyed innocence, her gaze met his for a second before she reached for him and pulled him over her, kissing him with ferocity that snatched his breath and tightened his muscles.

Struggling together they removed his formal suit, baring his hot skin. Aroused almost to the point of insanity after these past days of torture, he couldn't wait to be inside her.

And the feeling was mutual. Andi raised her hips, welcoming him as she breathed hot kisses over his face and neck. Sinking into her again was the best feeling he'd ever had. He guided them into a shared rhythm that made Andi gasp and moan with pleasure.

He wanted Andi at his side—and in his bed—for the rest of his life. She was perfect for him in every way. Brilliant, beautiful, sensual and loyal.

He eased them into another position that deepened the connection between them and made beads of delicious perspiration break out on Andi's brow. Her breathing was ragged and her lips formed an ecstatic smile. Pleasure swelled in both of them, thickening and deepening and growing into something new—their future together—as they moved together, clinging to each other with fevered desperation.

Jake held his climax off for as long as he could, until Andi's cries reached a pitch of pleasured anguish that sent him over the edge. They collapsed onto the bed together, panting and laughing, then relaxed into a sleepy embrace.

A sense of deep contentment settled over him, along with the languid desire unfurled in his limbs. Emotions he couldn't name flickered through him and illuminated his visions of the happy future they'd share, as he drifted off to a peaceful sleep.

Andi watched Jake's chest rise and fall, while silver beams of moonlight caressed his skin through a crack in the curtains. Her heart swelled with painful sensation.

It had been so easy. She'd told him she was tired and that she wanted to go to bed. Did he care? No. He had his own agenda and her needs were irrelevant.

He also knew she never had a prayer of resisting him. How could one person have so much power over her? He'd ruled her life for six years. Six years during which the joy of being with Jake was mingled readily with the sorrow of knowing their relationship was strictly business.

Now he'd followed through on his promise to seduce her into his bed. He'd driven her half mad with sensation—just because he could—and now he slept like a newborn, without an ounce of recrimination.

If only life could be that simple for her.

He didn't care if she loved him or not. That didn't matter to him one bit. He needed a wife and she was a promising candidate with a good résumé. Tried and tested, even, in more ways than one.

Jake probably didn't want to love anyone. Emotions were complicated and messy, and he wouldn't like anyone else having that kind of power over him. No doubt he preferred to keep things clearheaded and businesslike.

At least for one more day, she could manage to do the same. She couldn't bear to think ahead any further than that right now.

The next morning, Andi helped Jake host a palace breakfast for nearly fifty guests. Then they rode through the town in an open carriage with a procession of schoolchildren in front and the town's marching band behind them. Flags waved from windows and hands and the whole country seemed alive with enthusiasm and energy.

At one point Jake slid his hand into hers and warmth flared in Andi's chest at the affectionate gesture. But she turned to look at him and he was waving out the window with the other hand. No doubt the romantic gesture was just intended to look picturesque to the gathered crowds.

Her heart ached that she wanted so much more than a relationship put on for show.

Back at the palace a feast filled long tables on the patio outside the ballroom. She had her work cut out for her chatting with female guests—each of whom congratulated her on her engagement and wished her every happiness.

Are you happy? she wanted to ask each of them. Did these elegant women in their designer clothes enjoy close and loving relationships with their important husbands? Or were they content to follow along and smile, enjoying the gourmet food and expensive shoes that came with the job?

She envied the few women who were there in their own right as ambassadors or dignitaries of sorts. In charge of their own destinys and not dependent on anyone.

Whenever she glimpsed Jake, he looked right at home amidst

the glamorous crowd, smiling and talking and laughing—in his element.

By midafternoon Andi felt exhausted. Last night's late-night shenanigans hadn't helped. As servants cleared the coffee cups and the guests wandered out onto the lawn, she slipped back into the palace for a moment's breather.

"Hey, Your Majesty." Livia's voice startled her as she hurried along the corridor. "Playing hooky?"

"Getting something from my room." She just wanted to be alone.

"Don't you have servants for that?" Livia's brown eyes twinkled with mischief as she caught up with Andi and followed close by her.

"I'm used to doing things for myself."

"It must be hard to make the leap from PA to princess. Though I think I could manage it." She crossed her arms. "Shame Jake didn't notice me first. Still, maybe it's not too late." She raised a brow. "I don't imagine kings usually stick to one woman for the rest of their lives."

"Have you lost your mind?" Andi's temper finally snapped. She ran up the stairs, hoping Livia would not follow.

Livia laughed, climbing right behind her. "Oh, dear. We have turned into a princess, haven't we? I'm just saying what I've observed. It must be difficult watching your fiancé dance with other women almost every night. It takes a special person to put up with that, I'd imagine."

"It's just part of his job."

"And I suppose that putting up with it is part of yours." Livia followed her down the hallway to her own door. "Oh, dear, will I get fired for speaking my mind?"

Her voice grated on Andi's nerves. "Quite possibly."

"You must feel pretty powerful right now."

Not in the least. She wanted to cry. If she was just Jake's assistant she'd have had no difficulty issuing Livia some task, then talking later to Jake about how she wasn't working out. Now, somehow, everything seemed more loaded.

More personal.

"Don't you have a job to do?" Andi turned to her. "There's a big event going on and you should be running it."

"You should be attending it, so I guess we're both skiving off. I'm leaving anyway. Off to New York." She grinned and crossed her arms.

Curiosity goaded Andi. "You have a job there?"

"You'd know all about it. It's the one I told you about that you tried to steal from me. I guess it's lucky for both of us that I tripped you on those stairs in your silly dress."

"What?" Shock washed over her. "Is that when I hit my head?"

"Oh, did I just say that out loud?" She shook her head, making her red curls dance. "Must be loopy from packing. Certainly was lucky, though! I'd have said 'have a nice trip' if I'd known I was sending you into King Jake's affectionate arms. I saw you dancing around like a loon and him coming to your rescue."

Andi stared at her. "I think you should leave right this minute before I tell someone you tried to hurt me."

Livia just laughed. "I couldn't agree more. I'm looking forward to leaving this sleepy backwater and getting back to the big city. Ah, freedom!"

Anger flashed through Andi as Livia waltzed away. None of this would have happened if it wasn't for her interfering jealousy!

She couldn't help being jealous of Livia, now. If Andi married Jake she'd never get to live in New York again. Never be mistress of her own destiny again, with plans and hopes and dreams that could change on a whim.

She'd have duties. Responsibilities. She'd have to be loyal and faithful, serving Ruthenia and Jake until the end of her days.

While Jake danced and flirted and chatted with other women, day after day, night after night.

At least Livia wouldn't be around to taunt her anymore.

In the bathroom she splashed water on her face. She looked pale and haunted, so she slapped on a bit of her familiar blush. But even that couldn't pick up her spirits right now, though. She'd been in the public eye all day, and even though Jake was right there at her side for much of the time, it felt as if they were a thousand miles apart—her craving affection and love, and him needing a royal spouse to put on for ceremonial occasions, much like his sash and scepter.

Last night's intimacy didn't make things better. The closeness they'd shared for those brief hours seemed so distant now, like it wasn't real at all. The memory of his embrace still made her heart beat faster, which only made it hurt more that he didn't love her.

Were her suitcases still here under the bed? Sudden curiosity prompted her to look. They were. She'd only committed to stay through the end of today. After that she could pack her things—again—and get back on the track she'd planned before Jake derailed her for his own professional needs.

A wife by Independence Day. That's all he'd needed. If she wasn't around, he might well have asked Livia. It probably didn't matter all that much to him as long as she did her job.

Still, she did have a job to do for today. She dabbed on a little of her favorite scent, hoping it would lift her spirits. Didn't work.

Lying in his arms last night had been so bittersweet. A dream come true, but with the knowledge that it was just a dream. He'd slept with her to win her over to his side, much as he'd done while her memory was gone.

Any pleasure she'd enjoyed withered away when she remembered that.

She dabbed a bit of powder on her nose—it suddenly looked red—and steeled herself to go back downstairs again. She'd pushed herself through enough long and tiring events over the past six years; she could manage one more, even if her heart was breaking.

* * *

"Where's your fiancée?" Maxi sidled up to Jake as a waiter re-filled his champagne glass.

"Andi's around somewhere. It's a big crowd." Where was she? He'd been so wrapped up in their guests he'd only glimpsed her a couple of times through the crowd. Still, they'd spent a full hour together this morning being dragged through the town in the ceremonial carriage. Andi had been quiet, which was fine with him. He liked that she didn't have to chatter on all the time like some women. He hadn't stopped thinking about her all day, wanting to see her smile, her frown, hear her laugh and even her scolding. She was becoming an obsession.

"Daddy has a proposition for you."

"Oh?" Jake sipped his freshly filled glass.

Maxi nattered on about some proposed factory project in the eastern hills. He was used to listening with one side of his brain and making the right noises, while using the other side of his brain to plan ahead.

Tonight he needed to let Andi know how much she meant to him. He'd told her with his body, but Andi was a pragmatist and he knew she'd want to hear it in words.

I love you.

The truth rang through him like the old church bell tolling in the distance. Maybe he'd known it all along but not realized it until right now. The reality of it left him stunned and filled with a powerful sense of joy.

He loved her and he had to let her know that.

"What?"

He didn't realize he'd said the words aloud until he looked into Maxi's startled face. Her lipstick-painted mouth stretched into a wide smirk. "Thank you, Jake, I'm touched."

He schooled his face into a neutral expression. "Don't take it personally." He raised a brow. "I'm talking about the devel-opment project." He must be losing it. Andi had cracked open some tender new part of him that didn't quite know how to act.

He was so used to being all business all the time that it was hard to switch off that part of him and just be.

Andi certainly didn't have trouble reining her emotions in. She acted as if she was trying to decide whether to accept a promotion or not. It stung that she had no personal feelings for him at all. He could be alarmed that one slender woman had such a strong hold over him—instead he just wanted to kiss her again.

Andi stood there for a moment, incredulous. A cold, empty space opened up inside her. If Jake loved Maxi, why didn't he just marry her?

She stepped backward, shrinking back into the crowd before Maxi noticed her. Jake couldn't love Maxi, could he? She was insufferably arrogant and annoying—he'd said so himself. Unless he was just trying to throw her off the scent.

Maybe he didn't really love Maxi but just said that to her to keep her favor now that he intended to marry someone else. Maybe he was going around telling every girl in Ruthenia that he loved them and if only he didn't need a wife who can type and file efficiently...

Her mind boggled.

Jake was a master manipulator; that was how he accomplished so much and managed to get so many people on his side. Now he was masterminding his marriage, and his relationships with every beauty in the nation, with the easy grace she'd always admired.

Except that now she was its victim. So easy to seduce. Such a quiet and willing accomplice. Ready to sacrifice her life in his service.

Except that she had no intention of making that sacrifice.

She'd tell him why she was leaving, and give him a chance to reply, but nothing he said could now change her decision to get away before she signed up for a lifetime of heartache.

She made it through the grand afternoon tea and an enormous dinner. She barely saw Jake at all, so the hardest part was accepting the continued stream of congratulations on her engagement. She wanted to tell them, "I'm not marrying him!" but she didn't. Too well trained in royal decorum for that.

No. She waited until the last guests had left or gone to bed and she was alone with Jake. She let him lead her to his suite, steeling herself against the false reassurance of his hand around hers or his warm smiles.

Once inside she closed the door. "Independence Day is over, and I'm leaving."

Jake's expression turned dark. "You can't be serious."

"I am, and I'll tell you why." She straightened her shoulders and dared herself to look him right in the eye. He might have power over her, but she was stronger. "You don't love me."

"I do. I love you. I've been meaning to tell you." His expression was the same as always, bright and good-humored. Like none of this really mattered.

"But you forgot?" She forced a laugh, though inside she was crumbling to pieces. "You have been busy, of course. I overheard you telling Maxi you loved her. Perhaps you got us confused for a moment."

Jake smiled. "That's exactly what happened. I said it to you in my mind and it came out of my mouth in front of Maxi."

"You must really think I'm a total idiot." Anger snapped through her at his ludicrous response. "I know I've been pretty gullible, believing that we're engaged when we're not, and going along with your oh-so-convenient plan to get engaged in time for the big day, but it's all stopping right here."

"Andi, be sensible. It's been a long day."

"I'm tired of being sensible. I've been sensible to the point of madness lately, smiling at strangers while they congratulate me on an engagement I fully intend to break off. It's enough to drive almost anyone stark mad."

"I do love you." Jake's dark eyes fixed on hers and the intense look in them almost made her weaken.

Almost, but not quite.

"No you don't!" Her voice rose. "I don't think you even know what love is. All your relationships are carefully orchestrated for maximum effect. You stage manage us just like the seating plans at your dinners, swapping and changing people to curry favor when needed."

"I'm not trying to curry favor with you."

"Obviously not. I was seated as far as possible from you all day." She enjoyed the retort. "Maybe royal couples are supposed to be kept apart so they don't get tired of each other."

"You know that's just convention. You and I already have a close, intimate relationship."

"No, we don't." She cursed the way his words made her chest swell. "Just because you've seduced me into bed does not mean we're intimate. You think you can fix everything with sex. If you pleasure me in bed then somehow it will turn into a love that isn't there. It doesn't work like that. True intimacy is based on trust, and I don't trust you."

He stared at her, the good humor draining from his face. "I know I broke your trust. I promise you I'll never do anything to lose it again."

"Once lost, trust cannot be regained. Whether you love Maxi or not, I really don't care, but either way, I can't trust you and I won't live my life with someone when I don't know if I can believe what they say. It's too late."

Just the fact that she could even suspect him of carrying on with another woman made marriage to him a recipe for disaster.

"I want a normal life that isn't under any spotlights. I'd like to marry an ordinary man who doesn't have glamorous women kissing up to him all day." Did she? She couldn't imagine being involved with anyone after having her heart pummeled by this whole experience. She needed to get out of here before she burst into embarrassing tears.

"I've told you I love you." His features hardened and his eyes narrowed. Silence hung in the room for an agonizing moment. "I've given you ample proof that I care about you and think you're the perfect wife, yet you persist in wanting to leave. Leave then." His gaze pierced right through her. "I won't hold you here."

Andi swallowed. Now he was dismissing her.

Isn't that what she wanted? She'd already told him there was no chance. "I can't be the perfect wife for a man who really just wants a permanent assistant."

"Naturally." He seemed to look down on her along the length of his aristocratic nose. His eyes flashed dark fire. "I don't want you to marry me against your will."

"Good, because I don't think that would be right for either of us." Was she trying to convince him, or herself? "It's important to marry someone you care about. Someone you love." Her voice cracked on the word love.

Once she'd have thought she had enough love in her for Jake to sustain both of them, but lately she'd learned different. She couldn't stand by as the faithful wife while he continued to flirt with and cajole other women, even if it was just for "business" reasons. Not if she didn't know that alone, in bed, he was all hers, heart and soul.

She needed a man she'd believe when he said, "I love you."

"Goodbye, Jake." Her whispered words hovered in the night air of his dimly lit room. She pulled the big engagement ring from her finger and left it on the table.

He didn't respond. Obviously she was worth nothing to him now that she'd scuppered his neat plans. No more protestations of love, or even of how useful their union would be to Ruthenia.

Nothing but his icy glare.

Andi let herself out of the room and hurried along the corridor, grim sensations of regret trickling over her like cold water. She half hoped—and feared—that she'd hear the door open and sense Jake's powerful stride covering the carpet after her.

But nothing disturbed the small, nighttime noises of the palace.

She had to leave right now, even though there were no trains until morning. She didn't want to see him ever again.

Tears streamed down her face as she shoved her clothes back into her two suitcases for the second time in a week. How had she let herself get sucked into such an insane situation? Something about Jake Mondragon undermined all her good sense and left her gasping and starry-eyed. She'd already spent years hoping he'd suddenly fall madly in love with her, which was no doubt why his ridiculous and unsuitable engagement idea had been so easy to put over on her.

Her face heated at the thought of how happy she'd been back when she had no idea that their whole engagement wasn't genuine. He'd smiled at her and kissed her and held her like they were madly in love, knowing all along that the whole thing was a lie.

How humiliating.

She threw her hairbrush into her suitcase with a pleasant thud. Almost done with the packing. Her clothes would be really crumpled now after being shoved in so haphazardly, but she could iron them out again.

Shame she couldn't do that with her heart. She suspected it would be crushed and creased for a long time. Possibly forever.

There was still one thing hanging in the closet. The long, floaty pale dress she'd been wearing the night she lost her memory. She let out a long breath as she remembered why she had it on. She'd brought it with her to Ruthenia thinking she'd need something smart and beautiful to wear at parties now that her boss was a king. She'd chosen it after much giggling deliberation with a girlfriend, because it made her feel like Cinderella at the ball.

She'd never worn it before that night. Since she was staff, she didn't actually attend the parties. A crisp black suit had proved to be the most suitable evening attire as she hovered around the edges of the festivities, making sure everything was running smoothly and attending to Jake's every need. Her Cinderella fantasies had remained locked in the closet, just like the dress.

She'd taken it out that one night, just to see what it would feel like to wear it. The whole palace was wrapped up in the party happening in the dining room and ballroom, so no one noticed when she walked down the stairs, tiptoeing carefully in the silver sandals she'd bought to match the dress and never worn before.

She'd walked to one of the narrow casement windows and looked out. Pale moonlight glanced off the mountains in the distance and bathed the green valley in its soft glow. She'd grown to love the rugged countryside and its fiercely independent and engaging people. The palace and its nearby town were her home now, after three years. Leaving felt like stepping out of her own life and into a big, scary unknown.

Inspired by her pretty dress, she'd wanted to take one last walk around the grounds in the moonlight, just to let her imagination run free and think about what might have been before she left for the last time. The weather was surprisingly warm for so early in the spring and the soft grass, silver with dew, begged her to walk across it.

She'd crossed the wide terrace and taken off her sandals, not wanting to get the soft leather wet or have the heels sink into the lawn. Had Livia really tripped her? That's when her memory stopped. Sometimes the steps were slippery, the stone worn smooth by the passage of feet over two hundred or more years since they were built. She could see them from her window right now.

But she would never walk down them again. No detours this time. She had to get out of here and away from Jake.

She'd since worn far more fabulous and expensive dresses, tailored right on her body by Ruthenia's finest seamstresses, and she knew that they felt like the world's stiffest armor as she moved through her ceremonial duties next to a man who didn't love her.

She turned and scanned the room to see if she'd missed anything.

Her belongings had fit so neatly into her two bags, almost as if they'd just been waiting to pack up and go. Her heart sank at the sight of her empty dressing table, the gaping closet with its almost vacant hangers. Soon someone else would live in the room, and she'd never see it again.

Now all she had to do was get out of here without being seen. She couldn't bear to explain the situation to anyone. They'd be so shocked and disappointed. Disgusted even, at how she wouldn't slot into Jake's plans for the good of the nation.

Guilt snaked through her heart, or maybe it was just grief at what she was leaving behind. The memory of Jake's face—hard and angry—would stay with her forever. She shivered and turned to pick up her bags.

Even though it was well after midnight, she'd need to sneak down the back stairs. The cleaners sometimes worked late into the night, especially after a major event. If she could make her way to the rear entrance without being seen, she could cut across the gardens to the old barnyard and take one of the runabout cars kept near the old stables for staff to share on errands.

She grabbed the handle of each bag and set off, pulse pounding. No looking back this time. The pretty dress could stay right there in the closet, along with all her romantic fantasies. They'd caused her nothing but pain.

From magical fairy-tale engagement to shocking scandal overnight. She'd have to keep her head down for, oh, the rest of her life.

She let herself into the old staircase, dimly lit by aging sconces, and hurried down the steep, winding steps, bags thumping unsteadily behind her like chasing ogres no matter how high she tried to life them.

She held her breath as she opened the heavy wood door at the bottom. It led out into the back kitchen, which was rarely used, only if they were catering a truly enormous feast—like the one today. Freshly scrubbed pots and baking trays covered the sideboard and big bowls of fruit stood on the scrubbed table ready to be sliced for breakfast, but the lights were low and she couldn't see anyone about.

Lowering her bags onto their wheels, she crept across the flagstone floor.

One the far side of the old kitchen, she could see the door that led directly out into the kitchen garden. Before she took a step into the room, a burst of laughter made her jump. She froze, heart pounding, peering into the shadows. Voices reached her from the next room, the passage to the modern kitchen. She didn't recognize them, but the palace often hired extra caterers for big events. Were they already up, making breakfast?

She shrank back into the stairwell, but after an anxious minute, no one had appeared, so they obviously hadn't heard her. Bags lifted by her straining biceps, she crept across the floor. She lowered her bags for a moment and tried the handle—old, but well-oiled, the door slid quietly open, and cool night air rushed in.

She drew in a breath, then stepped out and closed the door quietly behind her. The click of the latch struck an ominous chord in her chest. She'd left the palace forever. She should feel happy that she'd escaped the building without being seen. Instead, she felt like a thief, leaving with stolen goods.

Which was ridiculous. She'd given years of her life to this place. Was that why it hurt so much to leave? And she wasn't gone yet. She still had to get across the grounds and past the sentries at the gatehouse.

She scanned the walled garden—a gloomy well of shadows in the cloudy moonlight—then hefted her bags past the menacing dark rectangles of the large herb beds. An arched doorway on the far side led to the stable yard, where the staff cars were parked. The ancient door creaked on its hinges as she pulled it open, and she shot a glance behind her. A lightbulb flicked on in one of the upper windows, and she held her breath for a moment. Was it Jake's window? Would he come look for her?

She cursed herself when she realized that it was on the upper, staff-only floor. Why would Jake come looking for her? He'd told her to get lost. Which was exactly what she'd wanted.

Wasn't it?

Heaviness lodged in her chest as she crept across the paved stable yard. She retrieved a key from the combination-locked box in the wall—they'd be sure to change the code tomorrow—climbed into the nearest car and started the engine.

Andi glanced up at the house to see if anyone would look outside, but no one did. Cars did come and go at all hours when the house was full of guests and there were meals to prepare. She didn't turn the lights on right away.

A sharp pang of regret shot through her as she pulled onto the wide gravel drive for the last time. A ribbon of silver in the moonlight, it led through an allée of tall trees. It was hard to believe she'd never see this beautiful place again. She certainly wouldn't be welcome back for return visits.

And she'd never see Jake again. She should be happy about that, considering what he'd done, but all the years they'd spent working side by side—and that she'd spent mooning over him and hoping for more—weighed on her mind. He was a good man at heart and she didn't wish him ill.

Don't think about him.

There was still one more gauntlet to run—the gatehouse. The guards didn't usually pay too much attention to cars leaving the palace, especially familiar staff cars, so she hoped they'd simply wave her through. She cringed, though, when she saw a uniformed figure emerge from the stone gatehouse and approach.

She cleared her throat and rolled down the window. "Hi, Eli, it's only me. Picking up a friend." The lie was the first thing that sprang to mind.

Eli simply smiled and gave her a little salute. She raised her window and drove out the palace gates for the last time, blinking back tears. In the morning, Eli and everyone else would know she'd run off into the night.

The town was deserted as she drove through it. She parked on a quiet street so she could walk the last stretch to the station. No need to advertise where she'd gone, since it would probably be hours until the first train of the morning. The staff cars were all identical Mercedes wagons and easily recognizable, and she didn't want to be too easy to find.

Not that anyone would come looking for her. She left the keys in the glove compartment. Petty crime was almost nonexistent in the town as everyone knew each other too well.

She groped in her bag for dark sunglasses. No need for strangers to see her red and puffy eyes. She wrapped a blue scarf around her head and neck. It wasn't cold but she didn't want anyone to recognize her if she could help it.

All she had to do was wait for the early-morning train to Munich, then book a flight to New York.

Her original plan had been to head to Manhattan and stay at the 92nd Street Y and temp until she could find an apartment and a job. She'd even had that promising interview set up. So, there'd been a hitch in her plans, involving all her lifelong dreams coming true and then turning into a nightmare, but she'd just have to get back on track and start rebuilding her life.

She glanced up and down the dark empty street before hurrying past the old stone buildings toward the ornate nineteenth-century train station at the edge of town.

She'd intended to leave Jake behind, and now she was doing it. So why did it still hurt so much?

CHAPTER ELEVEN

JAKE PACED BACK and forth in his bedroom, anger and pain firing his muscles into action. His wounded pride sparked fury inside him. He'd been mad enough to lose his heart to a woman, and now she flung it back in his face.

No one had ever treated him so coldly. He'd offered her his life and she'd turned him down. He should despise her for being so heartless and cruel.

So why did the thought of facing even one day without her make his whole body ache?

He'd have to announce to the whole country —to the world— that their engagement was over. People would wonder why she left and gossip would echo around the villages for months.

But he didn't care about any of that. It was the prospect of nights without Andi's soft body in his bed. Of days lacking her bright smile. Long evenings without her thoughtful conversation.

He couldn't force her to marry him against her will. Lord knows he'd come close enough by thrusting this whole engagement on her when she was indisposed by her lack of memory.

Shame trickled over him that he'd taken advantage of her so readily. She'd been so willing—in her lack of knowledge about their true past—and it had been so wonderful. A natural extension of their happy working relationship.

Idiot. Having sex with your assistant had nothing to do with work. Why had he tried to convince himself it was okay? If he really wanted to marry her he should have waited until she got her memory back, courted her like a gentleman—or at least a conventional boyfriend—then proposed to her.

Maybe he thought that as a king he was so special he didn't have to follow any of the conventions of romantic love? He certainly put a lot of energy into following other conventions, so why had he veered so badly off course with Andi?

He halted his pacing at the window. He'd been keeping an eye out for lights from a car traveling up the driveway, but had seen none. She was probably still here in the palace.

But she'd already rejected him and it was too late to change her mind. She needed a man she could trust, and in taking advantage of her amnesia, he'd given her good reason to never trust him again.

He'd given up a lot to take on his role as king of Ruthenia. Now he'd just have to learn how to live without Andi, as well.

Andi flinched as the ticket agent looked at her. She'd removed her dark glasses because, well, it was still dark outside. But there was no flicker of recognition in his eyes. Without extravagant jewels and fancy dresses she just slipped right back into the regular population.

As the platform filled with people waiting for the first train, she shrank inside her raincoat, raising the collar. The occasional stare made her want to hide behind a column. Soon enough they'd all know who she was and what she was doing.

She climbed onto the train without incident. Had she thought Jake would send the cavalry after her? The Ruthenian hills were notably free of galloping horsemen and the roads almost empty of cars as the train pulled away from the town at 7:43 a.m.

Perhaps he was secretly relieved to see her go. He could blame her for breaking off the engagement and carry on with his merry life as an eligible royal bachelor, with gorgeous women kissing up to him at every opportunity.

Her heart still ached with jealousy at the thought of Jake with another woman. Which was totally ridiculous since she'd just rejected him.

The train picked up speed outside the town and flew through the open fields and villages with their tall steeples, clustered at the foot of the proud mountains. She'd never even heard of Ruthenia until she met Jake, but it had come to feel like home and she was going to miss it.

She pulled a book from her bag, but the words blurred before her eyes and she couldn't concentrate. Tears threatened and she pushed them back. Was she making a terrible mistake? Would Jake have grown to love her?

She'd never know now, but it was too late to turn back.

It was midmorning by the time she reached the border crossing between Ruthenia and Austria. She held her breath while the border guards walked through the train checking passports.

The young, clear-faced guard looked at her passport, then pulled out his phone. He spoke rapidly in German and made a sign to another guard on the platform. The two elderly ladies seated on the bench opposite her glanced at each other. Andi felt her heart rate rise.

"I don't have anything to declare." She gestured to her two suitcases. "You can look through them.

"Will we be moving soon?" Her voice sounded shaky. Sitting here made her feel anxious, like she wanted to get up and run. Was Jake behind this? She cursed the pinch of hope that jangled her nerves.

Unlikely. She'd never seen him look so furious as he did last night. If only she could make that memory go away.

* * *

Jake's car swerved on a gravel patch in the road and he righted it quickly, coming around another of those hairpin turns on the mountainside. He probably should have taken the train, like Andi. It was the most direct route as it cut right through one of the larger mountains.

But he didn't want anything to hold him up. He also didn't want other people around. This was between him and Andi.

His pride still hurt at her forthright rejection, but something inside him couldn't let her leave like this. She'd said she didn't trust him, and that hurt more than anything. He'd broken her trust. He'd tried to keep her at his side using seduction and bargaining.

When he told her he loved her, she simply didn't believe him.

She thought his declaration was just more words. She didn't understand that his feelings for her had transformed him.

Swinging around another tight corner, he felt a twinge of guilt about using the border guards to hold the train. Another aspect of royal privilege he'd abused. Still, it was an emergency situation. Once she got back to the U.S., she'd be gone from his world, and he knew in his heart that he'd never get her back.

Then he'd spend the rest of his life missing her and kicking himself for losing the only woman he wanted.

He drove through the Dark Forest at warp speed, adrenaline crackling through his muscles, and emerged into the open plain on the other side just before noon. He'd had to stop on the way for one simple, but important, errand. This time he intended to get everything right.

He spotted the long train at the border crossing from quite a distance away. Luckily the road ran almost directly across the tracks near the village, so he pulled onto the verge and jumped out. Bright morning sun shone off the dark blue-and-gold surface of the cars and turned each window into a mirror. Which car was Andi in? And would she even talk to him after how he'd behaved at their last meeting? Every cell in his body, every nerve pulsed with the desperate need to see her and make things right.

The train was an old one, with individual compartments seating about six people each. The first three he peered into contained no familiar face, but in the fourth, opposite two older women in wool berets, sat a pale-faced and anxious-looking Andi.

He grasped the cool handle and inhaled. She looked up as he pushed the door open and he heard her gasp.

"I can't live without you, Andi."

He hadn't planned what to say. He'd done too much planning lately. "I really do love you." He prayed that the truth would ring through in words that now sounded hollow from overuse. "I didn't realize it myself. I've never known love before. I was raised to think with my head and not my heart. I spent so much time convincing myself I wanted to marry you because it was a sensible decision, because our marriage would be good for Ruthenia. The truth is that now my desire to keep you has nothing to do with Ruthenia. I want you for myself and I can't imagine spending the rest of my life without you."

Tears welled in her eyes for a moment and his heart clutched.

The two women opposite her suddenly rose, grabbing their carryalls, and hurried toward the door where he stood. "Please excuse us," one puttered in Ruthenian. He'd forgotten they were there. He stood aside to let them pass, eyes fixed on Andi.

She hadn't moved an inch, but color rose to her pale cheeks.

Hope flared in his chest. "I admit that our engagement began for the wrong reasons. I'm ashamed about that." Guilt stung him. "All I knew was that I enjoyed your company, and that once I kissed you…" He blew out a breath. "Once I kissed you, nothing was ever the same again."

He saw her swallow, fighting back tears that made her blue eyes glisten.

He ached to take her in his arms and kiss away her tears.

The few inches between them seemed an agonizing gulf. "I need you, Andi."

Her lips didn't flinch. Her silence hurt him, but she hadn't told him to go. There was still hope.

He reached into his pocket and drew out the item he'd picked up on the way here. The simple ring, the one she'd chosen in the shop that morning.

He knelt on the floor of the train car and pulled the ring from the box. "Andi, I know this is the ring you wanted. I made you get the other one because it was showier. I realize I was making decisions for you and trying to turn you into someone you don't want to be. I'd like to go right back to the beginning and start over."

She hesitated for a moment, eyes fixed on the ring.

His heart clenched. She'd already told him that she didn't want to be his wife. She didn't want a life of royal duty and an existence in the public eye. But that wasn't all he offered. How could he make her see that despite all the trappings of royalty, he was just a man? A man who loved and needed her with every fiber of his being.

"Andi, right now I wish I wasn't a king." It took effort to stop his hands from reaching out to her. "That I could promise you an ordinary life, in a comfortable house in some American suburb, where our children could attend the local school and play in Little League. The truth is I can't. I'm already married to Ruthenia and that's my destiny. I can't turn away from it any more than I could turn back the river flowing through the mountains."

He saw her throat move as she swallowed. Her hands shifted slightly, clutching at each other through her black gloves. How he longed to take them in his own hands.

"But I need you, too, Andi. Not because you can help me run the country or the palace, but because you're the woman I want to share my life with. That I need to share my life with."

Emotion flickered across her lovely face and made hope

spark inside him. "I do love you, Andi. I love you with all my heart and soul, with parts of me that I never knew existed. I tried to ignore the new tender feelings starting inside me because they scared me. It was easier to talk myself into using practical reasons to keep you. To convince myself I was still in full control of my emotions, that I didn't truly need you, or anyone else." He drew in a ragged breath. "But I do need you."

He paused, emotions streaming through his brain and mind. How hard it was to put into words things that he could only understand at gut level. "I didn't know until now that I've been living a half life, devoid of emotion and even of true joy. In your arms I've found happiness I never knew existed."

He blinked, embarrassed by his frank confession. "I know you no longer believe me when I tell you I love you." He shook his head. "I don't blame you. Those words have lost their power. They've been used too many times. I don't know how to express what I truly feel except to say that my life is empty and hollow without you. Please don't leave me, Andi."

Andi blinked, eyelashes thick with tears. The raw emotion in his voice stunned her. He was always so calm, so controlled, so in charge of every situation. Right now she could sense that every word he said was true.

No guile, no charm, no winning ways—just a heartfelt plea that shook her to her core.

She hadn't dared to utter a single word until now, and when she opened her mouth, the painful truth emerged. "I love you, Jake. I've always loved you." Why hide anything now? "I've loved you almost since the first day I came to work for you. You're kind and fair and thoughtful, and tough and strong when you need to be. I've admired you every day and dreamed about you every night."

Putting her thoughts into words took effort, but it was a relief to finally get them off her chest. "So you see, when my memories—and the resulting inhibitions—were erased, I fell so easily into the kind of relationship I've always dreamed of. I'm sure it was frightening to know that someone you've worked so closely with for years had those kind of feelings."

She shivered slightly. "I didn't want you to ever find out. That's one of the main reasons I wanted to leave. It was all wrong from the start."

"But it's not wrong." Jake kept his gaze fixed on hers. "I was wrong to take advantage of you, but we're meant to be together. I don't want a ceremonial wife *or* an assistant. I want someone who'll remind me I've never been up the mountain, and who'll take me there. I don't want someone who'll take good minutes on my life, I want someone to live it with me and make it fuller and richer than I ever imagined."

Unable to hold still any longer, Andi reached out to him and clasped his hands. He was still holding the ring, the pretty, simple diamond she'd liked, and the fact that he'd brought it touched her deeply. "I was already cursing myself for leaving you—and Ruthenia. I felt like I was leaving a big chunk of my heart behind." She hesitated and drew in a breath. "I don't want to leave you behind."

"Then don't. I'll come with you. Ruthenia can get along without me for a while." He rose from the floor and sat on the seat beside her. "We should visit your parents. It seems only right that I should ask them for your hand in marriage." A twinkle of humor brightened his eyes. "And maybe I'll have better luck with them."

He held up the ring between finger and thumb. "Though it would be nice to put this ring somewhere safe, like your finger, so it doesn't get lost while we're traveling."

The ring blurred as Andi's eyes filled with tears. She pulled off her gloves and held out her bare hands, which trembled. "I will marry you, Jake." Her voice cracked and a violent shudder rocked her as the cool metal slid over her finger. The act felt far more powerful and meaningful than the first time, when she didn't even know who she was. "I do want to spend the rest of my life with you."

Now that Jake had poured out his feelings, everything felt different. She no longer had any doubt that he loved her as much as she loved him. Sun poured in through the large railcar window, and the world outside seemed bright with promise. "I love the idea of going to see my family. They'll be thrilled to meet you. If this train ever gets moving again, that is."

Jake grinned. "Let's see what we can do about that. But, first things first." He slid his arm around her back and pulled her close. Andi's eyes slid shut as their lips met and she kissed him with all the pent-up passion and emotion she'd planned to lock away for the rest of her life. Relief and joy flooded through her and her heart exploded with happiness at the feel of his strong arms around her. When they finally pulled apart, blinking in the sun, she had a strange sensation of her life starting afresh from this moment.

"I love you, Jake." At last she could say it out loud without a hint of embarrassment or doubt. She'd waited years for this moment and it was sweeter than she'd ever dreamed.

"Not as much as I love you." Jake's eyes sparkled.

"You're so competitive."

"So are you." He grinned. "One more reason why we're perfect for each other." Then he pulled out his phone. "Now, let's see if we can get this train moving."

EPILOGUE

"OF COURSE YOU need an assistant." Jake leaned in and kissed Andi's neck.

Piles of envelopes and résumés covered her desk. The prospect of going through them seemed more than daunting. "But we already have a full staff. And three nannies."

"You need someone just for you." He eased his thumbs down her spine. "So you can come up with a crazy plan for the weekend, and put her to work making it happen while you and I go for a stroll on the mountain."

"That's too decadent."

"It's an important part of any monarch's job to be decadent."

Andi laughed. "Says who?"

"The paparazzi. They don't want to cover a bunch of dull worker bees."

"True." She giggled. "They did have fun taking those ridiculous shots of me sailing when I was eight months pregnant."

"See? You're helping people earn their livelihood. And what about the tourists? They want glamour and excitement, romance and majesty, not a queen who licks her own envelopes."

"I can think of better things to lick." She raised a brow.

"Now that you put it that way, I think I'll cancel this afternoon's meeting on foreign policy."

"Don't you dare." She shot him a fierce glare. "Just save your energy for later." She stroked a finger over his strong hand, where it rested on her desk.

"Have I ever run out of energy?" He growled the question in her ear.

"Never. Now I know where our son gets it from." Little Lucas was a tireless eighteen-month-old bundle of energy. They'd managed with just two nannies until he learned to walk; after that, three—plus Andi—were required to keep up with him.

A joyful shriek outside the door alerted her that his morning nap must be over. Jake dodged to the side as little Lucas barreled into the room, blond curls bouncing. "Mama, read me a story!"

"Of course, sweetie."

"See? You need an assistant so you have someone to read through all these résumés for you while you read Lucas a story." Jake chuckled.

"You're hired." She winked and gathered Lucas into her arms. "Lucas and I have an appointment with Thomas the Tank Engine."

"And James the Red Engine." Lucas's serious face reminded her so much of Jake's sometimes, despite the pudgy dimpled cheeks.

"This sounds like a very important meeting. Perhaps I should attend, too."

"Most definitely. Foreign policy can wait. Tell them Ruthenia just wants to be friends with everyone." Andi swept Lucas up in her arms as she stood.

"A very sensible approach. We'll just have a big party with cupcakes and tell everyone to play nicely." Jake squeezed Lucas's little hand.

"Chocolate cupcakes, 'kay, Daddy?"

"Hmm. Not sure. We might have to put a committee together to discuss the finer details."

"How 'bout rainbow sprinkles?" Lucas's bright blue eyes stared at his dad.

"If rainbow sprinkles are involved I'll just have to issue an executive order."

Lucas clapped his chubby hands together.

Andi shrugged. "I do like to be surrounded by men who can make important decisions without a lot of fuss. Really takes the pressure off. Where's the book?"

Lucas pointed at his nanny Claire, who stood in the doorway with a stack of paperbacks and a freshly made snack on a plate.

"Let's head for the garden." Andi moved to the door. "Claire, can you call ahead and have some blankets spread on the lawn? And maybe bring out Lucas's trike and stick horse." She tickled under his chin and he giggled. Then she glanced up at Jake. "See? I am getting better at not doing everything myself."

"Your efforts are admirable. And much needed since you'll soon be in the third trimester and Lucas isn't getting lighter." He picked his son up and held him in his arms. Lucas clapped both chubby palms against his cheeks and laughed aloud. "What if his sister has as much energy as he does?"

"Then we'll need six nannies. If we keep having kids there will be zero unemployment in Ruthenia."

Lucas arched his back, signaling his desire to be free on his fast-moving feet. Jake put him gently down and they both watched as Lucas tore off down the corridor with Claire running after him. "How do people manage a toddler without a nanny while they're pregnant?" Already she could get a little short of breath climbing stairs without carrying anyone.

"I don't know. I always had a nanny." He winked.

"It's amazingly easy to get used to being spoiled rotten. Where's my dish of peeled grapes?"

They both laughed. They knew they worked hard, for much longer hours than most people. Andi had come to enjoy the routine round of entertaining. It felt good to bring people into their home and make them feel welcome. As the host she took special pleasure in making sure everyone had a good time, quite different than when she simply had to make sure the events ran smoothly.

Her parents had fallen in love with both Ruthenia and Jake. With her father newly retired and her mom only working during the school year, they'd allowed Jake and Andi to give them a quaint house right in the town as a "vacation home," insisting they wanted to visit regularly without being on top of the couple.

Andi's sister and her husband flew in for the wedding, and their little daughter was a flower girl in the majestic old town church where they said their vows. They now also came to visit regularly, and the sound of little Lucy's childish laughter bouncing off the palace walls had urged Andi and Jake into parenthood.

Since Lucas was born the palace no longer felt like a place of business where people slept, but was fully a family home, where people also worked.

The difference was subtle, but transformative. Jake slid his arms around her waist. "Would you like me to carry you downstairs, Your Majesty?"

"That won't be necessary." She wriggled against him, enjoying the flash of heat that always sparked between them when they touched. "But you can kiss me."

His lips met hers and her eyes slid closed. She could always lose herself in his kiss. She'd dreamed of it so long and come so close to never tasting him again. Her fingers played over the muscle of his chest through his tailored shirt.

She pulled back, lips humming with desire. "Hold that thought. I have a story to read and you have to bring about peace in our time. I'll see you tonight."

"And every night." His soft glance was loaded with suggestion.

She glanced down at her hand, where the simple diamond ring she'd first chosen sparkled behind her engraved wedding band. A smile crept over her mouth. "For the rest of our lives."

* * * * *

MILLS & BOON

Book Club

Have your favourite series
delivered to your door every month
with a Mills & Boon subscription.

**Use code ROMANCESUB2021 to
get 50% off the first month of
your chosen subscription PLUS
free delivery.**

Sign up online at
millsandboon.com.au/pages/print-subscriptions
or call Customer Service on
AUS **1300 659 500** or NZ **0800 265 546**

**No Lock-in
Contracts**

**Free
Postage**

**Exclusive
Offers**

For full terms and conditions go to millsandboon.com.au
Offer expires October 31, 2021

ROYAL REBELS

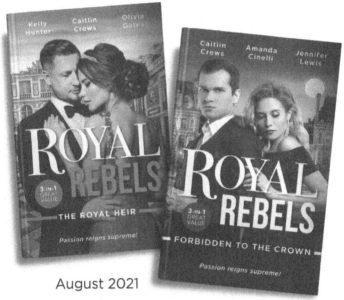

August 2021

September 2021

Passion reigns supreme
in these royal romances.

Available in-store and online.

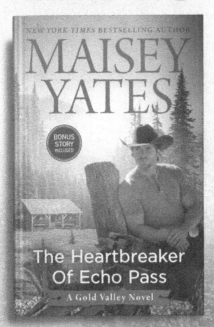

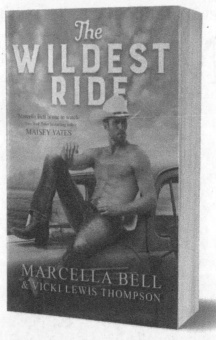

Diamonds Down Under

The cut, clarity & cost of family...

Set in Australia and New Zealand, these stories will take you into the world of the elite diamond industry and two feuding, wealthy families.

Available in-store and online.

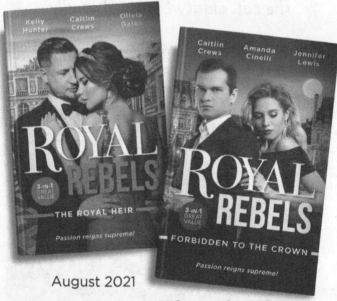

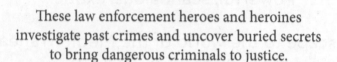

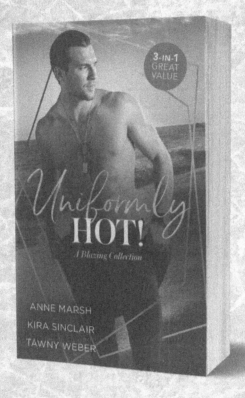

More LARGER PRINT books for you to enjoy!

Larger Print is now available
in the following series lines:

MODERN

Forever

MEDICAL

INTRIGUE

DESIRE

LOVE INSPIRED
SUSPENSE

LOVE INSPIRED
WESTERN

MILLS & BOON
millsandboon.com.au

LET'S TALK ABOUT BOOKS!

JOIN THE CONVERSATION

MILLSANDBOON
AUSTRALIA

@MILLSANDBOONAUS

ESCAPE THE EVERY DAY AT
MILLSANDBOON.COM.AU